HERE LYETH

Marrow Publishing
Here Lyeth
By Johanna Frank

ISBN: 978-1-7382907-0-3 Paperback
ISBN: 978-1-7382907-2-7 Kindle
ISBN: 978-1-7382907-3-4 eBook
ISBN: 978-1-7382907-1-0 Hardcover
Fiction/Fantasy

Acknowledgments, immense gratitude to:
Deirdre Lockhart, Brilliant Cut Editing – editing, patience, and inspiration
Damonza – cover design and interior formatting
My husband – a reliable, steadfast source of strength
ARC readers – feedback and suggestions, notably L.M. Spilsbury, Author
Victory Editing – Oops detection review
Book bloggers – for sharing reviews, very thankful
Family and friends – encouragement extraordinaire
Dreamstime – lavender illustration copy credit, Ernest Akayeu
Each and every reader! Without you, the question begs—why do this?

HERE LYETH

JOHANNA FRANK

A Lifeline Fantasy Series by Johanna Frank

Here Lyeth
The Gatekeeper's Descendants
Jophiel's Secret

Beloved characters. Stand-alone plots.

HAIL, Worthy Reader.

If you're like me, you find joy in diving into novels that take you away—like riding a gentle wave in the ocean of another world. Onward to a shore that captivates your senses, a place you long to stay. New thoughts, hopes, or even dreams, stimulate your imagination in ways it never has before. You've picked up *Here Lyeth*—and here's hoping your voyage thrills and delights you!

You will soon discover the rhythm and bounce of this creative story full of fantasy and twists to be focused on the spirited characters as they morph and bloom, and less marrow on language lingos and historical realisms. (Though please find a translation guide in the back of the book!) It is my wish you will enjoy the sparkles of divine happenstances, the pulls of Christian parallels, and the eager wonder of ever-after capers.

Although the third book published in *A Lifeline Fantasy Series*, *Here Lyeth* takes the position of first when it comes to the natural flow of time compared to its stand-alone novel mates, *The Gatekeeper's Descendants* and *Jophiel's Secret.*

I promise you, *Here Lyeth* won't leave you hanging, though it may unearth you a little. :)

May the following pages stir your thinking beyond the ordinary.

As always, yours with dutiful affection,

Johanna

for Stephie,
with Love.

CHAPTER ONE
A SUPERNATURAL DEATH

In the Germanic village of Vereiteln, 1670

WRATH HOVERED AS if alive by its own accord. Meginhardt best protect himself good. "Whatcha wait'n fer, Pa?"

Stilling his breath was the easy part. He came by it naturally, helped when his wits took to running. Plus, wise he was, he'd use both elbows to cover his brow, oversized just like Pa's and such an easy target, like shoot'n a weasel stuck in a trap. Never was he as ready as this. Muscles tensed with obedience, crouched in position, prepared for the wallop.

Distracting this time was the gnaw in his belly, a peculiar sense. An utter dread begged a rousing. Be it the faraway black in Pa's eyes? Nay, that was of no rarity. It be the iron skillet Pa gripped with both fists. Not any skillet, this one, full of schmaltz straight from the hearth. Mutton chops stuck to the bottom, hissing a dire warning.

Aye, never should'a poxed ya. Pa had this thing about curses. He believed them, obsessed even, like they were gospel. This night, something stirred his ire. Anger shook the man's body, a will to strike like never before.

Meginhardt ground his teeth against the words he'd already released—*"The devil's gonna come knock'n on yer stoop."* He couldn't take them back. Now, he had to face whatever came next.

The oil lamp flickered and went out, plunging their small farmstead into darkness. He was used to the dingy gray, but then strange balls of light appeared, floating around the room like glowing dust motes. That gnaw in his belly told him something big was about to happen.

Cry me a mercy, what's goin' on?

He jerked his arm to dodge a splatter of hot fat but didn't dare to look. More sizzling drops were likely to follow. He snuck a fist wipe across his nose and scratched an eyelid, then stayed. Nothing.

A smell hit him, like charred meat, harsh and foul. He checked his arms. All clear. Had to be Pa.

Moments like this were rare. A pause in the middle of correction? Unheard of. Meginhardt scrambled to his feet. Pa was frozen, not a single muscle moving. Even the fat slithering down the man's arm like a snake now seemed to hang in midair. Perfect chance to escape. A good slapping of searing iron like that would do some serious ruin, especially across the noggin, far more than he'd endured before. He barreled for the door, intending to make a run through the turnip rows, then disappear into the wall of cornstalks. A full night of hiding, staying out of sight, always worked to calm the devil in Pa.

But as he reached the threshold, something pulled at him, something unnatural.

Pa still hadn't moved. Standing there like a statue, locked in a moment of time.

"Pa? Why aren't ya moving? Ya teaching me someth'n again?" He held tight to the doorframe, eyeing the skillet, still a threat, as curiosity and stubborn loyalty took control.

Silence. Nothing.

Was this some kind of clay-brained trick?

Meginhardt crept closer, shivering at the twisted expression, a terrifying grimace. Jaw dropped like it was unhinged, possessed even.

Maybe talking to him would snap him out of this. "Ya would've done me in if ya'd gone through with it, Pa."

No response.

Meginhardt reached out. His finger tapped Pa's tongue. It barely moved, like a hinge left unused for years. "Ah, c'mon. Pa, stop it. Ya got me. You always said I was good fer nothin', so me putt'n a curse on the blood in yer veins shouldn't matter any."

Still nothing.

Meginhardt gave himself a two-fisted poke in the chest. "Go ahead, Pa. Call me pigeon-liver like ya always do."

He squeezed his eyes shut and braced for the hit. But nothing came.

Doggonit.

He'd almost forgotten the strange lights. They were everywhere now, swirling faster and faster, pulling everything into their trail—the wood table, the hearth, their straw mats. Even the doorframe. He grabbed onto the only thing not moving—Pa's stiffened arm. The second he did, Pa let out a bone-chilling howl. The silence shattered. The skillet swung down like a guillotine, and there was a sickening crack.

The room stopped spinning. The lights faded. The space sank back to dingy gray. Meginhardt felt nothing. Just a cold, horrifying realization of what had happened. No going back now.

Pa's arm fell like an ax when I grabbed it. Was that my doing? Had he been responsible for engaging that lever?

A body lay crumpled on the floor. Grease slicked its face, and blood seeped through matted hair.

Meginhardt bent for a closer look. He didn't recognize himself at first. How could he? He had only seen his image once, and that was a year ago.

His dead mother's room had a reflection glass, along with her other stuff kept locked away. But once, when Pa went to town, Meginhardt snuck in and saw himself.

So, was this mess of flesh and bones him? Had to be. That was his flannel shirt. No one else was here.

He squatted, bouncing on one knee, leaning on the other. The whites of his eyes were dull, and the stench under those flopped arms was unbearable. He leapt back, avoiding the sight of a massive purple welt forming across his face. Disgusting.

And Pa was still there, rigid in his after-strike pose.

"Yup, that's me all right. Pa, ya gone and done it." Meginhardt's mouth curled into a strange smile. An unfamiliar confidence bolstered him. Pa's rage no longer filled the space. Time had frozen when the skillet struck, allowing Meginhardt to separate from his body, numbing all the pain. And then time froze again.

A dark part of him awakened—a desire for revenge. He'd always dreamed of going head-to-head with Pa one day. Was this his chance?

"Guess'n ya can't get me no more, Wit–ford Di–*me*–trees."

But Witford Dimietris, locked in some kind of supernatural stillness, said nothing. His left hand gripped his right wrist, his fingers, one with the skillet. Eyes glassed like a demonized wolf, his mouth stretched open in a silent scream.

Meginhardt dared another look into the gaping mouth. A sickening stench of onion and fermented cider put a quick end to curiosity. At last, Pa's evil tongue-lashings had been silenced, and those steel eyes could rage against him no more.

"And that's just fine." Meginhardt jabbed Pa's stone-cold chest. "'Cause from here on, things are gonna be different."

Meginhardt might be dead, but he was free. In the end, Pa hadn't won. Meginhardt had.

CHAPTER TWO
A PECULIAR INTRUSION

In Vereiteln Dorf

AS MEGINHARDT REVELED in the newfound freedom, a flat and uninvited voice pierced his high spirits. "Different, you say. Indeed."

When had someone sidled into the room?

"Go your ways, or I'll whack ya too." He spun to confront the intruder. He puffed out his chest to appear tougher than he felt. After what happened, he shall be the scoundrel now and none shall doubt it. A louse was better than a nobody. Anyone sneaking onto their farm had to know they'd be taking a risk. They had it coming.

Cry me a mercy.

What beheld his gaze?

A massive, feathered creature loomed over him. A reptilian sort with sharp curved talons. An eagle's body, mostly. Arms of a man underneath folded wings. Despite an efficient flesh-tearing beak, oddly enough, a lazy expression in the eagle's eye erased any need for worry. The other eye shut tight.

Nevertheless, Meginhardt tensed. "Well, I be a calf lolly, *what* are ya?"

"Doesn't matter." A human voice came from the creature's short, thick neck. "I'm here to pick you up. Let's go. We're running late."

"I ain't goin' nowhere. Truly, nay with the likes of you." Nerves shaken to the marrow, he stepped back and clutched his father's statue for balance, or truthfully, more so for comfort. Mustering up another dose of courage, he puffed his chest out again. "I jus' got my life where I want it. Go yer way, whatever ye be. Git." "You just got your life where you want it," the eagle man mocked. "Really. Do tell."

Meginhardt ducked his head to avoid eye contact. He'd endured a life of abuse and emotional torture. Now, a miracle arrived. Magic. A super sublime something. He was free.

Still, the burden of Pa's rejection and his mother's tragic death while giving birth, his birth, ever present and unwavering. His worth was always measured by how much he could please Pa, a price demanding of his soul. Who wouldn't blame Pa for blaming him for her death? If it weren't for Meginhardt, their lives could have been good.

More alienated than ever, he scuffed his boot on a crooked plank. No one could lift his guilt. No one could be more unworthy than he.

He wrapped his arms around the statue of his father and squeezed tight. But frozen in stone with that familiar glare, Witford Dimietris offered nothing in return. Just as cold and immovable as always.

"I must remain."

With a natural, indifferent attitude, the eagle man claimed he was a courier with one job, to pick up Meginhardt and take him home. "Come on, dude. You loved him and"—the creature opened its arms in a gesture of empathy—"it was real. But time to go." His feathers ruffled as he stretched, looking majestic until a talon snagged a warped plank and he stumbled.

Meginhardt clung tighter to his father. "He's stiff. Tot, ain't he? It's my doing. I offed 'im good."

"Nah, you didn't." The eagle man adjusted his step to regain composure. "He's not dead." He leaned down and glowered at Meginhardt with his one good eye. "Besides, he slayed you. Get it?"

He had to let go of his father to cross his arms. "Pa ain't done no such thing." He pumped his arms wide open, inviting the creature to see for himself. "I ain't dead."

A choppy, uneven burst of laughter jolted the eagle man's belly like a bout of hiccups. "Sure about that?"

A talon hooked into the mound of flesh and bones heaped at Meginhardt's feet. He poked his beak around the body.

Did he have to do that? Meginhardt scratched an eyebrow. "I get it. I'm dead."

Strangely, the sight of his own body left him nonplussed. Still, the bird's intrusive pecking had to stop.

"Aye, got it. Halt, I'm dead."

"Check."

"And yer saying he ain't?" Meginhardt poked at Pa.

"Check."

"And yer here 'cause yer wanna take me somewhere."

"Check again, mate."

"Well, like I said b'fore, I ain't goin' nowhere." He raised his chin. He had a life to live, and this gift, peculiar as it was, meant a new life. But first, he had to get rid of this irksome bird. Just because he'd hitched his loyalty wagon to his father, didn't mean he'd be a pushover for anyone else. He tried to pry the skillet from Pa's grip, but it wouldn't budge, locked in place like mortar.

What else could he use? Ah, the ax, leaning against the hearth. He scooped it up and swung around to face the bird.

"Dude, you planning to use that?" Not a feather ruffled. "Come now, Meginhardt."

Meginhardt gulped at the sinking sensation, a wave of inadequacy. He couldn't even scare a bird with an ax. He needed to be more like Pa.

He took slow, deep breaths. No need to suppress anymore. Inviting years of pent-up rage to erupt, he cast a warning. "I'll do it!" He raised the ax. "Go on, git!"

The eagle man shrugged its feathered shoulders. "As you wish. I'm out of here." With a powerful beat of his wings, he shot through the roof like a phantom.

Meginhardt lowered the ax, his whole body sagging. What a day of utter madness!

He faced his father. "Now what, Pa?"

CHAPTER THREE
THE WORLD TURNS

In Vereiteln Dorf

MEGINHARDT CRUMPLED, TUMBLING backward, landing hard on his tailbone, the ax firm in a two-fisted grip. The dead body beside him—his corpse—needed protecting. No cunning bird was going to come anywhere near it again. *Gotta git past me first.*

His world hadn't changed much, still just he and Pa. Though reconsidering what to do now, Pa being a statue and all, needed some thinking.

"Hold fast. Best to keep 'em both safe." That was his duty to Pa.

One by one, spheres of light returned and created a dizzying atmosphere. This time, the circuit of whirling lights widened, disrupting everything.

Pa's rifle toppled by the doorframe. The table settings for the evening meal slid and crashed to the floor. The sideboard with his mother's dishes, the ones they never used, quivered as if to shatter. Even the smoky flame from the hearth trailed in sync with the lights until everything was a blur.

Angry blue streaks of wind roiled all in their rampage.

Meginhardt clutched Pa's legs for stability amid the chaos. The world blurred. Solid browns, iron, and copper dissolved into dots of nothingness. Meginhardt held on, unable to escape the madness.

His abandoned corpse disintegrated into nothing. Gone.

Sweat dripped from his trembling hands, challenging his grip. "Ya ain't goin' nowhere, Pa. I got ya."

The planked floor split open. His body jerked, at first his legs kicked like a mule at the clap of thunder, then the pair simply hung, suspended in midair.

Whew, Pa hadn't slipped away.

As quickly as the nightmare came, the dread of it calmed. He breathed easier, their bodies cradled in warmth. A storm of colors erupted. Hues he never imagined swirled.

"Pa, look!" A strange thrill shivered through him as his father became weightless and easy to ferry inside this spectral way.

A new ground butted up to Meginhardt's footing. He spread his feet wide in the freedom of the space. A moist surface waved up and down, he and Pa with it, rolling toward a shore that materialized out of nothingness. A sweet-smelling pasture of grasses covered the waves, invigorating him and making him heady.

He glanced at Pa's face—no expression, unmoved by it all.

Meginhardt sunk into an unexpected comfort, and his toes wiggled in their cry for him to remove his boots and socks to feel the inviting earth. Where were they? The farmhouse was gone, replaced by a wide-open field of countless textures and tones, varying shades of greens, and pleasing unfamiliar scents. Better than fresh hay.

He swerved with the comforting ebbs and flows, the corners of his mouth turning up. Till he caught a glance at his father, still angry. Didn't appear this mysterious other place was about to change him.

Meginhardt turned to the direction from where they came. *Cry me a mercy.* "You seeing that, Pa?"

A landscape of rolling swells dovetailed toward them. One after the other, right out of blackness, up and over a cliff.

"Pa, we're here. The end of the world." He engaged his shoulders with pride. He was smart enough to know the earth was flat. Plain logic it was, had to end somewhere. His father had at least taught him that much.

"Megs, over here." Cheery, the voice rang out from behind. His internal warning system set off an alarm.

Nay, anyone chipper as that kin be trusted. Another wise tip he'd learned from Pa.

The voice came from a different direction. Beyond it, a towering wall stretched far and wide. A single guarded gate at its center demarked some destination point. Could he sneak in like he once did to his mother's room? In the courtyard between him and this gate, people rushed about. But where and why? No one was pulling a cart or hoisting a sack of goods. And the way they approached each other? All so hail-fellow-like.

He twisted to check on his father. "Hang on, Pa. Somethin's not right about this place." But then he lost his balance. Thankfully, all that squatting, digging, pulling, and pushing work he did on the farm served him well. He managed his way upright, heaved Pa around—when had he become weighty again?—then set his gaze straight into the eager eyes of a half-pint woman, all smiles.

"Well." She planted her hands on her hips. "It's about time you showed up."

"Ya think I know you." Meginhardt tightened his hip muscles, readying to block her from Pa. Not good how her gaze lingered on him. What was she all in a huff about? Perhaps she didn't like the clots of grease on Pa's arm. More likely, she found the wide-open jaw silently screaming volumes disturbing.

Too bad for her.

Once she shifted her gaze from Pa, the woman stirred a smile. It spread so wide it plumped her cheeks underneath her eyes, like the chipmunk who lived underneath Pa's chicken coop.

"You've arrived."

Did she expect Meginhardt to know what that meant?

The ground shifted beneath him, and the powerful force swayed him forward by a giant leap. This rolling landscape would take some getting used to. Preoccupied again with catching his balance and keeping Pa from crashing, he shifted his footing to avoid further tipping.

The woman, however, remained steady and unfazed, clutching a bundle of parchment under her arm. Her head cocked to one side, and her ridiculous grin still claimed its place.

"You didn't need to bring him," she whispered with a head nod, her low voice seemingly an attempt to influence with some kind of secret, personal wisdom. Nevertheless, her blue eyes dazzled.

Was she trying to get into his head?

With muscles tight, a deep knee bend, and a strong hold around Pa's waist, Meginhardt achieved a backward jump, increasing his distance from this woman to show his loyalty. He would not fall into her trap. There would be no relationship.

No sense raising hopes he belonged anywhere but underneath Pa's controlling vises, even if one of them or both—given the uncertainty of the current situation—were dead.

"You did not kill your father if that's what you're thinking."

"Never said I did." He would prove her wrong regardless of what she might say. Besides, it was all a mistake. He hadn't wanted his father to die.

The energetic woman respected the distance between them, for now. "You feel responsible."

"Nay, ma'am. Ya got it wrong. Sees, he struck me. I'm the dead one." He jabbed a finger into his chest. *Dah, Pa always said women were dumb.*

Stroking her neck, she released a chuckle. "That so?"

Meginhardt turned his head one way, then the other. This was a trick of some sort. *Nay, I won't be made a narr.*

The situation was awkward enough—he was never much in a woman's presence before, not alone anyway. He fixed a gaze at Pa's vicious expression, anything to get his attention away from that nosy female. But then tears started to fall, a stream of them. *Cry me a mercy, now they come. Dern, grow up.*

Heat rose into his cheeks. He sputtered incoherently.

As if sensing his vulnerability provided an open invitation, she stepped closer. "You're free and very much alive, Megs. Come." She extended her hand. "And let him go. Not finished is he."

Megs? Nay anyone called him that, except the neighbor boy a few times. His *only* friend, if you could call him that. Their talk was rare and brief, mostly just nods when they sighted each other working in their fields. Sometimes his friend left notches in the fence by one of his frequent hiding spots. It seemed his way to acknowledge Meginhardt existed.

"I cursed Pa." *Dern.* He hadn't meant to release that.

The woman's lips remained tight. Like she was expecting more.

"Ma'am, I may be dumb'n all about the world and all this stuff." He freed one hand from Pa to wave to their surroundings. "But I know I don't deserve all what he did."

"Yet you hold on to him."

"It ain't his fault. Ma died when she done give birth to me. So mind yer own."

The woman took in a deep breath. It appeared to keep her calm. "It happens more than you know."

She was getting too personal. He twitched, ready to jump farther away. But Pa was too weighty, and the exhaustion of this day was becoming more and more burdensome. Surely, this woman could see he didn't welcome her empathetic stare, so why'd she think he'd accept the hand she extended yet again?

"I'm Aivy. And your pa is not ready. You know that, Megs. You must let him go."

Meginhardt produced his best bully stance.

Aivy relented her smile in exchange for a chin tuck. "We've been trying to wake him for some time now, my friend."

Friend? "I am Meginhardt Dimietris, and I do not know you. And Pa ain't sleeping." He bristled at Aivy's response, a miss-know-it-all simper followed by a shoulder-dropping sigh. Had the whole poxing business gotten him into this notlage?

She stepped closer to ride the same wave as he. Still, they weren't in touching range. She squeezed her smooth and perfectly thin sheets of parchment like a flat wooden doll packed tight to her chest. "So then, just where will future descendants come from?"

He shrugged. He'd never thought of anything like that—or

anything about Pa's future. "Like I should know." He didn't care. Nothing hid his involuntary gulp. Offspring? *That* was why she wanted him to let Pa go?

"Hmm." She tapped her foot. Those eyebrows arched high again. "Will you come with me?"

Something Pa promised came to mind. "Two more years, Pa said he'd get me a wife for my birthday." *My own kin would get to run the farm.*

Aivy sucked in her lips and held her breath as if to assist her to say what needed to be said. "And what then?"

"I'd get my own boy." Dah. What was with her questions and unsaid accusations? He twisted the toe of his boot and forced a hole the size of his foot into the soft ground. "Pa loved me just fine."

"Meginhardt, the man who begat you chose to avoid love."

"Ya don't think I don't know that?" He coiled his fingers into his palms, his face flushing hot. His heel tapped the ground where the hole had perplexingly repaired itself.

"Come." This time, the word came as a distinct order, and her fingertips paused mere inches from his elbow.

Nay, wretched woman! Whoever this Aivy was, she knew things. But did she know about the jeering, the clobbering, the hankering Pa had for the drink, the way he could charm a rat? Meginhardt's gut twisted almost confirming that, in some unexplainable way, this pint-sized woman knew everything.

He sought his father's stony face for some kind of permission. Pa always said, "Never let a woman push ya 'round. And never, ever trust 'em."

If only the day could start over and things to be different. Meginhardt liked the idea of one day having a boy, making Pa proud.

"No sense asking him." She kneeled to fluff the fresh grass emerging from the depression where his foot had been. Her fingers stroked as if the blades were an injured rabbit's furry coat. "Besides, he's going. Without you."

His eyes narrowed. Where was she thinking to send him? "Back home?"

"To earth, of course. Your farmhouse."

He almost pivoted at the urge to run. But with no field of grain corn to hide in, he wouldn't get far, not carrying Pa anyway. "Nay." He squared himself up, ready to accept the consequence. Whatever it might be.

"There's no need to prove yourself." She gave him her back and headed toward that gate.

She must be hiding something behind that wall. Well, his rigid body was festering for a row anyway. "I ain't goin' nowhere with you."

"Heard you the first time." She kept walking away.

"Send me back with him."

That stopped her. She turned her head. After a pause, the rest of her body faced him square-on.

She squeezed her lips till they had to hurt. "But why?"

CHAPTER FOUR
A DUBIOUS LIFE

In the Germanic village of Avondale, 1688

"YOU STOLE ME?"

Lexxie grinned at her bedridden father in return to his *scherz*, ranting on about her being taken as an infant. Rubbish. "Fever. 'Tis a sign of the supernatural. You know that, don't ya?"

She pressed her hands to the sides of his neck. No swelling. "And I suppose ye be a shifter now. You gonna tell me that too? Honestly, Harmon, I declare, Grossmutter's hemlock brew drowns ye senses." She waved a cooling cloth in front of him. "Do you know who I am?"

Any other time, he'd have jumped in with a one-up return to her wit, her father equally as clever and desirous of elevations to their mundane conversing as she was. Instead, he caught four of her fingers, enough to clasp her hand, but not her full attention. "*Meine tochter, hören mich.* I must transfer this knowledge. Quick. Now, before she returns."

She frowned at his gripping and scooted away. "Vater, shush. Come now. Get some sleep."

"I shan't leave this earth without you knowing your rightful lineage."

Of all the. . .! She gave him a stern look. "You are not to pass. You've only an ague. And a mild one at that." She wrung the cooling cloth. "And ye a baby."

Harmon Huber had a boyish way about him, so much so, most times she called him by his given name rather than vater for father.

"Lexxie, 'twas that mutton stew we had last night." He grabbed the cool cloth from her hand and plopped it on his face to hide a deep sigh at the nearing sound of a scrubber shaft jingling inside his mother's wash bucket. By its vigorous swinging, she was about to stomp into the room. He tilted his head as if wondering how much she overheard.

"Aye, she's here." Lexxie sang a teasing threat. "I'm gonna ask her myself."

Grossmutter entered in time to defend her cooking. "It be those eternally grazing sheep of yours. Yer lett'n them pasture in that field of weeds. The King in Heaven only knows what goes squeez'n through their intestines. And now—yers."

Lexxie's giggle burst free with its usual sunny energy. Then she squared her shoulders. "Well, my intestines are clean as a whistle."

"That's 'cause sparrows eat more than you." The cloth had already warmed. Repositioning it didn't help. Harmon wasn't about to apologize to his mother for joking about her cooking, was he?

"Yer probably right, Mutter. That mutton sheep must'a

got into something. So, I reckon I could die right here in front of ya both."

Lexxie shared a grin with her grandmother.

He continued. "Right here on this bench. How is it you two are gonna move me? Get along?"

They formed a family, tight with trust and respect, their homestead a contented one. Humor and jest kept them smiling and eased the rougher patches in life. Lexxie had never known her mother or her grandfather. The latter, Harmon's father, had been killed in a farming accident and the former giving birth to her. The two tragedies had been difficult, both occurring in a single year, and as Harmon had explained, were the reason they moved to Avondale to start anew. Since then, they'd forged a fresh path, the only path of life she'd ever been on.

Because of that traumatic year, she'd given up on learning much about her past. Pestering with questions—especially asking what her mother was like as she so often had—earned no answers. The big nothing unsettled her heart as much as her mind. Was there a secret? Something they weren't telling her? A part of her pined for something, she never knew what. Or for whom. But this business—her father telling her he stole her when she was a wee babe—preposterous! Just, fever brain.

Lexxie seized the corn broom and began her daily sweep of the room, spreading her caring aura about. After all, a radiation of positivity could always lift a mood. A peripheral view caught her father straining his abs to suck in a deep breath. "Harmon."

He welcomed her extended arm to lift his upper body and shift his legs till his feet met the floor. Apparently, still lightheaded, he rested his head in his hands, though a grin spread at the sound of her exhale.

"See, Grossmutter, our brawny boy here is all dandy again." Lexxie leaned on her broom, casting a smile his way. "So, all that talk ye littered me with 'bout being stolen as a baby? Fever talk, Harmon. I swear."

As though a bitter wind charged, the air chilled.

The incriminating accusation hung dead center in the room without so much as a peg.

Grossmutter's gaze focused on his full cheeks. "Unsinn." The growl came from the back of her throat.

That beard of his couldn't hide the way his jaw tightened. His movements were drawn-out, but he stood for the first time since last evening's supper, an unmistakable abnormality for this fit and dedicated farmer. Evidence of his ill-being lingered in his narrowed bloodshot eyes. He wobbled, uttered something incoherent, then stumbled out the front door of their simple log homestead.

The broom slipped from Lexxie's grip. As to why her words had been so deeply disturbing a cause for concern.

"Grossmutter?"

A purple vein in her grandmother's neck bulged. And those sparky glints in her bottle-green eyes had hardened into shiny black coals.

What the dickens? Lexxie touched her grandmother's arm. "You okay?"

Grossmutter jerked her arm free with an uncharacteristic snap. "He's fine."

"I mean *you*." Lexxie shook a finger at her grandmother.

Harmon was ill. That described his weirdness, but Grossmutter's jarring response?

"He went too far. Too far with his silly jesting. I'll speak to him. You stay here." When Grossmutter spoke stern commands, Lexxie obeyed. So would Harmon. Typically, anyway.

Now, he headed for the cornfield.

Pushing out the wood shutters, Lexxie poked her head out the opening to study the two people she loved and depended upon, the only two people she ever really knew. Grossmutter might be over fifty years of age, but that lady sure could move fast when she wanted to. Good thing too. She'd never have caught up to him had he entered that field of corn, his terrain of refuge. As of late, the nights had been cool, the days long and hot, making for an extra tall crop this season. Their words outside of earshot, their arms lashed about as if they were spears of accusations.

Was there a truth to be pushed and pulled about?

The late afternoon's excitement made for an uncomfortable and silent evening. No dinner, Grossmutter's discordant rocking in her sling chair commanded the mood. Neither Lexxie nor Harmon dared as much as stoke the embers. Grossmutter's anger kept them ablaze.

"Good night wishes," she chirped, hoping to break the silence, perhaps one of them might say something.

Historically, it was a first. A night without end-of-day prayers for peace and protection, without sleep-well blessings, and without Harmon's silly reminder—"keep yer horses tucked in good and safe. Otherwise, ye might suffer from nightmares." Lexxie would roll her eyes, and he'd laugh his way to his bed, skating the wood planks with thick stocking feet.

Of course, he *was* recovering from a fever, but still, a first. As blackness laid its cover across their sleeping loft,

Lexxie lay contemplating which of the two vivid dreams would consume the night. The one of horror—when a cavalry pounded alongside a ravine, their hooves making the dust fly as they raced on a wild and fierce mission to capture her. The front man, faceless, waving an ax about, chopping at airstreams, and a haunting voice begging her to komm. Or the one of royalty—when a carriage made of gold and crystals pulled by eight majestic white-winged horses bolted through a dark sky with a winsome coachman leading the way, flying to her aid with the same urgent cry of komm.

Both dreams stirring, each vying for her most deep and inner thoughts. Rare it be to go a month without at least one vivid as she slumbered. Was it time to examine their meaning? Could there be somebody out there searching for her? Calling her whilst she slept? Might what Harmon said not have been in jest?

Nay. Surely, there were no basis for such.

Finding comfort on her side, she fingered along a crevice between two stacked logs. Imagine, though, if she were a princess of some foreign place.

CHAPTER FIVE
A LANCE OF BETRAYAL

In the village of Avondale

SILENCE CHANGED EVERYTHING. Lexxie wiggled in place, even her own quietness disturbing.

Since Harmon's feverish utterance, all contentment disappeared. To where did it go? The corners of their one-room homestead reeked of betrayal. Days stunk of awkwardness. Uneasy footwork to avoid each other, and only mere squats of obligatory talk. Arms crossed tight against her chest, she rubbed her slumping shoulders while leaning into mournful watch by the open shutters. Another sunrise and there went Harmon, escaping into the cornstalks. In less than a week, they'd gained a fullness that swallowed him whole. How convenient.

She pushed away from the rough-hewn frame, leaving the shutters wide. "Good day Vater," she sneered. Three long days with no answers. It had to be true.

She was nothing but a scandal.

"Come, child," Grossmutter snapped. "This flax needs

another round of hackling." Her grandmother could do wonders with the resultant fine fibers for spinning. The process called for concentration and patience, but today, that would be an excuse to avoid chatting.

"Naturally." Lexxie ankled to Grossmutter's utility table on the front porch, aching already over the full day of bending and pulling in store. And thus, it passed in more agonizing silence.

Appearing hungry and haggard, Harmon sauntered back from the fields after she and her grandmother finished the evening meal, Grossmutter pretended it was always this way, that the three of them never shared time together. "Chores come first, Lexxie," she reasoned.

The tension only grew. Harmon wanted something off his chest, and Grossmutter wanted whatever that was kept buried.

"Genug!" Belly full of distemper, Lexxie kicked away her chair and relished the clatter scraping across the floor. "One of ya better bring the truth to light."

Grossmutter hardly moved, just stared ahead. If her lips spread any tighter, they'd surely snap.

Harmon stood centered by the doorframe. Blinking, a habitual tic when he fussed over a problem. Though his head faced Grossmutter, he refused to lift his face to Lexxie's. He'd been avoiding her gaze these days. Her cry for attention didn't change that.

Anxiety, the sick-knot-in-your-stomach kind, danced on a tense nerve. If neither were going to talk, she would. "Just what in the blazes does 'stolen as an infant' mean?"

Grossmutter sliced a hand through the air. "I forbid any further such discussions. My son's a blasted fool who's gone too far with his jesting."

Harmon winced, his jaw grinding so hard the clatter of his teeth hammered the room. It appeared her scolding burned him inside. But what was going on in his head?

Usually, Lexxie knew, but now? Not so much. Please let it not be guilt. That would mean he did something terribly wrong, and she'd have to blame him. Maybe even hate him.

He shuffled a turn and, with an odd hesitance, strode back into the drizzly dark of the night. His head hung as though a burden to his neck.

That was it? Nothing, no answers. The humid air inside the homestead clogged Lexxie's lungs, each breath bringing a horrid helplessness.

Grossmutter carried on, her head in another world until she, too, slipped out the door and into the dark air. A hopeful sign to end this conflict.

Lexxie edged open a shutter already closed for the evening, but only the shadowy crop line and the stump fence bordering their field emerged from the shadows. Low mumbling came from their sheep shed. She wrung her hands. Perhaps they'd agree. Wasn't it about time she knew?

But when the pair returned, Grossmutter bellied an order, "Child, the hour is past, get your rest."

Harmon nodded, adding, "Go on then."

Gawping, Lexxie blinked. Was she to blame for all this dispiritedness?

Each in their own straw pallet for the night, she lay awake. She prayed for a night dream to take her away—the horrible man with the ax or the well-attired man with the gold carriage—and best hurry it up. *I don't care which one, komm. I shall go with you!*

The next sunrise, the air was different, lighter. Grossmutter's silence proved to have ceased. She went on and on, insisting Lexxie's house skills needed perfection. Going forth, she would be in charge of all the cooking, all the cleaning, all the gardening, and even take it upon herself to master the spinning wheel. "It's time you grew some roots in this town."

Baffled, Lexxie rubbed her eyes. Did all that mumbling outside in the dark of night come to this solution? The reference to *roots* grated.

"I'll be minding my job now," the woman announced with a sense of distance.

Lexxie's lips curled up. Best she make fun with a mock rather than accept the betrayal knocking at her heart. "And what, Grossmutter, might that be?"

"Well, you'll be needing swaddling and slips and caps, of course."

Lexxie coughed a hearty chuckle. Aye, the suggestion gave her soul a much-needed lift. "Now, who's the narr, Grossmutter?"

But her grandmother stood firm without so much a lift to her brows. Lexxie's shoulders dropped. Grossmutter was serious, wasn't she? *This* was her plan to shake their little household back into a happy normal existence. Truly?

"We're good people," Grossmutter muttered.

"Aye." Lexxie nodded. What was she suggesting? And what plot was she concocting? Chores, babies, good people? Lexxie's eyebrows rose as high as they could go, challenging a feature in Grossmutter's face to move. Any feature.

"You'll be seventeen soon. It's time for suitors." Grossmutter's physical stance remained frozen. "We must prove you're a worthy catch."

Prove I'm a worthy catch? "Suitors? What?" Lexxie pivoted, arms waving over her head. So much for the fresh start this morning.

She rarely went beyond the church property at the edge of town. All their trading came about by the usual peddlers, weathered and ancient as the hills. They had what they needed to eat thanks to the animal feed Harmon sold and traded, the sheep they raised, and the garden Grossmutter tended. The same garden Lexxie would start tending single-handedly, as it appeared.

So, she knew no one, particularly any boy. Except for the back of that redheaded one she lauded Sunday mornings at church. She knew nothing about him beyond the color of the silky dyed-blue ties he used to pull and secure his thick wavy hair away from his face, the leftover strands tucked over his ears. And how he rolled his shoulders before sinking into the pew with sighs before his father elbowed him back upright. But his Sunday blouse was crisp, and he most likely bathed on Saturday nights. He'd be a fine suitor. If she wanted one, that is. Was Grossmutter pushing her out? Wanting her married off? 'Twas that what's going on?

The door opened wide, and a breeze circulated throughout the room, cleansing the tension of this farcical notion. The coolness revived her flushed face. Aye, perhaps Harmon could explain.

He seemed about ready to speak. But then he closed his open mouth.

Nay, nay, say something! What second thoughts had he?

He lowered his arms and set aside the long-toothed earth chisel he carried, only to grab it back and return to his outdoor refuge.

Some normality returned later that evening. Odd chitchat

about nothing but a shared evening meal at last. Things were improving, but still, so very off.

After a welcomed sleep-in the next day, a Sunday, Lexxie readied for church. She wire-brushed and polished her boots the night before, washed and folded silk stockings from the previous Sunday, and hung her remaining attire, ready and waiting. Now, she donned her high-necked smock, a simple affair with no lace, no gold trim, and no lavish embroidery.

She blew out the last bits of air in her lungs for sheer relief when Harmon approached, holding out his elbow for her. Was his arm his way of ending the burdensome conflict inside their dwelling? Were things to go back to normal? Her heart skipped, though her stomach tightened. Should she not remain stubborn, angry for answers? Should she be pleased to take his arm or defiant to reject it?

Her innate desire for peace won. She grabbed his elbow, then stepped aside, and pulled Grossmutter in to flank her other side, all while biting her bottom lip.

"Wait, child. I've something for you." Her grandmother yanked away but returned, caressing a package wrapped in silk with tucked-in corners, pristine and perfect.

"Commemoration isn't for months, Grossmutter." Lexxie leaned in for an explanation. Why would a parcel, a gift, come her way before the anniversary of her birth? But it was in her hands now, and her grandmother's eyes were warm and teary. Perhaps this offering was her apology for the harsh atmosphere as of late.

She fidgeted with the parcel and untucked the folds, her breath arresting upon its contents. "Oh, Grossmutter, such a beautiful shawl." Her heart managed to drain a tear gland before it sank.

It was the kind worn by a woman, not a child. Made of mohair, embroidered with mature peony blooms, all pale pink, and finished with green bobbin lace. She stroked it until Grossmutter placed it around her shoulders and then shifted it so it hung just right. Lexxie didn't need reflection glass to see how it accentuated her shape with elegance and grace. She fingered the fine deep purple cross-stitched emblem of an *H* at the bottom corner. Huber. The surname they shared.

But you are not a Huber! Her soul roared, scolding herself. Wake ye. Has not the past few days torn the edges of a secret?

She let the corner slip from her hand. "Thank ye."

This gift had nothing to do with an upcoming birthday nor either any acknowledgment that soon she would come into womanhood. This was about keeping her identity hidden. That whole time-for-marriage-and-infants thing, and now this? They wanted her to forget what Harmon said.

Too late. She knew now—she didn't belong to them. Didn't they realize she was ripe with wisdom to know the truth? Hadn't they themselves taught her well?

Unable to soothe the deep hurt, she avoided confrontation by keeping three steps ahead of her so-called father and grandmother. Their usual Sunday trek involved crossing their field, following a forest trail, and descending a sloping mountain footpath.

"Slow down, child," Harmon coaxed. "I've never known you to want to get to church so fast."

How dare they pretend as such? Hurt churned to anger. A gnawing inside wasn't about to slow. Should she carry on as if she were naught but a hollowed wooden gourd? Could she ever be whole, filled with the love only truth could provide?

Nay, there would be no act of forgiving. Nay would marriage or even wee babes fill her.

I shan't bury this deceit. Far too late for that.

Stopping on the forest trail, she faced Harmon and Grossmutter. But with a rigid posture, she continued with her steps, only backward, ensuring the chasm wouldn't close in. 'Twas only evil in their faces of empathy.

She tore the shawl off her shoulders and pitched it with as much force as her elbow allowed. It floated mere feet away, landing in a set of prickly thorns. The toss, although unimpressive, stimulated a self-satisfying boost of confidence. She shuddered, for Grossmutter would be appalled. No need to look to see the woman's jaw gaping, her index finger charging.

"Lexxie Huber!"

"I am not a *Huber*. Ye can't purchase me!" Her heart pumped too fast. Trembling with a sort of pleasurable rage, she took flight the rest of the way, leaving the only two people she knew and loved, helpless and stunned.

'Twas their time to bear the lance of betrayal.

CHAPTER SIX

TRUTH, AN AGENT
FOR CHANGE

In the village of Avondale

THE MODEST WHITE-STUCCO structure with red roof tiles and a tall matching red tower came into view once she veered onto the mountainside's well-traveled footpath. Its steeple meant something. Something special. A symbol of truth, hope, love and of Harmon's King. Lexxie grabbed the trunk of a sycamore maple to catch her breath and restore her balance.

What had she done?

Taking one section at a time, her fingers coursed through tangles of hair and smoothed the waist-length strands against her nape, settling pieces in front of her shoulders. A few heavy breaths led to a cough, and her heart rate slowed. The valley stretched out below as though it could have been hers. Why hadn't she immersed herself in the community's warm charm? Rows of white dwellings also with red-tiled roofs surrounded the church in each direction. Several even planted halfway up the mountainside lodged in between groves of wild greenery. Golden rays loomed across homes full of families, and the church bells would soon beckon all.

Tears flooded Lexxie's eyes. *You were never destined to be my home.*

She often wished they lived there, inside the nestling rows of townsfolk. Then she'd have made friends. Even a proper suitor.

Except for Sunday mornings, she never came to the village. Never had she been inside a shop, purchased goods from a market vendor, experienced the schoolhouse. Her eyes had only glanced down the planked walkway from the church, the heart of Avondale, while Harmon and Grossmutter held her elbows secure and coaxed her along. Arrive early to claim their regular back pew and depart early to avoid socializing.

If the priest hadn't visited their home monthly, Lexxie's fondness for the village might never have taken any root at all. When she was little, he'd pat her head, and as she grew, he'd wink. He'd described the shops, including the latest frequented by the most fashionable. With the little she saw and heard through stories, she imagined it well enough. As she matured, the priest's deep bows filled her with respect. Grossmutter prepared her best meals for his monthly visit and encouraged his stories. Harmon often took him for strolls around their land for what he called their discussion time.

A good distance ahead now from her father and grandmother, Lexxie resumed a slower pace down the slope. A seed of peace sprouted in her heart to guide her steps toward the church. The bells were not ringing yet, so she trod with a head full of thoughts. How to slow the wild circles in her mind? She must have a plan, so what came next?

Grossmutter had warned Lexxie about a grouping of girls who sat together each Sunday. "Idle and frivolous, good for nothing but gossip." Grossmutter insisted Lexxie wasn't missing anything by not knowing them.

A sunny ray surged at the crest of a cloud. Its light smattered her face as though to awaken a revelation. They'd been hiding her, keeping her away from everyone.

So obvious. Why didn't she—

"Lexxie," Harmon called out, catching up.

Just ahead, the gossipy group of five girls walked arm in arm in graceful unison. Hats bopped, skirts swayed, and a breeze carried their bouts of laughter.

Maybe some good ole gossip was what she needed. Lexxie stretched her spine as though she'd just grown two inches. They weren't girls—they were women. Just like she was. Practically, anyway. Perchance, they knew something about her. Might that be possible?

She set off toward them, heart pounding. Might they reject her? Even so, such a risk was worth taking. They'd no reason to turn her away. A quick and silent gesture of the cross for some blessing was in order.

After a head bob, she squared her shoulders and calmed herself to a pleasant ask. "Good morrow. May I sit with you ladies?"

Taking good looks at her up and down, front and back, two women loaned their elbows and grinned. Or perhaps they were smirks. Nevertheless, ever so thankful to be welcomed, she slid into their pew on the left side. Harmon and Grossmutter ambled into seats on the right wearing tight lips and imploring eyes.

Lexxie followed all cues, chin up, hands folded, head

cocked occasionally, and the odd shoulder shake to straighten a posture. She'd ignore the chance their excessive smiles were forced.

Payment, however, came due after the service. Stepping back into the churchyard, the women swarmed like flies searching for a place to lay their eggs. Her shoulders drooped. Her spine shrank. Her desire to disappear ached. She clasped both hands to her neck, their touch comforting but not enough.

"Exactly which farmhouse do you live in?" The boldest released the floodgates.

"Do you sew?"

"Will you join the community gatherings?"

"Is there a boy you have your eye on?"

"Why do we seldom see your father in town? Do you purchase all your supplies from peddlers?"

"Who owns your land?"

"Is that older woman you normally sit with your mother?"

Would their questions ever stop?

Lexxie answered as best she could with the minimum of words, for she had nothing interesting to share about herself and no gossip about any neighbors to part with. Perhaps she could interest the women in discussing the sermon? She raised that suggestion.

And they turned away.

When all five delivered their backside view, she reached out with her arms. *Come back.* Arm in arm, their distance only grew, along with the hope of friendship. How much dejection could one take? Should she tuck her head and stroll over to a watching father and grandmother or tell these ladies something exciting so they'd offer up another chance?

A new life. She needed to start somewhere. She pulled a

long breath deep into her abdomen and, along with it, drew in needed courage. Her secret, bubbling inside, pulsed to escape.

"Wait!"

The one in the center stopped and offered a graceful half turn of her head. The others followed like sheep.

"My pa says I was taken as an infant. Stolen from another family, and I don't know—"

The women surrounded her, met her eyes with eager oohs and aahs.

"Nay!"

"Really?"

"How so?"

"From where did you come?"

"You weren't birthed here?"

"You're just finding this out now?"

"Him—is that the man over there?"

"How terrible of him!"

"Do you want him punished?"

Cheek muscles tightened as shoulder muscles relaxed. Despite the overwhelm, Lexxie grinned to fit in. She'd never before needed socializing, or so she thought. And yet, a conflicting primal fear poked around her gut. Had she shared too much too fast?

Too late now.

The lioness of the group stepped forward. Margarita, on a hunt for facts just like the animal kingdom rulers of afar in Grossmutter's stories. If Lexxie were to be accepted into this group of gossip sisters, her courage would be challenged. Margarita's mane, loaded with brown curls, didn't sway like her walk did. The swishing of her hem on the ground did nothing to hide the clickety-click of her fashion boots. A good head shorter than Lexxie, she peered up with beady eyes set underneath thick dark brows, every bit intimidating, nonetheless.

Margarita extended a muscular hand. "Let's start from the beginning, shall we?"

The other four piled in behind, all bum rolls clashing, all ears straining.

It took Lexxie a mere two sentences to tell her story but forever to calm the heaving chest that spewed it out. As more questions pounded, redness and heat climbed. She couldn't answer any of them.

"Well, this just ain't right," Margarita snapped, four voices echoing in agreement. "You must at least know if your mama is alive!"

That shook Lexxie, waking her from a gossipy game gone way too far. She'd walked straight into it and now hadn't a way out. What had she done, turning loose this dark and personal secret? And yet, she didn't know so much about herself.

Mercy, was it possible? She'd yet to ponder the notion. But now . . . might her mother be alive?

Wafts of Margarita's fragrance found their way to Lexxie's stomach. An ill feeling took over. Violet perfume didn't mix well with the manure from horses surrounding the church. Unused to such an onslaught, Lexxie pressed a hand to her temple and searched for open space, somewhere to bolt. Somewhere to stop this madness, stop the whirling in her head, if that were possible.

Mother. Did she have a mother? Alive?

First walking, then sprinting, she left the women swelling with horror, casting accusing looks Harmon and Grossmutter's way. Lexxie ran home, halting to catch a breath numerous times, collapsing beside a few torn threads stuck in the thorns of a bush. Remnants of a fine shawl, another Huber façade! Grossmutter must have gathered it, taken it back.

At the farmhouse, Lexxie waited, each passing second stirring up a crippling anxiety. "Stop racing so, my foolish heart. I must demand answers and not accept anything but the truth."

Harmon arrived first. His body loomed in the doorway, a dark shadow, barely moving.

"Is my mother alive?" Surely, her squared shoulders made it clear she would accept nothing but a straight yes or no.

With a resigned attitude, he blessed her with an answer. "No, liebste, your mother is not alive."

He wouldn't lie to her, would he? Not now. Not about her real mother. At least he didn't say *my child*. She paced, circled the room twice, then slapped her hand—hard—onto the solid dining table, making a mockery of the house rule. She had helped tie the lumber with leather banding alongside him when he built it. The table was their place of peace, never to be any discontent. That felt like so long ago now, another life. Before the lies. But no, the lies had been there even then, hadn't they?

Gritting her teeth, she released the next livid question, each word spoken slowly. "Where . . . did . . . my life start?"

He removed his hat, stroked his hair, and hung onto the back of his neck as it fell forward. He reached for her. "Meine tochter."

"Don't call me that." She ground her fingernails into her palms. "I am *not* your daughter."

Watching him blink was painful. He cleared his throat as if to keep his voice from cracking. Would he now reveal what he kept from her since she was an infant?

"Vereiteln Dorf. Two villages over. Eastbound." He swallowed as though his words were choking. "Around the mountainside."

Vereiteln Dorf? Why was it she'd never heard of the place? She cocked her head. "And my father?" The toe of her boot carried on with a tap, tap, tap, satisfying the need of a nervous twitch. "My real father. Still lives, does he? Is he there now?"

She examined his face, his jaw stern, his eyes glazed to another place and time. His chest heaved and his hands tremored. She hiked up her shoulders once more and tightened her fists, fearful the emotion was contagious. This man standing before her, this father who raised her, who with such ease made her life light with laughter and wise with stories, was coming apart.

Grossmutter arrived, hair disarrayed and face flushed. From behind, she wrapped her sweaty arms around her son, the thistle-torn shawl balled and clasped in one fist. Harmon blocked the entrance to keep her from this come-to-truth space. "Na–ay." She employed that authoritative voice of hers. Only it cracked halfway through the single syllable. "Don't ya believe a word, Lexxie. You belong to us. We raised you. We be your family. You have no other."

"'Tis no life!" Harmon broke free from his mother's clasp.

Welts rose down Lexxie's neck and across her chest. She scratched the stress crawling on her skin. No going back now. She scolded her heart for its urge to console him, provide reassurance of her love, her dedication, her loyalty.

She fixed a shotgun gaze on this man who'd pretended to be her father. Since she'd been seven years of age, she called him Harmon. It had started as a tease, a game of pretend—she, the responsible one, and he, the playful child. Now, his name would no longer bear that loving jest.

"Truth, *Harmon*. I need the truth."

CHAPTER SEVEN
THE DOWNSIDE OF NO

In the Outer Courtyard of the Kingdom

AWARE THIS AIVY woman stood by watching, Meginhardt blubbered. "Pa says I should'a never bin born." His arms kept his knees hostage, pulled tight into his chest.

Pa lay lopsided. His body like a log swayed with the lift and fall of a wave.

"Enough already." Her cocked head dismissive.

Self-soothing came as natural as breathing. Won't she understand?

'Tis not on me I'm here. "'Tis fault of my neighbor, 'cause of his addlebrained advice."

"Seriously, that's what you bring, an accusation?" She huffed an exhale so loud everyone in the courtyard must've heard. Then her exaggerated shoulder shrug at a group in front of the gate had to be cause for alarm, curiosity at least. Was she telling them he was unworthy and hopeless? What business was he to them?

Uncurling himself, he fidgeted with grass blades, plucked one, and watched it grow back. The loose one dissipated into a tiny airy visible breeze. It left a scent as it whisked away like the fresh smell of their lavender bush after a rain, only better. He needed to stand, show any onlookers he wasn't embarrassed. But before he'd any chance to shift his weight, she touched him.

Aivy's palms warmed each of his shoulders. Except for the grab of Pa, no one had ever touched him before, 'least not that he could recall.

He likened this to how Pa's trapped varmints must have felt. He dared not move. While willing his heart rate to slow, he considered ways to protect himself, escape even.

Her hands were open. Still, best to remain alert.

"You always did what you thought was best." Aivy spoke soft encouragement. Her footing tucked in closer. "Megs, you showed desire, countless times, for something more, something grand. Can't you recall what?"

"Don't think I don't know yer plan'n to snap my neck."

Aivy jumped up to a stand and backed away.

He sprung to his feet, welcoming the shivers of freedom. Though her hands held high and open at her sides, he glared at her just the same. That threat might be over, but more was coming. Dern, the woman continued to say stuff that got inside him.

"Megs, won't you remember the voice that lifted your way of thinking?"

His throat tightened, making for an uncomfortable gulp. What was she getting at? How did she know about those mellow whispers in the night, comforting dreams assuring him of his worthiness, last-minute saving events from a wielding fist? Was all that this woman's doing? Supernatural stuff?

"Nay." *You ain't tricking me.*

Aivy grunted. Hints from her face revealed her resignation to continue down this path. "The King wants to show you some things. Far be it from me as to why. Come."

"I ain't going anywhere with you. Send me back. I know ya can."

"And why do you think I can do such a thing?"

"'Cause you said yer sending Pa back."

"His skull wasn't the one crushed in."

If he admitted this woman or anyone behind that gate could send him back, then he admitted this place held an all-consuming power. He scoffed, unready to believe that. Pa said all that church-and-king stuff was a way for priests to control folks and make a living. Tight lips barricaded Meginhardt's thoughts from formulating any words, his icy stare sufficient to project a firm rejection. If he bullied-up well and good, she might arrange to send him back. After all, a bashed-up noggin couldn't be all that bad. He'd hardied through plenty of wallops before.

Aivy raised an open palm, fingers tight as if glued. Then at a swift wave of her arm, a brush of air obeyed, strong it was. It lifted Pa good and high till his boots, dung lodged in the heels, swayed well above Meginhard's head.

What's she gonna do to him? His body leaned back, Pa was gone from reach. He fidgeted, his neck straining to watch.

A crisp petal fell off his nose. It had tickled upon its landing there. Then, more droppings, light as feathers. He blinked excessively, then wiped away the strange falling debris. The air was clouded, full of the stuff, dried-up flakes. Something was dying, disappearing.

"Pa? Nay!"

But the greasy fist that once held tight onto an iron skillet was already gone. Then his upper body, taking with it the bloated red face and wolf-black eyes. Finally, his breeches and worn-leather boots. Particles floated about, finding their way to join the accumulated puddle a short wave away from Meginhardt's feet.

The stabbing in his chest didn't stop him from attempting to gather the remains, but an aromatic breeze that swept every bit out of sight did. Pa, in his entirety, eerily erased.

Gone. His father was gone. And that Aivy done it.

Meginhardt's life as he knew it was gone too, his dreams with it. "Pa's all I had. I've got no one else."

She held her head high. "You cannot bring him with you, not like that."

He gritted an accusation through his teeth. "So, you just go around killing everyone ya don't want?"

"I did no such thing. Now come."

"Already said I'm not going with you, ya deaf?"

Aivy turned to the gate, her nod authoritative.

The rolling grassy waves had brought them closer to their destination. Now, the one guarding that gate, a well-muscled, sobersided man, snapped his fingers.

The elastic finger pluck placed an uneasy friction within Meginhardt. A muscular giant and a woman with some kind of supernatural power? This encounter wouldn't remain peaceful, nor be in his favor.

He sneered at Aivy. "I knew ya couldn't be trusted."

He curled into his protection mode, tucking in his chin and folding his elbows over his head. Something was surely to follow. A sinking feeling hinted whatever supernatural affray this place had in mind would be far worse than anything he'd ever experienced.

CHAPTER EIGHT
THE BEST LAID PLANS

In the village of Avondale

HOW WOULD LEXXIE get herself to Vereiteln Dorf? Harmon had spat its name as though ridding himself of poisonous saliva. She was no further ahead, no hints to guide her to the needed connections. Her mother was dead, her father alive and living in her birthplace. Neither Harmon nor Grossmutter would give more content.

Sickened by Harmon's eyes pleading for forgiveness and Grossmutter's silence rejecting unsaid accusations they'd done something wrong, Lexxie stood firm. She'd rely on anger and determination to get her where she belonged—with the father she was naturally born to. It would be up to her own doing to figure out how.

A long arduous week followed that grievous Sunday. And thank heavens for gossip. Hearsay being Avondale's communal network, the height of updates saved for after-church gatherings. After the excitement exuding from Lioness Margarita whence she and her cubs learned of her scandal, those ladies would surely oblige and have advice.

And they did.

"Nay, ye mustn't journey on yer own," the tallest asserted.

"Plenty of skirmishes still happening." The plumpest tucked a silky dark tress behind her ear. "Do ye not know that?"

"Not fit for any woman, even if one wasn't budding and beautiful." Now why did Margarita have to add that last bit?

The fourth woman remained quiet, her face oddly vacant. Her tight lips suggested she might be holding something back.

Lexxie smiled at the blond-haired woman, hoping to draw out the suggestion she was inevitably hiding.

And those lips relented. "Well, if yer truly hard for a way, my uncle's neighbor, a care doctor, travels regularly between five villages."

"The wanderarzt? Nay!" protested the tallest.

While the plump one nodded her agreement to that, the blond-headed one held up a hand. "He has possession of a country wagon, even a serf to drive. Ain't that what she needs? And she wouldn't be alone."

Margarita, the only woman Lexxie knew by name, watched her cubs argue.

"Who exactly is he?" Lexxie inquired.

"He wanders from clan to clan across the mountainside."

"A bit more than a healer."

"Lives here, but his travel is quite regular, though."

"I shall pay him a visit." Lexxie stamped her foot. "Perhaps he will allow me to transport with him. Where can I find him?"

Margarita took Lexxie by her elbow and whispered an

urgent message, a warning. "The man is not to be trusted with young women."

Lexxie's stomach roiled. "Perhaps not." Her shoulders dropped, closing off this option. Was that what it was like, this world outside anything she'd ever known?

"How about the post rider?" the enthusiastic suggestion rose from the huddle, again from the fourth woman. She seemed to have all the ideas. Had she thoughts to escape Avondale herself?

The excitement began again.

"He rides into Avondale at least twice a month by horse."

"Aye! Vereiteln Dorf is on his route."

"A two-day journey I'm told."

Saucer-pan eyes all around renewed Lexxie's hope. "Might I borrow a horse and ride with him?"

"He's too handsome." Margarita eyed Lexxie's boots and shook her head, dismissing this option.

The others giggled.

"Ye must consider!" one insisted.

"Do you even know how to ride?" Margarita challenged.

A good question. Though Harmon knew much about horses, they'd never owned one. Only a handful of sheep, cows, chickens, and a rooster.

"Nay. I could learn." She bolstered her head high. Stomach roils churned some more. Then she, too, gazed at her boots, where Margarita had made some kind of assessment. "Could I not take the stagecoach?"

That seemed the most logical and doable, yet now they were back to the beginning.

"Women may not travel by oneself." Margarita's narrowed eyes and raised chin declared her annoyance with such a simpleton attitude. "They don't sell passage to women."

Lexxie hadn't the coin to pay, anyway. Always having what she needed when their household could afford it, she'd never been in want of a purse. But now, more fuel poured its way into her belly fire. A grown woman she was. She should have her own purse.

How had it come to this? Her happy perceptions shattered. Harmon and Grossmutter now strangers who'd lied and kept her captive.

"Demand the coin from them," Margarita roared, giving some pull to her head-lioness position.

Logical advice. Lexxie would confront Harmon and request—no, demand—sufficient coin to purchase a stage-coach ticket. He owed her, and further, he must persuade the stagecoach to allow her single travel. This, too, be his duty. She'd put those begging-for-forgiveness eyes of his to the test.

When she returned to the farmhouse, Harmon and Gross-mutter sat lifeless at the table. For the first time, they'd missed their beloved Sunday service.

She marched to him. "Three coins. I'm owed at least this, surely."

Her chin held high, she wouldn't take no for an answer. The breath in her chest didn't move. She tugged in her bottom lip, foregoing a fresh intake. Choosing to focus on the hearth behind him, not his face, her side vision witnessed him cupping his mouth followed by a slow-stroking chin rub.

Why had he shaved his beard? It took great restraint not to giggle. More than ever, he sported such a baby face.

Somehow, she kept her stance firm. This business of being unfriendly and unforgiving expended so much energy. Resisting a dogged want to melt into an emotion she'd longed for, forget this nonsense, and go back to the way things were, she forced a frown.

Life was fine. Why'd he go and spoil it? But she couldn't—wouldn't—soften. This was not nonsense, and this man and woman were not her family. That was that. All those yesterdays were over. Gone.

"Not coming back?" he asked.

Angling a strained neck, she fiddled with gathered chunks of her dress. "What say you?"

"Three coins will get you there, count'n on you not eating anything and sleeping on the road at night, fight'n off coyotes and such. Never mind drunken men." His brows made that annoying *V*. Shaking his head would have sufficed. "Won't get you back."

Three coins were sufficient for a one-way, two-day stagecoach fare. Margarita had even said so. But she'd need more.

Chair legs scratched the floor when Grossmutter stood, hands gripping her hips. "Take her, then. She shan't go alone. Go on, Harmon. Ye started this business. You take her."

"*I* started it?" The wild glare at his mother didn't last long before he gave an obedient nod, then headed back to the field, even though it be a Sunday. Seeking refuge again in those tall crops of his.

Grossmutter returned to her sling chair and picked up her needlepoint.

Lexxie rubbed the back of her neck. It helped to loosen the lump in her throat. She'd not considered this, but she'd take it just fine. Such relief.

Though how long could she keep up this stiff anger toward Harmon? And what of his backlash suggesting it wasn't his idea to steal her away? Might all this have been Grossmutter's doing?

Craving the renewal of a fresh breeze, Lexxie settled on

the porch, alone, her body atremble. Dream time, now it be. What would he be like? Nervous as though meeting a prince of some fine land, she pinched herself and giggled. Soon, she'd meet her real family, her paternal father. And what a reunion!

She waded into that dream, the one of royalty. Imaginations of that carriage of gold coming to her aid lingered. *I'm coming, dear father!*

CHAPTER NINE
THE DANGEROUS PLACE OF HALFWAY

En route to Mittel Dorf

HEART PULSING, LEXXIE settled into place in the stagecoach, squished between Harmon and some long-bearded, gruff fella in a velvet doublet of all things. She gawked at his stained wrist cuffs. Grossmutter would never approve—strict she was when it came to clothes washing. Lexxie was reminded of the warning for female travelers when the man gazed uncomfortably long at her gloved hands. Perhaps rubbing her fingers for comfort was not suitable. She stilled them instead with a tight fold on her lap.

One far-too-eager gentleman across the way pushed his knees into hers. A hollow fluttering inside her chest, a churn of vulnerability struck a chord. She held her knees and feet tight together to avoid any further unwelcoming knocks. Thunderous clatter banged as they pulled out of the carriage station, playing even more into her isolated and panicky symptoms.

Never had she been outside of Avondale—well, that she knew anyway—this town, now just an empty shell, the place she thought she was born. No midwife here to attest to her birth. All lies.

The floor had fallen beneath her feet. What else did she not know about herself? Pushing Mr. Knee-knocker out of her mind, she forced deep swallows for later when she imagined a time to claim victorious glee. Such an adventure, a whole new life—a rightful one, the life this world offered—lay ahead. A two-day journey away.

Once outside the main road, the horses proved themselves relentless, pulling the wheels through ruts and divots, jarring each passenger. Heads bopping, buttocks shifting, and most annoyingly, knees knocking.

"Think'n ta marry her off in Mittel Dorf?" The man with the intruding knees nosed his business Harmon's way with an assumption more than an inquiry. Mittel Dorf was the halfway point to Vereiteln Dorf and their overnight stop. Young women, unmarried ones in particular, apparently had no business making the excursion from one village to another unless attendance for a professional matter was required. And even then, important affairs were reserved for a man's resolve.

Harmon offered a slight nod, obviously preferring not to engage in conversation. Most assuredly, she wasn't going anywhere to find a husband, so why didn't he stick up for her?

"She is rather . . . handsome. What makes yer think anyone there is gonna want her if you can't marry her off with yer own kind?"

Her face rendered an angry heat.

The nosy man suffered a disappointing retort when, in a sluggish move, Harmon tipped his hat so it covered the whole of his face. He'd always despised confrontation. That would be about as much conversation as the man would get. In turn, the man fixed his gaze on her, and the piercing stare made her spine shiver.

Forget etiquette. She glowered back, straight on. Examined his small eyes, agleam with malice, his thin upper lip atwitch, and his upturned nose, a deformed finger rubbing at its side. *You call me handsome? What nerve.*

The unkempt and patchy beard in her peripheral vision shook from a chuckle. It seemed Mr. Velvet Doublet beside her found Mr. Nosy Man's rudeness amusing.

A couple of hours in, and the dust was yet to subside. Apparently, it would not. Nor would the sticky insult balling inside her gut.

Aside from Harmon's utter silence, Mr. Nosy Man carried on. The cheeky smirking sound from his lip-licking disgusted her.

The temperature had risen, leaving her hot and sticky, praying drips wouldn't slide down her face. If only she dared remove her hat and gloves, but she mustn't give in to such unacceptable behavior. Then again, the very act might entice some engagement from Harmon. Would not any form of interaction be better than *this*?

She was ready for a stretch. Even that was not to happen soon. Limited stops, she'd been warned. Two only before arriving at Mittel Dorf, one every three hours to give the four draft horses a break before rotation.

When she attempted to remove a glove, Harmon elbowed her side. Quick to change course, she sat up tall once again. Envious Mr. Velvet Doublet had fallen into a deep sleep, attested by his hearty snores, she risked leaning her head on Harmon's shoulder.

Dusk fell before they reached Mittel Dorf Station where the other four weary passengers allowed her to disembark first. Mr. Nosy Man shoved a sharpened elbow into Harmon's side as Harmon stepped onto the footboard, his punishment for bringing her along. They then approached an establishment that advertised boarding rooms with bath on the main road. A few doors away, a bustling eating and drinking establishment offered its less appealing presence. The boarding-room place displayed window boxes with sparse flowers, a second floor, and a swept walk out front. Though the paint was lifting in layers, the bright blue the shutters and the front door sported must've given off a welcoming feel once upon a time.

Harmon's shoulders tensed from the alleging stare of the weathered-skin, middle-aged owner manning his front desk. So she jumped in. "I'm so stiff after sitting all day, Pa." Perhaps referring to him as Pa with casual conversation could settle any suspicious thoughts—an older gentleman with such a young woman. How odd, though, to start calling him Pa again, now of all times.

The owner gave a faux disapproving headshake, then smirking a grin, passed Harmon a heavy key.

Harmon fondled it. "Would you know, sir, if there be a couch also inside the room?"

"Sure, sure. There is—if'n ya need it."

Harmon, not having the coin for separate rooms, planned to sleep on the couch. She knew that much.

They settled into the room, each with a carry sack containing a single change of undergarments, a sleeping gown, and a few other essentials. Harmon kept his coin purse in his waistcoat and a Solingen utility knife in his breeches. He never went anywhere without it, his prized possession. Grossmutter had even sewn a leather cover for it.

The door creaked inward, almost too slow to discern the movement. Then a child no older than nine years stepped inside. She pressed her lips tight, her focus on a water bowl gripped with two pudgy hands. Her slow movements didn't jostle the precious sweet-smelling bathwater nor the unequal brunette braids dangling to her shoulders. She must've done them herself. She edged the bowl onto the side table, then let out a breath, seemingly the first one she'd taken since entering. Pivoting, now almost unable to contain her energy, she bounded over and handed Lexxie the washing cloth, her face, the palest of skin Lexxie had ever seen.

"I didn't spill a drop! I'm yer housemaid. You need anythin' just ring this bell." She curtsied and presented a brass service bell to Harmon. "Night or day, anytime, sir."

"Night or day, anytime?" He arched a brow.

Who would ring a bell for service from a child in the middle of the night?

"Yes, sir." The braids dropped as her head hung down.

"What's your name?" Lexxie offered a smile.

"Matilda." The worn cloth toe of the child's right shoe sneaked atop her left, her pasty face growing red. "No one's gone and asked me my name b'fore."

Lexxie knelt before the girl. "Well, Matilda, thank you for the bathwater and washing-up cloth. We won't be needing you in the middle of the night, so you needn't plan on it."

"Aye, ma'am." Matilda glanced sideways at Harmon. "Aye, sir." Then she scurried away.

Harmon huffed. After removing a coin from his purse,

he tossed his waistcoat on the couch. "Wash up, Lex, while I scout out something to bring back to eat."

At least they were communicating now. She took that time to exhale. They'd already devoured the barley biscuits and sour-milk cheese curdles Grossmutter packed for their journey. Lexxie plopped onto the plump high bed. Her first trip away. And this bed! She allowed herself a couple of bounces. Not like her straw pallet, low to the floor and lumpy.

After sliding to the other side of the room, she pulled back three layers of lace curtains. "Glass!" She stroked the bubbly panes, three of them, each set inside an iron grid. A layer of grime on the glass's outer side hadn't blocked the view entirely. Bustling, the street was, even at the supper hour.

So much to look at. Pleasant and fun to watch. Well, anything was pleasant after that arduous journey.

The metal latch took some fiddling. "Jawohl!" She picked out distinct aromas of cinnamon and pepper, roasting meats and salted fish, all raising her energy level.

"Du bist der fänger." A youngster waving a cap ran across the road. Three others chased him, all coughing with laughter.

Lexxie laughed along. "Run fast."

The edges of her happy grin fell in sync with her shoulders. What else had she missed? She'd had no fellowships. Harmon and Grossmutter had been her only friends. Now, all their time together rasped like betrayal in its rawest form. Deception. Lies to guard her away from the truth. To do that, they hoarded her to themselves, her existence private. They kept her a secret, their secret. When she let go, the lace curtains flopped back into place to cover her view.

She peeled off her dress. Hurrying before Harmon returned with whatever he rustled, she washed up and donned her nightwear straightaway. They'd regularly been in each other's presence in their nightwear. One couldn't avoid it in a one-room farmhouse. But tomorrow, she'd reach her desired destination. Vereiteln Dorf. "I'll find amity there."

She envisioned endless welcoming arms and eager ears to hear her story, eyes bulging with delight when she appeared. Someone they'd loved and lost.

Am I like my mother? Is my father still grieving for me?

So many questions.

How dare Grossmutter plot for Lexxie's children, saying it was about time, the next Huber generation. Huh! "Well, you're not getting that from me."

She slammed a fist against her thigh. "Here and now, I promise to be accountable. I'll not consider marriage nor a family until I know my true lineage. There shall be no descendants without ancestors."

A firm nod sealed the deal.

She hadn't noticed the mood changing outside until one disturbing voice caught her attention.

"Komm, komm!" A woman's shriek.

A glance through the lace revealed those same four boys rushing to the walk below her window despite a mother commanding they stay away. Rounds of cheering men resounded outside her line of sight.

Prying her window to open wider, she maneuvered her head and shoulders and strained to see the happenings below. Based on another woman's saucer-pan eyes, something horrific was going on.

"Dirty beau!" yelled one man.

"Arsworm," yet another.

A collaborating unison of voices cheered. A ringing circle

of yelling and shouting rose its way to Lexxie's ears, a cloud of disgruntled hot air, though she still couldn't see what was transpiring. A rivalry for certain. Some poor bloke being incriminated.

"Ye a schurke."

The harsh verbal abuse accompanied thudding blows and groans, and more shivers of speculation chased themselves across her arms. He must deserve it if the whole lot were against him. Likely, too much drink combined with disgusting behaviors called for such a response. She shook her head.

Then someone rapped at the door. At least he was back. Safe. He'd be cautious to respect her privacy, to ensure she wasn't in the process of undressing.

"Harmon, thank heavens your back." She ran for the door and flung it wide. "I was worried."

Mr. Nosy Man stood there. An evil grin revealed those lips he liked to suck so much. Deformed fingers clasped a leather flask.

No Harmon in sight.

"Harmon, is it?" he mocked her. "He ain't yer pa, little lady. You like 'em like me, don't ya? Experienced." His tongue slipped up and lodged itself between his lip and decaying teeth before making a sickening slurping sound, irking her and awakening her to danger.

She lunged in a valiant attempt to grab and force the door shut.

But Mr. Nosy Man's boot was already lodged in the frame. Bulging triceps thrust the door wide, and the cocky peacock strutted in. He sized her up, then down. Then his devilish eyes gleamed at the bed behind her. "Readying for a frolic, are we? Yer Harmon's busy, so I'm takin' his place."

He shoved her.

Another step and a push, and she'd end up trapped between the thick high bed mattress and her assaulter. A stink filled her senses, the stench of drink and a caking of dust.

She cringed at an image of poor little Matilda dealing with the likes of this brute. From the window still open wide came a swelling of voices, one becoming clearer and louder.

"You be leave'n her be."

A voice of distress. A voice Lexxie recognized. Her chest devoid of air squealed in horror. "Harmon!"

An image conjured in her brain and beat the insides of her temples. Harmon was the one being beaten and trampled upon, right there outside their rooming-board window.

Then came the howl again. "You be leave'n her be!"

That was the commotion. All such invective was toward Harmon, presuming his intentions with her were unprincipled. And now he knew the devil himself was in her room.

And that devil smirked and coaxed, pulling her waist tight up against his. One hand moved to his side, brandishing a familiar bone handle, Harmon's knife. How often had she seen him wipe it clean after trimming hooves?

Her recognition only broadened her assaulter's grin. His tongue showed itself between spaced-out, rotted teeth, allowing a whistle to escape with a lusty chuckle.

Cold churned through her veins, her mind, her heart. This was all her fault.

A clear voice with a soothing calm tone spoke from somewhere deep inside. "Alexien, my child."

Could it have been Grossmutter's voice? Nay, 'twas male.

Nor could it have been Harmon's—for he was yelling at his utmost, threatening bloodthirsty harm to her assaulter.

Alexien? That nickname was unfamiliar, but the voice reassuring, promising. Her father. Must be her true father. He must know she was alive and seeking him. He sensed this danger around her.

The devil himself was about to force himself upon her.

Harmon's wretched warnings detached, drifted somewhere in the distance, too far away. "I'll cut yer throat if ye touch her!"

As the life within him was suffering a butchering from fists and kicks, willing, he was, to kill for her.

The muscles in her cheeks spasmed to keep her eyes shut tight. Wetness accumulated and dripped off her face. Harmon's yelping churned to a whimpering melody. What happened below her window was too much to bear. A revolting priority occupied her mind. She cast her faux father's cries away, out to field with a blustering wind.

Her assaulter clutched his meaty knuckles around her throat to squeeze her body still. Sheer determination moved her lips, whispered up an ask. Trusting that voice inside her was the one she hoped it'd be, a true father's supernatural instinct, she surprised herself with assurances.

"Mein Vater. I'll be all right, and I'll find ye."

CHAPTER TEN
BEGINNING THE END

In the Outer Courtyard of the Kingdom

MEGINHARDT BOWED TO a cover position, an affray sure to be imminent.

An exhalation of gross proportions whistled across his back, bristling his neck hairs. Queerly enough, the tingling sensation felt clean and vibrant, neither evil nor threatening. Unlike the reeking odor of a distillery from Pa before an assault. Ignoring the danger foolish curiosity brings, Meginhardt pivoted to face the bedlam mobilized by the burly gatekeeper's electrifying finger snap.

And there it be. Mammoth white wings. *Oh, blind me. 'Tis a man? Nay, cannot be.*

Whatever he was—an angel, a beast—he was pure and colossal, covered with a glistening white robe and a golden crisscross sash across his chest. Thick blond hair whipped like a horse's tail, though groomed like a gentleman, an impressive well-built gentleman. One capable of socking a score of men if warranted. Even his bare feet boasted dense and developed

amazon.co.uk

A gift from **Kelly Lacey**

Enjoy your gift! From Kelly Lacey

Gift note included with **Here Lyeth (A Lifeline Fantasy Novel)** muscles. Each palm alone was larger than Meginhardt's skull. Most awe-inspiring were the tall silvery-white humps sprouting from his shoulders.

Because of his cowering, Meginhardt nearly missed something spectacular—powerful obedient wings folding into home position, hence the bristling neck hairs.

Drawing in a deep breath aided in relieving some nervousness. But the next warned him—*not-so-fast, you don't know what's coming.*

"Meginhardt Dimietris, this is Jophiel." Aivy planted hands on tiny hips and beamed. "You won't come with me. So, you shall go with him."

As if he dared to push his way out of this character's presence. *Go with him? Cry me a mercy.*

Anxiety helped itself to a chunk from inside his bottom lip, reminding him of that missing eyetooth a fist punch from Pa knocked out last year. Nay to grow back, he'd been told, and it hadn't. Nor did his confidence as to any sense of worthiness.

"He's going to take you. And then you will know."

He glowered at the chirrupy Aivy. "Know what?"

"You will know when you know." Her new singsongy tone grated. "Oh, and before you go, Megs, take a good look around."

That a warning? His legs set off with an unsteadiness thanks to a bloated ground swell. Pure instinct enabled his maneuver, adjusting and twisting his body to gain balance. Only then, he realized they'd arrived at the wave's intended destination. The ground swell he stood upon melted, leaving him to stand toe to toe with the gatekeeping guard whose stocky legs planted a firm stance before the entryway. A vibrant kingdom loomed on the other side.

The man wasted no time. "Take your boots off, son."

Son? You ain't no-one to me.

Where they stood, the ground no longer roiled with waves. The gatekeeper's voice came curiously, terribly familiar. Impossible. They'd never met before.

Bossier than before, Aivy caught up and pointed where she wanted Meginhardt to look. Not far to the right of the gate was a picnic area underneath weaving archways of artistically knotted branches that hosted white blooms. Or were they doves? A warm aromatic sensation drifted his way.

A woman sat alone in the farthest of the plain wood-benched tables. She, too, was watching but keeping a distance.

"Do I know her?" A balled-up pit inside him hinted he must.

Aivy pulled at his elbow and nodded at the border flowers lining their pathway. Something else she wanted him to see. Masses of tiny eyeballs, batting lashes and lids, fixated at his every move. Rubbing swollen puffs beneath his own eyes proved a failed attempt to clarify vision, so he patted down the wetness. Plants, flowers, all very much alive, each their own being. How did he not notice these before? "Are they true?"

The whole lot had facial expressions, each distinctive from the other—anticipating, disgusted, eager, empathetic, sorrowing. Blinking, cocking, jumping, straining. Mostly purples and blues, mostly jubilant, all giving him their full attention.

He hadn't the chance to remove his boots before Jophiel reached down for Meginhardt's chin and, with a finger, pushed his face upward. Blinded by a fury of white shades and yellow streaks, he was more confused than ever.

"Now. We must go."

The massive essence of a being was not to be disobeyed.

"Don't forget this place, Megs." Coming from Aivy, it sounded like a forewarning.

Sinewy biceps secured his waist. His feet slid from his boots, his body limp and swaying. He may have nodded. For sure, he swallowed. Hard. What else were his options other than to go with—rather, be scooped up by—this Jophiel?

Where were they going? Was he not coming back?

Majestic wings spanned a breath-capturing width and, with graceful force, headed toward the precipice, the end of the horizon far opposite that gate. At his glance back, Aivy neither waved nor watched. Rather, she strolled toward that familiar woman standing under those arched trees, who now clasped her mouth as though she just witnessed something terrible.

Straight ahead, a cliff to nothing, a fall into a vast midnight, a black-blue space of the unknown was coming fast. He sucked in to fuel his ask. "Are you taking me back?"

'Twas a hopeful thought.

No response. Only the deafening, swooning rushes of synchronized wing surges.

His uncut fingernails, still embedded with soil and grime, reminders of the life he left only moments ago—or was it hours now, days even?—dug heartlessly into Jophiel's forearms. With the cliff's edge fast approaching, certainty abounded. This was to be the end of his existence.

He couldn't settle it down, his breath. Inhales gulped too much. Exhales forced out too little. Was his heart even beating? What terror lay at the end of the world?

Profound silence supervened once the thrust of Jophiel's wings stilled to a glide at the precipice. A clicking gave the only hint of life each time Meginhardt blinked. Stopping his breath, he tightened his eyes shut.

This is it. Jophiel was gonna dump him.

CHAPTER ELEVEN
ONE WAY OR ANOTHER

In Mittel Dorf

A SOFT RAP AT the door. "Miss Lexxie, might'n want you some hot brandy?"

Lexxie was awake and had been most of the night. If not for the feeble sobbing fits taking such a physical toll, she wouldn't have dozed off at all. Straightening the blankets around her lap, she leaned her head against the planked headboard. She needn't fear. 'Twas only Matilda at the door, the young girl's whisper poignant with sisterhood as though they were close in age.

"Come hither. Step inside, child." Surprised and thankful to hear her voice full-bodied.

This young girl's action saved Lexxie from her assaulter last night, that appalling beast. Matilda had bolted into the street upon the ruckus and ruse. She encouraged—well, demanded—two muscle-bearing bystanders to "Rettet das fräulein!" the one the beaten man in the street was wailing about, so desperate for her protection. As the two men entered

Lexxie's room, they found Mr. Nosy Man brandishing a knife against her neck and trapping her tight between his body and the high bed's corn mattress. Mr. Nosy Man had been apprehended, and Harmon, whom she hadn't seen nor heard from since those afflictive whimpers, was reportedly at a local caregiver's home, his wounds being attended to until the traveling physician could arrive.

Last evening's echoes still haunted her, threatening her ability to maintain some semblance of emotional stability. She pulled her knees up to her chest, remaining comforted beneath the covers. Her hands shook as they yet again smoothed out the heavy woolen blanket.

A click to the outside latch, and Matilda peeked in, tray in hand, saucer eyes wide. She tiptoed to the side table by the settee and assembled a mug of tea. At dawn, this little Matilda was a godsend. After topping the mug with a hearty splash of brandy, the girl curtsied before passing it over.

As if I'm royalty.

A deep longing gleamed in Matilda's eyes. A dark sea of loneliness. Such innocence. Unadulterated, Lexxie hoped anyway. But this place was evil, as she'd discovered firsthand, so what had this child coped with? A seed of desire to protect this child snuggled its way inside her, looking for a place to root.

Thick brunette braids swayed. One fell loose at the end as she cocked her head, seeking assurances Lexxie was fine.

To prove she had, in fact, recovered from the night's trauma, she pushed the covers away, swung her legs over the bed's edge, and patted a spot beside her. With such an unhealthy pallor, the young girl mustn't eat proper.

Matilda accepted the invitation to plop herself down. "Yer man, you mustn't worry. I hear he's gonna mend jus' fine."

My man? Oh, this town thinks Harmon's my man and I'm some kind of frilly.

Lexxie wanted to correct her thinking, tell her Harmon was her father. Her pa. But that wasn't true either. She couldn't say it, not to Matilda. "What say you, dear child? Harmon is a kind man. A gentle man. 'Tis not what you hear."

Matilda's gaze fell to study her own feet as she nodded as though wanting to believe.

"Still, I despise him." More surprising words slipped from Lexxie's tongue. To keep from sharing anything further and risking this town criminalizing Harmon as some kind of ill-minded man of loose morals, she bumped her shoulder against the child's. "You, Matilda, you were brave. Thank ye. Your action led to my, ah, safety."

Matilda's dark-brown eyes revealed a spirited and mature soul, though lost. She was searching too.

Lexxie looped an arm around Matilda. "First a servant wanting to please so, then a bear with such bravery and bold-ness, and now you sneak in here as a compassionate little mouse."

Matilda grinned, revealing a mouth of crooked teeth and a faded bruise on her cheek. Her hands pressed into the mat-tress, and her short-lived grin churned to a tightened jaw. "So, why d'ya stay with'm? Yer old enough to go yer own way, find a nicer fella."

"No. It's not like that, I swear. He's helping me find my father."

"Huh?" Matilda's eyebrows arched high. "Did someone take yer pa? Threaten to kill'm?"

Lexxie stroked the young girl's head, now both braids coming undone. "Nah, nay that either. I believe him to be living, most possibly in Vereiteln Dorf." She grabbed the hair-brush on the nightstand offered as a convenience to room guests. "May I?"

Eager was Matilda's expression at this offering. She pushed her backside up against Lexxie and snatched the fallen and worn ribbon ties.

A calm rightness settled the room. Matilda sat still, eyes closed, while Lexxie brushed and stroked the thick dark strands. Empathy opened her heart, and compassion for this young girl snuck inside.

"Your mother, Matilda. Where is she?" Lexxie dared the ask, respectful and quiet-like.

Matilda raised her shoulders high and let them fall.

"Turn just to the left, so I can braid that side." Lexxie smoothed out the ribbon ties she'd brought for herself, then finished off Matilda's hair.

From the main level hallway, a barking voice gave extra duties. Cornmeal mush and brandy forthwith for three other lodgers, one required a boot shine, and after that a sweeping of the walk out front.

Matilda squeezed Lexxie's waist and, upon hearing this gruff call from the man who must be her father, darted out.

Other guests to attend to. Poor thing. And no mother around to nurture.

Those rough red hands that seized her waist were telling. Matilda had to be responsible for keeping the guest rooms up to a fine measure. Aside from scrubbing these floors, she probably even laundered the bedding. Of course, she would, for who else was here to do it?

Lexxie fussed with her own hair, braiding the long strands while sipping her beverage that had gone cold. She'd thought too much of poor little Matilda. Time to focus on what to do next. Might she exit and walk about the town to find Harmon? It could be challenging. While making such inquiries, she'd likely endure townsfolk looking at her shamefully. Her mug shook from nerves. If Mittel Dorf were anything like Avondale, tall tales about last night already got around.

"It doesn't matter." She sat up tall. "I am leaving anyway. They can think what they like."

She picked up the boarding room's handheld mirror. "I am on a mission. I haven't done anything wrong. I will simply explain, and Harmon will confirm it."

Nay, he wouldn't. If he refused to talk to her about her real father, he wouldn't do so to strangers. They might take him from the caregiver's home straight to the schulze. She drew her shoulders up again. "Harmon is better off to be involved no further. I shall continue to Vereiteln Dorf without him."

Besides you hate him now, remember?

"Yes, I despise him. This is all his doing." A single beating was nothing compared to a lifetime of lies.

After a pause, she stroked her firm nose and wide forehead. Lioness Margarita was right. Handsome. *I'm not delicate or comely.*

A nickering on the street enticed a look, a single pane still open. The stagecoach driver a few doors down was loading up overnight bags. She must go. Harmon would understand. After all, he already paid for the journey.

Harmon, please forgive me. She scooped up her carry sack and cut short her speedy plea.

Then an argumentative, yet deep and buttery monotone stilled her movements. Hark. Its source, too, came from beneath her window.

She drew the curtain across, and there he was. Had to be just over twenty years, average height and fit, untying his horse from a pitching post. With his square chin held firm, he made a swift move to point a finger at his chest. Matilda managed to occupy his full attention, begging for something he hadn't the least bit of interest to give.

Despite the oversized satchel on his back, an enormous size for any man to be burdened with, he heaved himself onto his horse and drew that pointed finger to her face. "I'm never late, girlie, and I don't intend ta start today."

Lexxie cranked the window wider to glean more of his face, but an extra-wide black brim hid that.

Matilda grabbed his wrist, the feisty mite, and yanked with full force. Their argument grew with intensity, as did Lexxie's appalled emotions. A bile rose at a flashback of last night's assaulter. Whatever for would that man argue so with an innocent girl?

Leaning from the waist beyond the open window, certain to catch the vagrant in some unkind act of naught, Lexxie bellowed a warning. "You harm her, and I'll see you charged, you villainous knave."

Matilda pointed up to the window, and the man's chin followed in sync, two pairs of eyes glared into Lexxie's.

The horse's head maneuvered an awkward sideways tilt. Harmon would say that meant unbalanced weight on the animal's back. A brass horn attached to a sealed satchel gave him away—the post rider, the much gossiped-about catch.

So that was him?

She clasped her mouth. Heat rose into her cheeks.

The post rider dismounted his horse.

An abrupt thrust to pull herself back inside resulted in a

bang, her skull colliding with the iron frame. She rubbed her head, the pain nothing compared to the foolishness flushing through her. One or the other caused a dizzy spell.

Breathe. No reason to be alarmed.

"Catch that stagecoach and be done with this town, including that post rider." *With the emerald eyes.* She snatched her bag.

What had Matilda said to him? Did that child betray her character? If so, Lexxie would be done with her too.

Two quick, meaningful bangs on the door startled her as she reached for the latch to make a fast getaway. Having already started to thrust it open, she blinked at—him.

His fists balled up, and he shoved a folding of men's attire into her chest whilst Matilda stood behind him, appearing hopeful. "Put these on and hurry it up."

At his command, Matilda nodded her encouragement.

Lexxie let the package of clothing unfold—trousers, shirt, underwear, and socks, all fit for the male species. They'd been laundered, most likely by Matilda. Lexxie shoved them back. "I most certainly will not. Now, move aside. I'm late for my coach."

Matilda played mute, shaking her head now.

"Nay, woman. No coach will take the likes of you." The post rider crossed his arms. "Now move it. I'll accept two coin, and you'll do as I say."

She needn't be insulted by this rude man. "The likes of me? How dare you."

Even his growl had harmony and reason she couldn't help but notice. But ride with him? Nay!

He leaned in. "The girl told me herself. Yer the unmarried sort, aren't ya? That reinsman don't take kindly to women travel'n alone, especially a maiden."

Matilda stood behind, nodding like a horse irritated with allergies.

"And if I be a man, that'd be okay!" Lexxie's upper lip drew close to her nose. Her sneer would let him know how she felt about him and his ridiculous suggestion. Awkwardness hung heavily. He too has heard a version of the assault. Still, something about him unnerved her—likely the fact it be the first time she found herself in direct contact with a stranger who wanted to help her. Was the wind changing direction?

"Five minutes, then I leave with or without ya. Preferably without." Leaving Matilda to convince Lexxie, he took to the stairs, two at a time, his mumbling distinct. "Villainous knave, my arse."

Matilda slipped into the room and closed the door. "You must go with him. He promised me he'll get you to Vereiteln. He'll take care of you, make sure yer not harmed or anyth'n. I made'm swear ta me and cross his heart. But ya gotta dress like him. Folks'll think yer his apprentice." Her brown eyes glowed, her fresh braids intact.

Lexxie clicked the heels of her boots and puffed up her chest. "I shall take the stagecoach. I shall demand the driver accept me. He'll understand if I explain. I have a paid ticket already. In fact, my ticket is for double his fare—two travelers."

Sinking in was her plan to do it, actually leave town without Harmon. She pushed down questions about her sanity and swallowed the answers.

Matilda pursed her lips and pulled at a braid. "Yer daft, fräulein. Not without a mankind, a guardian. Not here in Mittel Dorf. That reinsman ain't gonna let ya on 'iz coach."

Lexxie hung her head. "I can't dress as a man and go with that, with that . . . ruddy courier. I shan't." Not to mention how she'd embarrassed herself, calling him names, suggesting he had ill intentions with Matilda.

"You gotta if yer want'n ta find yer pa. Don't ya? Thought you was want'n ta know your kinfolk? That's what ya said. If ya please."

Everything in Lexxie stilled. What about the voice that spoke distinct and calming in her head earlier?

Alexien . . . The call echoed even now.

Above all else, she must find her father.

She eyed Matilda. "And what's in it for you?"

"You owe me." Matilda stormed a pointed finger Lexxie's way.

And that she did. If it weren't for Matilda, Lexxie's assaulter wouldn't have been stopped in time or arrested. Lexxie knelt to the angry girl. "Aye, you are right. I thank ye, Matilda. What can I do for you?"

Matilda crossed her arms over her puny chest. "After you find yer pa, come back here and git me. I've bin wanting a way out a long time now."

"What would your pa say?"

"He ain't my pa."

"Uncle?"

"Nah. I ain't got family, and I'm look'n fer one. You know, ta join." She cleared her throat. "I like you some. You'd be good family for me."

A whistle shrieked through the open window. The post rider was anxious.

Lexxie stood, and Matilda stole the clothes from Lexxie's grip. "Put those man clothes on now. I'll git some boots, a neckerchief, and a hat fer ya. I'll sneak them from my uncle's room, so don't let him see you. Git outta town as quick as you can."

"I thought you said he wasn't your uncle."

"He ain't. I told ya." At that, she ran off.

Lexxie scouted around the room. The sick feeling struck again, running off without Harmon. He'd worry. She'd have to ask Matilda to send him word. Lexxie undressed and redressed to the likes of a man.

Coin. She'd need coin. Stealing money from Harmon's purse—not a right habit, but a right cause. She took what she needed, what that ruddy courier demanded and a bit more for food.

Matilda returned in a flash. The boots were stiff and far too tall, but they'd do. Matilda grabbed a stool to stand on so she could pull a generous helping of Lexxie's hair into the wide-brimmed hat while Lexxie tied the neck scarf. A braided strand slipped out.

"Matilda, go get some scissors."

"What fer?"

"My hair. I'll be a high sign to the spur of a road agent." The very thought of another assaulter catapulted a series of shivers.

"Yes, ma'am. You wanna be sure ya don't look like a maiden, not to them. Yer face is okay, but like ya said, yer hair'll catch their eye." She flew from the room on a mission.

First Lioness Margarita and now bold young Matilda. Lexxie stroked her nose. Was it too big? Too long? Never mind.

Never would she dare the chance to run into a pack of road agents. Not ever having seen one before, she'd sure heard of them. They sat in the wings of wooded areas and trenches, targeting folks for the pleasure of their gain. The stagecoach was easy prey, given its pride in sticking to a public schedule of sorts. It was like hiding a sugared treat from a youngling, then telling them where to find it, according to post riders anyway. 'Course it was the post riders' livelihood being threatened.

That's why they kept mail delivery with a single man and his horse, more flexibility to take different paths, shift their schedules. Though given this ruddy courier's sternness, he must be on a schedule. Maybe he just needed to beat the stage-coach to each station to prove he could get the mail delivered faster than his threatening rival. Still, the plundering, murder-ing, raping road agents gave the post riders reason to keep their jobs, and gave good reason to be mistaken for a man.

Matilda hustled back into the room, eager to saw the blade's sharp edge through Lexxie's freshly braided hair. "Bend down."

With the trauma of her near-defilement last evening far too raw to argue, Lexxie leaned forward in obedience and shut her eyes tight. Heavy blond ropes dropped to the floor, fol-lowed by a handful of disheartened tears.

"Pinkie swear," Matilda demanded.

Lexxie swallowed a gulp of courage and stared at this bold young girl who somehow learned to make terms for herself. "For what?"

Matilda wrung her hands and yanked on her fingers, her voice not so demanding this time. "Ta come back fer me."

Lexxie gulped. She didn't do overwhelmed. Her life was simple—well, had been.

Muscles in her face pulled away from her cheekbones. Her eyes willfully shut. Too many emotional loose ends. Now this.

Nothing in her upbringing prepared her for anything beyond the farm. She coaxed her core to relax.

Focus, straighten out to the one critical matter of import. Though, no doubt, this Matilda needed a way out and none could blame her, getting to Vereiteln was Lexxie's priority. That was all she dared focus on right now. Even concern for Harmon must fade away.

Without as much as an inkling of acknowledgment to Matilda's plea, Lexxie's mind escaped to where it needed to be. If she were to dress as a man for the day's travel, how would she properly dress in Vereiteln Dorf?

Racing across the room, she shuffled through Harmon's carry sack. She snatched his coin purse, secured the coin she had taken moments ago back into the purse, and shoved the purse into her trouser pocket.

The post rider's annoying whistle rang through the window, and Lexxie, having pushed Matilda aside, bolted down the stairs.

CHAPTER TWELVE
THE RUDDY COURIER

En route to Vereiteln Dorf

RIDING ON THE back of a saddled horse was yet another new experience. Before long, a rhythmic throb in her chest snaked upward, burying a home inside her head. The aching motion mocked her trade in life—a once warm and happy heart exchanged for the hindquarter of a palfrey mare and a clutch upon a man with a brick heart. Had she manufactured all this? Her brain pained even more than the inflamed sacrum that burdened the weight of her bounces.

Hours passed. No stopping to rest nor speaking any word, though the latter suited her fine. They traveled through bush, tall grasses, wooded forests. Why they didn't stick to the beaten path she sighted now and again, she didn't have to ask. Road agents. A crawling itch on her right calf was making her dizzy with craze. She had to do something. Shifting her weight, she twisted and reached a slim hand inside her boot.

That was the last thing she remembered.

She awoke flat on her back. Stretching her legs felt so good, as did pointing her stocking toes away from her torso, her elbows clasping one another overhead. Lying there was such peace, even though the blanket beneath her was rough and smelled worse than a barn full of sheep. The breeze blowing across her face brought about her gentle awakening.

Then that dern buttery voice interrupted her pleasurable moment of revitalizing breaths. "Good. You're comin' 'round."

Her body spasmed into an involuntary stiffness.

Then his laugh.

It took mere seconds to sit straight up, on guard.

"I thought I was gonna have to leave ya here."

Judging by the sun, a valuable dose of time had passed. Protected from its high-noon position thanks to an oak, Mr. Ruddy Courier seated himself on a stump. With his wide-brim hat on the grass, leaf shadows flickered over a head full of hair sheared to short stumps, a rarity as far as she knew.

"Here." He handed over half a biscuit while his tongue muscled a nugget of something from his front teeth.

She nodded toward his canister, preferring a swig of ale.

He obliged and chuckled as she ensured the belting cord around her trousers was secure before accepting his offering.

The surrounding nature was surreal. Soft green moss blanketed a slight grade, lazily dipping to a rill where the mare rested beneath branches that ached with an abundance of leaves.

"It's lovely." The words slipped past her lips.

"Yeah, good place to stop. Think sometimes too."

"You? The thinking type, ha. What could you have to consider about, other than how to scrounge coin from women in distress." *Argh*. What say she? This whole discovery journey was changing her, not for the better.

He stood and, with pursed lips, stared at the stream. "All right. Let's go."

"Wait." She held up a hand. "I didn't . . . I shouldn't have . . . That wasn't necessary. Forgive me. I was wrong to lash out." Oh how she appreciated his look, somewhat of a message claiming to understand. "How'd I get here, by the way?"

"Ya fainted. Or slept and slipped or somethin'. I've never known anyone to ride and sleep at the same time." He chuckled. "That a talent of yours? If so, you're in need of a bit more practice, 'cause you fell off."

She blushed and arched her back to give it a rub.

He gestured to the tree. "I picked you up and tossed you over the horse to get to this spot. I had to lean you up on that trunk so's I could tie Sadie up by the stream, unsaddle the bags, and spread a blanket out."

That made her blush even more. She patted at her hot cheeks, feeling her hair tangly and wild from hat head, not to mention Matilda's uneven butchering chop. "I must be a sight, dressed like some cattle herder. You must think I appear so foolish. And my hair—"

"Nah."

She held a hand over her chest but wasn't prepared to go as far as offering a tentative smile. The whole dress-like-a-man-thing was on him.

"You left your father in a state."

"He's not my father."

"He's not my father. He is my father. I'm look'n for my father." He waved both hands at her. "Make up yer mind, woman."

Nope, still don't like him. Excessive grunting was unavoidable as she hoisted herself up. Ugh, her boots were no longer on her feet. Regardless, once her shoulders were square and hands clutched firm at the hips, a scowl was easy, but her voice wavered. "Harmon raised me from a babe. I'm looking for my real father. Good enough for you?"

"Yeah, I heard. He's supposedly in Vereiteln. And worth leavin' this Harmon like that after the beat'n he took for you?"

"Dah, you were the one in such a hurry. And if it weren't important, why the dickens else would I be ridin' with you of all people?"

No reason to acknowledge the leaving-Harmon-behind accusation. That part she wasn't ready to contend with. Groaning, she stuck her stocking feet into the tall, stiff boots and tucked the trousers inside.

"Well, you ain't paid me yet."

She tossed a coin at his feet. "You get the rest once you deliver me."

Hands on his hips to match her previous stance, he rocked back off his heels, not even stooping to pick up the coin. "I've earned extra carrying yer off the horse and letting ya sleep while I've a tight schedule to meet."

She tossed another coin at his feet and stomped over to Sadie, the much nicer of the two.

Mr. Ruddy Courier claimed his coin, tended his horse, resaddled his postbags, and secured his lot of packages before tightening the belt holding his pistol. After mounting, he reached for Lexxie's hand to heave her up. "What's his name," he asked. "The real father of yours, that is."

Her shoulders hugged her neck. A wet gloss fogged her eyes. "I don't know. Harmon wouldn't tell me."

He tipped his head over his shoulder. His quizzical face could almost be mistaken to have a streaking of care woven within. "So how do you know it's Vereiteln Dorf you ought to be look'n?"

"That's two villages east of Avondale, isn't it?"

"That's it? That's all you got, two villages east?"

It must sound vague and foolish, but it was the foundation of her existence. The grass was cut from under her feet, and she must find a new and stable ground.

He shook his head. "Well, if'n he's from Vereiteln, it might be some witch cast a spell on him."

Though his chuckling chest proved his sarcasm, her face cooled at the suggestion.

"'Course, I don't believe in that stuff, but the folks in that town, well, they sure do. They're full of 'em, plenty of witchy goin's-on."

She looked up in silent prayer.

"By the way, my name's Jonne."

At that and a tug on the reins to cue Sadie, they galloped. Another five or six hours till they'd arrive at Vereiteln Dorf post station.

CHAPTER THIRTEEN
AT THE PRECIPICE

In the Outer Courtyard of the Kingdom

TOO LATE FOR regret. Eyelids clamping, brain spinning, primal instinct kicked in. Intrusive thoughts.

No time to debate his next panicked move, absurd as it was. Meginhardt released his life grip on Jophiel. If he'd kick up a fury he'd leave the mammoth bird-man with no choice but to drop him, an accident of sorts. Not on purpose. That way, he needn't be shamed his life ended by way of some kinda failure on his part. Aye, then, his demise would be *their* accident, not an execution. Still, his life was about to be tossed into an endless sea of nothing like a bag of chicken bones. So would it really matter?

His breath suspended. Despite the want, his eyes wouldn't shut.

Air propelled around his body, increasing his lift. That paradise of opinionated flowers was no longer beneath him, rather their blinking faces all left behind. Jophiel carried him across the threshold and straight into what had to be the absolute end of existence. Or at least, the outside boundary of this kingdom. Headlong into fast and strong winds.

A thunderous anger of lightning raged above, and irrational fear raged within. Meginhardt abandoned his hideous plan and hung on to Jophiel. Tight. He prayed, to whom he wasn't sure, and neither did he trust all would be well.

Why was the bird-man increasing their height, straight into the thunder? Who needed more height when a sea of abyss lay below? Likely, it made for a more terrified victim.

"I give. I give! I'll go wherever she wants. Just don't drop me."

Jophiel's hearty belly chuckle shook Meginhardt's forearms, adding more vigor to the unpleasant free-hanging sway. Apparently, there was no going back.

Jophiel continued to climb, Meginhardt clenched as prey. They barreled through the storm. The deafening shrieks of howls and piercing needles of shivers becoming their sole atmosphere until it wasn't. Above the storm, a platform of calmness, a ledge of pure black. Jophiel aimed toward it, and though he'd nothing solid to land on, his captive's sway lessened.

Soaring churned to an effortless glide. Turbulence smoothed to tranquility.

Meginhardt dared a look. Beyond the viewing platform of blackness, a deep sea of nothing but blurs. Conscious his heartbeat slowed some, but not enough. Still nervous. The height alone with no control and this eerie blackness was mind staggering.

"Why . . ." He choked. "Up here?"

If you're plannin' ta dump me, you'da done it by now. I'm not dumb.

"When the enemy attacks, you fly higher," Jophiel said.

Who was attacking? Best leave that one alone. Meginhardt had enough to deal with, never mind the introduction of yet an additional assaulter.

Jophiel employed a gentle pace with rarely a flap for a period. "I've no intention to drop you. Examine carefully. Tell me what you see."

They were quite a distance from the luxury of something solid to stand upon. And oh how Meginhardt longed for it! Was the courtyard the last time his feet would touch solid ground?

Despite the swelling waves, it'd been a paradise indeed, hadn't it? Would he get the chance to go back? And what of Jophiel's instruction? What kind of enemy lurked in a sea of nothing? That must be what he was hunting for.

Not going to drop me, yeah right. He still thinks I'm idle, nothing but a narr.

With the distant storm clearing, Meginhardt braved a glimpse into the vast vacuum of nothingness below. Surprised he was, eager to widen his curiosity.

Ribbons of colors spread horizontally, one atop the other without blending or patterning. Each color gleamed, alive with its own personality. Coming to play from four corners of the vastness, flopping and bowing to one another before merging systematically and elevating in an orderly manner. Moving in united harmony, the multidiverse rainbow drifted upward.

From here, he appreciated the telescopic view, details becoming clearer when he laid his glance upon a section. In the farthest corner, bubbles of light, not dissimilar to those that entered his farmhouse when Pa—

Meginhardt dropped that thought, his separation from Pa still pain-filled. Besides, too much to focus on here.

Hundreds of them, bubbles sputtering into the dark atmosphere at rapid rates from open-ended cylinders, a chaotic eruption of splendor. He zeroed in on one in particular, the beauty as the bubble unfolded and birthed into a strip of color stunning beyond words. The streamer came into its personal hue, then yielded in line with the others and spanned as if to spread wide its arms, so welcoming, so graceful.

Meginhardt's mind spun. Who'd ever imagined such magnificence?

These casts of hues had traveled from somewhere and were on some kind of orchestrated mission. "Where are they going?"

Wait. He'd released the tension from his grip. When had he accepted that Jophiel's secure hold and the buoyant capabilities were sufficient? For yes, he hung in utter awe and safety.

A glint from Jophiel's sleeve flashed as he lifted an arm toward the cliff, reminding Meginhardt from where he came before being ambushed and forced to confront a storm headfirst. He tightened up his grip on Jophiel's forearms and zoomed his vision to the rising distant strips of colors, focusing on the one next in line to reach the cliff's top outer edge.

Displaying hints of its innermost soul, the glowing strip of revitalizing green curled loose into itself, again another transformation. A circular wind of calm blues with the optimism of yellow streaks and tinges of ruby red swirled up and over the cliff in exuberant energy, landing soft onto a waiting ground swell.

Gadzooks. Meginhardt's jaw hung agape.

The what's-it transformed to a who's-it. The orb of energy unfolded with grace, a human being appearing. Order and routine, one after the other, he witnessed a dozen before formulating any kind of question. Each ribbon unraveled its array of color like a peacock, then transformed into a person. A living person, having some kind of escort, most of which were like the eagle courier who attempted to pick Meginhardt up at his farmhouse. Other escorts resembled Jophiel, more man than eagle, but from what Meginhardt witnessed, none of them measured up.

"Arrivals," Jophiel responded.

Meginhardt didn't have to ask.

So many questions churned, but his voice was stuck under a rock at the bottom of his gut. Was he supposed to arrive like that? What color was he? Did he miss his chance?

Now what? Maybe, just maybe, Jophiel would take Meginhardt back to Vereiteln Dorf to be with Pa. Things could be different—no, things *would* be different. *I'm wiser now.*

"Time to go. Hang on, boy." Jophiel repositioned his arms to increase the snugness, extended his legs, and swooped. Down in circles, the grandeur of his wings spread with majestic strength. The pair soared through pure black and deep-blue hues before uniting paths of gassy atmospheric color layers. Boundless waves of magnificent color.

An ear-to-ear smile stretched out Meginhardt's lips, and blissful laughter threatened to break free. Never had he ever imagined something so uplifting and natural as they dove into a lemony presence. His head went dizzy with the fresh and tangy aroma of citrus, like someone peeled a luscious, sweet pomelo, a scarce rarity where he came from.

Drunk on the sunny surprise, he luxuriated in the radiant

yellow. They had entered the first-in-line color ribbon, more of a yellowish gaseous mixture with fine sprays of liquid than a solid. He absorbed its presence, so personal. It had a life of its own—it *was* a life of its own. Eager and cheery. An unexplainable, envious zest.

Had he known someone like that, could his life have been different, better? Could a person like that have helped him change Pa? How often had he lingered awake, pondering what his mother was like and imagining how their lives would have been had she not died at his birth? If she were anything like this fair, fine, and fresh energy, she would have lightened the mood every day. She would have taught him things.

But now Jophiel's feet extended downward again, and something pinched Meginhardt's chest over leaving that sunny presence. Alas, the choice was not his. They swooped and entered the next layer—green. Or perhaps blue? This mixture of hues was more complicated. Graceful wings smoothed away turbulence.

Now soaked in a murk of turquoise, Meginhardt jolted at Jophiel's breath close to his right ear.

"Can you feel it?"

"These are people. Each color, each layer," he answered, as though something so mystical was common knowledge.

"They're coming home. You're in their path. Tell me—what's this energy struggling with?"

Instinct kicked in. Female, perhaps past childbearing stage. A mother, likely. "She's afraid." Once Jophiel's sideways nod confirmed his assessment, Meginhardt concentrated some more. "She don't think she's enough. Her mind's so occupied. . . . She thinks she's not lovable."

Jophiel's squeeze suggested empathy for the woman and pleasure with the assessment.

Meginhardt's head rose. His taut muscles loosened. "You're not going to drop me."

"Not going to drop you, boy."

They swooped through more layers. He absorbed the energy and, amid each, worked on describing the fruit and fears of its presence. A skill within him awakened. He never had an inkling it existed.

The experience continued, exhilarating and rewarding in its challenge. Then came along a thin purplish brown strip.

"A young lad, around eight to nine years of age. Kind-hearted." Meginhardt's voice churned to a whisper. His chest constricted, his heart walloping its walls. "Badly beaten. By someone he loves." He wanted to embrace this energy, scoop it up into his soul, comfort it. "I wish . . . I would like"—he swallowed hard—"to have a boy of my own."

But the reality of his past . . .

He squirmed to see Jophiel. "Will you be taking me back?"

If only that was the plan. If only Jophiel could return him to the earth, so Meginhardt could finish his walk there.

"I know more now." His heartbeat steadied. He drew in deeper breaths. "I'd be better at it. And I want to have a family. I promise I'll cherish them. Going back, right?"

"Walking in the paths of others has helped you."

How wise Jophiel was. Still, he hadn't answered the question.

Breaking the silence with a deep sigh, Meginhardt regarded the young boy's energy as it orchestrated in harmony, arching and aching to reach the top edge as the others before him did. At last, he flipped over and landed on top. The energy transformed into a young boy, one who could barely contain his excitement as he clambered onto a ground swell to balance.

The boy would next make his way across the field, riding that wave through the courtyard under the careful eye of his eagle courier and be awed by those chattering border plants. Then he'd land at the gate where Aivy and that gatekeeper would greet him and offer him further instructions.

Meginhardt exhaled. "Why didn't I arrive like everyone else?"

"You refused. It wasn't your will."

How was he supposed to know how everything worked when you died? Or almost die. "So then I can still go back?"

He fisted his hands. No way would he let a little smack on the head stop him.

Several more layers came and went, but no response from Jophiel, no more analytical assessments regarding the energies. Purple, emerald, pink, turquoise, another yellow, red, a murky brown . . . then a pitch black.

"Whoa." Meginhardt fixed his curiosity on the approaching ominous black wave and tugged on Jophiel's forearm.

"Not sure you're ready for that one yet, boy."

Still, Meginhardt arched toward it with such eagerness he coerced Jophiel to skip the other energy hues and swoop directly to the heaving blanket of thick darkness. The heavy, boggy energy slowed the lineup of energies below it, and Meginhardt gasped. Tears dripped fast and steady down his cheeks.

"What in the blazes has caught your mind?"

"Is this my pa?"

It *must* be. It *had* to be.

"What? No. Your pa, he's still—well, why ask that?" Though it seemed Jophiel knew full well.

"It smells like him." Twisting his mouth, Meginhardt

stilled his core. His arms and hands readied to protect himself. "I feel anger, anxiety, jealousy, and . . . and . . . *hatred*. This energy wants only to destroy. Not just others, but himself. Something's terribly wrong here."

Jophiel hauled Meginhardt out of the black layer, turned him around, and held him up so they'd be eyeball-to-eyeball. "Sorry, kid. You had a rough ride. But that is not your father." He drew his shoulders up and cocked his head. "A sort like your pa, I suppose, but not him."

"A stenching foul breath, just like his." Meginhardt wiped his eyes, then blinked at the movement upon the cliff's edge. A pink energy had gathered to shape and formed a young female. She was shaking herself off and getting her footing and balance, ready to ride a rolling grassy wave across that field like the others. A gentleman was next, forming a shape from that turquoise energy, on his knees, preparing to stand and balance. Inevitably, he, too, would roll his way inward.

With that black energy still spinning Meginhardt's thoughts, he nodded toward them. "Who can actually arrive, then?"

Jophiel held Meginhardt face-to-face in midair. "They've completed their earth journey and come home. Well, some aren't from here, but they are arriving here." He carried out a head tilt, his words dipping. "And some from here don't come back."

Meginhardt twisted his face up for the missing parts of his confusing explanation.

"Never mind." Jophiel winked. "TMI. But you get the Arrivals part, right? Tell me you got that."

TMI? What kinda ciphering is that? Meginhardt wobbled his arms and kicked his feet to see his own body. "What color am I?" His gaze burrowed into the gleam of Jophiel's eyes. "I must be something. I deserve my own."

"Calm it. You absorb too much of this blackness, and it absorbs you. That's why—" Jophiel paused as though he nearly said too much.

Then he took a butterfly stroke to remove him and Meginhardt farther out from the grim strip of dark energy. "I knew you weren't ready." He shook Meginhardt albeit with gentleness, enough to give the sense he needed to rethink his pride and self-pity. "Onward. To the next stop."

"Wait." Meginhardt wiggled as if he could hold the behemoth back. "Tell me. Exactly. Why all this?"

Jophiel maneuvered one full and powerful downward flap of his wings and swooped up, high, back into the darkness. A rapid swerve. Already, they were above the cliff again and heading in the same direction as the Arrivals.

Whew. Maybe Jophiel would dump him right where he scooped him up by the gate with that finger-snapping burly guard and the bossy Aivy woman.

He'd get another chance.

Beneath the glide, the Arrivals, each on a wave, one in front of another, peered upward, displaying a sense of awe. A boy carried along by one with an essence as Jophiel was one of many astonishing revelations they'd encounter. Now, they were fully formed and appeared how they likely did when they separated from their earthly bodies. One moment, there. The next, here. Awed with unbelief yet nervous and cautious, as he was.

"I get it—I refused," Meginhardt hollered up to Jophiel. "So do I get another chance?"

Ah, there stood Aivy, fully immersed and preoccupied with other Arrivals.

If a second chance was coming, did he want it? Could he trust himself to comply? After all, trusting was dangerous. Trusting your neighbor was never a good thing. How many times had Pa said as much? Definitely not advisable as far as he was concerned. Even after what Meginhardt experienced, he'd rather take that experience and go back home where he belonged. The farmhouse in Vereiteln Dorf with Pa. Stronger now—wise even—Meginhardt could handle Pa better, if given the chance.

Again, Jophiel ignored the question. He swooped across the courtyard, took a right turn at the gate, flew past the picnic-table area, swooned a glide around a winding mountainous path, and landed inside a fog-filled aromatic outdoor arena, Meginhardt in tow.

A circular maw yawned in the ground before them. More beings like Jophiel, wings and all, climbed out. Some dove in.

No human-looking beings anywhere.

Something was amiss. Meginhardt's heart commenced to hasty pounds, and a flush of excitement coursed. A cold sweat trickled fear to his limbs. His usual retort was to cower and protect his head. But this was quite different.

"Your turn next." Jophiel dropped, then pushed him to his knees.

The shallow fog lay heavy.

Meginhardt sank to all fours, his hands clouded out of sight, though the ground was solid and warm. He could've kissed it, thankful to be back on land somewhere, anywhere. He resisted.

Glares from the other escorts bore into Meginhardt after Jophiel signaled them to wait. At his urging, Meginhardt crawled slow till he encountered the opening's edge. No more opportunities afforded discussion or negotiation. This was it. An open mouth with a hungry throat waited to swallow him whole. No jumping required. A magnetic force drew him close. The outer walls of the opening swirled. If there were a throat, there'd be a belly of space to land on, right? Would it digest his very existence? Would it hurt?

He regretted handing over precious shreds of trust. He took them back. "I ain't goin' in there."

Jophiel shoved him into the tunnel.

CHAPTER FOURTEEN
A NEW ARRIVAL

En route to Vereiteln Dorf

THE LATTER PART of Lexxie's journey to Vereiteln Dorf, although excruciating to her back and buttocks, extended more pleasantries. Somehow, following a broken and icy start, she allowed a grudging respect for Jonne. Tit-for-tat arguments offered a connection of sorts, the repartee of home.

Though what had brought a turnaround in Jonne's attitude? Had he, too, suffered a disenchantment one day, a reckoning of not belonging? Or akin to Matilda, a yearning from a desperate heart. Why else would he be so keen to know more about Harmon and Grossmutter and what life with them had been like?

It mattered not. She could appreciate his interest, and this must be how it goes with friendships.

She no longer despised holding him around his waist, and he had placed her boots in one of the courier bags, acknowledging her discomfort inside them. Hospitably, he checked with her frequently to see if she needed any nourishment or a stretch break.

Now, a weary Sadie trotted into the rural edge of Vereiteln Dorf, and the sun hung in the west, promising an hour, perhaps two at the most, before the gray dusk cooled to a black night.

"Yer want to go straight into town, secure a room for the night, and remain there till morning," Jonne called over his shoulder. "I know a place that'll take ya if I talk to them first." Having traveled from village to village regularly, he must know all the folks who ran shops and inns, whom to trust and whom to avoid.

Yet, he claimed he hadn't heard a thing about any infant going missing in this place. That story should have fussed up a dose of gossip for years. 'Course, he would have been just a boy then, not old enough to be caring about scandals.

"You never heard of any rumors?" She tightened her hold on his waist, clinging to hope a repeated question could birth a new answer. "You must've heard something, or do you post-courier-bearing types not care about stolen infants?"

"I deliver parcel bags of mail to the town post office. How would I know?"

"Well, it's more likely you don't care to listen. I imagine horse thieving is of greater interest."

He chuckled and stopped by an iron gate where the words *Vereiteln Dorf, where Justice Comes First* branded a wooden sign. "Look, I ain't into silly entertainment like you."

"I am not the gossipy type." Though if not for Margarita and her pack of lionesses, Lexxie mightn't have had the courage to make this trip nor known how to go about getting here. A purpose there be for community gossip, so why was it so demeaning to the menfolk?

"Besides," he added, "ya must be talkin' over eighteen years ago, long before I was a post rider, ye must have been a child yerself."

Wee daft, are ya? I'm barely seventeen. He was fishing, but her age wasn't any of his business. She swung one leg free.

"Look." He reached to recover her awkward dismount.

Etched beneath the branded claim lay a simple map, worn and less distinguishable. The sole road into town ended as it ran into another where a cross marked the town's church. Before the church, a lineup of farmland, then the town with the post station marked the clearest. Left of the crossroad, northbound—some kind of noteworthy water hole. Right—some etchings of workshops and houses. A second marking of a cross farther away from the main road.

Lexxie scooched closer. "Two churches?"

"Yeah." He pointed to the second marking, a fresh scratch of a cross. "That one's new. Won't be having too much history there for ya."

Huh. She accepted the hint to start with the town's primary church. Catholic churches kept records of the local folk. There, she could find her roots. They'd know about the births and deaths going back several decades—not to mention any infant snatching. Made sense. Her shoulders squared up as she reveled in the deep relief of their arrival. So close now to finding her proper family, she never expected it to be so simple. Problem was, though, she sure couldn't march into that church looking like she did. A man and filthy at that.

"'Bout a twenty-minute walk from here." Jonne twitched his fingers, coaxing her to get back on Sadie and ride along.

Lexxie planted her feet. If she was to stay in this town, investigating however she might, she must arrive as a woman, not posing as a man and rousing mistrust. "I lost my clothing due to you, all that business about attackers. Huh, there weren't any. The very least you shall do is find me something womanlike to wear." She bit her lip, hardly believing her firmness.

"All right, then. Yer the boss. I'll deliver up the post, then fetch ya some proper clothing and come straight back." He winked and tipped his hat. "Then I'll be expect'n my trousers back."

"Don't ye be dawdling." She rubbed her shoulders, shivering. She'd be left to fend for herself, vulnerable and unprotected. But staying back was her idea. She couldn't flip-flop when she best be determined and focused.

"Ah." He grinned. "I know the seamstress. She runs a market stall with textiles and basic garments. Hats too. She'll do anythin' for me."

Lexxie shook her head, figuring the worst of that. "I don't need a hat. I need a skirt and bodice, whatever she may happen to have prepared." Definitely a ladies' man, as the lioness of Avondale claimed. Her sensible solution seemed foolish. She'd also need a shift, footwear, and a scarf, but to ask Jonne to obtain these things as well?

But what other option had she, being caked in earthy dust, hat to stockings? She dare not embarrass her rightful father. She raised her chin. No, that shall not be. She'd make him proud.

Alexien. The name rolled silently around her tongue, and she reached for more coin from Harmon's purse. "That ought'ta cover it, something simple-like. Practical." She cringed over this man picking out her clothes. "If it must be a dress, nothing with a cinched waist."

He shook his head and laughed. "There won't be much. You'll get what she's got. Might even let ya borrow somethin' of hers." He leaned on an elbow. "But don't worry. I see yer measurings."

He found this amusing.

"I'll be back before the sun sets." Straightening up, he pulled the rigid oversized boots from the satchel and tossed them at her stocking feet.

She dipped her head to hide her warming cheeks, a handsome man knowing her measurings.

"Ya may as well start yer research here." He smirked and jerked a thumb over his shoulder. "It's where they bury thieves and witches."

"How dare you." Employing an annoyed voice, she scolded a return, though surely his comment was meant to be a tease.

At his lead, a weary Sadie begrudged a trot down the tree-lined dirt road.

Pressing a hand to her mouth, Lexxie stood in place aside a patch of unattended land cramped with crooked, flat stones and knee-high weeds.

A graveyard? Disgusted from the stench of her hand, she unclasped her mouth and spat. The only burial place she'd known was behind the church in Avondale. She'd never known anyone who had their life sucked from them and needed a burial. When the cart drove the dead through Avondale's countryside, it never came by way of her farmhouse. Harmon and Grossmutter seemed pleased to avoid those funeral corteges.

"Guess'n none of you were godly." She frowned at the lot of them. Folks unfit for the church graveyard were buried at the edge of their towns.

Her fingers struggled through a knotted clop of unevenly

chopped hair. Squeals thickened her throat. The painful matting left her almost thankful the strands no longer hung waist-length.

Despite her exhaustion, the curves of her lips rose. She did it. Here she stood at the edge of Vereiteln Dorf, set to embark on a journey of discovery. Of truth. Amazing. No one around to watch, she did a little dance in her stocking feet before yanking on those tall man boots.

"Okay, spirits of the dead, maybe y'all know something. Speak to me. And if'n ya know anythin' you better tell me, and it better be good because I've paid a steep price to get here."

Her half-joking plea returned what she expected—the calming sounds of nature.

Interrupting the serenity was a keen awareness. Had it been there all day? Or just coming to haunt her now? An iron ball inside her gut shifted.

Harmon. She left without even checking if he was okay. She took his purse.

And what of Grossmutter and her plea for Lexxie to let things be?

Would they ever behold her yearning? Doesn't matter. She must do this.

She scolded the annoying ping in her heart, shoving it underneath the mission, her priority, to find some kind of new life. New people to love. Her flesh and blood. Her true father. Whatever joyous connection awaited.

At that, she tucked her wide-brimmed man hat under one elbow, squeezed her only provision—the coin purse in her trousers—and marched into the overgrown weeds.

Had to be close to eighty or so gravestones. She could review each and get back to the road before Jonne returned.

Should she be concerned with Jonne's scherz, a witch interrupting the peace of her family? Rarely did there arise any talk of witches in Avondale, 'least nothing she'd heard. Had Harmon and Grossmutter sheltered her from such things? Huh, what if they were witches?

Nay. Couldn't be. An imagined vision of Grossmutter secretly brewing potions and ointments delivered some well-needed humor.

Overgrown devil's nettle outlined the narrow plot except where a man-made wall of rocks separated it from the road. Two oaks flanked the yard, one at the narrow unmarked east entrance where she stood and the other on the west-most point of the strip's end, which bowed into a decline. The lowering sun behind the stone markers coaxed her to hurry. Long shadows already challenged her ability to read the engraved records of life.

Well, dear Jonne, I've a brain in my head, and I'll attend to my own research just fine.

While she could blame his mocking as a way to fight hesitation, this was the first real step in her investigation. Other than making her way to Vereiteln Dorf, that is.

A quiver spurned across her shoulder blades, though not from any cold air. Quite the opposite, the late summer air hung heavy and humid.

The human skulls and bones lying underneath her feet belonged to criminals, evildoers, and the unbaptized—anyone not in right standing with holy men. And witches. "Plenty of witches in this village, more than any town's share," Jonne had dared claim. And he would know, given his job.

She craved the mohair shawl, the one she spurned and ruined. A symbol of maturity in Grossmutter's eyes, a symbol of deceit in Lexxie's. Could it be regret and comfort were companions?

Never mind, keep going.

A cumulative calming effect consumed her as she went from marker to marker, reading the information each stone provided, letting her vivid imagination complete the rest. 'Twas good in everyone. Harmon taught her that. These poor souls buried here were simply misunderstood. Or misguided perchance.

Or maybe not. She stepped back from the clear inscription on an oversized slate:

HERE LYETH ABE STRONG
Age 23
Hung August 26, 1651
For the Murder of Jess Furling
Witnessed by Carl Hock
JUSTICE SERVED

Next to this murderer, another criminal:

HERE LYETH MARK "MUGS" BRUGGS
Horse Thief
Age 19
Hung August 26, 1651
JUSTICE SERVED

That must have been some day, two hangings. Were the crimes related? Had to be a story there.

Shaking it off, she continued her stroll. What was the penalty for an infant thief? If she found her true family, would somebody be hanged? Might that someone be Harmon? And what would they do to Grossmutter?

Lexxie firmed her chin. She mustn't reveal herself, neither where she was raised nor why she came to this town, not until she found her family. The truth. Despite the betrayal in her belly, she couldn't allow further harm to befall Harmon, never minding charges and persecutions of infant thieving upon him and Grossmutter.

For now, she'd keep her past a secret. For their sake.

CHAPTER FIFTEEN
TIME PASSAGES

Somewhere on Earth, another place, another time

THE DISTURBING SOUND of Meginhardt's body as the hungry mouth sucked it into the tunnel popped his eardrums. Eerie silence followed, then a stunning transformation. Freedom and weightlessness. He'd closed his eyes and melted into the warm sensation of floating. Even the rushing winds whisking his mop of hair and flapping his trouser legs provided such relief.

The time spent in this blissful state before landing wasn't long enough. Annoyed he was when Jophiel blew in his face, awakening another new reality. Meginhardt's body lay heavy upon a stony ground, which made for a clumsy scramble to an upright position.

But where were they now? Wait—the bigger question was *when* were they?

"What in the dickens?" He fixated on a metal horseless carriage having thick short wheels, enclosed forward-facing seats, and a steering column.

"Welcome to 1952." Jophiel spread his arms. "And that, my dear boy, is an automobile." He crossed his arms over a full chest and bounced head nods as if he'd invented the thing himself.

Meginhardt shuffled himself around the vehicle, examining angles and details, glass and rubber. His saucer-sized eyes glowed in reflection on the shiny surfaces. "Whoa, what the devil, ya brought me to the way future!"

He paid no attention to the two men arguing until Jophiel's sharp elbow redirected his interest. A father and son in the laneway. The latter stomped toward the vehicle following harsh words spoken by the former.

Perfect. Meginhardt slid in behind the steering column. But the son's harsh movements brushed him over to the passenger side. The son slammed the door. The unexpected clunk juddered through Meginhardt.

Why such fuss? Fathers and sons argued all the time. Besides, neither were aware of his presence nor of Jophiel's, two unseeable airy beings. Colorless energy, maybe. To be sure, Meginhardt waved an abrupt hand in the son's face.

The son just shoved a metal key into the steering column. A motor rumbled. The son whipped around to face the back window. The automobile exited down the laneway, flashing signals of warning—imminent danger. Such an angry force sourcing something powerful.

Meginhardt attempted a scramble out the front window, though several balls of light appeared from nowhere and began a wide spin. Nay, he sighed. He knew what would happen next.

All surroundings froze. The energy in the front seat became visible, and an expanding mass of haze spread between the son and Meginhardt. Dark energy. Meginhardt understood given the absorption, a waft of the son's anger. Wrathful and unforgiving.

"He hates his father," he announced to Jophiel.

Jophiel nodded and snapped his fingers. The scene unfroze.

The son, having no concept of the temporary immobility, cursed under heated breath, words unknown to Meginhardt escaped into the air. Accusatory anger was a universal language, despite the letters and syllables used. All too uncomfortable and strange. And far too familiar.

The automobile jerked backward. He braced to avoid collision with the front windshield, but he passed through it without effort. Phew.

Steadying himself in front of the automobile, he eyed Jophiel. "So, what's all this got to do with me?"

Shrugging those wide shoulders, Jophiel used hand gestures to emphasize words Meginhardt had never heard of. "Embitterment. Exasperation. Peccability. Who knows? Fathers and sons. Sons and fathers. Could be any sort of thing."

The son rolled down his window. "Die, old man!"

Meginhardt's pa tickled his senses, specifically, their last argument. A nasty finish.

A woman bolted out the front door, apron flapping and a full head of brunette curls pinned up. Likely, she'd heard the screeching tires when the son took off. "Charles." The word came with a boil rising from her belly. "What have you done? Franklin is all we have now. When will you accept that? When will you figure that out?"

The father, this Charles, released dismissive words. Their son must've escaped like this countless times. The many burn stains on the pavement said so. "He'll be crawlin' back before the sun sets. He ain't goin' for long, Maggie."

A slow, sweeping shake overtook Meginhardt's head. "I'm sorry for her. He's left. It's in his head—he ain't com'n back no more." He gripped both sides of his head to still it. "I felt it. He's been pushed too far."

With how Meginhardt ached to have known his own mother, this struck a nerve. The woman reentered their bricked homestead where she'd probably been cooking up a meal. A mother's love. Instinct told him this woman was not estranged to sorrow. This scene simply added one more, if one could use simply when adding up heartaches.

Anger pushed empathy aside. "I've done nothing wrong. Why'd you bring me here? Who are these people? I want to see *my* pa."

Charles marched right through an invisible Meginhardt and stormed up the laneway, then stopped, and turned around, pausing as though he might have felt something.

I know him.

Jophiel picked Meginhardt up by the scruff of his neck. "You're not getting it."

A massive entourage of light balls swirled the scene. A weak and dizzy Meginhardt collapsed, making Jophiel's job simpler as he swooped him off to their next stop.

CHAPTER SIXTEEN

THE TRUTH SNATCHED

In Vereiteln Dorf

LEXXIE COULD HARDLY relax—not from lack of luxury, the room Jonne arranged being the choicest, but from the night before, the terror in Mittel Dorf still afresh. Gawping inside the reputable Coaching Inn, she brooded. Would there be another fight outside her window? Heaven forbid, another drunken intruder?

Jonne had assured her not. Vereiteln was a market town, popular with the rurals. That, according to him, meant they were more eager to please than to deter prospective buyers. "I hear business has been slow, and that's to yer advantage," he told her before escaping his way to stay farther in town. He insisted they room at separate boarding houses, given the gossip. He had a reputation to keep. Lexxie stifled a tee-hee, nodding to the reputation he already earned according to the Lioness of Avondale.

"To my advantage, nay. I'm still a woman. Unescorted. They'll still look at me with furrowed brows," she announced as though the vacant room could give a cock-a-hoop. She tossed her carry sack onto the floor. Gossip be the least of her worries. If only Jonne were closer—down the hall or even on the floor below, anywhere within screaming distance. Her room may be one of the finest in the town and fit for a princess, but that didn't assure safety.

Yet, even supposing such perils, the room was dandy. A pleasing of high class. Did that man think her some Miss Chock Full of Coin? Mercy. How was she to pay?

A capacious exhalation pushed such fears away.

Jonne had worked it all out. Rather than leaving her to peel away the filth in the graveyard, he snuck her in the back-alley entrance and straight up three flights of stairs. No one would ever see her in those man clothes. She hadn't met the inn owner yet and imagined another servant girl like Matilda working for some scoundrel, an anything-but-nurturing, so-called-uncle. But the warm air of a hot-water bath captured Lexxie's senses, and the soft Marseilles soap tingled her skin, activating her muscles to liquefy. A soft pastel blue dress with ruffled puffed sleeves and a navy satin sash hung on a wall peg. A shift and stockings folded neatly in a package atop the hardly used settee.

How did Jonne arrange all this? *Why* did he arrange all this?

Scrubbing her skin had never felt so good. The cleanse, however, couldn't brighten the wits that darkened her mind, bobbing from one to another. The traumatizing attack on Harmon, Grossmutter's betrayal, what Jonne might dare to expect in return for his strange kindness, and those haunting words Harmon first shared, the ones that erupted this campaign.

Was telling her an accident? Did he mean for her to discover the truth?

Only when she dragged a lofty armoire to block entry to her room, as though that would prevent destructive thoughts from entering her head, did a yawn grant her a much-needed full night's rest.

The neigh of a horse the next morn cut short the deep slumber, prompting her to a high alert. Along with a loud snort, the sound of that familiar, buttery click-click triggered a panicky heartbeat. She shot to the window and pushed aside a raspberry drapery panel.

A stream of bleached sunlight poured in, spotlighting dust particles moving at random rates.

And Jonne galloping away.

Her shoulders dropped just as fast. He did tell her he'd be leaving at the crack of sunrise. He'd said so right after he burrowed a stern look straight into her soul and ordered, "Watch yer back."

"Ye may have a reputation, Mister Jonne the post rider, but I appreciate what you've done for me."

An inkling penetrated, she and him, courting. She shook it away. Naught. She lifted her head upward with a resounding self-directed command. "First, I must know who I am. And that means I must unite with my father."

As she slipped on the new dress, her cheeks heated, for Jonne had picked out a style and fit—along with the slip and new stockings. Even pins and a bow for her butchered hair were supplied. How did he explain these purchases? The bodice fit snug.

She stepped forth to admire herself in the long-framed reflection glass. No longer a child who belonged, but rather a woman who didn't. "So, you are courageous, Fräulein Lexxie. Don't you worry none. You'll find yer belonging."

Hmm. Clicking her tongue, she searched the room in stocking feet. Those ill-fitting man boots stood firm in the corner. She shivered. As long as she could help it, never would she slip her feet inside those again. She mourned for her own comfortable low leather boots left behind in Mittel Dorf with Matilda.

Dern him. Did he not think she'd need something on her feet?

She rummaged about. Aha, tucked against the wall under the settee was a tied sack.

She unknotted it to reveal the most stunning pair of footwear. Even the wealthy women back in Avondale's church never wore shoes this exquisite.

A note pinned to each, one for the right foot and one for the left. Whoever thought one needed to be concerned with matching a shoe to one's foot? She slipped each on and, after wincing at the tightness in the toe area, strutted around the room.

Oh how the embroidered beading and dazzling buckle offered a sudden burst of renewal! How incredible she felt, not a mere woman, but a beautiful woman. Not manly looking. Having no claim to any sort of fashion brilliance, she yet knew these shoes were far too elegant for everyday wear. The curves of her mouth lifted once again, only this time more generously.

Puffing her chest and smoothing her skirt, she was ready. Today was the day.

She headed down the polished wooden staircase, extolling every clunk her brilliant new shoes sang out at each step. She'd nearly made it out the front door when the rich, full voice of a female called to her ears. "Think'n ta start a family, are ya?"

Lexxie dared a curious turn. A woman at least a dozen years her senior, perhaps more, sported a straight-line grin between dangling chandelier earrings.

Taken aback, Lexxie pressed a hand to her chest. "Forgive me, madam."

"Giselle." The woman tilted her head, her eyes locking on Lexxie's stomach. "Jonnie says yer here to observe the place, see if it's suitable fer a family."

Lexxie's mouth fell open. What? *That* be his story to explain her away? Mercy.

Turning motherly, Giselle's expression reminded Lexxie of tender moments with Grossmutter. "Fear not, liebste. No one shall hear a word from me."

Lexxie took a step back. "My family. I'm looking things over for my family, my parents."

The woman nodded, and her grin line shifted. Unbelieving.

"They're not well, my parents. They couldn't take the journey." If Jonne could tell a story, so could she. And hers would trump his, but this Giselle woman still nodded and still smirked. "I hear you have a good physician here in Vereiteln Dorf."

"Nein, the doctor comes from Avondale once a week, but we've got plenty of midwives."

Right, how could she have forgotten? Lioness Margarita had even said such. The doctor for the region lived in Avondale. She'd even heard a whispered warning about him. She needed to sharpen up her storytelling.

Giselle laughed, though Lexxie wasn't sure why. "Jonnie's paid you up for a full week, so guessing he's picking you up on his next run through. I'm to collect his clothes and launder 'em."

"I wish you a good day." Hiding a clenched jaw, Lexxie stormed to the street. How dare he make things up like that. And coming back for her in a week? Did he think her to fail in her search?

The iron latch on Giselle's Coaching Inn boarding house was loose and jammed from Lexxie's urgent exit, catching her dress on the heel of her right-foot gilded slipper shoe. She flopped onto the front walk bench thanks to a twisting stumble. She wasn't used to wearing heels of any sort, especially the fashionable thin-heeled kind.

Whilst rubbing her ankle, she gasped. Could Jonne be of the impression the attack in Mittel Dorf was worse than it was, that perhaps . . .? Oh my, he thought the attacker . . . He thought it possible she could be with child. That's why he was being so nice to her. Pity. He pitied her!

Tears whined, wanting to flow. A bout of lamenting cast its knot, undeniable rejection, unexplainable grief.

No more. I must be courageous, and narr to no one.

She sprang afoot and stomped along, bypassing shops and brewhouses, paying scant attention to the stares. A two-wheeled carriage steered around the threat of her gait. She elbowed her way through shop owners to the end of the road. The T-intersection, where the wide stone steps of Vereiteln Dorf's well-established church commanded all to clamber up, or perhaps even crawl their way, to the ornate lumbersome doors.

Grabbing the morning-cold iron rail, Lexxie stalled on its first step. Paid her up for a week? Jonne paid for her stay, not knowing if she had the coin to reimburse. She wouldn't be here if not for him. She ought to be thankful.

Anger tucked aside, she scurried up without bothering

to read the inscriptions on the risers. Needing the strength of both arms, she pulled the door open wide. The haunting drawn-out creak confirmed a renewal of focus on her single priority. *Find my lineage, my true father. Then new life is certain to follow.*

An entrance hall revealed itself, though dark with looming shadows. Unable to avoid inhaling the displeasing odor, a mixture of lingering day-old incense and strong lye soap, her throat did a gaggle. Nothing like the sweet-pine pews inside her white-stucco church.

Attempting to step quiet-like, she still clicked her shoes against the marble floor, her feet inside all that lavish commenced to swell and pine for attention. *Huh, stomping through town in modish spikes, 'tis not wise.*

A figure across the room sat up on its knees and twisted a neck to inspect the visitor. Even in the darkness, the woman appeared maturely aged.

Unfolding with a painful slowness, the woman stood and rubbed her hands into her apron. With such a crippling figure, she couldn't have had an easy go at life. Her head, a weighty slump, her neck, cranked to one side. Had she eaten in a while? So thin. And dressed in all black. Scrubbing a floor that already shone—preparing for a wedding or cleaning after the ceremony of a disposed corpse perhaps?

"State yer business," the woman gnarled.

The plucky tone surprised. "Guten morgen, I'm, ah, here to examine the registers for births and deaths—if I may." Politeness best protect her from being turned away. Harmon always said one achieved more with kindness than with harshness.

"Yer a stranger." The woman's shaking middle finger accused.

Huh. This woman the epitome of the latter.

"Madam, 'tis that I am. Please be, I intend no harm. I assure you. Just seeking. I shan't be long." Should be easy to check births around the time of her own, though this woman need not know that specific detail.

"Seeking? Huh, seeking ye what?"

Was it so wrong to seek? Lexxie sucked in a full breath. Her throat irritated by resins, she stifled a cough. But nay, she hadn't come all this way to permit some grumpy old spinster to blockade her. *Forget the kindness of honey, Harmon. Time for some harsh vinegar.*

"Are ye cloaking history? Is that what you are saying, madam?"

The old woman shot an indication to a wooden door hidden beside the nave.

Lexxie jockeyed between pews in the direction the bony finger specified, stifling the clicks of her shoes as much as possible.

Whew. She knocked.

"We don't lock history." The old woman's crusty voice echoed, having the last word.

This door, not nearly the heft nor clangor as the one fronting the church, Lexxie nudged and invited herself in. Larger than one might expect, the narrow room hosted wooden shelving loaded with books up to the ceiling sidelong. A movable ladder rested against the end wall, and an unlit kerosene lamp awaited on the single high table.

Help would be nice, some guidance as to the order of records. Lexxie glanced back where the scowling woman gave her a second glance. Then again, Lexxie could figure it out herself. After lighting the lamp, she shut the door for privacy.

A musty flavor and layers of dust from decades past awoke and scurried about. No window to allow a breeze of any sort. Once her sneezes settled, she walked the length of the room, thankful now for those daylong lessons in reading and writing with Grossmutter. 'Twas the age of enlightenment, Grossmutter would say. She kept at least one lesson ahead of Lexxie, so as to in turn share the blessing.

A thin cotton curtain covered one section of shelving beside a nailed sign—Prohibited Books. She edged closer to shelving with books of various sizes, difficult to distinguish due to caging, each row with its own locked latch. *Huh, don't lock history, say you?*

She wandered to a series of consistent volumes laying heavy on their own, their leathery pasteboard covers bound with cord and red edging their pages. Numbers stitched atop.

Years, yes! Those ones were organized by years. They had to be the records she sought.

All she possessed now was her birth year. Harmon wouldn't have lied about her age, would he?

A shiver ran through her veins. There had to be over seventy books, each covering a year, each varying in thickness.

Here it be: 1671. Energizing another dust cloud with a loud exhale, she heaved the book off the shelf and clutched it tight to her bosom. Her heartbeat thumped against the pasteboard cover. The registry for the year she was born must speak to her, reveal information she was desperate for. Vital to get on with any way of future.

She released her gripping hug, placed the heavy book on the table, and wiped dry her sweaty palms down the skirt of her new frock.

Overwhelm assaulted her. Harmon, the loving father she

adored all those years. Grossmutter, the wise, gentle, and kind grandmother, her only female influencer. Was it true they be not her family? Would opening this book mean turning her back on them?

'Course, she'd already done so, hadn't she?

If only they were cruel or unloving. Made her work like a slave. Cussed and cursed her day in and day out. This then would be so much easier. Her fingers twitched to shove the book back onto its shelf. Her legs urged her to take flight, run all the way back to Avondale, and bury this outlandish nonsense.

But nonsense, it weren't.

The pounding in her chest begged to keep going, threatening to explode if she stopped now. She almost missed the rubbing of hinges, the only door to this library tomb opening, a male figure entering, the unwelcoming floor-polishing ogre poking her head around him to catch a glimpse.

"Searching, are we?" The man's monotoned query struck an unexplainable chord.

Not just any man. The priest wore full garb, black on black, and spoke with more than a hint of accusation.

Lexxie clasped her hands so they touched neither the book nor the table it lay upon. She absorbed the coldness in his eyes, the lack of kindness or gentleness. The tiny hairs on her nape stiffened to attention. This man was not like the priest back home. After a few blinks, she pushed her head up high and dipped a curtsy. "As a matter of business, aye, I am researching."

"Researching? And what, my child, is so dire you must arrive unannounced and unescorted?"

Lexxie raised her chin. "Are these records not public?"

"Oh, they are records. My records. Births, baptisms, marriages, and deaths of my flock. None of which concern you. I know my flock, my dear child, and you are not one of them." His steps toward her were seamless as though he were gliding on ice. He reached for the book and, despite its weight, tucked it effortlessly between his chest and his crossed arms. "Unless, of course, you have come to our quaint populace of saved souls with your parents? Perhaps you are resolving to become one with us?"

Disheartened, yet bold, she swallowed. "Perchance."

Instincts warned to keep a firm guard. She wasn't about to glimpse any records. Not right now. She nodded to the priest and bid him a good day.

Her smile not returned, the elderly woman clasped and rubbed her palms back and forth as though washing away Lexxie's intrusion to their holy atmosphere.

Now what? She'd not come so far to fail.

CHAPTER SEVENTEEN
TIME PASSAGES II

Somewhere on Earth, another place, another time

WAR WAS THICK in the air, friction obvious. Not the kinship-feud sort. Nor land control or religious wrangling amongst villagers. This conflict was far greater, state to state, maybe even country to country. The atmosphere, full of tension. Its color, ashen.

This time, Jophiel and Meginhardt's travel was anything but breezy as shooting streaks of lightning and vicious, jarring winds dominated. They'd crossed a series of ocean swells at one point, a variety of lush islands. Then dove into a countryside homeland disturbed with scorched blotches of land, battered barns, and blitzed stone houses.

Meginhardt struggled to find his legs, even more so to accustom himself to this alien scenario. Such a forbidding place. Blowing out air and shaking his head to clear his mind, he suffered an elbow jab from Jophiel, who seemed less interested in the environment and more interested in the young woman.

She sat next to a boulder lodged aside a tree stump and a rotting wooden plow. Unmanaged stubbles poked through fields on either side. The woman with her face buried in a tattered skirt, shivered in the winter cold.

Meginhardt refused to let his impatience go. "And so now what? Who is this woman to me? Why bring me here? Why should I care?"

"Look closer. Inspect."

Unaware of her invisible visitors, the woman jerked to sit upright as though she sensed their presence, then quivered, and returned to wringing her hands inside a balled-up apron.

Meginhardt kneeled in front of her. What an uncanny resemblance of his pa's facial features! The way her eyes sat close to her nose and the way her upper lip curled.

He lifted back. "Is this my mother?"

With a curt wave, Jophiel dismissed the guess.

Shrugging, Meginhardt shifted toward the young woman's face again. A blotchy redness was nearly hidden thanks to frizzy curls. "Still, she kinda looks familiar." Though he couldn't know why. "What's her name?" Not that he cared. "Just curious."

"Her earth name? Sarai." Jophiel kept an arm's-length, matter-of-fact distance. "Another member of the family line you bedamned."

Meginhardt couldn't stand up fast enough. "No such thing. You're lying. I don't even know her. Why would I cast a curse her way?" The words *another member* whirled.

Jophiel remained tight-lipped, almost bored.

Meginhardt sank back onto his knees.

The woman was now peeking around a tree trunk to eye the farmhouse at the field's far end. Those final words to his pa surfaced and circulated. How could anyone know about them? He, himself, had practically forgotten. "Who told ya that?"

Dern, I told that Aivy too much. "Er, wait. Pa ain't got no family. Just me." He smirked. They must be sending him back. Of course. If these folk Jophiel showed were Pa's descendants, they'd need him to go back and carry on.

Confidence tickled at his skin. "This still the future?"

Hard to tell, being surrounded by barren farmland. But those twisted wires forming cables for fencing and that big porch on the homestead . . . He'd never seen the like in Vereiteln Dorf. He sprung up to a tall stance. "I get it now. This woman, Sarai, is one of my descendants. Like a grandchild or a grandchild's grandchild or such. Right? And that Franklin lad we met probably is too." He bounced foot to foot at this notion of his own life somehow continuing—he, Meginhardt Dimietris, would leave such a legacy! A family line for decades to follow. Nothing could be more pleasing.

Jophiel's furrowed brow and raised chin paused Meginhardt's blissful glory. "No."

The single word destroyed it with completeness. He stilled, needing an explanation.

"There's someone else."

Someone else? Pa ain't got no one else.

A sick, horrible realization loomed like a dark shadow.

Does Pa have other children I don't know about? Nay, I'd have known.

"Yer lying to me. You made that up, 'cause you don't *want* to send me back." Far too natural, his jaw and chest protruded. Fists coiled and forearms tensed. Survival instincts. He shoved his missing-eyetooth clench upward to catch Jophiel's undisturbed facial expression. Cocking his head just like Pa used to, he poked an accusing forefinger into Jophiel's chest. "You said we were going back. So, Mr. Whatever You Are—Take. Me. Back."

"Anger controls you."

"Of course, I'm angry, dah. Yer mess'n with my life. And it ain't none of yer business."

"You were handpicked to come into a life of flesh, the grandest of opportunities."

"Stop changing the subject." *Handpicked? My arse, such talk.*

"Resentment and self-pity overflows. Too much risk, roots too deep." Jophiel stooped to look squarely into Meginhardt's eyes. "Handing your anger to future generations would have knocked them off track. As it is, they are suffering enough."

Meginhardt clenched his teeth. Still, words spewed free. "You don't know me."

He stomped in a circle, shaking his head, tightening, then loosening his fists to calm himself. It didn't work. He shoved that accusing finger back into Jophiel's chest. "Ya know, he always told me all you—whatever you are—were useless. So high and mighty. He scoffed at you all and yer idea of some afterlife kingdom. And you know what? I believe him now. Pa was right."

Seeming unaffected, Jophiel rubbed his chin. "Suffering makes people knock. You did it yourself."

What a ridiculous comment. It meant nothing.

Sarai moved to her knees as though she'd heard something and spied the distant farmhouse. A series of shots flared from the same direction, as did the voices and cries of men.

Meginhardt had forgotten about her. She was in the midst

of her troubles now. He no longer cared. She was Pa's descendant, but not his. He liked her better when he didn't know any of this.

"For what exactly did you bring me here?" He waved both arms. "Never mind. Let's just get out of here. Take me—wherever. I don't care."

"She could use a little encouragement."

"I don't care."

Jophiel scratched his jaw and shook his head, then grabbed Meginhardt by the scruff of his neck. Employing majestic wings, he was about to leave Sarai behind in some kind of danger and fearing for her life.

Haunting Meginhardt's mind in secret was whether he should care or not. *She ain't my kin.*

Jophiel was right. He couldn't control his anger. All those years of being bullied built a rebellious mechanism.

But right now, I don't give a rat. "I thought you guys were supposed to be all kind and helpful. All that King-and-heaven stuff, just rubbish and all. Yer just gonna leave her. Yeah, real noble of ya."

"She's not alone." Jophiel huffed.

Meginhardt fixed his gaze on the woman as they lifted. Just as Sarai wasn't much more than a thumbnail, another of those light beings glimmered beside her. Clear as anything, the shiny near-translucent man waved upward, a cheerful and casual see-ya-later kind of gesture.

CHAPTER EIGHTEEN
OATH TO SELF

In Vereiteln Dorf

'TIS A SADDLE goose am I.

Examining Vereiteln Dorf's church records was Lexxie's surety for answers. Knowing to whom she was born called for a simple record check. How could they deny her such a privilege? Why had she assumed all would be eager to help?

Dern, narr I prove to be.

The question resounded again: Now what?

She paused on the ground step and stretched onto the tiptoes of her shoes for a perfect view of the town's hub. Shaking off embarrassment from her abrupt morning parade, she focused on merchants and traders sweeping the walk before their establishments and leaning signboards against barrels and posts, announcing they were open for business. Might her father be an operator? A cheese emporium, a baker's shop, a candlemaker, the general store. A furrier aside the butcher, a blacksmith, a wrought iron decorator, and a market stall with textiles, hats and gloves. Was that where Jonne purchased the frock she donned?

An uncomfortable brush of silence prickled her backside. She didn't have to look to sense the priest behind her, up those steps leading to the church's lumbersome door. His glare scored the back of her head, protecting his flock's cherished records, as though she had no right to know who she was.

This would have been so much easier if Harmon were with her.

'Course, if Harmon were with her, he could've told her himself who she was.

To keep from sobbing in sight of peering eyes, she ambled alongside the church where a worn path led to a sacred burial ground. A pasture of the holy dead. A grouping of boulders among some trees offered the perfect place to stifle sniffles, firm-up strength, and concoct a plan.

Forget what happened in the past, including who she was. Now, she would embark on something new. Once she found her true father, she'd assuredly enjoy a whole completeness within and a bright future.

A warm breeze brushed her face, and a few loose hairs escaped the imprisoning hairpins. More restrictive and tighter, given the shortness of her hair. The gentle current felt on side with her, lending renewal. A lean back of her neck allowed the morning sun to change her mood. The luminous ray on her face and happy chirrups of hedge sparrows in her ears reminded her of home.

Stop it. I won't quit. Not now.

But had she ever felt so alone?

King, you'll help me, won't you?

That's what Harmon would have done, looked up and

asked for help. Not an inkling of comfort came from Vereiteln's priest. Excusing his creepiness came half-heartedly though, he'd a weary job. Often, justice for the righteous fell onto the laps of his kind.

A pack of crows screamed in unison from the tidy graveyard's farthest corner. Squinting against a ray of morning sparks, she spied a small frame below the flurry of black. Shabbily dressed, as much as she could tell, a man waved fists about a gravestone, hollering a demand to its occupant of six feet under, a vehement: "Leave me be."

Kicking off her gilded slipper shoes, more for comfort than the call for quiet, she tiptoed in the grass, still dewy in shady sections. She employed the trunk of a linden tree for cover to view the bizarre scene. Indeed, an angered man crouched there. Likely inebriated or crazed and in dire need of bathing and a shave, not to mention some fattening up.

"*Giiit.*" The command, followed by an authoritative swig from his leather flask, could've awakened all the dead in the graveyard, not just the targeted dweller.

Lexxie aligned herself with an extended shadow, taking a covert position. Herr Priest entered the graveyard and strolled toward the man. Best he didn't know she was there, watching his precious flock in distress no less.

With nary a word nor any visible prejudice, the priest snugged the raging man into a shoulder hold until he calmed, then escorted him off the grounds. His easy approach indicated he'd done this before, maybe several times. The priest then stood at the church's front property line watching the hunched man shuffle up the main street.

Lexxie's heart ached. He was probably all alone in this world. A feeling she'd come to know herself.

All chirrups had ceased, thanks to the landing of several crows. She stopped counting at six. How oft had Grossmutter said such a number of ravens and rooks was a bad omen, warning of a pending death?

"Well, dah, we're in a graveyard." Lexxie shooed them away to clear her path to the stone markers in the back corner, the one with the accused of haunting beneath it.

The row farthest from the road must be reserved for the wealthy. Most were the sandstone caskets with fancy scripting on the tomb's cover, several decked with twigs of rosemary and cypress. She touched the carved handiwork. Someone in this town was talented. Around the aboveground caskets lay gravestones marking the deceased buried below. These markers, too, displayed an impressive size, indicators of wealth.

The dead man she was approaching must've lived a rich life full of self-righteousness and undue pride, most likely the reason for sucking the life from his crazed visitor. The marker boasted no everlasting greenery though two pebbly stones were tucked firmly aside it. Grossmutter once claimed that, when a stone was left at one's grave, it bound the deceased to the one who left it.

Hah, two stones. Someone truly loved would sport a whole pile.

Lexxie stood in the footprints that poor wailing soul left moments earlier. "Now tell me." She confronted the occupant. "What did ye to traumatize that man so?"

Tucking at her dress to allow a squat, she let her fingers trace each line below the ornate winged death head.

HERE LYETH
Gillam Huber
Murdered 1671
Season of Planting
Having one wife, Meredith
Having one son, Harmon
Landowner, 2 lots, East Path
39 and half years

She failed to cover her mouth in time to mask the screech. "Harmon? Meredith?" Be there another Harmon and Meredith Huber in this King-forsaken town? It couldn't be her Harmon and Grossmutter, for Harmon's father died in a farming accident.

Another lie. Surely, it be them.

Her tongue lashed out with heaves of cusses, surprising no one more than herself. This falsity another stab in the back.

She read and reread the shocking and informative engraving. Running her index finger inside the indentation of letters, M u r d e r e d, she gulled herself to a cool head. The inscription said nothing about justice. Had justice not been served? Was the one responsible for taking this life still free to harm another?

Summoning her recent pact, she snapped back to an abrupt stand. "Why should I care?" She took a turn at scolding the man beneath the gravestone. "Ye be not my grandfather. Nay shall ye be my concern."

There it was again, another glare. Her instincts heralded someone was watching. What if someone learned she knew Harmon and Meredith? Might that be good or bad?

A glance to the side confirmed the priest, standing with an eerie calmness. Still and in deep contemplation. Watching her.

In dewy stocking feet, she strolled to the next gravestone with a casual air, stooping and pretending to read the marker, then strolled to the next and the next. Best the priest make no connection to her and this Huber family—the name she'd been raised with, the name that, like the shawl tossed into the prickly bush, she hath shed. Though this murderous information embroidered more threads to her frayed identity, she'd no idea how large or complicated this shawl—or be it a tapestry?—might get.

But she did have a plan. The village stonecutter. He, of all people, would know. He would have carved all these stone markers, and if he hadn't, chances were his father would have passed along the skill and would know. Had she not passed a sign pointing down a side road? Therein would be her next stop.

CHAPTER NINETEEN
TIME PASSAGES III

En route from one season of time to another

ANOTHER TUNNEL SYSTEM, equally mystifying, yet Meginhardt rathered focus secretly on the musket shots heading the way of that Sarai woman, a so-called descendant of his father's. *Did Pa go and get a new family? Cast me off like a bad lot?*

Jophiel propelled with efficiency. One space in time to another.

On edge from constant jolts and thunderous crashing outside the tunnel's throat, Meginhardt hugged his arms inward. At times, the inside walls were hot to touch, at other times, a frosty chill.

Jophiel smirked through it all. Ugh, he enjoyed Meginhardt's nervousness.

He fancied to smack a blow to Jophiel for the rough travel. He was doing it on purpose, was he not? Trying to make him squirm like a wiggler in the dirt.

The angry friction from that Franklin fellow set the next

foot in his mind. So hampered down and oppressed that boy was, Meginhardt got a charge from the drama. He envied Franklin for having the pluck to bog off from his parents.

He's making a life of his own like I should'a done. Sticking around Pa only got me here, ending up with this Jophiel birdman.

Something eerie seeped inside the tunnel, a foreshadowing. A series of howling screeches bucked at Meginhardt's misgivings. But Jophiel waved his arms about to clear away the invading murky fog, so he allowed his mind to drift back to that war-torn field and that Sarai woman. Scared, she could only run into the field. And so barren it was. Oh how he related! Her energy said it all—nothing good could happen, there was no way out, and no one cared. Even that light man just stood there, waving, like nothing was wrong.

Meginhardt was a little like Franklin and Sarai, or were they a little like him? Angry and fear trapped. A weak kinship brewed.

But they're Pa's descendants, not mine.

Wherever they were traveling this time, Jophiel must be taking a long way. This was the least enjoyable. A third stop was coming up. For what sake must Meginhardt meet people he'd never know?

He shooed away intruding empathy for Franklin and Sarai. They were nothing to him. With jaw clenched, toes and ankles stiff, Meginhardt prepared himself for the next *whoever*. A hardened heart was the most reliable way to get through. With Pa gone, the only one Meginhardt could ever trust assuredly was himself. He'd no time to be concerned with others.

An upward gale of forced air chilled his calves and sent him leapfrogging atop Jophiel. The traversable passageway cracked, and the tunnel's protective wall split wide open. Shards of light blinded Meginhardt as he and his guide were forced out, ejected through the fissure and into a vast blue arena of nothingness. It happened so fast—the sudden pleasantness of the atmosphere was quite confusing. Nearing to faint, he drifted, no longer gripped by Jophiel, but airborne beside him. As if he were an angel falling from the heavens, he was left to his pumping blood. Behind him, their travel tunnel shriveled and disappeared.

How was it terror could be so magical? A calming sensation prevailed. So much so, he released the shock stemming from such a tumultuous dump. A little warning would have been nice.

A gush of wind revved by, so powerful it stopped his breath. Struggling to catch it back, he pushed his arms out and shoved his head high, then laughed. Twists and turns were controllable! Soon, Jophiel's hold around Meginhardt's waist held secure again. A good thing, given the delicate action of landing was just ahead. Inevitable doom be it otherwise.

Now he daren't get carried away and tricked into anything. *No one matters but me. Focus. Survive.*

The landscape formed a colorful blur, variations of greens, browns, and blues growing in clarity as they descended. Forests, farms, barns, roads, a town, a church steeple at the end of a main road.

Wait? Could it be? Was this—*Vereiteln Dorf, my dwelling!*

He hooted at the prospect of getting back to his life. "'Tis my fate, renewal. Thank ye! This time, I ain't gonna be no gauchmann."

Jophiel squeezed him but chose to remain silent.

Whether they caught a downdraft or were the downdraft, it didn't matter. So much was recognizable. All the smells and odors had given him hope back then, hope he'd have his own life once he got more years under his chest. And a family of his own. But he would be different. He'd take his boy to town every week and teach him stuff every day.

And now he'd another chance. Jophiel and that Aivy must have come to their senses. Amid a magical contentment, Meginhardt hid a smile and employed his facial muscles to pull down the corners of his mouth. If they thought this pleased him, they might change their minds.

Jophiel steered toward the main church.

Gadzooks, lookie yonder. Meginhardt never even knew a second church stood away from the main road. Much smaller and less impressive, nevertheless.

Pa never stepped a foot into any church for all Meginhardt witnessed, though many folk knew his father, their greetings being either disgruntled or empathetic. Just another one of those mysteries, like why some townspeople gawked at him. Sometimes even stepping around him like he was bad luck or something. That was another thing he always held onto. Folks knew Pa, and he belonged to Pa. That was something.

Powerful winds trailed them atop the bustling town. Three women even grabbed their hats as Jophiel and Meginhardt rushed past, likely blaming a blast of late summer air.

Carrying his curious and roused cargo, Jophiel swerved north where the main road met another at the foot of the main church. A crowd had gathered alongside the deep reservoir. A wooden platform, decked out with celebratory decorations, stood as the obvious main attraction overlooking the water's glistening violet hues. Three men, official-looking townsmen, would soon be making some kind of public announcement.

Meginhardt blinked, gawked, blinked again. "Pa?" Nay, couldn't be. His throat grew tight. *Cry me a mercy.* "'Tis him!"

But there Pa was on the platform, all official. In breeches and a cassock? Cleaned up like never before, hair slicked, mustache manicured, shoulders high, sash shiny. His shoes even shone, not like the muddy boots Pa always had his woolen socks and feet tied up inside. "Ha, I bet yer trotters don't stink from them there shoes." An odor he could never get used to.

Jophiel landed before the wooden structure. Meginhardt kept his focus steady on his father, so proud he was to see him up there on that platform, looking so dapper and important, so darned impressive.

Whoa. "Councilman." Close enough to see the gold and silver badge, he knew what it meant. "I'll be darned."

Wait. He pivoted to Jophiel. "This be another prank of yers?"

Jophiel must have noticed his furrowed, suspicious brow. "Just watch, boy."

Reluctant to accept the caution, Meginhardt examined the healthy version of his father. Was this the way things could have been if Ma hadn't died?

The other two men, one labeled Burgermeister, Master of the Citizens, and garbed proud in a loose black gown, and the other, an ominous fellow in ill-fitting black trousers, a harsh steepled hat and a long cape that partially hid an over the shoulder satchel appearing to hold considerable coin. Each shifted their footing to space a perfect distance apart from the other and employ the entire width of the high staging as though nothing could be left untried.

The burgermeister raised his staff while the man in the steeple hat called for attention from the chattery crowd. "The mayor speaks."

A thumping inside his chest, Meginhardt fixed his gaze on Pa. A councilman. Who could believe it?

Wide muscular palms belonging to Jophiel maneuvered Meginhardt's head, forcing him to face the reason for the gathering. Five women, each dressed in only their shifts and stockings, stood along a precipice at the water's edge, bound hands at their backs. Ten men, two for each woman, held the end of the ropes as if anticipating a tug-of-war of some sort. Three of the men appeared apprehensive as they wiped sweaty hands on their trousers, while the others smutted variations of grins.

"What's going on?"

But no response came from Jophiel.

Meginhardt examined Pa's face. Somber, but more curiously, dead sober.

When did the audience expand? Had to be the entire village. Men, women, and children grew quiet, a sea of muted heartbeats. The whine of a single mosquito crossed Meginhardt's path before landing on the neck of the woman second from the left. Churning as best she could, she rubbed her head on her shoulder. Forgetting the pesky insect, she fixed her attention straight at him.

"Can she see me?"

"No." Jophiel then waved toward where a carry basket waited alongside the platform, an infant sleeping unaware of the impending doom that would change the course of his life.

Her icy glare moved from the swaddled infant to Pa, who would only look down at his shiny black leather shoes to avoid the defeat in this woman's eyes.

Something ain't right. Horror struck a new beat. It hit him. How he knew, he had no idea. But this woman was his mother.

"Ma?" Emotion coursed, a lump caught. This woman resembled the one who waved at him from the picnic table by that gate. "Meine mutter!" The longing of each syllable barely escaped his lips.

Jophiel indicated accuracy with a simple nod.

Shouldn't the fellow appear more empathetic? Meginhardt stiffened. "What's this bodge?"

Jophiel motioned that Meginhardt calm, then pointed. "Listen."

And the burgermeister stepped forward boasting a victory posture. "Ladies and gentlemen, my very fine people of Vereiteln Dorf, our troubles end herewith—*this very day*. We've been infiltrated with a grand share of witches. Troublesome spells they cast on every one of you."

When he pointed his finger to the sky, the ominous-looking man in the steeple hat aside him sported a toothless grin, and Pa held his lips tight and stared at the bare feet of Meginhardt's mother.

The burgermeister continued. "Shall we stand for this?"

The crowd roared a thousand noes.

"As long as I am the master lord, I will ensure our township will be purified again and again. We shall become the envy this side of the mountain and beyond all marks of land. Why?" His arms stretched out to the five women roped and accused of witchcraft. "Because every suspect of witchery will undergo a trial. Justice. That is what we, the very fine folks of Vereiteln Dorf, are about."

The crowd roared their approval, stamped their feet, and shook their fists in the air, casting waves of invisible angst above them. "Jus–tice. Jus–tice. Jus–tice."

Meginhardt shivered at their blackness. An energy field he'd seen. How could he have forgotten so soon those ribbons of colors, particularly that ribbon of blackness, the one with the hardened and unforgiving heart? Similar to what he'd known for most of his young life—when he had a physical body, that is. The feeling was fiery and wound him up.

"This is their trial." The burgermeister gripped folds of his loose black gown. "A fair trial, accepted across this superior and just empire. And you, the outstanding citizens of Vereit-eln Dorf, shall witness the purification before your very eyes. *You* shall come to know how pure we become. How safe you shall be in your homestead, how fruitfulness shall bestow your harvest, and how profit will boom in your business and fill your purse. You will send your children off to sleep each night with confidence. Why? Because they will be safe. No witch shall ever come to steal them away as you slumber."

In a barrage of near-contagious excitement, hats and hands waved feverishly in the air, and cheering and howls rose even higher. All while, the crowd jostled closer to the water's edge to witness what would come next.

"I shall hand over the proceedings to our village treasurer and terminer of witchcraft, Jake Richter."

At that, the burgermeister stepped backward, and Herr Steeple Hat swaggered forth. His bony fingers pinched his nose and hid his smirking grin. His satchel of coins jingled.

Pa managed to stand tall and proud, yet Meginhardt sensed a discomfort, a discoloration around his being. Pa would be squeezing each thumb one after the other, repetitively alternating grips behind his back to stay calm. Like a duck's feet paddling water to resist its own body from sinking and somehow adding to it a calm demeanor.

"A witch, say you? You sloven dirty beau." Meginhardt, firm and quiet-like, scowled at Jake, this man who visited their homestead frequently and now remained oblivious to this unnatural visit.

"Quiet," demanded Jophiel.

Jake explained the rules, and the ten men holding the ropes took their positions. At the command, with wooden shields to protect themselves from any evil spirits that leave the women in an attacking plight, they took a running leap and shoved each into the judging waters. A seven-foot drop into the deepest section known to be at least twenty feet, the most treacherous part of the landscape the region boasted.

If nature accepted a woman as pure, the woman's body would sink. Should nature refuse a woman's body given its contamination with evil spirits, it would spit her back up to the water's surface, having rejected the fleshly impurity. The men equipped with the ropes were further charged to hoist a body up at a reasonable time should a body sink and not surface. Then and only then, would that woman be innocent in the eyes of the villagers and free to carry on as one of them, restored of dignity. Presumably, anyway.

But what was a reasonable amount of time? Jake would announce when such time was "reasonable in the eyes of godly justice."

Meginhardt's world was collapsing all over again. The echoing *splosh* of bodily masses entering their watery graves sickened his core. "Ma!"

Despite them never having a life together, his dreams and thoughts of his mother warmed him regularly. Happy thoughts of an imagined nurturing figure coexisted inside his hopelessness, the two emotions inseparable.

He elbowed Jophiel's hip good and hard. "Do someth'n."

Jophiel remained still.

Disoriented, uneasy, and confused, Meginhardt couldn't think. He pivoted to Pa. "Pull her up. Pull her up, I demand you!"

Meginhardt ran to the edge. His mother's body hadn't bopped up to the surface. She'd survive this trial and prove them all wrong. Facing Pa once again, he pushed a command straight from his abdomen. "*Now!* Pull her up before it's too late."

Jophiel scratched an earlobe. "He won't hear you."

"Please, please!" Meginhardt begged. If only Jophiel would reset the clock of time, allow him this desire. "*Do* something."

The unnatural contortion of Jophiel's face said it all. He wasn't going to do anything.

An animalistic shrill caused women to cover gaping mouths and their children's eyes. The first woman to appear on the water's surface kicked her legs like a lassoed bull. The men hoisting her up and over the edge treated her about as much, dragging her dripping body across the stony ground and kneeling on her back in front of the podium. Then the second woman, the same thing. The crowd was roaring—or were some sobbing?

These two women failed the trial and were due to be hanged in mere hours, which was, according to Jake, sufficient time for folks to get to town for some well-needed drink and nourishment.

Meginhardt returned his focus to the water's surface. *Mother, if you rise, you will fail this trial. Please hide in the deep long enough to prove your innocence, but come up before . . . Please don't drown.*

Could they begin their lives anew, but only together?

Three women left beneath the surface. Pools of gurgling bubbles, their only signal of life.

Roaring ceased after rags were forcefully stuffed into the wailing mouths of the two captured so-defined witches. All gazes once again patrolled the plunge area where connecting ropes to the other three lazily coiled. Was it not time to pull them up? Tracking the seconds a person was capable of staying below the surface was in the hands of the black-attired Jake. He clutched a pocket watch within his hungry grip, the power of life and death within his evil tongue.

"Irrsinn!" Meginhardt's fist rose high. He jumped up to the platform. "Stop, Pa. Yer in charge. What are ya thinking?" He glared into the eyes of the man who raised him, recognizing the shape, the hue, the depths. The natural curve of his upper lip. A flash of Sarai came and went.

Sure enough, this was him, but not the father he'd grown up with. This man looked frightened, regretful, hiding in a stance of authoritative strength. The eyes of the pa he knew flared with rage, revenge, angry remorse. Hatred even.

Which was better?

Unaware of his son's apparition, Witford Dimietris dismissed a bloodsucking pest from employing his nose as a place to rest.

"Yeah, like that's more important." Meginhardt booted his pa, his ghostly leg passing right through a set of shaking knees. The inkling notion of a life with his mother, fully alive, drove him on.

Frustration kicked into rage. He pounded his father with every cell of energy he could muster, striking him with his right fist, then his left, then a right punch, and another and another. A shoulder push sent Meginhardt straight through. No one gave the slightest notice of his foolish handglide across the platform, other than Jophiel releasing a disappointed sigh.

Finally, Witford Dimietris cleared his throat. Was he, too, anxious each excruciating second?

Jake motioned to two of the three remaining sets of men. "Get ready. The countdown now begins. After which, you are to pull in your accused. Should these two women be yet alive, nature will have spoken clear—nothing evil within these natural beings."

What about the last woman, Meginhardt's mother?

"Jake." Pa spat. "Come now. My wife, add her to the countdown."

Meginhardt anchored himself back on his feet. Pounding some sense into Pa didn't work. He'd try a different strategy. He whispered into his father's ear. "Forget the countdown—go, pull her up."

An unheard but satisfying command. Tragically, also ineffective.

Jake slithered behind Pa like a snake in tall grass, leaning in close. "'Tis my belief yer heathen wife should steep a bit longer, Witford. Might teach somebody a lesson."

Teach somebody a lesson? Meginhardt chewed his lips. Was his mother being tried as a means to teach Pa some kind of lesson? A horrible punishment with generational consequences.

"Nature's accepted her gladly." Pa's neck veins bulged. "There ain't a heathen bone in her body."

"Huh. So, you say. Yet, you alleged her, Witford. Or have you forgotten?"

"Pull her up. Or I shall take you down with my very fist." Pa tightened a fist behind his back, his threat meant for Jake, not for the crowd to witness.

"First you mock my trials. Then you threaten me. Maybe

I should be putt'n you at the end of that rope with yer wife." Face pasted with a smug grin, Jake strolled back to his position of public authority—overseer of the annual water trials. That is, when he wasn't collecting taxes from the merchants and farmers.

Was his father being blackmailed? Meginhardt could see Pa's relief to have the stench of Jake's breath removed from such proximity, but his face remained worried, worn, contrite.

Jake cast a brief look at his pocket watch, then spied the water's surface for added crowd-pleasing intensity.

Voices rose with wild screams. "Not yet, not yet!" For if they pulled the sunken women too early, they might never know if these women were innocent, and suspicion that witches lived among them wouldn't cease. No, it'd be best to wait, give the women more time to prove their innocence.

Jake held his palms high and spoke. "Come now. It's time. Gentlemen, countdown starts: Ten. Nine. Eight . . ."

The infant in the basket aside the podium began a piercing cry. Glancing at the young girl in charge of his care, a child herself, Pa cast a firm look instructing her to quiet the boy down.

"Shush, Meggie-boy." The girl crouched to hoist him into her arms. Though the babe was near half her size, she managed to bring him close to nuzzle her neck.

"Meggie-boy? 'Tis that baby me?" But that meant—

Was he present at this contemptible trial, sleeping and fussing, all while his mother was yards away, drowning? Pa said she died in childbirth. "Ya lickorous, lying glutton!"

Queasiness consumed Meginhardt. He wanted to shake that infant silly. *Slumber naught. Be aware!*

He ranted, instructing Jophiel to reverse this senselessness.

The one shushing—Emmaline, his mother's sister—called him Meggie-boy. She came by plenty of times to cook and clean for him and Pa. She saw all this and never told him?

"Of course, Einstein, that's you, and that's our cue. We gotta go." Jophiel scooped up Meginhardt, stealing him away from the tragic moment that set the course of his life, Meginhardt kicking vehemently to stay.

"I command you to drop me!" he hollered as they rose. "I wanna talk to Pa."

The entire sickening ordeal made him dizzy as it swirled and swirled, becoming tinier and tinier till it was no longer in sight, leaving him traumatized with generous bouts of nausea. A battle brewed within. Hopeful thoughts for any kind of joyous future no longer existed.

CHAPTER TWENTY
CUTS OF A CARVER

In Vereiteln Dorf

THE BRISK WALK did much for Lexxie to bandy about the morning's learnings. This murder business of Harmon's father, Gillam Huber, circled madly. For what reasons had Harmon and Grossmutter lied of it? Might *they* have killed him? Plus, the murder happened in the year of her birth. How did one fall upon the other? Presuming, of course, her birth date was correct. Huffing, she dismissed all the intruding muses.

She almost didn't see the man, crouched on the ground, concentrating on a laid-out-flat grave marker. She halted to avoid toppling into the glow of a blazing metal brazier. Evidently, pedestrians were used to making broad strokes around the grinding and cutting, though she had missed the telling worn walk-around path in the dirt road.

"Woman, what's ailing ya? If ya don't need a carv'n fer yerself, ya should be fine." He snorted a chortle. A wearing to the man's physique showed decades of slouching. His narrow-fronted shop, though small compared to the others, must be the noisiest and messiest. A sign spread beyond its borders, declaring: Ye Carver and Stonemason of Vereiteln.

Her lips curved upward. Well, something was on her side. Mindlessly led to the village's stonecutter. Pure fate. 'Course a sign *had* directed her in this direction.

"Guten tag, mein herr." She curtsied to the man who'd surely have some answers, a lift to set her free from this trap of unknowing. By his shabby clothing, his living must be meager, and this livelihood of stonecutting, a backbreaking craft.

He peered up at her, blackened fingertips, one curious extra-long nail on each stubby hand, and an eye patch covered his left eye, likely from a flying stone chip. But his grin be genuine. A sparkle in his uncovered right eye and three spared teeth flashed into sight. "Huh, no one's ever gone and done that before. What can I do for ya, gracious lady?" When she didn't respond right away, he studied her face. Did he recognize her? "Don't mind if I don't stand up. Legs gone crampin', and it ain't pretty. Not like you." His mouthy grin even bigger now, his tools placed within easy reach by his knees.

She blushed. She hadn't been out and about in any town, much less met strangers who told her she was pretty, so the increased blood flow was unmanageable. No sense to stand tall and businesslike. This man was on the ground and willing to help. So, tucking her skirt, she kneeled to begin the unfolding of an unusual request.

"A pleasure to meet you, sir. I've been admiring your handicraft in the graveyard garden."

"By me troth, been doin' it forever." He chuckled. "Whatcha need? No deaths lately, I'd know. So, yer settling here? I ain't seen ya before. Need yer farm name on a boulder or someth'n? My Gypsy works fer hire too. Ya need her?" His waist allowed him a half turn.

Gypsy? Ah yes. A glance through the split slats underneath his sign revealed the mule inside his shop. "Thank ye. Nothing to hire right now, sir. I'm doing some research. About townsfolk. You know, simple things like births and deaths."

"Ree–search? What fer? Anyone who's anybody 'round here already knows everything. Who in the blazes else would wanna know stuff like ree–search?"

"Me?" She smiled flirtatiously, hoping to get around this stumble. She sure didn't need another blockade.

"Oh well, depend'n what yer after. What kin I do fer ya?"

"Mr. Gillam Huber—the family man murdered in 1671. Why doesn't the stone marker show the words *justice served* like others I've seen?"

The creases in his neck unfolded as his head drew nearer to hers. "You ain't from 'round here, are ya? 'Cause if'n you were, you'd know justice served only goes on the villain's marker. And those there villains ain't gonna be buried over there. I kin tell ya that much."

Dah! This time, the heat rising up her neck tingled. "Of course, that makes sense. And they'd be buried out of town on the west edge."

"That's right. Ya bin there yet? Ya must've bin if you saw justice served. Some of my finest work is there too, ya know." He sat tall and proud, sucking in something stuck in the long fingernail of his left hand.

Lexxie stood, doubting why she thought this man could be helpful with information to lead to her identity.

"But yer not gonna find the killer over yonder either."

Oh? "What do you mean? Justice was not served? His killer never found? On the loose maybe?"

Huh. Maybe it *was* Harmon and Grossmutter.

He curled the finger belonging to that long fingernail on his right hand, instructing her to get back down to his level as if he had something to share.

She squatted, attentive ears waiting, breath held.

"That Gillam Huber ya talk of, his kill'n was the work of witches." He sat back, chest puffing. "Best not even mention that name, gracious lady." The single window to the man's soul transitioned to a horizontal slit as his friendly information bordered a warning.

She leaned back on her knees and wrenched a twist, ignoring whether it be appropriate. Surely, it wasn't, but her body needed the stretch. Her toes were aching from the new shoes and her stockings still wet in the feet. A hearty inhale, followed by a puffy exhale.

Witches! There wasn't any talk of witches in Avondale, certainly not by their priest. And a man of his station ought to know. Even Jonne speculated it was a way for people to blame others for crimes they committed themselves. And Jonne, being a traveling man between five villages, would have a good sense to the manner of the world—as did Harmon, it seemed. She shoved the latter from her memory. And Jonne too, for that matter.

"Sister witches." The carver tipped his head, his eye looking to read Lexxie's.

Mercy. Her inhale and exhale lengthened. "What do you mean?"

"That poor bloke, he married one of 'em. Not knowing

she be a witch. Then he gone and married the baby sister. She was a witch too, a worse one. He didn't know it."

"Gillam Huber had two wives?"

"Nein, gracious lady, the killer. Possessed he was, by his wives. Sisters." The fragile man's shoulders shook with a violent shudder. "Devil's daughters."

Devil's daughters? "How do you know they were witches? Do they look different—er, did they?"

"Noth'n kin tell them apart from real folk. It ain't right. They've no place here. I bury 'em. Then I burn my clothes." The muddy gray that sparked a moment ago in his visible eye churned to a glossy black and glared as if he desired to be sure she was paying close attention. "They make ya do things— even after they're buried."

At that, she stood and smoothed her dress to hide a shiver. "Really." Honestly? She allowed herself a delicate snort. "They make you take someone's life."

He waved her disbelief away. "Ah, yer one of those. Go away, then. Please yerself. Ya come to me fer answers, didn't ya? Don't like what ya got, fine." Picking up his tools, he resumed to chisel away at the laid-out-flat marker.

She remained. Watching him work. Despite his dismissal, her instinct insisted she stay. She wanted—*needed*—more information. If these so-called sister witches—devil's daughters, heaven forbid—had something to do with the killing of Harmon's father, then they might have something to do with her being snatched as an infant and with such secrecy.

"Who was the killer? The possessed one, that is." Though she asked politely with an attempt to reconnect, he ignored her, his focus on the half-finished gravestone.

Annoyed with a bee wavering around her knees, she

slapped at it with her coin purse. The bug dazed like a drunkard and fell to her feet, bouncing onto the marker. The carver's hand brushed it off. Something about the inscription caught her attention.

No name, no age, only a date—a *future* date.

"That's three days away. How do you know someone will die in three days?" She probably should've apologized for her insensitivity before making another inquiry. But this demanded an explanation. And he best not claim the sister witches were behind *this*.

The carver dropped his tools and grunted, contorting his facial muscles, and maneuvering his thighs and ankles till he took a full stand. The permanent arch in his back kept him to a height equivalent to three-quarters of hers. And she must've set off some kind of emotion inside him—anger, maybe—to make him struggle as such to wake up those shaky knees. What warning would he bequeath this time?

"Ree–search. Bugger ya. Yer one of those advi–cates. Ya don't think we gotta business keepin' our village pure. Ya know full well, don't'cha? All sorts o' people come to town to watch. Why? 'Cause they applaud us. We got the best water trial around. Take no guff. We round 'em up every harvest. If'n the pure don't want 'em, the waters spit 'em out. Then we hang 'em." That long right-handed fingernail waved in her face, his warning stern. "You better watch yer tongue."

Far too late to apologize for any insensitivities, she quivered from this man's crusty gall. Water trials in three days followed by hanging for those who failed. This man was preparing the grave markers before the deaths. As she hadn't left, he seemed the need to continue.

"We don't hold much regard fer your sort."

"My sort?"

"Yer sort. Ya think we donna know what were doin'. Yer in favor of yer witches, ain't ya?"

"Nay. No, sir. I don't know what to think. You've taught me much today, and I thank ye. I bid you goodbye." She curtsied and walked with a determined briskness back to the main road's walk. She hid behind a trio of women, strolling as though she were one of their group. When one caught her eye, Lexxie choked on the morning's experience and took to running the rest of the way to the safety of her private room.

An unwelcoming priest. A madman in the holy graveyard. A murder and another lie from Harmon. Daughters of the devil—sisters, even. Water trials. An upcoming hanging. And was that a threat from the stonecutter—"watch yer tongue"?

Might any of this, all of this, have to do with her? She hoped none, but her instincts hinted otherwise.

CHAPTER TWENTY-ONE
UNCOMFORTABLE HONESTY

In Vereiteln Dorf

LIGHTHEADED FROM OVEREXERTION, she cursed her shoes, elegant as they were. Had she been wearing her regular leather tie-up boots, her feet could have kept up to her mind. She stubbed an already swollen set of toes on the stoop leading into the boarding house.

Grabbing the doorjamb, she eyed Giselle's gilded footwear. Quite similar, only higher heelwork. Had Jonne purchased a pair for her as well? How dare he.

But why should I trouble my thoughts? Still, she carries herself better in them than I.

"Goodness, liebste, let me help ya." Giselle aided Lexxie to a relaxing lean against the frame before collecting spilled coins that rolled away from her fallen purse. "What's gotten into yer goat? You're all pale." The back of Giselle's hand stroked across Lexxie's forehead. "A fever? Come, sit down."

Thankful for a much-needed caring, Lexxie massaged her knees with sweaty palms, allowed her breathing to settle, and nodded to accept the invitation to a vacant plump parlor chair. The hugging deep-blue velvet, far too luxurious, but oh so welcoming. A sweet undercurrent of fragrant oil reinvigorated her senses and worked hand in hand with the relaxing room. Generous floral wall coverings egged Lexxie on to smile. Permitting mindlessness, she waited for her heartbeat to slow while sipping a mug of warm ale Giselle had fetched.

Feeling Lexxie's forehead once again, Giselle opened her pursed lips into a line of inquiry. "Well, better now. An ailing, nah. Did ya see a ghost or someth'n?"

Aside from annoyance earlier over the ridiculous with-child remark, Lexxie hadn't taken much notice of Giselle. Particularly, the blue in her eyes that shone pure compassion. How that deep-purple glow in her pupils gave full and meaningful attention. Appreciating both, Lexxie broadened the examination. Those hair twists pinned with equal tension revealed a perfectionist by nature, and how was it possible to smell so nice? Best of all was her smile. Like one a mother might gift each day to her young child, full of approval, no matter what. Something Lexxie never had, a mother, much less a mother's approval.

Why'd she so rashly paint the woman with an ill impression? Lexxie's gaze fell to her lap, barely noticing Giselle's hands had clasped her own.

"Now, liebste, what's got yer goat?"

Lexxie needed a friend. Someone to confide in. Someone to help her muddle through this. "I haven't been truthful," she squeaked.

"No one comin' to my boarding house ever is." Giselle chuckled.

Lexxie eased her hands from under Giselle's. "Can I trust you?"

Giselle pulled back. "Why on earth wouldn't ya? If there's a master secret holder in this town, it's me. You don't stay successful running a boarding house if ya can't be trusted." She leaned in close, genuine-like. "And don't be daft. I may not know why yer here, but I can tell you I know yer not checking into things for yer parents."

Slipping shoes off never felt so good. Lexxie crossed her ankles and stretched her toes wide inside her stockings, dampness still clinging to both feet. "I'm not with child like you think."

"Oh, too bad. Thought maybe Jonnie was gonna, you know, settle down." Giselle winked. "He is a good-lookin' man, you gotta admit."

"Have you . . . ?" Lexxie couldn't finish the question.

"Me? Hah, nay."

"Did he gift you those shoes?"

They took a moment to compare footwear, both having the same fine leather stitching and similar beading.

Giselle clasped her mouth to hide a giggle. "Yup, but not what you think fer. He must have a load of 'em. You can't get these here, not in this town. Lora-Lee's got the same ones too."

"Lora-Lee?"

"She runs the market stall with all the hats. Where the frock you got on must've come from. I think he was stuck on her for a bit."

They bonded over a good laugh at his expense. Giselle must know as well as Lexxie'd learned that below a coarse kind of mannerism, he was kindhearted and, despite his reputation, a gentleman in many respects.

"Another cup of ale, might ya?"

"Nay, thank ye."

"Then go on. Tell me what got ya so pale and shivered such a fright up yer spine."

"It's a bit of a story." Lexxie shifted in her seat and furrowed a brow. The business of running a boarding house must be of great demand. Wasting time over her dilemma seemed selfish.

A slow double-blink disclosed Giselle's understanding. A half grin spelled curiosity.

Jealousy struck. Even the way Giselle pressured her knees, giving her shapely frame a push up, was carried out most elegantly, not to consider how well the woman managed on those heels. After a glide onto the walkway, she flipped a hand-painted sign to closed, then skated a return, and settled in with an embraceable eagerness. "Go on then."

A salty drizzling accompanied each facet of Lexxie's story. She spilled it all, starting with that day, the horrifying—perhaps accidental, perhaps not—slip of the tongue from a man she thought to be her natural-born father. Deceit led to this quest, the need to find her genuine family. "It's been a dogged journey. Why was it so necessary for me to dress as a man? The embarrassment of it all."

Giselle slapped her lap, chortling. "Sounds like Jonnie!"

The shared laughter offered a blessed release.

Giselle tsked a serious tone. "Tell me what did you this morn'n? What have our townsfolk put into your silly little head?"

Silly little head? Lexxie's shoulders took a pulse, her wanting to share, a pause. She pushed flat against the chairback. "What think you? That I pay attention to everything everyone tells me?" *Spew.*

"Don't go gettin' your gird up. I know what goes on out there. Who you bin talking to? Someone shook ya up."

With a breath to push the guard down, Lexxie leaned forward. "I upset the stonecutter. I set out to inquire of him why Gillam Huber's stone hadn't the justice-has-been-served message."

Giselle's torso stiffened. "Gillam Huber? Why . . . ? How . . . ?" She clasped her mouth, and the rosy pink drained from her cheeks.

"Did you know him?" Wiping sweaty hands down her skirt before leaning forward on her elbows, Lexxie pressed again. "Do you know what happened to me?"

Giselle stood and, as if in some kind of trance, walked over to the front desk and positioned herself behind it. Her mouth remained covered though clearly not for ladylike shyness.

Lexxie's breath was as fast as her steps. Facing Giselle across the slanted counter, she placed a two-handed grip on the woman's forearms.

Giselle's eyes glassed.

"If you knew Gillam, you must have known Harmon. Why did Harmon take me? I must know."

Giselle freed her arms. Grasping the edges of her desk, now a protector of sorts, she shook her head. "Want my advice? Leave town. Go back."

How cold, how dry her voice had become!

"Huh?"

"We shall speak no further of this."

TWENTY-TWO
YOUNG AND RESTLESS

In Vereiteln Dorf

BACK AND FORTH, Lexxie paced her room, regrettably quiet. If she were wearing her old boots, she'd have the satisfaction of some stomps, not those silent mopping marks her damp stocking feet left. She tore her stockings off and tossed them against the flowery wallpaper.

Gillam Huber had been an unwelcomed reminder. But why? Was he some kind of lying cheat? A deceitful knave? Did he deserve to die at another's hands?

"Nay." Silliness, if that were so, he'd not be lying in the holy graveyard.

Outside her window, the street was still busy with Saturday marketgoers. Why couldn't her life have been normal like she presumed theirs were? A chill of invalidation and aloneness called for a bout of sulks. A fresh woodpile lay in the hearth, a perk of staying in the top-floor suite. She collected her stockings and hung them on the mantel.

Yanking away the bow and pins, she freed her butchered

hair to lay as it wished. She gave the gilded slipper shoes a shove back underneath the settee and cursed the moment she'd found them. Then she pulled up her bare legs, curled into a ball, and fit herself perfectly inside the settee's arms. Who cared that her head crimped the fashionable look-but-don't-use cushions?

"Murder, secrets, witches—devil's daughters." She rocked back and forth. "Stolen, deception, attackers, and accusers."

Did Harmon survive well enough in Mittel Dorf to get back to Avondale? Was young Matilda being harmed this minute? What did Giselle know? And what of Jonne's generosity?

Working to sort out one's life sure took a toll, particularly when exerting energy to stay angry.

The next morning came fast. She bolstered up to get out and try again.

The clatter of carts and carriages brought a smile, a familiar joy of Sunday mornings, or so it was in Avondale. *Am I homesick? Surely not. Well, maybe a little.*

Removing her frock, she waved and snapped it about to smoothen the crinkles and freshen it up. At least she had crisp, dry stockings.

To avoid that priest, she'd attend the alternate church. She set off to stroll through town. At the crossroad, she pushed her head high to snub the place that so dashed her hopes and then veered right to stay clear. Others, common folk, on the same dirt path were not dressed in fancy attire. A short stretch away, a Protestant pastor invited the strollers and stragglers, circulating his arms to lead his flock. From the path, one might have overlooked the church, a derelict structure, set back a ways from the road. Lexxie scouted the yard at its side for another graveyard to explore. But nay.

She entered the side door and eyed a pew, wary of more conflict. Ah, the spot behind a thick wooden beam. Surely, no one would fight her for a seat with a blocked view. She sat tall and focused on staring forward, obedient to cues from others for standing, singing, kneeling, and folding hands in prayer. Her goal was to be unnoticed by villagers, particularly the gossipy sort. No one glanced nor even looked her way, which added to the accumulating aloneness.

Finally, the last belt of the closing hymn rang out. She snuck out the same way, the side door, avoiding the pastor's handshake and all the after-church backslapping. A raw and emotional knot in the pit of her stomach flashed an image— Harmon and Grossmutter leaving their beloved church in Avondale and strolling home for lamb stew and the much-anticipated Sunday biscuits. How sad to think of them. Alone. Without her.

Her fists balled and her pace quickened. They shouldn't have lied to her.

Where now? It was the King's Day, and she was hungry, her immediate needs comprised sustenance. Whatever Giselle would be cooking for her boarding guests, Lexxie could dine on in her room.

Still, she'd yet to have a plan, even an inkling of a next move. Employing an efficient, clipping pace, she headed toward the Coaching Inn.

A scuffling of footsteps caught up, and a cry to wait arrested her attention. A lad, a few years younger than herself, took a place alongside her, a jog to keep up. "Yer new. I'm supposed to git yer purpose."

His teeth were big. At least, the front two were, the rest appearing crooked. Thin lips stretched from one ear to the other, matching the horizontal lines on his forehead. His hair was tied back and was that—? Yes, fuzz around his chin. A boy man. He looked harmless. She giggled, and without realizing it, her handgrips loosened.

"My purpose?" she inquired at a standstill, allowing the lad to catch a breath. "Who shall have such privilege of knowing?"

"Ah . . ." He huffed, turned his shoulders to the church, and pointed at a gathering of men on the yard. He collapsed to a lean, resting his elbows on his knees, still huffing, his piercing eyes checking for a reaction.

"Well." A dignified Lexxie resumed her pace. "You be telling whichever male is inquiring that I'm not lookin' for a husband."

How dare a man send a boy to seek her acquaintance! She'd not yet had the chance to be courted, but this was clearly not a suitable way nor was the timing. She shooed the lad away.

"He only wants to meet you." The lad put effort in to keep up with her mean and long strides. "What's yer name?"

"Why wouldn't he come himself?" She shooed him away again.

This time, he stopped in his tracks. "Ah, come on. He's busy. He's my . . ."

I'm sure he is. "Well, you tell him I'm a proper woman. I've no intention to have anything to do with him. You go and give him that message. And he—nor you, his little messenger for that matter—needn't know my name." She quickened her pace to gain some distance.

The lad waved a bug with his cap. "So why did ya come, then?"

Was everyone compelled to ask this? "Nay ye business."

"My pa likens to know every person who comes to our church."

Her steps stuttered. "Our church?"

"That's what pastors do, don't ya know? Daft, are ya?"

Mercy. She swung around. "Your pa's the pastor? He's the man? Oh my. Wait."

The lad had already squared his shoulders to face his father's church.

"Wait if you please."

He stood, hands in his pockets and neck arched to hear her out. He waited this time for her to come to him.

And she did. Sheepishly. "I'm sorry. Really. I'm just . . . this town . . . Forgive me. What's yer name, by the way?"

"I'm supposed to give you my name, just like that, am I?"

Ouch. She deserved that. "Please, I am truly sorry."

He kicked some dirt around. "GC."

"GC, what's that supposed to stand for? Why'd they call you that?"

He shrugged.

Her turn. She reminded herself of the need for manners. "I'd be delighted to meet your pa."

"Next Sunday, then." Obviously fed up with her, he nodded in suggestion she continue going her own way. "I'll prepare him for ya, let him know he's got a wild one to tame."

"What? Me? Now listen here, I'm no wild one."

His legs, which scored more inches than his torso, and his knees, a bit knobby, began the trek back to the lingering gathering in front of his pa's church. He weren't a farmer. That's for sure, too thin and tender footed.

She marched up behind him and squeezed his right

shoulder. Bony, this lad didn't know what work was. Must be a mama's boy. If so, then, he must know a lot of people stuff.

"GC, I'm new in town. Might you show me around? Tell me about this place. I surmise it's got some good history, maybe some stories."

He paused at least to consider her invitation. Good.

"C'mon. I said I was sorry. I imagine you know what things happen 'round here. Plenty of keen stories?"

His eyes opened wide with an eager want. His lips pursed.

"I won't be telling yer pa anything you tell me. Don't worry 'bout that."

Anticipation practically bled down his cheeks.

Yes! He be the gossipy type. A little encouraging push might do it. "I promise, anything you share'll be our secret."

If there be one thing this town wasn't short on, it'd be stories. And secrets. She pressed a finger to her lips. Would this be what she needed—homespun tales of village villains?

His eagerness befell the lad. "Aye, I know more 'bout the secrets in this town than the devil himself. We've got plenty of the unhallowed. Where ya from anyway? Yer new, so yer gonna be a story on yer own. Everyone's gonna be asking Pa. He'll be pleased if I can give him something about you, so's he can pass it on."

The boy was negotiating.

She waved an invite at herself. "Ask away."

"Fer starters, where's yer kinfolk?"

"I kinda thought you'd ask what my name was first."

"Good gracious, what's yer name *and* where's yer kinfolk?"

No way could she give him the truth and risk him shutting his mouth and walking away like Giselle did. Her pause made the boy restless. She caught the pastor's fixed stare on the two of them.

"You in trouble, young man?" After all, the pastor had his elbows and his eyebrows both angled at a stern dial.

Another shrug, this time a single-sided one. "Says I don't show 'nough interest in his flock." He flapped his arms and squatted around. "Quack, quack."

How's that fer commonality? His eyes sparked, his personality coming forthwith, and her laughter burst loose.

He beamed. "Look, not sure what yer look'n for, ma'am, but if I can assist, I will. But you gotta spin me the yarn 'bout ya so's I can share with my pa."

"Deal." She curtsied for fun and opened her elbow, inviting his own. "They gonna miss you?"

By now, the whole dern gathering in front of the church was glaring.

"Nay, mostly cuz'ns." He looped his arm through hers, and they kicked off a happy step.

"So what ya wanna know? Kill'ns, thieve'ns, outta-wedlock illegitimates?"

Fortuity at last. How blessed she'd been. Could he unknowingly give notions as to her identity? Depending, of course, how far back his stories would be. She needed a history greater than this lad's years. "Let's start with nasty massacres, might you have stories going back as far as, say, twenty years or so?"

"Aw, marry come up, I kin go back a hundred years." He jumped into a famous resistance when some early settlers tried to convert a bunch of Alemanni. "A slaughterhouse." The lad spoke as if he himself had been there. "My pa says we gotta be thankful. That's when Vereiteln got its own marches."

She kept her lips tight and pretended a keen interest. Harmon had always preached peace and negotiated land boundaries to be the better path. "Anything between villagers perhaps?" Her open hands gestured for more. "Like when the murderer was never brought to justice?"

The lad came to a standstill, perhaps insulted, his face morphed to a scrunch. "Ma'am, we are a town of pure justice. No one 'round here gits away—no, ma'am, not here. If'n yer damned, yer damned and buried. And we got a place for 'em. We clean 'em out every year."

Clean them out? "And just how do you do that?" She held her breath, afraid she already knew the answer—water trials and hangings. Ignoring a quiver, she awaited his version.

"Ya daft? Ain't you here for our festival? We git plenty'a strangers this time of year."

I'm not daft, young man. She sucked in and tightened her lips. "Festival? What festival might that be?"

"You missed the banners? Ma'am, yer ears full'a somethin'? I told ya—we clean 'em out every year. The Justice Festival. Big hang'n, day after tomorra." GC looked back at the watching crowd. Then, with a tilted head, he turned his gaze to her. "What's yer name again?"

"Lexxie." She spilled her name, the stonecutter's work on her mind. Surely, though, the town didn't make a celebration out of such a disturbing ordeal, much less promote it?

"Lexxie? What kinda name is that?"

His squinty eyes didn't bother her much. Rather, she wanted desperately out of any Justice Festival discussion, just thinking about it sent shivers traversing her spine. "Huh." She chuckled. "Yer really gonna fish for answers the whole time we talk, ain't ya?"

"That, I am." He puffed his chest. Apparently, he needed the gossip on her to prove his worth.

Chatty, colorful, and eager to please—both her and his father. She didn't fight the uncontrollable smile, so innocent and harmless the lad was. As her face curved up, her mind transformed along with it. It might be a good day after all. Now, she'd have to devise a tour of this place for the damned. Once there, she'd slide in a request as to where Gillam Huber's murderer was buried. See what came from that. There must be a story connection, maybe even a child-thieving one. Though GC's reference to "illegitimates" plagued her somewhat. That being a possibility she hadn't thought of.

"I'm waiting. Ya haven't told me anythin' yet about yerself, Lexxie, ma'am."

Hesitation made it obvious she was guarding her identity.

"Well, I'm nineteen," she lied. "So, your turn. Why's it called the place of the damned, and I presume yer speaking of the ole graveyard at the end of the stretch of road?"

"Why'd you lie to me?"

"What?" By no reasoning could he know she lied about her age, not that she could imagine.

"Ya've bin on this road before, so why'd you say ya presumed stuff, when ya already knew?"

Oh, that lie. She didn't like his smug expression.

"Right. Sorry. 'Tis the only way into town, this road." No one entered or exited Vereiteln Dorf without traveling past the unconsecrated graveyard.

"Ya can't read, kin ya?" GC looked at her sheepishly.

"Sure I can." She cast him a wide-eyed glare. "My grandmother taught me well, I'll have you know."

"Well, ya missed the banner and the sign at the graveyard.

It even says, Place of the Damned. Sooo—wait. Hey, who's your grandmother? She live in town here?"

Dern. Hemmed in. Best allow GC to think she couldn't read. She lowered to a gaze of shame at her feet. "Might you take me there? To this place of the damned. I'd like a story-teller like you showing me around in that graveyard."

Good. He took her request as a heroic gesture.

They spoke little other than chitchat about the weather, crops, and moon phases as they strolled past the shops. All closed for the day except for Giselle's boarding house where new people entered the front doors, likely to seek a wash up or a meal or both. Certainly, the rooms to stay the night would already be filled.

The road winding upward softened, its curbs of gullies loaded with wild cornflowers, their deep blue feeding a tran-quil and promising emotion to its passersby. Wafts of clover scented the air. Lexxie breathed in deep the carefree scent, a merry feel. Until GC started chatting her up again.

"It's tough to pull a wagon on a cow path, so yes'n, the stage and the postie com'n go on this road. I reckon you came with postie as you sure as anyth'n weren't on the stagecoach. How d'ya know Jonne?"

Forsooth! He'd figured enough already. How did she know Jonne? She'd have to answer this question carefully. She'd already become a village story of interest herself. She told the priest she was researching. He didn't accept that explanation. And what about that stonecutter? He thought her an advo-cate—for witches, of all things. And Giselle? Simply hearing Gillam Huber's name clammed her up. And oh, then Jonne. Jonne. How shall she explain him?

"Ah, the post rider, Jonne. Yes, I missed the stagecoach at

Mittel Dorf. He offered to bring me here." Might that be sufficient? She plucked a ladybug off her shoulder, blowing it away
and wishing it would return with some fortuitous happenings.

The lad scratched the back of his head underneath his cap.
"Rumor has it, he's good with the ladies."

"Nein! If you're going to be rude, young man, you can
march right back to your pa and ma. I'll speak to them myself
about your manners."

"Easy." He tossed a piece of grass he'd been chewing on
and picked up the pace, so her intent to shut down this topic
was successful. "Seeing it's a Sunday, no bushels fer sale today.
Guess'n we go straight to those dead damned ones." Then his
pace slowed. "You'd like that, wouldn't ya?"

Their arms had been unlinked for a while now. Her hands
found her hips given his accusing sarcasm. "And why would
you say that?"

"'Cause yer a liar. You ain't from Mittel Dorf, bin there
myself with my Pa plenty'a times. Never seen the likes of you
there."

"I didn't actually say . . ." Too late to explain.

"Yer a fake, and yer hid'n someth'n."

"GC, don't be a narr."

"I ain't the narr." He stretched his neck forward, shoving
narrowed eyes into her face. "Yer a witch—and you've come
back to steal a child."

CHAPTER TWENTY-THREE
FROM PREY TO PREDATOR

At the River of Times, the lowest level of the Kingdom

YESTERDAY, A WEB of lies, Pa, its orb-web spider. Decades of deceit made from sticky long strands. The circular grid entrapped Meginhardt inside a spinning world.

For years, he berated himself each day. He deserved every thrashing from Pa, because if not for his own selfish existence, his mother would be alive and Pa would be sober and kind. 'Least that's how he steeped. But now, the truth unveiled. *Bollocks!*

His mother hadn't died in childbirth. She drowned at Pa's hands. Jophiel whisked Meginhardt away before witnessing the traumatic ending. Was that oversized, smart-aleck creature with an overstuffed feather appendage out to get him too?

Yet, Meginhardt pined for this old version of his life. His mother had died in childbirth. His pa needed him. He and Pa shared the grief, shared a victimhood. Not ideal, but he'd learned how to manage it. He coped, he survived. He had dreams, hope that, one day, it would all change. It would be good. Routine to excuse Pa's behavior became easy. He endured a life of tongue-lashings and boot-kickings because the man didn't know how to cope, much less raise a boy. Meginhardt gave his darndest to churn misery into happiness. Not what some folk would call a good life, but he considered it a purpose.

Hope and purpose. Turned out, for nothing.

And now, he lay flat on his back, emotionally detached. Mending energy from the cool and aromatic grass underneath him tempted his senses. A river, a gentle slope away, offered lullabies in a restorative gurgle. The silvery edge of every leaf hanging lazily above him sliced the breeze, showing off some kind of synchronized dance. Somewhere in the distance, a thousand chimes, faint and orchestrated, offered up their own way of soothing.

Cry me a thousand mercies.

He resisted bliss of any feel or sound. The harshness of truth was worse than the harshness of deceit.

From behind, the surprising softness of Jophiel's voice interrupted the dogfight ranting inside his head. "You carried her forward with your own life."

Now you make like ya care. And what does 'carried her forward' even mean?

Not only did Meginhardt mistake his father's guilt for grief but also he'd allowed all harmful behaviors to be reasoned away. So now, time to despise himself for being such a narr. For being nothing but playful prey, easy pickings for his predatory father.

Nay, never again should he be snared. From now on, he shall be the one who does the trapping.

And who best to teach him? He'd take his breeding from Pa's doings, commit to self-absorption. Concern for anyone else? Futile. Not only that, he'd double-cross these kingdom beings. It was time he got what he wanted.

The argument within settled. He just needed someone to teach him the ways of this new world.

"Don't lecture me. It's my life," Meginhardt responded to Jophiel's witless views as he finger-snatched chunks of grass to sabotage its scent of succor.

He didn't deserve comfort. Comfort could only serve to weaken. Tossing the freshly ripped blades onto his torso, he ached to hide like when he took refuge shielded by the stone pile behind Pa's farm when the cornfield was bare. Bury himself forever in a whole pile of this aromatic greenery, and sob with no one knowing. He could have done it too, for the grass blades grew back as soon as he ripped them from the soil.

But as far as his life went? Wasted. It wasn't to grow back like these grass blades, nor was he ever going back. No chance of that. He was dead. He needed to become a predator of sorts. Attack others for the sake of nothing but simple, pure revenge. Some laughs. Yes, that would be nice for a change. He reveled, imagining this new bold version of himself.

Finally, a long exhale. His breathing pattern, much like the flow of the nearby river, wasn't going to settle, not while he fought the curative surroundings. Rushing, then slow, rushing, then slow. He propped himself up on one elbow and eyed Jophiel sitting large and cross-legged close to the river's edge.

"About done?" Jophiel said without as much as a twitch.

Couldn't he at least pretend to care?

"Pardon yerself." Sarcasm fit comfortable on Meginhardt's

tongue. "Ya made me watch my father execute my mother. Was that yer job? Make me watch'n squirm?" His forearms initiated the process of forcing his weight to a standing position, a warring sensation arising within. "Why? Why did I need to see that? And fer what purpose am I here with you?"

Boldness broke free from a suffering stupor. He stepped down the slope and towered a stance behind the sitting, slouching Jophiel. Enough was enough.

"I ain't moving till ya tell me."

Jophiel seemed intent to keep his eye on something at the river's edge, a churning swirl of water with murky threads running throughout. Whatever it be, it meant something disturbing, to him anyway. Rubbing his chin and sighing, he might've even whispered to it.

"Huh?" Meginhardt snapped his annoyance. "You say'n something? C'mon, ya owe me ta answer."

Jophiel shushed him. "Sit."

I am not a child. Still, Meginhardt took a spot and pulled his knees into his chest. Waiting. Something must happen next. Surely, some answers would come. They must, right? Some afterlife.

What was going on with Jophiel's features? Saddened and worried. Kinda distraught. He rubbed his face even harder and stared across the river, teeth clenched.

Meginhardt saw nothing on the other side. What was he looking at?

"What's got yer goat over there?" No response. Wait, why should he care?

This called for a closer examination. He stretched his neck to get a face-to-face view. The big infallible guy was sucking in his lips. "Are you—?"

Cry me a mercy, the oversized bird man is shedding tears.

"Temptation." The word barely escaped Jophiel's tight throat.

Well, if yer tempting me to be compassionate, it ain't gonna work. Having had enough, Meginhardt scrambled to block Jophiel's view of whatever he was staring at. "Enough. Spit it outta ya. Yer supposed to be showing me amazing things and telling me everything I need to know, ain't ya?"

"What do you want to know, boy?"

Aye, finally. "Start with my mother. You said she died in childbirth."

"I never said that."

Right. Pa did. "So why didn't anyone tell me the truth?"

Jophiel laughed. "Did you seek it?"

Meginhardt plopped back to the ground. He wasn't getting far with answers, but he'd keep trying. After a period of quietude during which he minded Jophiel inspect that water swirl as it grew wider and deepened with murky blotches, a plug of anxiety within himself released. "Was my mother a witch?"

A broad smile swept across Jophiel's face, and was that a burst of light emanating out the top of his head? "No, dear boy. Your mother was loyal, assigned to you she was."

Assigned to me? He best chew on the meat of that.

"Now, lookie here." Jophiel pointed to the water swirl, now appearing muddy and ominous, a rotating saw cutting deep into the riverbank side, only not getting anywhere. "That, right there—now *that* is a showstopper."

Whether Jophiel was avoiding his questions or more preoccupied with some circular current of water, Meginhardt wasn't sure. Curiosity enticed his cautious move to the river's edge. He peered into what was now, according to Jophiel, a portentous obsidian churn. Within the whirl, he glimpsed a fleck, a shiny glint—no, a tiny, tiny flame encased alongside a stone. The stone was being tossed ferociously, caught in gravity. It tumbled, trapped inside the swirling water torrent. Prying, he leaned over the bank.

Cry me a mercy.

"Are those eyes?" Aghast, he pivoted to Jophiel. "That thing, that stone—it's alive."

"Her."

A her. That stone was some girl. "Still, do something. She's trapped. You're gonna just sit there?"

When Jophiel didn't move, Meginhardt did. Three steps closer, though none did any good to slow the heat rising in his head. "Aye, I'm on ta ya. You're gonna let that life suffer, just like ya let me suffer my *whole* life, caught inside a world of lies."

He reached in with an outstretched hand. Perhaps if he could scoop up this living, gasping stone, she'd be saved from the tumultuous swirl. Then he would toss her into the clear stream, which swam in the river's center, far more inviting with crystal clarity.

But wait. He was no longer the compassionate sort. Remember? The merciless echo haunted between his temples.

Jophiel yelped a single, commanding word—*stop.*

Meginhardt did.

There needn't be further instruction. Jophiel's tone frightened Meginhardt to a back shuffle from the river's edge.

"There are rules. Besides, she's not stuck. She's on the search."

Even more questions pounded at his brain.

CHAPTER TWENTY-FOUR
YER A WITCH

In Vereiteln Dorf

MERCY, HE'S GONNA *wallop me one.*

Lexxie's impulse to tense an ankle scared her even more than what GC was planning with those balled-up fists. If he hurtled a punch her way, would she kick him?

Was anyone nearby? A farmer, a wanderer, or better yet, a wagon with family folk coming up the path? Anyone!

Nay a soul to be seen, just grazing cows across the road. Any chance of aid was left far behind in town.

"GC, don't be ridiculous." Somehow, she employed calm maturity, though preferring to whip the scrawny lad on his buttocks and send him off whining. "I've had about enough of this town."

His stiffened torso wasn't about to loosen up. "I ain't narr."

"What if I am a witch? Is your fist enough to send me away?" Her lips spread into a sly smile. "Who are you to dare mess with me in the physical realm?" Did she really speak such atrocity?

Tension maneuvered through his body, his fists went limp, his frame held tight, and his mouth fell, stretching wide. But the fear in his eyes brought to mind her horror with her assaulter, Mr. Nosy Man.

Mercy, what had she done? Exhausted in spirit, she dropped the act. Needful, he was for something true. Facts to deliver up to his pa, proving his own value. Time to talk her way out.

"GC, please, I am simply exploring. I understand I have relatives who lived once in this very town, your beloved town. I'm not here to cause trouble. I just seek familial roots. You see, I was . . . adopted." That was about as close to the truth she'd give. 'Twas a decent gift for his pa.

She eyed his fists to be sure they hadn't gripped again. She'd rather see him tug his loose trousers, so they'd anchor more suitably around his slim hips.

His body resigned to a slouch though he raised an eyebrow. "So, is it stories ya want? Or are ya look'n fer yer family up there?"

A trick question. If she agreed to the latter, she'd be a relative of the damned. Which, surely, wouldn't help her cause any. Besides, she wasn't anyway. Was she?

"Just stories." She clasped the back of her neck with both hands. "I love a good story. Tell me the juiciest ones, of course."

Good. His eyes brightened again. She'd won him over.

"I've bin to practically every burial fer the past five years." He puffed his chest, explaining his job shoveling the earth onto their boxes. With those slim forearms, though, he mustn't have carried that burden alone.

At the entrance, the spot where Jonne dropped her off the

day before yesterday, GC pointed to the farthest row. "Over yonder. Plenty'a stories there."

Those responsible for digging and placing markers must carry out their job with such haste. Zero regard for alignment. Many grave markers crooked, one even backward. As they strolled the maze, GC sluiced a bucket of stories as promised, many of which must be exaggerated, others downright unbelievable. Imagine what the tall oak trees had seen over the years. Those big ole knotty eyes knew the truth.

"Most were jist swill-bellies accord'n to my pa, but them ones, over there, horse thieves and cattle stealers. The worst."

All justice-was-served recipients, apparently. GC hadn't talked about child-thieves or witches. She was counting on an inkling of such. A thread she could pull to unravel something knotted up in her tapestry shawl. Needing to neither sound eager nor be mistaken as looking for her own "damned" relative, she practically sang the words to hide a shiver. "Cattle thievers, you say? Any child thievers 'round here? Bet they'd be hung and buried too."

"'Course, they'd be here too. But we ain't got any. Not child thieves anyway. When it comes to taking chil'en, that's the work of the devil's daughters." Through squints, he eyed her face-on, fists ready to coil if called for. "Fräulein Lexxie, were you taken as an infant, stolen from your family? Or were you adopted, like ya said?"

"Me? Oh goodness, certainly not. I went to a paid carer, arranged in secret, nothing like"—she gulped—"nothing to do with anything like . . . like devil's daughters, I assure you." As GC's posture eased up, she dared another ask. "So, who are these evil women, anyway? They sound horrible." She bit her lip. *Please, Grossmutter, let you not be one of them.*

GC perked up. She'd asked for something delicious. "Ya serious? Ya really ain't heard of 'em? Sister witches. They come back and git their own kind."

Lexxie's head spun. Get their own kind? Could she be from a family of witches?

He must have noticed her fallen face. "Don't tell me ya ain't got none where you come from. I bet yer town does noth'n about it. Ya needn't worry 'bout it here in Vereiteln Dorf." His eyes still glowed. "We hang 'em. Then we burn 'em up, and now, we even bury their ashes. No way now any daughter of the devil kin come back to get their chil'en, nor any chil'en for that matter."

The lad stood there as tall as could be, his face all confident and proud.

"Bravo," she squeaked. A gulp relieved some tightness in her throat. "Where, ah, might they be buried? Those sister witches you call 'em." She didn't like the familial referral to the devil, but if all this had something to do with her own tapestry, she must unknot it.

He pointed down the hill and two disheveled rows over. "Yonder. There's a pit in the south corner. Pa said there was a time once when a gust came and carried the ashes away, so like I said, now the ashes are buried good and deep. But some folk think it don't matter, say they still kin git free." He gazed upward. "Yup, their spirits are here."

"That so." She didn't believe such. "Shouldn't you be afraid, then?"

He hesitated before claiming a tough stance. "Nah. What fer?"

A warning crackled nearby. Then another, ending in a booming pop. A branch fell, dropping its brittle oak bones and bouncing twice before settling at his feet. A wind picked up and swayed the plentiful leaves attached to the fallen limb. Tall grasses surrounding nearby grave markers blew in helpless circles, their roots aching to be released from the soil.

The rosy red drained from his face, leaving widened eyes in a ghostly pallor. Seemingly on instinct, he heaved in a breath and charged a shaking finger at Lexxie. "Liar!" His attempt to scram backward was almost hilarious. His gaze never left hers, even when his footing caught another loose branch and he fell against a cow thief's marker. "Yer a witch, and ya come to talk to yer folk."

He scrambled out of the graveyard and back down the road. A cloud of dust trailed the lad.

She rubbed her forehead, mouth gaping. This would not help her cause. More curious than even before, she examined the fallen limb. Dead limbs fell off trees all the time. Something got this town spooked. And her too.

Another crackling pop in the distance, this time more subtle. As though the lone tree beside the pit was calling her, she slipped off her shoes with a mind to head toward it.

A single gentle step.

Then a second.

And another.

The wind picked up. Brittle skeletons of leaves, having survived cold seasons gone by, came from nowhere and swirled in tight formation around her. An icy chill snapped up her spine. Absent was a comforting shawl to tighten around her shoulders, which rattled a bone of self-resentment.

She gasped a sharp inhale. The air didn't feel fresh as she remembered from that day Jonne had dropped her off, a day now eons ago. Drawn to that dreaded pit, she stepped with caution ten more times before stopping in her tracks.

A whirl of black ashes rose at excruciatingly slow speed. A pair of eyes from the ashes blinked. The assembled mass flared high, then fell just as fast, returning into the earth.

Just as quick, Lexxie recanted. Maybe she didn't need to learn anything about these "sisters."

"Ah." She searched for words, but none came. She instructed her shoulders to relax. Those eyes were not only sad but also in desperate want. And to whom did they belong? A mystery. But there they were, their glare burrowing into her soul. But it wasn't what one might expect from a devil's daughter. It carried a hint of kinship and an odd familiarity. "Sorry to disturb you," she whispered.

A bigger mystery, even she chuckled about, was just where her courage came from. She'd never needed it in Avondale.

"Forgive me for having disturbed you." This—whatever it was—was enough to take one out of their own head.

Backing out with dirt-sopped stocking feet, she chose the same footprints used in her approach until she could snatch her gilded shoes and sprint back to town.

CHAPTER TWENTY-FIVE
FEAR NOT

In Vereiteln Dorf

MONDAY MORNING WITH the early meal a solid hour away, the birds at her window fluted as though warning of danger. Lexxie slipped on her gilded slippers. The balls of her feet screeched instead for those old soft leather boots. She'd rather be loosening cords and spreading toes to make more room. She paused at the noisy blow of her own exhale, and suspicion entered with the next intake of air.

After yesterday, anxious thoughts surfaced and bobbled up and down like drifting wood in deep waters. The apprehension that something evil had formed her past offered. What an unsinkable thought.

Could it be possible—her birth mother, working the devil's bidding? She shivered anew at GC's words—*"When it comes to taking chil'en, that's the work of the devil's daughters."*

Assuredly not. She stiffened her spine. Her mother didn't

even have a sister. Her shoulders sloped. Would Lexxie not know if she did? She knew so little of her mother.

GC's nonsense seeped into my brain. I'm as forlorn as those eyes in that whirlwind of ashes. Mind trickery, simply a reflection of myself.

The cool floorboards felt good on her bare feet. She pulled back the curtain and soaked into the shaft of sunlight as if it were a wise advisor. "If witches were real, would Harmon not have told me so?"

Then came back to one unavoidable suspicion—Grossmutter. Witch or not, she took Lexxie.

Still, all wasn't weaving up the way it should. So, who would know more and not be afraid to talk?

Nay. A nervous laugh challenged the answer as it came to mind. *Might those sad and searching eyes communicate with me? Mercy. What if that was my mother in that ash pit?*

What was wrong with her—hinging identity on some cackling sounds and eerie winds? Nevertheless, she now had a plan for the next step. And that was something. She needed to tie off this crazy option before it wove further into her soul. Next, would be a return visit to a pit of witch ashes.

Giselle continued to avoid Lexxie, their conversations kept at rooming-and-board business, mealtimes, and hot-water delivery. So, it should have been easy to escape the boarding house unnoticed. Dern if Giselle wasn't out front sweeping away the dust blown in from the evening before.

"Lovely morning, Giselle, just going for an early walk." Lexxie chirped out words to lighten the mood between them. How she'd cherished that previous touch of friendship, something she desired more of right now, a friend. Though preference would be a confidante who shared information and didn't judge.

Giselle's dark brows gathered tight across her forehead, framing eyes that churned their soft blue to a steely gray. "I know where yer go'n."

A jolt scored through Lexxie. How could she know?

But Giselle had already turned, granting the view of her backside, and slapping the bristles of her corn broom across the walk.

So Lexxie had become the present-day story. GC must have gone straight to his pa.

Witch news traveled fast. And there's a new one in town.

"I'm not what you think."

"We are what we are." Giselle didn't miss a swish.

Best Lexxie get this sorted. Then everyone would change their minds. "She was only seeking her family," the villagers would say and accept her as one of them.

Up the main road to the outskirts, she headed. She carried an empty basket to disguise her business—a stroll toward a local farmer's field. Yesterday, a table at the farm's edge was empty. Today, it would likely be filled with fresh beets.

Though what was the use for a disguise if the whole town heard she was a witch? Whatever thoughts circulated wouldn't be in her favor.

At least she could bring some beets back to Giselle. Perhaps that could help their friendship?

Without incident of watchers other than those same grazing cows, Lexxie arrived at the graveyard and placed her empty basket underneath the solace of the oak tree. A low-lying fog and plenty of dew cast a heavy blanket on a sleeping sum of souls. The sun's rising cast awakening shadows over their stone markers. Birds chirped, hundreds of them.

"So *here*, you sing beautiful?"

But it provided a pleasant atmosphere. Even the crooked rows of grave markers held an eerie beauty. This was home to these poor souls whose lives went astray somehow. Harmon taught her to be neither quick nor harsh when it came to the judgment and the damnation of others.

Well, curse him anyway.

An echo of a man's voice disturbed the scene. A distance away, it spoke calm and continuous as though explaining something complicated.

Removing her shoes provided the advantage of tiptoeing freely. Not that her heels made any noise in the overgrown wet grass. *Argh.* This frequent ritual of trekking in the dirt was causing the washing up of stockings to be a daily chore.

She crouched to keep her shadow from stretching too long and giving her presence away.

It was, indeed, a man. He sat cross-legged beyond the hilly decline before the pit.

Dormant, it was this morning. No volcanic eruption for him. How busy with visitors could a pit full of witch ashes get?

As best as she could tell, he was talking to a tiny marker sticking out a foot or two behind it, his neck stretching forward to communicate directly. He practically sat within the gray murk.

She crept closer.

The man was pleading, a genuine pouring out of his heart. Between mumbling slurs came only a few words—*mah child* and *never should've*—and then an accusation flash of sorts with arms waving above his head wild enough to cause crows to adjust their perches.

A cold wetness soaked through to her thighs. The dew saturating her dress mattered not. Her heart warmed. `This man cared for his child. She strained to hear more.

"If'n we kin jus' . . ."

The madman! Yes, same overalls, same gritty hair and facial scruff. The same flannel shirt, soiled and checkered with black and grays, though the grays may have once been white. He must be alone, no wife nor direct family. Why else would he be so distraught? No family, she could understand that.

He couldn't be a threat, not if that priest handled him with such gentle mannerisms.

Remaining as silent and hidden as possible, Lexxie arched an ear to catch another single pleading word.

"They say ya kin come back."

Now, who would be "they" to tell him his child may come back to him? Perhaps other witches? She shuffled to reposition her footing but snapped a twig.

The grieving man stood. His crawling gaze surveyed the graveyard. Then he bolted into the field beyond its edge. Rows of grain corn swallowed his profile.

"No. Wait!"

What would make a man so afraid he'd run into a field as such? Another curious and discouraging event. Was he connected to those witches? Perhaps more children had been taken as she'd been, only his to a lonely grave.

But this victimized, pleading man might not only have clues to her own identity but also be sympathetic to her situation and help her. He seemed the right age. He'd have been around when she disappeared. He must be a kind man. Otherwise, why would he spend time in such a place as this and be in such a pleading pursuit of his child's memory?

She stood where he'd sat. The inscription so tiny, she leaned over the pit and squinted at the epitaph:

DIMIETRIS INFANT
ALEXANDRA
LIKELY A WITCH
BORN AND DIED 1671

"Likely a witch? How dare they—a mere newborn." Of greater significance, the year of this child's death caught a lump in her throat. The babe born the same year as she!

She must meet this man. The poor soul, she'd pour him an empathetic presence. They had something in common. Something terrible must have happened that year of her birth. Harmon had once told her how a ferocious plague lingered inside his home village not many years before she was born, many died from fever and swelling in the neck. Or perhaps there was some kind of revolt, leftover conflict from the war.

Whatever it be, 'twas still her to acknowledge. And it didn't necessarily have to do with any witchcraft business.

Employing the balls of her feet, she gazed across the horizon of purple tassels. Now, to which direction had the poor soul of a man escaped? The corn ears, waving to the same breeze, offered no clue. He'd vanished.

Finding him again could be difficult, but not impossible. Her headmost task was to converse with him—gently, of course. Like a skittish sheep, he might bolt again, or worse, give her a good headbutt.

She smoothed her damp dress, and her legs flopped to a drop. A heavy loneliness burdened her. Fidgeting with a chunk of coal alongside the grave of some innocent babe, she stretched her arm to place her hand atop the marker. "You poor little thing. I pray you're as natural as a breeze and go wherever you want. I hope you are loved, and mostly, I hope you know who you are."

She'd not been a person to pray on her own much. Mostly, she listened and followed along to Harmon and Grossmutter. She bowed her head and spoke to the divine being Harmon and the priest back in Avondale had said was the king of all. "King, if you are there, may this innocent child—whoever she be—be yours."

The grave marker was stone cold. Much colder than the morning air.

She pulled back her hand, and as she did, a coldness stabbed like a dagger. Anger, betrayal, hurt. Why hadn't she paid more attention to that longstanding niggling notion something was amiss?

As a young girl, she'd dreamed a faceless kingdom dropped her from a carriage held with gold wings, but then left her in a cornfield, alone, to find her way home. Well, right now, that niggling seed deep down had grown into reality. She was indeed alone and lost. Even so, although jumbled, threads were appearing, and soon she would weave them all together. Yesterday was yesterday. She'd now stepped out of that corn-field called Harmon and Grossmutter. Her future promised she'd return to a kingdom where she belonged.

The soul inside her smiled. She was going to find it. She'd find her way home.

A warm breeze swirled atop the pit, stirring the cold inside her. Ashes rose and blew in distinct form, circling her and the infant's grave.

Mercy, nay happenstance. Not twice, ashes rising and swirling like that. She couldn't move a muscle for fear.

This time, the sad blue eyes were absent. Instead, a beckoning and tender voice whispered from within the blowing ashes.

She trembled. *What say you?*

The tender voice repeated. "Come near, child."

CHAPTER TWENTY-SIX
PRATTING WITH THE DEAD

In Vereiteln Dorf

LEXXIE MUST HAVE appeared quite the sight for Giselle to drop her coolness and be genuine with concern.

Out of breath and leaning against the hitching post, Lexxie nearly fell into a pot of overgrown flowers. Pale and sweaty, she was thankful Giselle guided her inside where the other guests were finishing up their morning platters. A cup of ale was offered, and Lexxie's weak and shaky body accepted. She had run the entire way.

"Child, talk'n to the witches?" Giselle announced.

How was it this woman knew everything? Once Lexxie's breath settled, she needed to know. "What makes ya think I was?"

She took a huge gulp of ale in an effort to hide the choke in her throat. Still reeling over that distinct voice and those words.

Towering over Lexxie, Giselle brushed her hands down her skirt. "Well, girlie, look at ya. Blackn'd from ash and soot."

Lexxie released cheeks full of air. "Aye. I'm getting desperate. No one's helping. No one cares. All so suspicious—what threat can I be? For kingdom's sake, I've not done a thing." Her voice churned to an accusation. "Is it so wrong to wanna know who ya are?"

When Lexxie's spewing caught the attention of the other guests, Giselle grabbed her elbow, dragged her into the reception area, and plopped her down where guests couldn't gander. "Listen up. Ya better stop visiting that graveyard, you hear? Folks are already unsettled. Besides, you are who you are."

Lexxie acknowledged with a weak nod, but Giselle wasn't finished with this little rant of wisdom, was she? At least she was taking an interest.

"Better shush or tomorrow's noose is gonna have yer head in it. Can't you see that?"

"Tomorrow's noose?" *Mercy.* "You can't be serious."

"The townsfolk are already talkin'."

"Hanged?" Stuck on the noose bit, Lexxie released her question slow. "Me. Why?"

Giselle gave her shoulder a push. "Yer daft." Exhaling a long sigh, she pulled up a chair and sat uncomfortably close. "Look. Did ya notice all the folk in there?" She pointed toward her tables, all full, all new faces chomping down a potato mash of some sort, some people with a duffel sack at their feet, but all, chatting their excitement.

"Marketgoers?" Lexxie surmised.

Giselle shoved her palm against Lexxie's forehead. "Wake up, girlie. Market was Saturday."

Oh, wait. "Right, the inane Justice Festival."

"Ain't that what you come for too? It's that time, just before harvest, our village clears out the bad. How do they do that is what you should be ask'n. A hanging . . . of witches. It's become an annual thing. Folks come from miles."

Dismay pushed its way inside. "And you think that's what I came for?"

"I dunno, some kind of ugly curiosity, more than likely revenge."

Lexxie pressed a hand to her chest, holding down her horror. "Revenge? Praise be, whatever for?"

With a wave of a hand, Giselle shushed her again. "Yesterday's stagecoach was chock full, and it don't normally run on Sundays. This mornin's too. These folks here traveled all night. Another com'n this afternoon. Darn good for business. Only thing is—there's no witch to hang this year."

She leaned in. Her lips push hot breath into Lexxie's ear. "You can bet the bonnet ya should be wearing our town priest is eyeing you up. He came by to question me 'bout ya just after ya left." Her shoulders shrugged as if to support the holy man's visit. "He'll look as though he ain't do'n his job if he can't produce a single witch."

The priest's unfriendliness and suspicious attitude . . . the stonecutter's nameless grave marker with a death date of tomorrow . . . and GC's accusation yesterday . . . beyond the pale. Heat surged in Lexxie's body. "So why me?"

"That's easy. You arrive here unannounced or expected, no man at yer side. And Jonne don't count. He was just yer ride. That's enough to get the folks talking. You claim to be doing what? Research? C'mon, no one believes that. Yer spying on someone, and you've come to cast a spell—that's what they say."

"I've never, such ever, a thought."

"But yer asking questions 'bout Gillam Huber. Axed to death in his own kitchen he was. A witch ordered his death—that's what folk say. Then you had the pastor's son take you up to the burial of the damned. What were you thinking girlie? And why, pray tell, did you need to go back this morning?" Giselle's gaze met Lexxie's. "Did anyone see you whilst you was up there?"

Axed to death? Oh, poor Grossmutter, poor Harmon.

Giselle snapped her fingers, wanting an answer.

Lexxie squirmed. "Well, just, er, the one they call the village madman."

Giselle's jaw fell at least an inch. "That's ole Dimietris. Did he get a good look at ya?"

"No. He ran to the fields whence he saw me."

"Okay, good."

"Why?"

"'Cause you look an awful lot like Emmaline." Giselle blinked a few times, then paused as if to take the name back.

"Who's Emmaline?" Lexxie's heart quickened at the name.

"I said too much already. Look." Giselle's eyes engaged sufficiently to pour genuineness into her advice. "You ought to get out of town."

Then she stood, securing her hands to her hips, this time avoiding Lexxie's gaze. Apparently, she'd say no more.

Nausea rose. More foppery to absorb. That Justice Festival banner she'd been ignoring was one thing, but the town wanting to hang her? And now she looked like some Emmaline? Was Giselle on her side or not? An unthinkably large divide was growing fast.

Lexxie versus the village.

She fixated on her lap. "I'm frightened. Will you help me?"

The bore of Giselle's eyes was uncomfortable. Lexxie kept her gaze downward, hoping this awkward pause would soon pass.

Menfolk anxious to get on with second helpings banged tables with their mugs.

"More ale," one yelped.

Another chimed just as loud. "How's about some of yer stew and cake over here?"

Giselle slapped a nearby hand towel like a whip and headed back into her serving room. "Stay put till I figure out a plan." Then she muttered something under her breath, something like . . . "Ya should'a gone with my expect'n an illegitimate."

CHAPTER TWENTY-SEVEN
A STONE IN A STORM

At the River of Times

"RULES?" MEGINHARDT'S ONE-WORD query came unrushed as he almost feared the answer.

Jophiel stood guard over the area of activity, keeping that stone with distressed eyes under his surveillance. All while Meginhardt's head swirled as murky as that water with competing thoughts.

What does he mean—my mother was assigned *to me?*

The watery tornado sprouted a funnel tail. Its hungry power sucked up a dark murky substance from deep in the river. A tiny flame remained still and calm in its center, the suffering stone caught in the swirling walls. A prized captive. If only that stone, whoever she was, made her way to the storm's center by the flame, she'd be safe.

Not stuck, just seeking. Meginhardt barely moved his lips, mindlessly muttering advice. "Get to the middle, then look up."

If only she would. Looking down into the dark narrowing

tail, so ominous, and that way out, guaranteed ruinous. Instead, the stone remained trapped within the deadly tempest walls. Thrashed about. Helpless. Her wide-eyed gaze, searching and fearing, seared into Meginhardt's head.

"Wait." Illumination flashed. "That stone represents life. Is it my mother?"

"What made you think it's her?" Jophiel progressed from disquietude to his educational mien.

"It's obvious, isn't it?"

Seemingly ignoring Meginhardt's sarcasm, Jophiel instead swiped a gentle wave suggesting Meginhardt lift his watch higher to the grandness of the river.

Countless living stones floated along, some by the edge, some bobbing up and down like bottom-feeders, some raced, some meandered.

He inspected the bankside. So many others, stuck in their personal watery storm, emanated the same bizarre look of fear. "These stones represent people's lives. Don't tell me I'm wrong. I know it in my bones."

Jophiel's arm rolled around Meginhardt's shoulders. "Not bad, kid. You're a natural. What else?"

"First, answer my question. Is that my mother?"

"I already told you she was fine. You saw her for yourself. Remember?"

"She was about to drown. She's not fine." Meginhardt's frustration grew. He wouldn't get tricked by this Jophiel. *Don't trust him. Don't be a narr.*

"Think. Remember, we are above time."

Above time? Inconceivable. Though an image drifted into his thoughts. "The woman in that courtyard by those picnic tables—that was her, wasn't it? Take me there."

Jophiel pointed at the stone in the battering storm. "And her?"

"Why should I care? C'mon, take me to meet my mother."

"Meginhardt, within yourself, you have a genuine desire to heal others. Shall you not employ this gift?"

And here it comes. He's trying to trick me again.

"Gift. Yeah right. Look, I don't know what yer after, what you expect of me. So, let's get out of here and head back to your little lady friend, Aivy." At Jophiel's responsive chuckle, Meginhardt turned to give the know-it-all his backside. "Besides, didn't you say something about rules? I'm not supposed to touch anything in that river."

Audible gasping deafened their ears, the stone vying for attention. Jophiel gave no explanation for the heavy breathing that filled their space.

"This some kind of test?"

"No test. Surely, she is struggling." Jophiel nodded to the gasping stone in the turbulent swirl.

But Meginhardt wasn't thinking of her. Sure, that she-stone was in the midst of trauma. But why this pressure to presume he could help her? And why her when hundreds of living rocks remained stuck up and down that riverbank? To feign interest, he kneeled close to the river's edge. "Who is she, then, if not my mother?"

At least, his mother was okay.

"Oh, dear, dear boy, she's another one you cursed."

He scrambled to his feet. "Will you stop with the curse thing? I never . . ."

Jophiel's shaking head displayed disapproval. He swirled a circle with his right arm, creating a moving image against the backdrop of a bank of evergreens. Meginhardt's last moment on earth. Him cowering under his pa's threats and his response ringing out—"I curse you and all the blood in yer veins!"

The image disappeared, sparing them the scene of a searing iron pan and sizzling fat crashing into his temple.

He digested for a time. "So, like you said, Pa got himself a bloodline of kin. Wasn't just me." This only strengthened a personal and repeated battle. He never mattered. And knowing what he knew now made it even worse. *I'll never matter.*

"One other."

"Let me guess. Her? She's the special someone else." He pointed to the struggling stone. Even faking an empathic notion became impossible.

"Yes. Her," Jophiel confirmed. "She was born after your journey ended. Your pa married again. They had a child."

Meginhardt turned his back to the river. "Again, why should I care?" *Aha, I knew you wanted something from me. You want me to help her.* He crossed petulant arms over his scrawny chest. *Well, I ain't gonna.*

"So, when you didn't know who she was, you wanted to help her. Now that you know who she is to you, you have no such desire." Jophiel scoffed. "You may be smart, but you're still a fool."

This was about more than he could take. Meginhardt slammed a fist against the earth. It would have been better to have lived with a severe head injury than to go through this.

The truth was cutting. His life was a lie. Everything, so unfair. So confusing. So uncertain.

"Enough!" He glared at Jophiel, who examined his own hands as though his translucent and gleaming fingertips might have a speck of dirt somewhere.

Pushing his fists into the ground, Meginhardt impelled himself to a stand.

The ear-piercing gasping ceased, replaced by Jophiel's booming voice. "Sit! We go when I say we go."

Meginhardt collapsed as instructed.

Time lingered. Luring babbles and delightful fragrances wafted.

Meginhardt resisted their wallowing effect. A power-filled rush of a waterfall rumbled somewhere distant, as did an abundance of laughter. Emotional exhaustion prevented him from diverting his attention, yet inner calm was not to be.

Jophiel broke the closemouthed hush. "You should be pleased with yourself."

Meginhardt's sarcastic tongue got the better of him. "Cry me a mercy, Giant Birdman, tell me why."

"You're a natural." Seemed Jophiel would ignore the insult. "I speak what I know. You picked up on the energy colors of the Arrivals concise and quick. And you figured out the gist of the living stones in our river."

Meginhardt did his best to stifle a smile. "Simple, like I said, each reflects a life."

Jophiel gestured toward the water. "That river—it separates us from them."

"Them?" Who was he talking about?

"Look yonder." Jophiel nodded across the waters. A curtain of fog lifted, enabling a glimpse of an army of bodies. "Rebels."

And there they were. Dozens upon dozens of armed and armored beings, all similar sizing, none with a distinguishable face, mere blurs of eyes and mouths. They stood in neat rows, one behind the other, spread across the river's edge watching Meginhardt and Jophiel. Waiting, it seemed, for something to happen.

How long had they been there?

"They're always watching." Jophiel spoke as though having read Meginhardt's mind.

"What do they want?" Meginhardt had scrambled to his feet, on guard himself.

Sensing danger, he moved one backward step at a time, till his back met the welcoming embrace and sweet smell of a big old oak. Quite the contrast to the barren, leafless forest on the opposite side, like a fire had rushed through and left nothing but smelly black shadow branches. A pongy stench drifted toward them, assaulting his senses.

"You." Jophiel responded too casually. In a bored fashion, he uncoiled his body as he rose. Tall. His wings unfolded one position, then snapped to attention, full width now greater than thrice his height.

Impressive. Good thing to be on Jophiel's side of the river and under the bird man's protection. "Sorry 'bout the giant-bird-man thing." *I sure could'a used you when Pa took a turn at me.*

Jophiel's arms crossed against his chest and did a slight grin sweep across that steel-firm face?

A simple nod. A firm directive. Meginhardt was to step forward to the river's edge.

Cry me a mercy, he's serious.

Meginhardt dared not disobey.

CHAPTER TWENTY-EIGHT
A TIME TO RUN

In Vereiteln Dorf

FIRST THINGS FIRST. Lexxie packed her belongings, not that she possessed much, just a few hair clips, a brush, and Harmon's coin purse. Time to flee this unsafe town. If Giselle's words were true, then the priest or even the town authorities could come soon to arrest her, claim she was a witch. They'd only one sundown before the so-called Justice Festival where all expected travelers were promised they could gather and witness the bold annual cleansing.

Schadenfreude. *My demise will be their gain.* Her hands pushed the air in front of her, fingers spread wide, halting her movements. *Breathe. Stop. No time for crying. Think. Where to go. Who can help?*

Giselle had instructed Lexxie to move to the cellar and hide there till she came up with a plan. Dare Lexxie trust her? No, too uncertain. Giselle had proven that.

And GC? He blabbed her out, so not him. Would Jonne be back in time? No, not till Friday, too late.

"I could be nothing but ashes by then." She punched two fists into the air.

Besides, could she trust him? Did she even want to?

She couldn't answer that one. Her heart and mind being so at odds raised concern.

That village madman, Dimietris—he was her only hope! The feeling was instinctive. She wanted to meet him.

She must find him. He lost a child to death, so he'd understand, protect her. A tinge of excited joy mixed well with the urge to save her life. A next step, just what she needed.

Shouldn't be hard to find him. Perchance, he'd hide her. Huh, perhaps in return, she could nurture him back to a healthy mind.

She dared not use the road heading out of town, especially since travelers were still arriving. Neither could she head into town. Her plan must then consist of ambling through the farmer's fields—discreetly. She'd wind her way to the unconsecrated graveyard, slip into that grain cornfield, and mayhap trace the madman's steps. It might lead her to his farmhouse. Assuming there was one, it couldn't be far out.

If only she had her own boots. Her gilded slipper shoes would have to do.

With carry sack cords wrapped around one wrist, Lexxie strolled through the hot boardinghouse kitchen and straight out the back exit into the alley, the same door Jonne snuck her in only days ago. Eager customers demanded much of Giselle's servitude, distracting the woman.

The back lane stunk. Ew. Nauseating. A soggy mixture of half-eaten meat pies, porridge, and pudding overflowed a trash bucket. The surroundings foretold this was not a rare occurrence. After a skid, Lexxie caught her footing and edged into the passageway.

Only a deep rumbling in her stomach stopped her. She hadn't been eating much as of late and nothing at all this morning. Given the mental and physical energy she'd spent, she'd need sustenance. Reversing her steps in the alley, she spied a sizeable chunk of bread crust atop a bit of porridge. Seeing no one around, she grabbed it.

Ach du lieber! What had she become since arriving at Vereiteln Dorf? Would this destination deliver what she sought?

She ground her teeth, for it must lead to the discovery of who she was, by finding and meeting her true lineage. Some kind of royalty, she dreamed.

Though right now, keeping from being hung was the higher priority. And that required ongoing doses of physical and mental energy.

Heading westward, opposite to town and straight for the witch pit, she could either stay on the road's north side, where livestock farmers resided one after the other, or traverse up the road's south hill through fields of wheat and grain corn.

She rubbed her shoulders, her skin already imagining the crawl of insects. Again, she craved Grossmutter's shawl, not that the covering would have protected Lexxie much. It simply would have felt like a warm hug, something she needed right now.

Because that man, Dimietris, escaped southbound, the insect path made sense. But an incoming onslaught of travelers caused her to stick to the north side where she'd traverse in the gully until she could cross the road without attention.

She imagined the town crier ringing his bell, warning all to be cautious and report any sightings of her. Or was she overimagining things? *Stay safe. Get up the hill back to the old graveyard and scoot through the field where he entered.*

She didn't get far before she needed to pull her dress around her hips as tight as possible. The flowing garb caught splinters on a boundary fence beyond which a herd of cattle munched on tall grasses feet away. All, but one, paid her little attention. The watcher of the herd minded her presence, its pricked ears and flicking tail warning her to get out of their space.

Another lot of travelers passed. Then she high-stepped out the cow patch and clipped across the road. After all, a barrage of insects would be better than a charging steer.

Although the grainfields appeared bountiful with uniformity to any curious onlooker, the ground was uneven and rough on her footing. *Dern these shoes.* They had become a burden. Shoving them into her carry sack, she'd have to manage in stocking feet. They were already filthy anyhow—as if that mattered.

Rocks, mud, and divots were nothing compared to snakes and groundhogs. The crouching navigation was tiresome. Hot. Itchy.

A thirsty and silent cry out to Harmon and Grossmutter only angered her more. She was in this predicament because of them, their selfishness. No, she shan't forgive them, not after this.

"Stop it." She battled the unsatisfied craving. "Forget them. They deceived me so." She must meet her own needs now.

Whoever thought the Place of the Damned to be a pleasing destination? Soon, she could escape into the grain corn and start her tracking, only upright as the harvest-ready plants had met a plentiful height. Her back muscles were already singing a song of relief.

Where Dimietris had entered, just feet away from the ash pit, temptation loomed. Dare she approach, speak in return? So gentle was that voice. 'Twas female too. What if it were her mother? Who else would call her child?

Nay. She'd best dismiss the idea.

Curiosity drew her to the infant's gravestone. She plopped with relief, deserving a rest. Not a sound in the graveyard. Where had those chirpy birds gone? She rubbed her feet, disgusted at herself, so disheveled, so black with filth. Maybe she should remove her stockings? But nay, one glance at the grainfield convinced her better of it. She'd need that scant layer of protection. The balls of her feet ached from stony ground.

What would Jonne think if he saw her now?

And what of those gurgling words she heard the day before—*"Come near, child."*

Mercy, pray tell, she wasn't asking me to join her.

That gave Lexxie a shudder. A better option, perhaps the voice was calling her to come closer, hear that all would be okay, or all would not be okay and her comfort was a mere motion away.

Did she even hear it right? 'Course, she believed so, but what good was it, if she didn't know what the message called her to do?

"Ma'am?" Lexxie whispered, then grimaced.

Calling to a woman's spirit from the past caused a shiver. This action alone was sufficient to be called and condemned a witch. She yanked fistfuls of grass as silly thoughts hit a deep nerve.

She imagined her mother. Would they meet one day? Find each other in another life?

Another glance around proved still no one to be seen,

thankfully. A mere single crow cawed, warning of his watchful eye. His cohort hoarded the top branches of the old oak.

"Ma'am, I'm keen. Tell me more."

Treetops bristled. That same crow cawed as if to give her away. This felt wrong, to speak to the dead. That priest would have every right to hang her should any soul be witness to this.

Just one more try. Then she'd go.

"Ma'am, might I ask you to repeat yourself? Might you be wanting me to know something? A warning?"

Nothing.

The sun was climbing and fierce. High noon. Hadn't days passed since she awoke in a comfortable room this very morning, a room she now couldn't return to. So where would she sleep tonight?

Dizzy with exhaustion, she doubted not only her decision to bolt but also herself. *I'm delusional. Thinking I heard a voice here earlier. Mercy.*

Fixing upon the infant's meager marker, she stooped to touch the stone and whispered what came to mind. "You're precious and loved. May you have much peace."

She then wiped a tear from her dirt-smudged face and gave her itchy scalp a harsh ten-finger scratch. It felt good—until a rumbling bray close by ceased the pleasurable distraction. Then an excited horse's snort.

A surge of energy woke Lexxie's tired muscles. She jumped up, never minding the two swollen feet that wanted nothing more than a long soak. With haste, she shoved them into her shoes.

Watching from the road were three horses, each with a rider. The priest dismounted and aimed an accusatory finger at her. "That is her, the woman I fear." His voice rang with suggestive instruction for the other two authoritative-looking men. "Imprison her before she is detrimental. I must question her."

Question me, my arse. Yer gonna hang me.

Following the footsteps of Madman Dimietris, she leaped like a scared deer into the grain corn and busted a run for her life.

CHAPTER TWENTY-NINE
A BEACON OF SMOKE

In Vereiteln Dorf

FATIGUE FORCED LEXXIE to stop. She lay her elbows heavy against her knees to relieve the lightheadedness. Waiting for a heart rate to slow only seemed to open opportunities that begged her attention to other physical discomforts. Throbbing hamstrings were nothing compared to the bruising pain on the balls of her feet.

Her mind flitted in circles as she tossed a fist upward. *In truth, King, 'tis this my journey in life?*

Her plea did nothing but tip her balance. Wiping a swath of dirty sweat from her forehead, she listened. Anything?

Only the buzz of thrips and greenflies. Needing to confirm she'd be safe to rest, she risked a brief look above the strangles of tassels.

No one.

She collapsed and took to massaging ankles to stop their complaining. An accusation thudded between her temples: Giselle. She pointed the authorities in Lexxie's direction. "'Tis good for business," Giselle had said of the town's absurd Purification Day, a hanging of witches to begin their weeklong Justice Festival.

This year, there's only one witch. Me.

Lexxie pulled spikes and florets from her hair. Mercy, what wouldn't she do for a good brushing and washing up right now? Tucking that quench to the bottom of her priorities, she encouraged herself to keep going. Her carry sack had been left behind in her escape at the old graveyard, along with essentials, of vital importance was Harmon's purse. No amount of coin could save her anyway. Hold fast. She had the afternoon before daylight waned and disappeared.

First, she must find Mr. Madman Dimietris and a place for the night. Surely, of all people, he'd understand and hide her. He wasn't like the others. She witnessed him enough to believe him vulnerable and insecure. And alone. Given his charging dash upon seeing her, she must first assure him she wasn't a threat. After she found him, that is.

Perchance, by some miracle, he might even know her true father and take her to him.

If only she could've focused on the madman's tracks when she escaped from the priest and his apple polishers. Now, behind her lay naught but a trek of rapid steps and torn plants.

"Too obvious. They'll find me." She waved to stop a hover fly buzzing around her head, the pest lending an idea. "Distract them!" Yes, that she must.

She ran in circles, dashing this way and that, trusting any seekers following her tracks would arrive at confusion and pure frustration. Apologizing upward for the damage its farmer would one day discover, she tiptoed out of the trampled section and, using the sun's position as a guide, proceeded in a direction away from the graveyard. A way that might lead her somewhere fruitful. Faith she needed right now, so she fixed on that.

What felt like hours later, no one seemed to be following. Perhaps she overthought the whole thing. After all, imagination could play havoc on one's mind.

'Twas an ease to go mad in this village.

She trudged on.

A surprising intense energy blasted her face after she brushed aside a grouping of wild sunflowers. Succored by the sunlight's bathing and the cool afternoon breeze, she reveled in its healing wrap. She made it to the other side. The thick wall of grain corn had spat her out, weak knees and all. Tottering on its outer edge, she indulged with a long intake before exhaling the breath.

Relief washed away the nagging concern she'd been traveling in circles. But where was she, and where to now?

An endless row of hedging lay in the short distance beyond a ditch with thinned-out bush. She crossed with a dogged gait. Beyond that, another farmer's field. A spicy, pungent whiff crossed her senses, and her stomach growled. Rows of purple and green, a field of turnips. Perfect. Her fingers shook as she dug a large one, peering each way before launching an attack. She devoured the crisp white flesh, not convinced her stomach was thankful given its gassy talkback and her still-dry throat.

She searched the puffs of her sleeves for a clean spot and employed it to wipe the grime from her eyes.

Even now, not a soul could be seen in any direction, though a thin strip of gray smoke rose toward the horizon. A straight plume, a good omen. A farmhouse stood in the distance. Someone had started a late afternoon cook fire.

If she traversed a path to cross the rows of turnips diagonally, she could arrive at the homestead before darkness fell. Doable. What she would do then, she'd figure out on the way. In the meantime, plenty of dead trees scattered throughout the field offered hiding places if needed. This farmer must be poor and without animal power to clear the stumps. Why else would he allow his trees to rot?

She coaxed herself to keep moving and tried not to consider what the farmer would think, should he spot her, a strange woman, coming out of his field. A woman head to toe in filth and just as the sun started to set, no less. If she didn't know better, she'd think she was a witch too.

Not funny. With no other plan, she couldn't worry about that right now and quickened her pace.

The rows of turnips were endless. At least, the ground churned softer and was more predictable than the cornfield, her footing thankful. Sunbaked and parched, she fought dizzy spells. Perhaps collapsing would be better than the risk she was about to take.

Another row of hedging rose ahead. Two farmhouses stood side by side not far in the distance with more hedging between. One appeared stately, yet long abandoned while the quite meager other one had a nice fire brewing inside, its smoke a lovely blend of blue and gray. The familiar smell of burning wood reminded her of the fires Harmon used to make. She missed him. She missed Grossmutter.

Mercy, stop.

There and then, she committed herself—once more—to feel nothing but anger when those two family members of yesterday entered her mind. There be no reason to forgive them either.

Crouching, she followed the hedge up toward the houses. Studying the empty one took only moments for confidence of abandonment—windowpanes cracked, moss climbing the sides, weeds overtaking the yard. A plow rusted from years of rain and neglect in front of a decrepit barn, its doors wide open. Surely, no livestock inside. A wealthy home. Why would anyone leave such behind?

Someone must be present on the other property. The smoke lingered.

She crept across a dried ravine and paused behind an overgrown patch of bushes. Lavender. The aroma made her want to smile, something living on this otherwise dead and forgotten property. Now wasn't the time for pleasantries. A hedge hungrily grew over a rotting property fence. Visible was a lineup of notches nicked across the top strip of wood. On the opposite side lay a hefty rock pile. A coveted hiding spot! She scampered over the rotting wood and ducked, sheltered by the stacked mass of stones, every size imaginable harvested from the farmer's field.

Beyond the open wood shutter, an oil lantern took to moving, an arm swinging it low. Then a mumbling of voices gripped her attention. When she reached cautiously to spy, her left hand inadvertently pulled on the pile. Loose rocks fell, and chickens in a nearby coop began to rustle, one particular clucking up a panic.

Mercy. Lexxie lodged herself farther into a tighter space, the sweet smell of metallic grit from the rocks on one side, a musty odor from the rotting wood, the other.

Three men exited the simple farmhouse and entered the yard where she hid.

Stifling a gasp, she plastered her mouth with her filthy

hands. The madman! She'd stumbled onto Dimietris's homestead. 'Twas destiny in her favor after all?

Ducking back into the shadows, she dared not look. Rather, her ears perked.

The voice of one man, highly recognizable, rang loud and clear, and far too close. "Now, Witford."

The priest. Oh heavens. That dern eerie monotone.

That priest was right there, stepping even farther into the yard and scowling a warning. "Should she reach yer doorstep, repeat to me what you are gonna do?"

His lantern's soft glow landed mere inches from Lexxie's ankles. She stifled a breath, paining from the awkward crouch and needing to be dead quiet.

"Hold onta her. Won't let her git away. No, sir, Father."

Curses. How might they have come to know I'd be looking for Witford Dimietris? Giselle, that biddy. Quite the chiseler.

"But, Father, I don't think any girl is gonna come here, look'n fer me. Don't know why ya think I got anyth'n to do with this."

Lexxie shook when a third man threatened a warning. He must have been leaning on the stone pile because his voice boomed straight above her head. "Never ya mind, Witford. Do we have yer word?"

She tightened her abdomen, refraining from want to exhale.

"I said yeah, Jake. Yer deaf?"

Hmm, Dimietris didn't like that Jake grobian, whoever he was.

The chickens settled, and the three men, once satisfied nothing threatened the livelihood in the coop, reentered the farmhouse.

Relieved they hadn't seen her, she blew out a load of pent-up tension. *Okay, now cry.*

No, nein. Grow up. No crying.

Her ears rejoiced in the clip-clop music of hooves. Trotting never sounded so good. Horses extracting the presence of the priest and some Jake-scoundrel away from the Witford Dimietris homestead. He wasn't like their priest back in Avondale, a man respectable and wise. The dark of night had fallen, the only light now from the oil lamp inside the farmhouse.

What to do? What to do? Dare she approach him now that he'd been threatened?

When so uncertain about something, Harmon would always say, "Ask the King, wait till morning, an answer will come."

But dern you, Harmon. No, I won't do that.

Still, logic warned her speaking to this Witford Dimietris—a man, said to be mad in the head—wouldn't be wise tonight. How would that look if she came to him in the blackness of the night? He'd surely think her a witch. She'd have to wait till the sun rose.

The glow from within the farmhouse flickered, startling her meditative angst. The back door creaked. Witford Dimietris stepped outside, oil lamp in hand, appearing to move discreetly.

Why did he sneak so?

His gait shaky, he stepped, balancing one foot at a time—directly toward her.

Lexxie gasped. He knew she was here. This was her chance!

CHAPTER THIRTY
ABOUT THAT STONE

At the River of Times

JOPHIEL'S COMMAND WAS a dead-serious one. Meginhardt must approach the river's edge all while across the waters an army of rebels stood at attention. All eyes on him.

Watching. Waiting. Wanting.

Much like a vulnerable and timid buck, Meginhardt nudged himself to meet the embankment. He stood there, fearful of more exposed truths or perhaps even more rejection. Another firm cue from Jophiel suggested he take additional steps down the grassy slope to where a shallow pool had formed. Sizing up the hordes of faceless armed beings on the other side, Meginhardt swallowed down the swell of anxiety. "Are you handing me over?"

"Never."

Whew.

He'd rather have Jophiel's favor, especially now that he

had to trust him. He slipped with an awkwardness down the slope. His toes dug into the gooey wet shore.

In fending position, Jophiel cast another instruction. "Upstream two steps, then take what is yours."

Upstream? All righty, then.

Wary of slipping, Meginhardt made two knee-high steps to his right, one eye watching each foot plant, while the other kept a peripheral spy on that rebel army. What could be his?

Then he saw it. A swollen stone atop a dry mound blinked. Eyes fluttering and its sides breathing. Living.

"It's you, kid." Jophiel loomed over him. "Yours to deliver. Now pick it up."

Mine. Me? Cry me a mercy.

"If'n I grab it now, will I ever be able to go back?" He still held hope of returning to his life, a second chance.

"Meginhardt, you know the answer to that."

And he did. It was finished. His life on earth had completed. Still . . .

The side-shuffling of that army across the waters was quiet and efficient. Shivers crept up his spine. And him a constant in their direct view. But surely, Jophiel would counterattack if needed. Meginhardt crouched low, and his heart thudded an endearing kinship. His own stone. A living rock, twitching. No time for sensitivities, he sensed the pressing need to pick it up. A sense of wonder beheld him. The markings on its surface, and the way it sat inside his cupped hands, comfortable yet vulnerable. *You belong to me and me alone.*

The emotional connection caught him off guard. Some kind of bond, the kind he'd craved his whole life. Someone who knew him. Understood him. He rose from his crouch with heedfulness, his precious stone cupped secure. Then he examined an inscription carved on its underside.

"Shhhst, ye shall not read it aloud," Jophiel warned.

Meginhardt sounded out three syllables in his mind, casting an inquisitive look Jophiel's way.

"Your eternal name, providing you come with me, that is."

The rebels, enemies as Jophiel warned, stood watching.

An intuitive bragging burst free. "Hah, I got it!"

Meginhardt couldn't help it. Winning this strange battle felt too good. No sooner had he boasted, the eyes on his stone ceased to blink, and the exhale-inhale motions stopped. Its energy attempted to merge into his, resulting in yet another odd sensation. Afraid of something coming at him, he stopped it.

"No. No, no, you don't." He wasn't ready to trust anyone yet, including some stone. "I own you—you shall not own me."

"Come. We'll now enter the gate," Jophiel instructed.

A single rebel lowered himself down his side of the embankment and called attention to Meginhardt's ear. "Come back. Meet me here—without him." He nodded reference to Jophiel. "Listen to what we offer, for what we offer is greater. We'll give you everything you desire and more. Bring your stone."

Bring my stone? Who'da thought a dern stone was so valuable up here?

"Including your pa. You want that relationship back, don't ya? But in harmony, this time?"

"My pa?"

"Yeah, doesn't he deserve another chance? Don't go selling him out, bud."

Angular crinkles pinched Meginhardt's forehead. Maybe those lines of doubt encouraged the rebel who then explained more. Over the river's active movements, he coaxed Meginhardt closer. "They're not tell'n ya everything, bud. Come later. I'll be right here, wait'n for ya."

A booming echo behind Meginhardt rang out another of Jophiel's commands. "Tuck your stone in your pocket. Come hither, boy. Time to go."

"Aye, coming." Meginhardt's voice warbled a higher octave than usual. With a blank stare at the winking rebel, he wasn't so sure what to think. Particularly as its presence felt familiar.

"Psst. Whilst yer gone, want us to get rid of, he-he, you know, the girl? We'll call her to come close, get good'n stuck." The rebel chuckled, nodding downstream at the turbulent swirl and furthered his offer with a convincing shrug. "If you can't have Pa's descendants, why should she? You're the one who put up with him all those years. We can make sure she goes nowhere."

Another someone who understands me. My stone and, now, this rebel guy. Guess this place ain't so bad.

Knowing Jophiel wouldn't be pleased, Meginhardt granted the rebel a subtle but distinct nod, hiding an all-too-easy agreement to "get rid of" the girl. If this guy wanted to get rid of her, why be it Meginhardt's business to stop him?

He scrambled back up the embankment, feeling pretty good about things. Those rebels weren't so terrible. On his bouncy way back to Jophiel, he braved a last look across the river, but that curtain of fog had fallen, covering the entire army. Gone from sight.

A gurgle caught his attention downstream, that fledgling she-stone trapped, struggling inside a muddy swirl. He watched, then shook it off. That rebel was right. She shouldn't get what was rightfully his.

He thumbed his own stone, safely tucked and stowed in his pocket. It was safe. She wasn't. Still, he felt proud of himself for the win. He owned his precious stone. Jophiel would protect him. The rebel said he could reconcile him with Pa. What more could he ask for?

Assured he was making good decisions about his future, he commended himself for ignoring the trap to care for that struggling woman or any of her descendants. A gurgle of guilt surfaced, but he pushed it down, drowning it and trusting it would never surface again to challenge his judgment.

"The only way out is through," Jophiel preached.

What did that even mean? Meginhardt swallowed. Had Jophiel any insight into his thoughts? Might he have seen Meginhardt nod to that rebel?

He shook that off too. *Cry me a mercy, I don't care if he did.*

Jophiel's wings lifted, maneuvering to a place atop the river above the turbulent swirl, where he murmured aloud. "Though she's not ready for that just yet."

He held his right arm in the air, and a brilliant whiz of color circulated and formed his hand into some type of glove made of gold metal. He placed that glove into the river near the tumultuous swirl, then whispered into the mouth of the storm. "Come this way for safety."

The glove's gentle paddles urged surrounding waters to loosen the sawing swirl. As it gyrated, the stone drifted away from the muddy side, though surely the assistance wasn't enough to get it to the center of the river where it could be whisked far from danger.

Engaging was such skirmish over a stone.

Although Jophiel had no hat on his head, he motioned as though he were tipping it, as if to say "You're welcome, ma'am."

Jophiel's attention moved to Meginhardt, casting a steely gaze. "Now, you. Come."

The golden glove no longer on his hand, he spread his wings out wide in low flight and reached for him.

Meginhardt accepted the gripping lift with one hand and checked his trouser pocket with the other, his own stone still safe. Even so, he'd remain silent and ask no further questions about anyone's descendants, including reasons why he would never have any. Rather, he'd fix his focus on sneaking back to the river to hear out the deal the rebel claimed to offer.

CHAPTER THIRTY-ONE
A PILE OF STONES

In Vereiteln Dorf

LEXXIE HELD HER breath. Witford Dimietris was approaching the stone pile she hid behind.

She wanted to pop up, surprise him. Greet him warmly, let him know she was on his side, whatever that was. Opposite to the village's priest for starters. For sure, he couldn't be like all the others. They'd have an understanding, right?

Excitement churned to apprehension. What if she were wrong? What if she couldn't trust him?

Looking for distance in case of the latter, she sprawled onto her stomach and snaked through dirt and undergrowth beneath the wooden fence till she stretched out flat underneath the wild lavender on the abandoned property side. A fierce argument pounded inside her head.

Just stand up. You're here because you want to meet this poor soul.

Aye, but if he wants to turn me in, I'll need to dash away.

Just the thought of another urgent getaway drained her

brain. Besides, where would she go? Back to the cornfield for the night? She shuddered at the intrusive notion.

Madman Dimietris spoke, interrupting her battle of wills. "I wanna talk to ya."

Mercy, he knows I'm here. She positioned her elbows, readying herself to stand. Surely, he knew what it were like to be separated from family, be it from death or otherwise.

Oh how she appreciated the advantage the high pile of rocks and the property fence between them provided. 'Course neither mattered anyway since the fallen darkness sufficed as a buffer.

"Meginhardt," he continued.

Huh? Who was Meginhardt? Was someone else there with him? She kept to a squat and quietened her breath while straining an ear.

Dimietris was mumbling, incoherent even. Was he inebriated with drink? The first time she laid eyes on him, he was yelling at Gillam Huber's gravestone at the church, demanding to be left alone. Then he was pleading at the old graveyard at the edge of town, begging for his infant child to return. Now he was talking to this pile of rocks as though this Meginhardt, like the others, could hear him.

Dimietris grabbed a rock from the pile, only to whip it right back. It ricocheted off the pile and into a wooden plank by the coop. A panic of clucking erupted.

The man snarled and spat. Muttered curses suggested this Meginhardt was good for nothing. The man then made angry stomps back to the farmhouse, leaving her to linger in a shadow of confusion.

Peering through the fence, she witnessed his outline in pure aggravated form as he punched the back door and spat in a nearby bucket before slamming himself in. "Truly deranged."

As the words slipped out, she stood, shoulders and jaw sagging. Was her all-afternoon trek in the field for naught?

One dern noisy hen just wouldn't quit with restlessness and clucking. The others settled back into a night calm. Likely, Lexxie's sobbing kept the mother hen on guard, but Lexxie couldn't care less. She pushed her shoulders back, feeling tall in the dark. Sticky twigs on her bodice flew with a single hand swipe, as did a layer of dirt from her forearms.

That did it. Whatever internal machinery she used to process emotions and realities was surrendering. Sorrowful about the past, fearful of the future, lost to the present—too many vulnerabilities to break down. Far easier to transform into anger.

She eyed the farmhouse that swallowed Witford Dimietris along with her hopes to resolve her self-indulgent conundrum. Giving the madman her back, bottom lip helpless in a quiver, she made her way through the blackness of the night toward the abandoned farmhouse.

Somebody's family must have called this decrepit structure home years ago. There had to be a corner somewhere inside where she could hunker for the night. She would blubber all she wanted then.

"Everything will be better in the morning—yeah right." Each word etched in her head thanks to Harmon now quashed by sarcasm with every stomp. She shook her fist at the very thought of that man pretending to be her father. And Grossmutter. What kind of deceitful people went about stealing another's life and affection?

Hinges creaked. Of course, they would. The door hadn't been used for years. Utterly drained, she took no mind to feeling her way, fingering the deteriorating leather strapping and swiping away cobwebs.

A family of squirrels scattered, and to the large one that chattered a hiss, she enjoyed the motion of an imaginary rifle in her arms shooting it dead. "You don't belong here either," she hissed back.

The bright moon enabled sufficient light to make her way up the stairs. They didn't have many two-level farmhouses in Avondale. She snickered at the progressiveness of Vereiteln Dorf. No attempts did she make to soften her footing when floorboards and risings creaked. An eerie instinct led her straight into the first room on her right. Discovering a straw mattress in a cramped space and too discouraged for further exploration, she plopped onto the pallet of dust and hopelessness.

Fatigue and sore muscles didn't offer sleep right away. When it did arrive, hunger pangs disrupted its peace. Shouldn't despair do that to a body, make one pass out pure and simple?

Frustrated, thirsty, and ravenous, she swore again there'd be no more tears. She'd fallen into a whirlwind of danger and had nowhere to go, no one to trust. Something scurried beneath the bedstead, dashed across the room, and bolted down the stairs. Nestling her legs to her chest, she pushed up, back against the wall. In that position, she fell into a slumber.

Hours later, she awoke, and her groggy eyes adapted. The blackness of night now a mere curtain of gray fog. Hiking from a slouch, she placed her bare feet on the chilled floor and took a moment to recall removing her stockings to dry them sometime in the night. Aye, and she'd left her shoes by the fence. A reminder of the lavender scent lingered. The only nicety of recent, it lifted the corners of her mouth.

The mattress itself lodged against the windowpane provided viewing access. Perfect viewing access, in fact. Whoever slept here overlooked Witford Dimietris's homestead, including the yard in back. Wiping a circle for clarity through the once fancy, now dirt-caked glass pane, she focused on that pile of stones beyond the property fence.

The first crack of sunlight appeared on the horizon. It targeted the pile with a sharp splinter of glint.

She must've finally slept deep. Who could believe the events of last night? Nor the whole of yesterday? Indeed, she'd like to wish it away entirely.

And now it was morning, another day. To where should she go?

She peered out the clearing she'd made on the windowpane. There was something about that madman's farmhouse. A piddling instinct suggested a clue to this tapestry of her personhood could be unraveled within its walls. A strange connection tied her there, something she couldn't ignore. *And just who are you, Mr. Dimietris? Are you truly mad?*

Perhaps she could hide here, use this farmstead, keep an eye on this Dimietris, assess further. Maybe all hope was not lost.

Her gaze fixed back to the stone pile. She enjoyed some mindlessness while the rocks churned a gold color thanks to eager sunrays. *And who, pray tell, is Meginhardt? Might some poor forgotten soul be buried under those stones?*

She shivered before chuckling at such imaginary thinking that followed. *Could the madman be a murderer? Mercy. Nay, I say.*

It wasn't the greatest plan, but it tested as sound as anything. She'd hunker down in the abandoned house. When the opportunity arose, she'd sneak an exploration inside Witford Dimietris's farmhouse. She needed a better sense of who the madman was and if he were safe to approach.

CHAPTER THIRTY-TWO
PERPETRATORS AND APPARITIONS

In Vereiteln Dorf

"AYE." LEXXIE TAPPED the glass, her finger covering the nearby farmhouse entrance. "I shall survey your abode once you leave, Witford Dimietris."

Something wasn't right about the whole madman business, about how he spoke to the dead with no consequence. Should not the priest report him for arrest? Then the coincidence of Dimietris's child dying the year she was born made for certainty this man knew something about her past. It was a clue, and she had no other.

An urgent banging shook the wall she'd been leaning against, shuddering her nerves. An angry caller at the door? A tension pulled at her wary insides. Forearms flexed and fists clenched. How dare she let her guard down?

The door to the backyard creaked, then slammed. Solid-heeled boots slapped the wooden floor. An angry perpetrator on a mission with a target. The owners returning? Nay, brain-less thought. They needn't knock.

The intruder's footsteps stepped with intent to threaten.

She wrestled the urging to freeze. Who predicted she'd be here?

Couldn't be Witford Dimietris. She'd been watching out the window. She'd have seen him coming.

Mercy. What if it were that Jake, the priest's henchman?

Her heart pounded in her throat. Whoever it was, the intruder threatened to harm.

Where to hide? She closed her eyes tight.

Think. Look up. That's what Harmon would say.

When her eyes opened, she blinked several times. No words could explain the oddity hanging in midair before her.

A hand, transparent, oversized. It gestured to her. "Come."

A golden glow surrounded the apparition.

Just how she felt about moving transparent visions, including an unattached floating hand, now was not the time to wonder. The way the palm and fingers motioned expressed genuine aid. Without even a whisper, its come-this-way-for-safety coaxing was unmistakable.

She tiptoed in the direction the hand led, biting her bottom lip. Reminders of Harmon claiming one could never find human logic when it came to divine intervention pro-vided some balance of mind. 'Twas this what he spoke of?

Breathing heavy and placing internal queries on hold, she crept into the hallway, following the apparition's calming gestures. A glance down as she hurried past the top of the stairwell exposed a long shadow against the bouquets of faded wall covering where the natural light of the early morning sun would have blessed the dining room's occupants in days gone by. The narrow shape of a musket preceded the meager frame of a man. Harmon had one just like it. Except he shot rabbits and groundhogs.

The apparition—thick, muscular, and masculine—waved, demanding immediacy from her. It escaped into a room two doors down, the master chamber.

She followed, though its strong promptings for her to hide caused an agitated search around the room along with a riled whisper. "Where?"

Eyeing the high bed, she stooped low to scramble underneath.

The hand blasted a determined Stop motion.

Nay there. She took in the rest of the chamber. A franticness tore apart the threads of calm keeping her together. No choice but to place complete trust into this hand, a comforting vision so unnaturally familiar.

It pointed its forefinger to the bottom drawer of an armoire—a drawer far too small.

And she whispered up a fury. "Yer crackbrained."

A ghostly forefinger scolded in return, sending her into deeper frenzy while a deliberate clunk of a boot slammed the foot of the stairs. Holding in a breath, she opened the lower drawer.

Aye, it be deeper than she'd expected. She glanced at this limb of a ghost directing her every move. Then she cursed beneath her panting. Stepping into the drawer, she forced a collapse forward and curled as she imagined the likes of an infant in its mother's womb. Facing the back of the armoire, she felt the drawer glide to a floating close.

"Thankee," she whispered, then amended with a silent, "I think."

Without intention, she clung to a leather-bound journal, raised initials on its cover. A spool of lace and some leftover embroidery thread became her only companions, the other contents aside her shaking body.

The supportive planks backing the drawer had shrunk, perhaps from humidity. It didn't matter why. Generous buckles and gaps allowed for air to flow, even though the armoire closet backed a mere inch or two against the bedroom wall.

The invader made it clear with an evident thud on each stair—he was coming for her.

Heart racing, she willed herself to calm. Had she gone mad also?

Pressing eyelids tight together, she gave up a prayer. *Please, King, I'm so confused.*

A grounding sound preceded a metal snap. A recognizable threat as the rifle cocked into firing mode. The intruder was in the room where she'd slept, a short hallway stroll away. Panicking only made her space feel smaller. Would he find any telltale of her presence? Did she leave anything behind? Would she die in this dresser drawer? Would anyone find her? Or care?

Her stockings! She had removed them to dry.

She wiggled her bare toes, though she couldn't see them. All ten performed an eagle spread beneath the knees snugged into her chest. Their freedom regretting the trail they left behind, gilded shoes in the lavender patch, stockings in the other room.

"Well, lookie here." The drawer muffled the intruder's voice. Was that Dimietris's taunt? Whoever it was must have found her stockings.

I've done nothing. I shan't be afraid.

Scuffling noises and huffs—he must be checking beneath the straw bed she'd slept on. Maybe a varmint would sever his nose. A girl could dream.

He'd soon discover the clearing she made on the window spying into the yard next. Then he'd come here, to the master chambers.

Hot in the drawer, she twinged. Her skin crawled with a sweaty itch, though no bugs were visible.

The pounding in her chest would surely give her away. Attempting some logic, she listened so as to time her quick and deep gasps. Such would aid to keep still once he discovered this room, cocked rifle, and all.

His purposeful stomps through the hallway, anything but quiet, caused her to pause. Perchance, if it were Dimietris, might he be just as frightened?

The violent crash of the chamber door rattled her spine. Right off the hinges.

'Twas a madman for sure. First that Mr. Nosy Man assault and now this.

She steadied watery eyes through a crack in the back of the drawer where deeply pink peonies blooms graced the wall covering. The image reminded her of Grossmutter. She adored those pink blooms. Her bedding quilt back in Avondale had been embroidered with a similar design.

"I know yer in here, ya menacing woman."

Menacing woman? Did everyone in this forsaken town think so ill of her?

If there'd been an inkling of doubt, 'twas gone now. *Witford Dimietris, to think my heart ached for you.*

No time to wonder what else she'd guessed wrong.

More scuffling. He must be checking under the high bed,

the armoire certain to be next. This time, his boots kicked the wooden floor as he shuffled back to his feet, slow, penetrating steps one by one to where she hid.

Her face sopping with tears, she imagined her own hanging. Alone, no one who cared about her to watch. It'd be better if he shot her dead right here and now.

Why had she doubted the love of Harmon and Grossmutter? Nay, no such thoughts! Curse them both for leading her to such harm as this.

If only she could find her real father, he'd protect her.

Cabinet doors atop the enclosed dresser drawer whipped open. She stopped her breath from any necessary moves. Sounds were obvious, the end of the musket scraped the inside walls, tapped the ceiling, and poked the back two corners of the cabinet space. The man swore and tossed some left-behind dresses, sending cast-iron pegs tingling as they skidded across the chamber's plank floors.

Cussing like she'd never heard proceeded a harsh boot kick at the drawer, shoving a sharp pain into her back. Her forehead thrust into the crack, splitting the back of the drawer wide open. A nauseating metallic stream of blood spilled down her forehead and wet her cheek.

She held her eyes tight and instructed her breaths to run shallow. A way to cope with the pain of a fresh wound. He wouldn't see her unless he attempted to open the drawer or move the heavy armoire enough to check its broken backside.

With the drawer now jammed, her ears became witness to the villainous man's transition from evil killer to a wallowing wreck. Releasing the toxic mixture of a mildewy distillery and yesterday's smoke, Dimietris succumbed to his early morning meal of fermented cider.

A groaning followed by a lineup of overzealous cuss words, then a telltale vibration. Dimietris had slumped onto the floor.

Lexxie wiped moisture from an ear, careful not to give her presence away, but needing to hear what this man mumbled. The movement of his rocking jostled the floor joints. In a state of shock and curiosity herself, she was certain he was self-soothing.

Had the danger passed? She couldn't stay in a cramped drawer much longer.

Surely, he thought she got away. Wouldn't he leave soon so she could escape this private hotbed and wipe away the oily mixture of blood, grime, and tears from her face? She gave up another "thankee" to the hand.

How was it Dimietris had no interest in kicking the drawer a second time? He must've presumed, as she had, nobody could fit inside.

Sounds rose above his self-pitying mumbles—racing hooves pounding the distant dirt road. The thundering clamor increased and, soon enough, trembled the chamber's single windowpane.

His grumbling suggested he heard it as well. Was he expecting someone? She could only hope he'd leave to meet them. He stumbled to the room's opposite side and the window where it faced the road. He must've taken one boot off—a clunk then a drag, another clunk, another drag and again and again.

She smirked, imagining he'd hurt his foot when he kicked her drawer. Served him good.

"Ah, the ratbag priest." He minced no words this time.

So—devoted, he's not. Hmm, that dislike be in her favor. Forceful negotiations with the window jambs underway,

Lexxie managed to shift with the noise and maneuver her head around, daring a peek through a crack in the drawer's facing. She eyed the musket across the floor by a single boot.

So determined he was to push open the window, he spat on one of the hinges to get it moving. As he did, the metal and wood frame released its grip and outward flew a dusty sash. He poked his head beyond the frame, his stocking foot resting on his booted foot.

Soft snorts rose from the horses. Their hooves crunched gravel as they halted. Must be more of them than just the priest.

"Over here," Dimietris yelped.

Meandering hooves followed his voice.

Attempting to overcome a dizzy spell, she shut her eyes and slowed her breath. Silent cries for freedom from this confinement, for fresh air, and for a good body stretch threatened more tears. Humorous how priorities change.

"I reckon ya got her."

Her eyelids charged to a widening attention at the distinction of the priest's nauseating call.

Dimietris scratched the back of his head. "Nearly."

"Nearly?"

Scuffling noises suggested at least one rider dismounted. A second, with a slower and lower octave joined the conversation. "She'n there?"

Ah, that scoundrel henchman with the gravelly voice.

"Was. Must'a slept here last night. Gone."

"Event's at sundown. We need her alive. Got it, Witford?"

Sundown. It's Hanging Day. Justice? Hardly. Best grab that musket and shoot them all.

"I'm think'n ya better double up the reward," he responded with hardly a hint of any drunkenness.

Reward? There was a reward to bring her in?

"I'm think'n ya better get out there to track her down," Jake called. "I ain't patient like yer priest."

"How'd ya figure she found this place, Witford?" the priest probed.

Witford took a leaning to the side of the window. "Ya said she was head'n my way, and ta watch fer her, didn't ya? Looks like she come. And now she's gone. Now I gotta hunt her down? That's different. Worth at least double, I'd say."

"How about we let you stay a free man?"

Horses whinnied in sync. Hooves churned the gravel.

"Event's at sundown." The priest finalized the discussion. "Bring her to me alive. Lest it be your neck in that noose."

Jake's hoarse chuckle churned her guts. The pounding of their horses racing away left Witford with a blank stare, forehead pressed against the windowpane. They had something on him. But he didn't succeed in his negotiation to double the reward money. That was the only silver thread on this, Lexxie's dark day.

CHAPTER THIRTY-THREE
RICH YET POOR

In Vereiteln Dorf

"HOW IS IT the priest is always one step ahead? It's almost like he's been expecting me." She spoke freely now, alone in the chamber.

After Witford grabbed his boot and musket and left the abandoned farmhouse in a scuff, she goaded her way out the drawer. His straight-on toe kick had splintered the side panels. A few shoves with her knees and she released herself. She rolled, then lay still on the floor where he had been.

"They're hiding something. Not just Witford, all of them." Safe for the moment, she spoke to the empty room.

Despite the filth and thistles, she used the fullness of the skirt to wipe down her forehead and neck before bunching the hem to muffle uncontrollable sobs. An emotional breakdown. She cursed this King-forsaken town. The priest back home was kind, humble, and honest. A genuine gift to their community, Harmon used to say. But not here. How misguided these Vereiteln folks were!

Seeking stability, she scooted on her buttocks across the uneven planks to lean on a bedpost. Her breath tight, she worked through the cramping in the back of knees too long bunched up in that drawer.

"Get yer feet under ya. You're on your own," she snapped at her courage, calling it to attention and propping up her body. Then she scouted the room for that ghostly image, the hand that came to her rescue. "So, where are you now?"

Funny how the mind goes when in dire situations. Though it did protect her from being captured, so she whispered up another thank ye just in case she hadn't imagined it.

Lack of water and nourishment must've caused the light-headedness. She remained still for it to pass.

"No more crying." Lips tight together, she gave herself some much needed spurring. "First, you need something to eat."

But what and where?

Returning to where she'd slept the night before, she dared a spy out the circular clearing in the windowpane. Witford strode toward the fields, musket in hand, likely searching for her.

Hungry eyes diverted her attention to the crab apple tree outside his back doorstep. Her stomach growled.

Disgusting varmint actually took her stockings. No longer were they hanging on the peg.

Barefooted, she slipped down the stairs, then paused to admire the kitchen, at least what it had once been. Such an impressive hearth, as wide as the room. It would have kept the occupants warm even in their beds on the high floor. The pedestal dining table confirmed a wealthy landowner had lived here. Every cooking tool one could think of and more she couldn't have imagined hung from the ceiling, now covered in layers of sticky dust. The floor with a black mush, leaves from last year's fall. Pairs of critter eyes peered out behind a corn broom. There had been an odd warm feeling about the house. It let her sleep. It protected her. Abandoned love in this dwelling somehow embraced her. Whatever happened to its family?

After checking each way before slipping out the back door, she crossed over the dried ravine to the property's border and back under the lavender bush. Chances were her shoes were still there.

Huh. Those nicks in the wooden fence this side of that long rectangular stone pile caught her attention again. Her bare toes bore into the soil, a comforting footing for once. She pushed aside the overgrown lavender. A perfect spot for spying, a spot someone had obviously found before her. Fingering the etchings, she speculated the carvings were made with a sharp stone or more likely a pocketknife and by someone schooled.

M doth Sleep. H.

M doth sleep. H? Whoever *H* was, might he have been cursing a deathly fate to fall upon *M*? And this *M*, it must signify the Meginhardt fella Witford was keen to harass last night. Maybe he lived with Witford, in his time.

The *H* brought a sigh, but no sense lingering over the *H* insignia on the shawl Grossmutter had given her. Though it too exhibited embroidered pink blooms, much like the wallpaper in that master chamber. Peonies, a sign of prosperity. But such details weren't important now, not with her life in imminent danger. Still, she couldn't stop other symbols from flooding her head. The journal in the drawer, those initials on its leather cover, another *M* and *H*. Then that spool of green bobbin lace and deep-purple embroidery thread . . . same thread as the shawl Grossmutter gifted her.

"Huber. M H—Meredith Huber." *Mercy, could it be?*

And then the H etched into the fence . . . "H—my Harmon?"

The unwilled shriek echoed. Her hand flew to her mouth to stop it from furthering. She pulled herself back to a crouch and labored to catch her breath. Aye, had to be. The pale-pink peony wallpaper—so like Grossmutter. Despite its condition, the oddly warm and protective feeling was a sense she'd recognized, grown up with. That was where Harmon grew up. Of course. Had to be. The house, the kitchen, his father—oh, mercy, Gillam met his death by an ax there!

And Harmon. Did he know this Meginhardt fellow? Did he curse him?

Oh, such thoughts. So disturbing.

If she were right, Harmon and Grossmutter left behind the abandoned farmhouse, once a grand property. From wealthy landowner in Vereiteln Dorf to meager tenants in rural Avondale.

She plopped on her behind, well beyond the point of caring whether layers of filth could ever be removed from her new attire, never mind her skin. This place was once the Huber homestead. Still, it was supposition, all of it. But a guess her gut couldn't deny. But why would they have given all of this up? For what cause would they walk away?

"I could have been the princess I'd always dreamed about if we lived there."

A shift in thought surged an abundance of energy, this time pulling her up to tower on both feet, fists clenching and unclenching. "Nay. That would *not* have been my home." The harsh reminder, a dagger to her heart. "Harmon and Meredith Huber are not my family. They are nothing but child-thieving liars. Rich with everything but children."

Then it hit her.

"That's why they took me."

CHAPTER THIRTY-FOUR
NOTHING YOU CAN DO

In the Outer Courtyard of the Kingdom

MEGINHARDT DIDN'T HAVE to hang on. Rather, he could feel the anger in Jophiel's grip, a purposeful clench. "Argh."

Another spell of dizziness invaded. He'd best not look down. Though he swung like a sapling in the wind, his mind was stuck good and firm. Some girl would carry on with Pa's descendants, and that was not fair, plain and simple.

Sailing above the outer courtyard of the kingdom brought little comfort. The nerve of Pa having another kid. Did he batter her up too?

A rough landing, Meginhardt rolled sideways after the harsh touch down on his back end. For sure, Jophiel released that grip of his earlier than he should've on purpose. Still, Meginhardt didn't shake it off. Did Pa quash her dreams like he did Meginhardt's?

Don't matter—I despise her anyway.

Soon enough, he'd get back to the river and hear the rebel

fella's offer. A future of some sort. He'd negotiate, getting as much as he could want.

Jophiel ushered Meginhardt to where they first met, the kingdom's outer courtyard, far above the River of Times and a lifetime away from Vereiteln Dorf. Leaving him in Aivy's tiny hands, the massive sort cawed a mouthful. "Relinquishing." Then he gave an abrupt wave with no indication as to where he was heading and left the scene like a fox from a fire.

Aivy said nothing.

Was that it? Would Meginhardt see Jophiel again, that is, if he wanted to?

Meginhardt rendered motionless, blinked, weighing up. These two thought they had some kind of sneaky way of communicating? Jophiel must be going back to that girl. What would he find? Had the rebel already done what he said he would? By now, she'd be good and deep again, stuck in that embankment and going nowhere but inside her own dark, little, murky world and never be able to see her way out. Self-satisfaction earned his grin.

Aivy cleared her throat. The back of her hands pressed against each hip spoke volumes. She was not impressed. She couldn't know about his coming river meeting. She introduced herself to Meginhardt again, this time emphasizing her role—his transition agent.

Fiddle-faddle. She rattled on.

He caressed the stone in his pocket, affirming his decision to trust neither Jophiel nor this Aivy. He would trust only himself. That got him through his past life. It would get him through this new one. Besides, Pa had ingrained clearly that women had no authority. Liar though Pa be, he couldn't have lied about that.

How comforting to know Meginhardt's stone was there, deep in his right trouser pocket.

He jerked his chin up. "I ain't transitioning anywhere. So, I don't need you, ma'am."

He diverted his focus to the woman by the picnic tables. She was still there, waiting for him. *Mutter.*

He headed away, straight toward her.

Aivy threw up her hands, stepped aside, and busied herself with another incoming Arrival.

Each step heavy loaded with emotion and questions, he raked his fingers through his hair. Perhaps that would make him more presentable.

'Twas this really happening?

What if she doesn't approve of me, thinks me disappointing?

Will we have stuff to talk about—did Pa beat her too?

Then she might think I'm gonna fist her!

What if she really is a witch?

What if it's not truly *her?*

The shake of the woman's head was even more gentle than her smile. She must have recognized his pondering expression and oversized wrinkled forehead.

That was all it took for him to defy all negativity. With no further delay, he clasped his arms around her waist. Her hands, warm and soft, held his head against her chest.

"I watched you drown." He sobbed, eyes soaking her shoulder.

"Shh."

"I've dreamed of this. Never, did I think it would come true." He pulled back to study her face. "My own mother, so eye-catching, more than even make believe."

She laughed. "And you, my son, are a sight."

What did she see? Windblown hair, torn shirt, dirty trousers, bare feet?

She held up his chin. "What happened here?" She examined his mouth, more likely the gap where a front tooth was missing.

Don't she know Pa knocked it out? Her knowing suggested she understood.

She invited him to walk with her, to head to the gate together. Meginhardt insisted on sitting and waiting outside instead. Holding hands across a picnic table was so magical, leaving him in love with the moment, each nurturing with their words, gleeful with the anticipation of this new everlasting reunion. He pushed down the troublesome sea surging beneath his hardened and scarred heart. That was not to ruin this moment.

"My dear boy, waiting for this time to arrive has been excruciating. I pained over all that burdened you so. Still, wanting an arrival is not something one rushes."

"I thought you died giving birth to me." He choked, needing to hide the angry swirl stirring his soul.

Not her fault. A lie, it was an evil lie. He found comfort in her smile.

"Nor were you a witch." He extended an upturned hand, inviting, rather insisting, her confirmation. *Tell me I'm right.*

Ignoring his silly bait, she scolded him. "Meginhardt, letting go of such lies and self-reproach is what you must do. Else, you be inviting what is evil to remain within you."

His stone might as well be in his throat, the struggle to swallow near impossible. *A lecture from my mother?*

This was a first. Women weren't supposed to tell men how to sense. He pulled back.

"I understand you've learned many truths. Caution is still an utmost priority. Avoid the temptation to trade in your empathy and forgiveness for anger, or even worse, revenge." Having said her piece, she leaned back and sat tall.

He broke their eye lock to examine the picnic table's intricate design. Let go of her hands to rub his chin, wring his wrists, anything to rid the striking bolt of nervous energy. How dare she scold him and tell him how to feel?

She wasn't there. So many words roiled on his tongue, circulating and unspoken, dizzying his mind. *You didn't stop the way Pa treated me, so you ain't got the right to tell me noth'n.*

Pa always said women were jus' bossy prating knaves. The mother Meginhardt dreamed of was comforting, someone to run to, to take his side. Not this. Not someone to tell him what to think and how to feel. Pa may have made him a fool, but she wasn't adding up to what he expected. Did she know about Pa's other child or even Meginhardt's agreement with the rebel to harm her? With a scratchy voice, he clarified, "It's not revenge."

"How can you be certain? Do you truly know yourself?" Her gaze bore into him.

Aye, she knew.

Guilt stirred. How could the slightest of nods cause him so much grief?

Best to accuse another's wrongdoing rather than admit yer own. Good thing Pa taught him that too.

"How can you not be angry? After what he did to you? Being called a witch and dying at his hands." He lowered his head, recalling what Jophiel had shown him. "Lest you did drown that day, didn't you?"

"And you have not caused anyone to drown?"

Frequent blinking did nothing to wash his guilt. That girl, yes. He wanted her stone driven into the mud so she couldn't surface, maybe even never.

Did I agree to drown her?

He fought the temptation to cower as though preparing for a wallop, only it was he himself, the angry assaulter. Pa, responsible for his mother's death. And now, himself responsible for that girl's demise?

No longer dare he look at his mother's face. Telling words slipped from his tongue. "I've become my father."

Twice, he'd said that now.

Meginhardt shirked the very thought of that rebel at the riverbank. Should he stop him? Could he stop him? Did he *want* to stop him?

He leaned in close to his mother. This was not the moment he'd dreamed about when face-to-face with her. He slapped the picnic table and jerked his body to a full stance.

Before he could speak, she reached out. The tips of her fingers met his arm. Warm and soothing. What he wanted to say might have been a lie anyway, a made-up excuse for his behavior.

"I fear that look in your eye," she said. "What's in that mind of yours to do? And don't tell me nothing. I may not have raised you on earth, but I understand you. That head of yours is spinning." She added a finger shake. "You know that's where the battlefield is, right? In the minds of those walking the earth."

He hadn't thought of it that way. Pulling his arm back, he mustered a turn to walk away.

But she grasped the back of his shirt, then his shoulder. "Come with me inside the gate. Go through. It's time."

"Nay, I won't. I ain't like you!" The tail end of his outbreak melted with meekness from fear of sounding as though he accused her of not doing anything, and rather forgetting it all. Once one entered the gate and delivered up his stone, he, too, would belong to the King's family. A kingdom citizen. And that meant total forgiveness, handing over all injustices.

Not ready. Meginhardt spent his earth journey excusing Pa. Now that truths and realities were unfolding, he couldn't let it all go. He refused to meet his mother's pleading eyes. "Nay, Mother, I shall not enter."

"Able you'd be to come and go to this outer courtyard anytime you desire. And inside, there are so many ancestors eager to meet you."

"Yeah, and because of you and Pa, I'm the end of the line." Heat charged through him, clenched his muscles, knotted his stomach and fists. "No family of my own. No descendants."

He couldn't explain his need, this deepest desire of his heart, to have a family. To teach them, take care of them, love them. The complete opposite of what his life had been.

A distraction at the gate caught him up. That burly gate-keeper was employing his extraordinary belly laugh with some new Arrival.

Meginhardt's mother pulled him back to face her. "It's in your blood." She pointed to the happy ruckus. "Your experience balanced you rightly, guarded and aware, so much so that now you won't allow harm to enter. I hear the King has something in mind for you."

Did he deserve her words of purpose? He chewed the inside of his lips.

"What ails you? Why hesitate? There's nothing more for you to do." She raised her brows. "Interfering and interventions are neither for us to carry out."

Nothing more for you to do. The phrase backchatted over and over, causing his head to shake.

He gave her his back. *It ain't finished yet, not fer me.*

CHAPTER THIRTY-FIVE
GREENER PASTURES

In the Outer Courtyard of the Kingdom

"MOTHER, YOU GO on in. I need time, but I tell you, I will enter." Fingers crossed behind his back, Meginhardt coaxed her to enter the gate on her own. He'd come later. Possibly.

Gotta get me back to that river. He must hear what that rebel had to offer. Why not? A future, one perhaps more deserving, awaited him there also. A gentle squeeze of the stone in his trouser pocket provided some comfort. Still there, still safe. Both sides of the river wanted him—him!

Though amused, he realized the critical value of that stone, a mysterious living representation of himself.

His mother cast a cautious glance where Aivy stood cross-armed by the gate. Aivy, that pint-sized tempest of a woman, could help him with what he needed to do.

Could being the opportune word. Whether she would or would not being the challenge.

Aivy was waving, time to reenter the kingdom. His mother leaped at Aivy's command without even saying goodbye.

His throat tightened.

Was that it? Would he see her again? She just up and left at that woman's command?

Tingles of abandonment trickled up and down his spine. He sucked in deep, another protective layer of coating to harden his heart. As far as his own stone went, he'd reserve his decision till after this conversation with the rebel. If he stayed on this side of the river, nothing disastrous could happen, right?

People tarried in the courtyard. He forced the air out his chest. What's this all about? Social connections were foreign to him. The interactions in the courtyard made him lonelier than ever, especially now that his mother pranced away, leaving him—voluntarily this time. How he despised that familiar sickening pain. This place was beautiful, so joyous, and bitterly, not for him.

The disconnect, like a sharpened ax, sliced nicks at his soul.

Back at the picnic table he'd shared with his mother, he observed the horizon where that cliff met the universe of nothingness. The amazement unforgettable. Ribbons of living, energy-filled colors gravitating to reach the height of this land, transform into beings, and ride those waves inward.

Eyes closed, he welcomed a magical breeze on his face. Freeing and abnormal. For an instant, it removed his angst. No one could argue—everything here was incredulous. Particularly the waves of brilliant lavender in the distance. They reminded him of the purple aromatic patch beyond the property fence back home. He used to sit there for hours, either hiding from Pa or spying on the neighbor boy, Harmon.

Pa never approved of Harmon, so they seldom talked. Yet Harmon was the closest thing to a friend Meginhardt ever got.

Don't be fooled. Bolting upright, Meginhardt shunned any such trappings of complacency. Instead, he ran toward the gate, insisting he speak with Aivy.

She appeared in perfect timing as though expecting him, any previous smiles reserved for her precious Arrivals, wiped from her face. "Stubborn and determined."

Ignoring her attitude, he lifted his chin enough to avoid her gaze. "So, what does a transition agent do?"

"One's arrival and entrance require careful planning, coordination, and aid."

He didn't like the way she cocked her head. "Well then, I require some aid."

"Oh, really?"

Nor did he like her sarcasm. No doubt, with the way she shifted her feet and pushed both fists into her hips, he was in for some sort of lecture.

"You know," she started, "the early completion of your journey may not have been a component of the King's plan. Still, good always comes of such things."

This ought to be good.

"You were saved from a lifelong influence."

"A lifelong influence. Do tell." His turn to be sarcastic.

"I don't like your tone."

He paused as if to study the horizon before waving for her to continue.

"You were vulnerable and about to choose a similar path as your pa. Not having anyone close enough to influence you any other way was not for lack of trying. It was certain you might have—"

"Might have what?"

"Well, develop bad habits."

"You mean the drink."

"I mean the mindset. Anger. Hatred. And worse, such pride and self-righteousness." Her eyebrows rose. "You have an assortment growing quite well enough, I might add."

"And murder," his guilty conscience spat the self-accusation.

She faced him square-on. "Oh, taking another's life, is that in your heart?"

Wiseacre. He calculated her charging look. He'd had about enough. This woman was naught but a block. He increased the space between them. "So, is that Jophiel bird around?"

When she took a half turn away, Meginhardt breathed a little easier.

"Jophiel is assigned elsewhere. I'll call a courier, but he is not in the same category as Jophiel. Couriers carry and deliver and wait if instructed. They won't lend advice."

Good. "Even better."

She marched off into the kingdom to arrange a courier, giving him another chance to look around. The place was stunning, miraculous even, like nothing he could've invented. Far too good to be true. Nothing this upright or magnificent happened upon him, so dare he trust it? Too risky.

His mother had said the city inside was a place no one ever desired to leave. The only reason some ventured into the outer courtyard was to await a loved one, and even then, most prefer to wait inside.

But was that even his real mother? Deep inside, he knew full well it was. Still, the arrows of doubt casting upon him felt more natural, more trustworthy.

I'm a good person. Although, a niggle haunted—he *was* becoming more and more like Pa.

But all he'd have to do was take back that silly nod of agreement to harm the girl. That's all. Then he'd get back to himself, feel right.

The burly gatekeeper sent him stares, so Meginhardt slipped to his side to chat, perhaps even quiz the man. Maybe he could offer some advice.

Short and stocky, the gatekeeper stood with his legs well-planted. White hair fell past the man's broad shoulders. Fat toes stuck out from dusty sandals. As each of Meginhardt's steps brought them closer, access to the entry he guarded closed in. The gatekeeper folded his arms, his words terse and cutting. "Think you gotta prove yourself, do ya?"

The interrogating comment halted Meginhardt's steps but not his tongue. "I woulda thought all you people here would be, ah, a little more kinder maybe?"

"Why's that? So young foolish lads as you can do as you please? Ha, you arrive, and suddenly, you got to go figure it all out so's it fits in your box of thinking. I don't care what they say—you're not fit for this."

Meginhardt swallowed the dismissal, reliving the all-too-familiar humiliation he'd experienced during his life.

The gatekeeper blew an offensive huff Meginhardt's way. "Now, step aside so's I can get back to business that matters."

Business, which apparently included conversing with Arrivals and scanning their palms for rays of colors, of all things.

Fit fer what? Meginhardt backed off, preferring some space between him and the gatekeeper's scolding outburst. *Aivy's got a sick state of mind. She thinks I'm to enter? Hah, I wouldn't get past that old garrison. All he's guarding is a bolted-up hatch.*

As he sulked, another attack materialized, this one physical. A weighty mass struck the side of his head, sending him flat on a jarring skid for several feet. A flurry of feather underlay threshed across his nostrils. His back ached.

Propping himself up, he met the set of beady eyes studying his face. Ugh, another one of those creatures, an oversized eagle bird.

The bird brushed itself off, then glowered. "You Meginhardt?"

"Aye." Caught off guard, though catching on quick, he chuckled. "Guessing yer my way."

Perfect timing. Now, he could get away from the bully gatekeeper and the foolish-minded Aivy.

The yellow in one eye gyrated to green whilst the other squinted to a full shut. "You the same Meg–in–hardt who told me to get lost earlier today?"

Ah, was that just this morning? And should he deny it? That whole scene may as well have happened a lifetime ago, and yes, he did insist the bird leave empty-handed. Without him.

Meginhardt recanted, "About that—"

"Never mind." The bird gave a one-wing flap, saving him from concocting an excuse or apology. Astounding, especially since Meginhardt had threatened the bird with an ax. "Where to?"

Where to? "The River of Times."

With a whoosh, the eagle courier clutched Meginhardt in his talons and swooped him away. When Meginhardt glanced down, Aivy ambled over to that bully gatekeeper. They hugged, and she leaned her head on his muscular forearm.

Cry me a mercy. The pair of 'em, in this together?

Even here, he was labeled for rejection, an outcast.

Fighting loneliness drained him. Temptation niggled. Connecting with the rebels would allow him to lower his guard. Aye, he'd keep a ready mind. If that rebel was straight-forward with answers and his offer was right, he'd stay with him on the other side of that dern dividing river. Who needed this other nonsense?

CHAPTER THIRTY-SIX
A BABY ROBBED

In Vereiteln Dorf

LEXXIE RAN A finger inside the rough edges of the *H* carving. Having presumed wrongly a few times, she was discovering a weakness, her fast jump to conclusions. Anybody could be H or MH, for that matter.

For a time, her gaze remained fixed upon the rocks and stones, as though it were some kind of mesmerizing landmark. No sign of Witford returning.

She figured and counted on another presumption. He likely went to that old graveyard to look for her. He'd likely gone asking the talking pit of witches for help.

A chuckle escaped, him finding her carry sack and coin purse.

Sarcasm heightened, encouraging a challenge to her imagination. Did she actually hear a voice there? Nay. Lack of water could do that. Her sanity was not disappearing with her identity.

"If that's where he be, I have time."

On hands and knees, feeling around the earth, she found her shoes. After pushing her toes into the tight confinement of ornamentation, she hiked over the property fence.

Pulling two crab apples off a tree, she scooted through Witford's backyard. She devoured one in five bites before she opened his back door and stepped inside. Throttling a tart chunk down her windpipe, she shut the door and let her eyes adjust to the cool darkness within the timber-framed farmhouse.

Tiny molecules attacked high inside her nose. Even the abandoned farmhouse had a better scent. A toxic odor of ale, burnt wine, and body sweat hung like an invisible veil. The ceilings were not much lower than the farmhouse in Avondale, though she could never recall such dark dankness.

She cracked open a wooden shutter and pushed a tattered hanging cloth aside, admitting some light and a chance to hear anyone coming. Several floor planks were buckling, most discolored and thick with dirt. Did he never sweep?

Her stockings. Bunched up, they'd been tossed atop a cabinet loaded with dishes, dishes that couldn't have been used for years given the dulling thick covering of dirt. Each plate crisscrossed with precision one over the other. The whole thing, the cabinet and dishware included, were out of place with the rest of the room. She grabbed her stockings and rolled them on with an eye out the window the whole time. Once upon a time, had the place been an outbuilding, something to suit and service a wealthier home? Like the abandoned place next door.

The man obviously lived just in this room. Worn attire slung in various places, a wash bucket, wooden table, and basic but heavily used hearth. With the floor planks so uneven, that husk mattress jammed against an interior door was lifted on one side by a number of bricks.

On a peg in a darkened corner hung a pair of outdoor overalls, boots, and a cap, all much like a younger person might wear, a boy. She leaned in and, just as quick, backed away, holding her nose. Those clothes couldn't have been worn in years. Perhaps Witford had a son years ago? Only a single pewter plate and knife on the table. Dinner for one, not two. This was the home of a man with no wealth, no family, lost to wander in the present.

An imagination of his pain swelled inside her. Was that priest and his henchman, Jake, blackmailing Witford? Had he become a madman because he'd no one else to turn to?

Empathy followed, filling her veins.

"Stop it." Her outside voice took over. This madman would have killed her had he found her in the armoire a mere hour ago.

"What are ya hiding?" She stomped to the blocked entrance of the second room, drawn to whatever mystery lay beyond the door. A split and broken beam braced against its padlocked entrance.

Shoving the mattress and kicking the bricks out of the way was easy. The challenge was the broken beam and a padlock, the kind with a spring and a hinged shackle. What could be so secretive to a poor madman, that he needed a padlock for his second room?

Crazed and determined, she heaved the rotting beam out of the way. Next, the padlock. "Well, I'm about to find out."

Best she not find anything grotesque, like the crow-eaten skeleton of this Meginhardt fella.

After a furtive glance at the cornfield and satisfied there was no sign of Witford, she scoured through a pile of tools and spied a crowbar. Imagining him chatting up or more likely rebuking some poor soul beneath a gravestone somewhere, she leveraged the pry's flat end between the padlock and the shackle. She applied full body pressure and challenged the shackle to release. Her attempt failed and ended with a buildup of frustration.

She stepped back to examine the latch. Aha, the wooden doorframe itself was warped and bowed. A hammer. She needed a hammer.

Focused on finding one, she paid no mind to see if Witford was nearby. But a maul was. An eager grab at its handle and a good three swings later—success.

"Hah. So much for yer padlock, Mr. Witford." After winning this battle, she pushed her palm against the splintered interior door.

It creaked, though she expected as much. The smell was different, not pungent. Leaving the door propped open offered some lift to the blackness. She glided straight to the shuttered window and pushed aside heavy blackened curtains. A cunning blaze of sunshine, long forbidden an entrance, streamed in. As her eyes adjusted, she managed another quick scan. No Witford. Good.

To another, the room could be a pleasing piece of history, a yearning wistfulness frozen in time. To her, it was an ancient cave, an undisturbed slice of somebody's yesterday.

Though badly chipped, a carved high bed made of cherrywood was dressed in a threadbare, four-block quilt and two tall matching cushions. A round rug, hand-hooked from worn-out clothing gathered a thick layer of dust in the center of the room. A lower, narrower bed stood aside the back wall, a nightgown hung on a peg above it.

Definitely for a youth, and given the overalls she'd seen previously, Witford had a son, Meginhardt apparently. "Solves that mystery. But where is he now?"

He, too, must've died.

A dresser held figurines and a music box atop it. Such oddities.

Scratching an itch on the back of her scalp, she struggled to understand just who lives—more likely, lived, past tense— here. This room, also abandoned like the farmhouse next door, imprisoned nothing but memories.

With another fleeting surge of empathy, she better understood this Witford Dimietris. Terribly sad. He was in sorrow for a wife and son, both gone. Plus, an infant daughter beneath that grave marker. No wonder he was a madman, no one to help him with such a burden of grief.

Absorbing and steeping in such trauma, she couldn't imagine. This was the logical reasoning how Witford Dimietris churned into the town's madman and why townsfolk left him be, despite his constant conversing with the dead. But whether this could have any connection to her own dilemma?

She sighed. Likely not.

Fawning at the sight of an ivory hair comb, she gave in to unavoidable temptation. For whom would it harm if she used it? The initial pulling stroke to detangle grubby distresses from her scalp was much harsher than expected. She needed a step back to keep her balance, ending in a trip over a knee-high wooden structure resembling a food trough. Within it, a folded lap quilt covered the body of a hand-sewn doll as though it were sleeping.

A kinderwiege.

Telling herself to breathe was becoming a norm these days,

particularly this day. The ivory comb slipped from her hand and tinkled against a floor plank, freeing her to explore the tiny bedside crib. Drawn to it, she stroked it to lift accumulated dust on its sideboard and, with the other hand, fingered the simple decorative carving. The infant Dimietris. This must have been for her. Little Alexandra.

Such presumed enlightenment begged more questions. 'Course many infants died before getting the chance to even yawn at their first nightfall. But the way Witford cried and pleaded to his infant's grave, it had to be more than a natural death. *Pray tell, it wasn't at anyone's hands.*

Picking up the doll, she brought it close to her chest. She filled her nostrils with the earthy essence and nestled her chin around its soft head. Her stomach roiled with a grief she'd never known and realized. This was that "something missing." A mother-child love like no other. They'd both been robbed, this infant Alexandra and herself. Acknowledging the room, she imagined love filled these walls at one point. It had to have. She rubbed the doll's nose with her own. Her body relaxed, a slight smile crept across her face.

A rifle snapped and cracked behind her.

CHAPTER THIRTY-SEVEN
A DREAM SHATTERED

In Vereiteln Dorf

"TERN AROUND. GOOD'N slow."

Nowhere to run. A man with a cocked rifle blocked the only way out from this somber room with the haunted past. Too late to hide. No golden hand apparition to guide. And no reason to call out. Who in this forsaken town would come, even if she screamed and even if they heard?

The click of the rifle echoed the threat of what comes next. A single thunderous blast. She knew it well. Harmon shot at varmints to keep them out of Grossmutter's garden. That was different. Harmon may have lied to her, but he wasn't a madling.

Would this madman standing behind her shoot a woman?

Evoked with hatred and a voice throaty, Witford Dimietris repeated his order. "I said, tern around. Ya deaf?"

Intrusion. That be her crime. It's punishment? A public whipping.

The room spun with a negative energy. So dark, so angry. Witford's eyes would be beady black. A scowl would be squeezing his eyebrows to his chin.

Stay calm. Change the direction. Change the story.

A crackling in her ear chattered from a dry swallow. The gulp felt good.

She caressed the stuffed doll and straightened its dress, then pulled the wool hair back to reveal its full face. A yellowed pale with soft painted-pink cheeks, tiny lips, and blue crisscrossed stitches for its eyes. The doll quivered in her shaky hands.

Traumatic grief had turned this man to evil. She'd be kind, be humane. Relax. He wouldn't hurt her. No reason to be afraid.

Still, she couldn't be sure. What if Witford murdered them all and was not an innocent victim gone hardened and mad? Nay, look at what he'd been hiding, nothing but a history of pain in this room.

"Ya dumb-witted woman. I said, tern around."

"You don't have to be afraid of me." Her voice emerged firm and confident, her eyes shut tight. A deep breath. Then another. She must turn this conversation around into something, anything, other than what it was.

"I ain't 'fraid of ya. And I don't take kindly to intruders. Show me yer face."

She cast her gaze downward, a disguising act of submission, stalling first at the bedside crib intended for the man's infant daughter. With a slight backward glance, she could see Witford's boots firmly grounded, securing his body in ready-to-shoot position. A stench of sour breath crept into the room, this sanctuary, his private little graveyard.

He must have buried his hurt real good and deep inside. Otherwise, why keep this room so? A moment frozen in time, a time when perhaps he was happy? This man, perhaps not so mad, rather chock-full of grief and guilt and an inability to cope. Weak-minded.

She counted on it.

"I'm no intruder."

Her shoulders jerked back when the cold poke of the rifle jammed smack between her shoulder blades. Her lips tucked swift inside her mouth. Drawing breath convinced her to speak with boldness. "Mr. Dimietris, I don't want to harm you."

Hot sour breath stirred the hairs on the back of her neck.

Her heart had never felt so bold, her veins loaded with a whole new sense of self-worthiness. "I want . . . to help you. You see, we have something in common."

"Sure do." The rifle eased from her back. He discharged a big spit of saliva. "Reward money. Yer giv'n, and I'm get'n."

Body weary and filthy, hair full of thistles, stickiness where she had rubbed the blood off her cheek, she turned. Her hips made the first move, twisting the balls of her swollen feet next. Clinging the doll tight to her chest, the rest followed.

Those eyes. Words wanting to choke their way out her throat tightened and begged otherwise. *I know you, but that's impossible.*

Witford hardened his look. His body stiffened as if he just figured something out. His movements were swift, that rifle back in shoot-ready position. "Priest said yer come back. I didn't believe him."

A bead of sweat slid down the side of his chin. A purple flush swallowed his otherwise dull-gray skin. Like blue worms, his neck veins swelled and contracted. His body convulsed, and once the rifle took to shaking, she grabbed it from his loosened grip.

The man had transitioned from malicious to mush upon sighting her face. Then he scattered out the room, fast—as he did that day in the graveyard. Why?

She tossed the rifle and doll onto the bed and went after him. She couldn't let him go.

Whoa. An abrupt halt jerked her knees at the broken doorframe.

He faced her head-on again. Wild was he, an ax high with both hands.

Okay, the whole madman thing made sense now.

"I buried ya once. I kin do it ag'in."

"Huh? Wait . . ." Her palms attempted a gentle slackening. *Buried me once? Who does he think I am?*

"Gillam was noth'n but a cow pie. Ya should'a just kept yer fat mouth shut."

Gillam. He knew her grandfather? Er, not her grandfather. "I–I, ah, I never said anything. I don't know what you're talking about."

Witford let the ax fall to a slumber swing at his side. He leaned forward to examine her features. The ax dropped. He grasped both her wrists. "You ain't gonna trick me ag'in."

The surprise grip to his advantage, she wriggled for freedom. She bit his forearm and broke thick layers of withered skin. Drips of blood escaped.

Growling, he hard-kicked her knees with his own. He had aimed higher, but she buckled to the floor, giving him the perfect opportunity to disable her temporarily with a strong kick to the back. As he balanced his knees on her backside, he ripped his shirt enough to get a decent strip to tie her wrists.

Lifting her off the ground, he bullied a commanding yank and pulled her into the main room toward the cabinet with the fancy plates. There, he apparently stored a variety of utility resources in the drawers. Rope in hand, he dragged her back into the museum-like chamber and propelled her onto the bed.

She gave her darndest to struggle free, but he won. He tied her firm, face up and spread eagle, to the four-poster bed. Her nose twitched from years of accumulated dust trapped in the straw mattress.

"What happened to the woman of this household?" Her vocal cords couldn't vibrate properly, her voice dry and weak. It was her best crack at sincerity.

"Don't git smart." He shoved another torn strip of his filthy shirt into her mouth.

The notion of him as the victimized sort sickened her.

"Want yer little baby doll?" He mocked and plopped to the floor beside the empty crib attached to the bed, the rifle and ax laying heavily, each at a side within his easy reach.

Lexxie's head was pounding. Water filled her eyes. This Witford Dimietris is truly a bedlamite. Her childhood terror, a faceless man raising an ax. 'Tis *him*. That was a warning dream. This man was lawless and heartless. It was all weaving together, pieces of an unlovely tapestry. Not only would he harm her, for certain, this madman axed Gillam Huber to death.

The floor of her heart gave way. That M and H. Without a doubt, they lived right next door in that abandoned farmhouse. The Huber family, Meredith and Gillam and Harmon. Their lives, thrashed as heads of wheat in a stone-grain crusher. Did Harmon witness his father's ghastly slaughter? A grievous calamity, too much to sort out, at least right now.

"You should'a listened, Emmaline." Witford started again, this time with a strangely calm voice, as though lecturing a child. "I warned ya to stay away from those folks, more means than brains. They don't know what people like you and me are like. But you went and got too close, didn't ya? They told ya a bunch o' lies 'bout me."

Emmaline? Of course, Emmaline. The woman of this household. Hadn't Giselle said Lexxie looked like her?

"We couldn't have them tell'n folks I slain my son. You know as well as me, that dern Meginhardt was always tempt'n fate. Talking to his dead mother all the time—well, that's punishable by law. That sister of yers was a witch. She come and got him. You know that. Guess'n she was jus' saving him from the law."

Done in his own son? Mercy, he murdered his boy too! Who couldn't blame anyone for taking up conversing with their dead mother? Hardly a reason for taking their life. A murderer this man be.

"You jus' wouldn't listen, would ya? So caus'n of you, I had to shut him up. That Gillam was gonna ruin us, everythin' we had." Picking up his rifle, he gave it a petting stroke. He cocked the gun. "That wasn't enough fer ya, was it? Ya still listened to that good-fer-noth'n know-it-all buttock and tongue he married. Lucky fer ya, a woman's word means noth'n, 'specially a widow."

Meredith Huber. He must be talking about Grossmutter.

Lexxie groaned. How could she convince the madman she wasn't Emmaline?

"Terns out, Emmaline, you was a witch too. Jus' like yer big sis." He tsked. "Ya know what really got my goat?" He stood to approach Lexxie's side, hovering his face over hers.

"Ya took Alexandra, my baby girl. Ripped her away like a crow to a field mouse. May the devil rot thee."

He spat in her face. With a dogged gait, he left the room.

And there it hung. This man, a cruel slaughterer.

No wonder Grossmutter and Harmon left. This man would have killed them too.

Lexxie struggled to wipe her face with her shoulder, which only helped partially. Meginhardt's mother and the mother of that little Alexandra must be those they call the sister witches. But verily, were witches real? Nay.

What Jonne had said replayed, there being no such sort. Rather, they were someone to blame for another's crime. But that look on GC's face when he thought Lexxie was a witch— frightened for his soul he was.

Another attempt to wipe her face failed, her shoulder now aching.

Witford Dimietris killed Gillam Huber and Meginhardt, his own son. He admitted as much. But not Alexandra. He blamed her mother, this Emmaline, claimed she was a witch, and took her away. How then did the wee babe meet her demise? Poor little thing, "likely a witch" on her grave marker.

Lexxie yanked each fist and both ankles. Dern. The knots were tight. Well, that little Alexandra Dimietris was better off dead than having that madman a father.

And then horror struck. She looked like Emmaline, the babe's mother.

King forbid. I am *Alexandra!*

CHAPTER THIRTY-EIGHT
I AM

In Vereiteln Dorf

MERCY. IT HAD been right there in front of her, all those hints. How did she not see it?

Working harder to breathe only made things worse. Heart pounding, lungs collapsing. Gasping, not possible with a torn shirt stuffed in her mouth.

Hush. She soothed her panic to quell, coaxed the pounding in her chest to slow, instructed her shoulders to relax. Once a rhythmic cycle filled her belly with air through flared nostrils, she allowed her mind to pick up the horrific reality.

Alexandra. Lexxie, a mere nickname.

The room was spinning.

It made sense, but her mind didn't know where to go, preferring to float into a sea of nothingness along with the tidal wave of remorse.

She had it wrong. So very wrong.

Grossmutter and Harmon stole Lexxie—*Alexandra*—away. Then sheltered her life. Too much exposure, and someone might have figured it out. Witford would have come after them. They raised her as Harmon's own. They left their lovely farmhouse, their land. To protect her. It would have been better to let her be. To suffer her fate.

She deserved this punishment.

But then who was underneath that grave marker if not Alexandra Dimietris, the babe known to be "likely a witch"? A snickering from an attempted laugh provided some unexpected relief. *Me, a witch.*

Lexxie threw imaginary punches at her mind till it hurt. She had seen the familiarity in Witford's eyes. Giselle had even mumbled something about looking "just like her." Emmaline, Lexxie's mother. And the priest? He recognized Lexxie. He knew her to be the infant. He could even be the one playing up the witch stories. Even Witford believed it.

Worse, the thought pounded between her temples wanting to escape and vanish, wishing it were not so. Witford Dimietris 'twas her natural father.

All those lectures from Harmon about battling inclinations of anger, the importance of doing good and being kind no matter what . . . Aye, he was concerned she carried borne traits of her natural father.

Tilting her head sideways to better direct a stream of tears, she glimpsed signs of Emmaline, her mother, the mother she never knew. *Were you harmed on this very bed? He treated you sorely. I know that now. Why must you have married such a man?*

Her back ached from his kick. She wretched a stretch as best she could. *Perhaps it was the best way to watch over Meginhardt, your sister's child.*

That brought a warm, kinship smile to Lexxie's heart, a selfless act by her mother. But where was Meginhardt's body now? There had been no sign of his existence in either graveyard.

The wound she earned from the splint in the armoire sent fresh, hot blood streaming down her forehead. Hah, where was that magical hand now?

A ruckus arose at the front door. The belligerent Witford returned, staggering and clattering through the main room and back to her bedside. Quite pleased with himself, a jug in one hand, a mug in the other, he plopped against the wall under the window.

"I always thought that dern priest were lying to me. Holy, holy, holy, says he, the masterful hypocrite. Said you'd come back one day. Put the town on watch fer it, warned everyone that witch Emmaline's gonna come back and take yer chil'en if you don't keep pure." He took a big swig from the jug, perhaps saving the portion in the mug for later. "Gotta commend him—he were right."

This time, he raised the mug to his lips and gulped away. He wiped his chin. "What ya got to say fer yerself? Ya witch."

Was he expecting her to respond? He must have forgotten he shoved a fistful into her mouth. Extreme with discomfort, Lexxie emboldened herself to muscle up that courage she was convinced lived somewhere inside and dared not shut her eyes. Another drop of blood seeped. She rolled her head to the other side, hoping the gore wouldn't impact her vision.

"Why'd ya go to see the priest anyway? Ha, ya jus' wanted to taunt him, didn't ya?" Witford howled. "Wish I'da seen his face when ya tramped inta his church."

Lexxie muffled a groan, urging him to remove the mouth gag or wipe her face or do something remotely human.

"Ah, don't matter. He and Jake'll be here soon. I'll get

my reward coin, and you'll go back to yer home in hell." He laughed heartily and took another swig. "And all the chil'en in this town will be safe. Thanks ta me," he slurred, the drink getting to him as he finger-pounded his chest.

Lexxie kicked her legs to get his attention. Hadn't the priest said she needed to be delivered alive? She pretended to be gasping for final breaths of air. Sadly, it took naught much pretending. She gasped and kicked away until Witford stood and glared glassy-eyed.

"Should jus' bury you straightaway and never mind all this." He yanked the wet balled-up piece of his shirt from her mouth.

Lexxie continued to gag and finally spat.

"Watch yerself. That's my proper quilt." He wiped her brow with the stank cloth.

Heaving, she choked out. "I'm not Emmaline." She breathed in fast to catch some air in case he had a mind to shove that cloth ball back down her throat. "I. Am. Alexandra."

He said nothing.

So, she added. "Your daughter."

"No, ya ain't. Shut yer lips up, or I'll jam this right back down yer throat."

Lexxie revolted, and with pure facial expression, she committed to remaining silent. Breathing was much easier when her mouth wasn't obstructed.

His body swayed, but his gaze remained fixed on hers. He returned to his seat on the floor and back to the wall, easier to balance there probably. Picking up the jug of that amber cider, he commenced an obnoxious drunk laugh. "An' ya know what? The mockery 'tis mine to suffer. 'Cause they haunt me, ya know. Yer dark sister, Lilith, and that dark Gillam. They're always watch'n me." Liquid splashed from his jug as he accentuated *always*. "'Course, ya prob'ly tell them to. Ya always were the bossy one."

A weary Lexxie did not attempt to respond. He obviously wasn't finished.

"Do ya believe in ghosts? 'Course ya do. Ghosts are like cuz'ns of gore ta witches." He broke out laughing as though he made the biggest jest of the century.

An onslaught of uncontrollable hiccups assailed her lungs. A mixture of blood, dirt, and tears forced her eyelids to lock down.

"Ah, shites." Maneuvering against the wall to stand, he went to her. He held her head up and rubbed his forearm across the grime on her face.

Squinching, she accepted when he offered a sip from his bottle, anything to remove the nauseating remnants of his shirt from her mouth.

Then he tucked the doll back into the bedside floor crib, smiling as if it were a real infant, only to snatch it back up. He waved it at her. "Yer mother made this yerself, ya know."

Back into the bedside crib the doll flopped, this time with careless regard.

Aha. He does know I'm not lying. He just admitted I'm his daughter! A warm thought that her mother made the doll floated in her mind. So precious.

Back to the floor, he rested his head on the wall.

Liquid swished as it lifted to dump its contents into the man, fueling his heart and head with heated hatred.

"What now?" She labored but got her question out.

"Keep that loose mouth of yers shut."

She listened to his moans of satisfaction as the pourings down his throat took a break.

"How old are ya?"

"Seventeen." Well sort of. In a couple months, but no matter now.

"Yer mother was past twenty when we married. An old maiden. She was always com'n around, felt sorry fer the stupid boy. I made her believe me." A sick grin spread across his face. "I had nothing"—he accentuated the word with his hands in the air—"nothing to do with his dis'pearance. Wolves got him."

He broke into a roaring belly laugh.

Lexxie dared to ask. "So, no one knows he's there? Buried in your yard."

Meginhardt's body must be under that pile of stones. That's why he talked to it that night.

"Nein, and don't go tell'n anyone. The whole village thinks his witchy ma came back from the dead to git him."

"What was she like? My mother." Reeling, knowing this madman was her natural father, she craved now more than ever any tidbit as to what her mother was like.

They couldn't have been married for long, the calculation hurt. Lexxie's mind spun, so many questions. But she must keep Witford on this track of thinking, letting it sink deeper and deeper, so he'd realize he was harming his own flesh and blood. His daughter. But would that matter to him? Right now, it seemed her only chance.

Amazing he could stagger to his feet. Once he did, he pointed a shaking index finger at her, nearly falling on her. "Yer ma come to figure it out, thanks to that mouthy brat next door, Harmon. He gone an' warned my Emmaline, told her I was a cold-blooded murderer, that I'd gone and done Meginhardt, buried him under that pile of stones."

"That's when you killed Gillam?"

"I was after his boy. Would'a got that little ratbag if Gillam didn't get in the way." Witford's creepy laugh rose and subsided. "Aye, Gillam got what he deserved."

Lexxie's gut roiled. Just the thought of Harmon and Grossmutter coming to grips with such horror. No wonder they refused to speak about it.

"We was short a witch and festival was comin' up. Yer mother got what she deserved too." He slouched back to the floor. "Had to postpone that year so's the baby could be born. My Alexandra, she went and died the same day. They buried her before I had a chance to see her, said it was fer the best." He glowered at Lexxie, probably striving to connect the wee babe he never knew to this woman claiming to be his child, a woman he'd bound.

That's when it happened. Grossmutter and Harmon took her the day her mother was—oh, mercy!—hung a witch. This truth, how was she to digest?

"You never loved my mother, then?" Lexxie mustered the question out, her throat gruff and dry, desperate to hear more, much as he would tell now that he was too drunk to know he was sharing.

"Nah, I liked her good." Witford pointed the top end of the jug toward her to emphasize his point. "Alexandra wasn't supposed to die. When Emmaline died, I come back. Like I said, she was gone."

"You mean when Emmaline was hung."

"Yeah, she failed square as anythin', hung and buried. Jus' like her meddl'n sister."

"That priest knew all this? About your murdering Gillam and blaming my mother?"

"Hah." The swish of the bottle was loud. "Was his idea."

He slammed it on the floor. "But, girlie, yer in trouble."

A long unbearable silence followed. Then a crash. His head against the floor.

Witford had passed out.

Wrists and ankles secured the bed, she laid her head back to mull all that happened today, all that had been said. So much to absorb. An overwhelming weariness was winning. A wallowing of sadness manifested its way through every fiber of her being, a heavy fatigue tempting deep slumber. But that was not to happen, not yet anyway.

Her ears harkened. Interrupting her fall into sweet darkness was a distressing strike of panic, a rushing charge that warned her the worst was yet to come. Dreadful strides of pounding hooves pealed forth, the devil himself was coming near.

CHAPTER THIRTY-NINE
WAKE UP

In Vereiteln Dorf

"WITFORD. WITFORD!" LEXXIE shrieked. Her abdominal muscles strained to support her arching neck. His head had knocked hard on the floorboards, but surely, he'd hear her screams if they were loud enough. "Witford!"

Out cold, he was.

Hoofbeats coming up the road, unmistakable and determined, conjured up terror and angst.

Her kicks were furious, her ankles sore, her knee joints jeopardized. She tightened her buttocks and thrust her legs as forcefully as she could muster. Hoary dust flared out the mattress. The bed jerked and moved. An inch, then another. Like the claws of a wildcat, bedposts squelched the wooden planks.

"Ah, come on, ya old narr. Get up!"

Her bone-tired body tackled its rapid heartbeat. She banged her head backward. He ought to hear that.

This is it. This is it. Inordinate helplessness seized her muscles. The impending doom too traumatic to grasp, her own end too near. She clenched her teeth. If only one wrist were free. She focused on using the sweat on her palm to free a hand.

The horses' pounding pace slowed, gravel crunching underneath their hooves. A jingling of stirrups made the skin on her back shudder with cold.

They'd arrived. She swallowed the increased saliva flow. Her mouth breathing sent unwanted gulps of air to her stomach.

The priest and that Jake crank were right out front.

All limbs stayed securely fastened. Witford must've done this before. The very thought brought a disgusting flash to mind—her mother, tied, helpless, and vulnerable. "You animal. You did this to her too, didn't you?"

Not even his soul made a stir.

A snort from a horse, she recognized it. That same edgy snort she heard from the Huber farmhouse. If there were any chance the visitors outside could have been anyone other than the priest and Jake, this crushed it.

If she were dead quiet, perhaps they'd go away.

A horse whinnied. A man whistled. Jake's gravelly voice called out. "Witford, ya old dog, komm. We're waiting."

Her shoulders twitched. Bolts of shivers took the place of determination. Her deepest mind screamed fear.

She willed herself to pass out. The inability to get free physically couldn't stop the inability to free her soul—her only way to escape. Could she do that?

"By all saints, Witford."

Nay, Jake's holler heightened the alarm.

Don't come in. Don't come in. Please, mercy, don't come in!

No escape, even in spirit. Dirt and bloodstained tears, fresh ones, seeping, stung her eyes, and her with no ability to wipe the sledge away. Her heart ached for safety, the kind of safety that came with love and hope and respect. Even if untied, that safety wasn't to be found in this house.

More whinnying and some stomping and jingling. The men, two of them, dismounted from their horses. Stones crunched beneath their boots.

This hardly being a friendly visit, the men, avoiding the front door, repeatedly slapped the exterior board siding as they headed for the back. As far as Lexxie recalled, that back door was wide open.

The door to this chamber suffered a battering, though still shut. Pure luck, he'd closed it upon his last entrance. Maybe, just maybe, the priest and Jake wouldn't open it. What a sight if they did, Witford passed out on the floor and she bound, a limb to each bedpost.

What would they do, take Witford or her?

Her.

Nothing on this journey compared to this moment—wanting only to retreat into a void of nothingness and remain there, frozen. Be done with life.

The echo of boot heels scuffing the floorboards in the main room pounded inside her chest. Heavy steps trod the main room.

Deathly still, she wallowed. Of course, they'd see the padlock had been tampered.

She strained to recognize the muffled noises beyond the wall, voices murmuring, planks squeaking, a belt shifting, a pistol triggering to ready a bullet, a soft brushing at the door.

"Eh, Witford, ya got company?"

Ye pig.

The door creaking resounded like an explosion in her ears, sending shards of stone to every part of her brain. She willed herself to die. But such an escape wouldn't come.

King. No! Don't let this happen, I beg of you. If you're there, really there, please, please, hear me.

"Well, well. Lookie here. Witford wanted ya fer himself."

The revolting hiss of Jake's voice gathered phlegm at the back of her throat. Even if she wanted to look at him, she couldn't. The discharge from her eyes blinding, the secretions from her nose choking.

She turned her head as far as it allowed.

The priest brushed past Jake and went straight for Witford, searching for a pulse on his cold, sweaty neck. "He's got sense about him. He may be mad, but he's no fool. He's got her for us." Then he stood and stared at Lexxie seemingly forever.

"What?" she demanded.

"What'ja do ta him?" Jake accused.

The priest held his hand flat out, commanding Jake to mute. "Ya shouldn't have come back." The priest's calm thoughtfulness regarded her. He rubbed his bearded chin. "But your timing is heaven-sent."

He then nodded to Jake. "Untie her from the bed. Time's getting short. We'll strut her through town and take her to the back of my rectory."

"An' Witford?" Jake jerked a thumb toward the madman's living corpse.

"Leave him be."

Jake dutifully cut the cloth ties on each of Lexxie's limbs with his pocketknife. Four quick slices.

Crushed with exhaustion, she sagged in place. If only she

could run. Rather, she pulled her wobbly legs into her chest and rocked, then rubbed her wrists.

The priest fetched a linen cloth and brought it over to meet her face.

She pushed his arm away. "You're only getting me ready for some big show of yours. You're going to tell everyone I'm a witch. Desperate, aren't you?"

He tossed the cloth on her lap, so she wiped her face herself.

"Aye, feisty mouth." Jake chuckled and yanked her off the bed, tying her wrists in front of her in a crisscross formation.

Her puffy-eyed gaze wandered to the long rope he attached her to.

"Like I said"—the priest's monotone manner came through—"ya shouldn'ta come back."

Jake gave Witford's feet a nudge with his boot, hard enough to shake his entire body. But Witford didn't waken.

"Let him sleep it off. Wait!" An odd excitement had risen in the priest's voice. He eyed the armoire, opened it, and reveled in what he saw. Dresses.

Her mother's frocks.

He grinned, chose one, and tossed it onto the bed. "Put this on."

He then slapped Jake across the head. The strong hint to avoid watching jostled his satchel of riches.

Then they walked her to the waiting horses like leading a mule. The priest instructed she ride on the back of Jake's horse until they got to the edge of town. "You pull her from there. She'll need her energy for the crowds."

His malignant grin must've satisfied Jake who nodded with yet another annoying chuckle.

The town was spirited. From where had so many people come? The streets were full—men, women, children, carrying sacks, packages, boxes, or bottles, many pulling carts. Carriages making their way through hordes of walkers, horses clicking and maneuvering down its center, one way. A barrage of visitors collected around peddlers on each side. Promotional banners strung high across the main street. Other than a few gashes and discoloring, they seemed to be in good shape.

The words *Annual Justice Festival* sewn in scarlet on white silk flapped against a bright blue sky. While vivid gold silk lettering—*Purification Day, Come One, Come All*—on another banner invited revelers to the main event.

Today, the town would sacrifice a witch, restore its purity, and keep itself safe from supernatural evil for another year. Congratulations to the town leaders. They'd receive immense celebration. Purification Day. Beer and burnt wine would flow like a river. Musicians would play as long as their fingers could endure. Ladies would dance into the night. Most notably, all in honor of the priest, the restorer of holiness, and Jake, the keeper of the tax purse and terminator of sorcery.

Who were these people to sacrifice a harmless woman? They must be blind. She should pity them.

Crowds gathered, wanting to catch a good look as the trio approached the banners.

Jake whined. "Enough, I'll drag her from here. 'Tis what they all come fer."

The priest's headshake, a sliver of relief to Lexxie, appeared to suggest he changed his mind. She avoided Jake's anger-hungry gaze as the priest helped her off his horse and decidedly kept the rope of victory for himself.

Leading their parade, the priest sat tall, one hand on the

back of his saddle, making it easy to glance at his prize. Lexxie, barefoot, walked behind his horse. He had pinned her hair himself, tight and high, so she couldn't hide behind any straggling pieces. He wanted people to see her face. He wanted her recognized. What a pleasant score for him, she looked much like her mother. Witch Emmaline returned.

Flocks roared. Gatherings grew. Onlookers crowded the roadsides. There, a building on the left, the Coaching Inn, Giselle's boarding house. Lexxie sought with pleading eyes for that familiar face. She needed some warmth in her veins. Giselle's gleaming eyes could provide such, at least an inkling. There she stood, sheepishly behind her guests.

Giselle? Lexxie fixed on a glimpse, hair perfected as expected, but Giselle's head hung low, her eyes wouldn't rise to look. Lexxie's hammered heart suffered another kick. Giselle was profiting from this.

A woman on the road clasped her mouth, covered her shock, and grabbed her children tight to her skirt. The next woman used a crucifix to point. Men pumped fists and yelled, "Hang, burn, bury!" One even screamed out her mother's name. "Emmaline, nay you take our children."

Lexxie winced. *I've not come to take anybody's child.*

No sense in even wishing they could understand. Her fate was sealed. Though she felt close now to her mother, imagining the horror she'd gone through. Worse, she walked this same road to her death some seventeen years ago, knowing she was leaving a newborn behind. Lexxie.

The excruciating parade would have been better had Jake dragged her through the street at a galloping pace. The priest took his time. All the seeming faithful went crazy with delight.

CHAPTER FORTY

DECISION DAY

At the River of Times

MEGINHARDT'S TRIP FROM the outer courtyard to the River of Times had been strikingly
different this go-around, the courier taking a
separate route. They entered and exited several tunnels before
gliding into another heavenly fall with fantastical views.
Distant peaks of ice from towering mountaintops. Rotating
pinwheels of lights with spiral arms. Then out of nowhere,
a narrow strip ran across the horizon, no beginning and no
end—lush greenery, banked with a perfect line of flourishing
trees on one side and a fast-flowing, crystal-clear river beside.
As they neared, Meginhardt recognized the pasture to the
water's edge and nothing but a thick curtain of fog opposite
the river.

"Dude, this spot okay?" The eagle courier scanned the
area, moving his head left and right as he approached to land
regardless.

Aye, that's the river. Extreme excitement tickled

Meginhardt's neck. "Good as any." He cast his voice upward, humiliated somewhat, sensing it wouldn't have made a difference had he refused. His guide had already positioned his wings to drag their speed. Had he the option, Meginhardt would have preferred to travel up and down the bank to find the spot where he'd been earlier.

In view now were plenty of gurgling swirls and trailing streaks of dark matter with twists and bends like snakes doing their best to interrupt the paths of clear waters. Their landing was much too quick. His knees rubbed against the rich soil. Then his shoulders and head plopped into a patch of blue ornamental grasses as clawing talons freed their grip.

"Sorry, dude." The courier chortled. "Nearsighted." After strutting away from the riverbank to the bank of trees, he stretched out on his back beneath arching branches, perched his talons into the air, and spread his wings behind his head for a cushiony nap.

Just how had a clumsy bird with a vision disturbance landed a courier job?

"Call me when you're ready to go back." With that, the bird blinked on purpose, leaving a translucent covering over his eye sockets. "Don't think I can't see you, dude, 'cause I can."

Then he became disengaged to whatever it was Meginhardt was there for. In seconds, the oversized courier bird was snoring.

Pulling into a squat, Meginhardt brushed himself off before attempting a full stand, still dizzy. Those airborne journeys spun a head like a top. There'd be no harm in sitting.

But he was here. So now what?

The meadow smelled incredible. Fresh and tender and full

of bounce. Desiring to relax his muscles, he lowered his back to lie down and soak up the invigoration. That bird had a wise idea.

Meginhardt's own body felt overwhelmed by the temperature and atmospheric changes endured, his mind still foggy, his limbs heavy, first his legs, then his arms. Once his shoulders sank into the edifying earth, a long exhale escaped without choice. The soft vegetation pillowed up to meet the gaps under his neck, his lower back, and his knees. Oh how tired he was!

A quick lie-down couldn't hurt. Where did he need to be, anyway? His eyelids closed, and he melted as if in a floating, warm bath of bliss.

But his deep snooze was not for long.

A breeze tickled his nostrils, then slapped his face. Literally. He bolted upward onto his elbows. *Whoa, cry me a mercy!*

Awake and in panic, he scrambled to his feet. *The hog, the hens.* Wiping his clammy hands down his trousers, he remained bent over till his heart settled. *I sacked out. Gotta get at chores . . . before Pa.*

Not desiring a whipping this morning and in a stupor, he darted three strides, tripped, and fell flat.

"Dude?" A croaky voice not far away echoed. "What's wigging out with you?"

Wigg'n out? What did that even mean? Wits returned, the fog of his yester-life dissipated.

Meginhardt anchored up to a stand. *Oh, ya narr.*

He shook his head and cracked his neck once, each side. "Nothing, I forgot. I'm dead. And I'm here." He added a sneer, then a shrug. "Sorry I woke you, bird."

"'Bird,' huh. I'm going to let that go. Besides, dude, it's

not that bad." He laid himself back down, covering his eyes with a wing. "Another thing, look around. Look at yourself. You're anything but dead. Silly fool."

Meginhardt coiled his fist. Never had he even an inkling to think what death might be like. Even so, this was not what he anticipated. "Thanks, Einstein." He repeated the new phrase, not knowing what an Einstein was.

"Ha, you've been hanging around Jophiel too much. He calls all his smart-alecky Arrivals that. 'Cept Einstein ain't even walked the earth yet, not in your time."

"Okay, fly rink. Fine."

Enough. Meginhardt dismissed the courier. A stroll along the riverbank was in order. "Got someth'n to do," he tossed a vague intention to the courier, but the bird had already drifted into another set of snoozes.

Meginhardt walked as though balancing on a beam, one foot in front of the other, a habit of his from those days on the farm when he walked the rows of turnips, more for amusement than any other reason. Toe-heel, toe-heel. Perhaps a direct straight stride would stop his mind from reflecting in circles. A large hand had slapped him awake from his peaceful moment back there. It simply whizzed out from the breeze. *A purpose for that?*

A new bluster picked up, another oddity, only this time more than a scolding breeze. Churning from clockwise to counterclockwise, a wind whirl wrapped itself around his legs. As it lifted upward, his shirt puffed, and then his hair fluffed. It leveraged off the tip of his head, leaving him to shake like a wet farm dog.

Now where'd that come from? Some crazy air waves were giving him a message.

Surroundings shifted and morphed. A veil lifted. The riverbank was no longer a private sanctuary to stroll, rather a busy place, like a town center on market day. Guardians having enormous wings, similar to Jophiel only not as large, escorted or hovered about individuals. Those beings, the humankind sort, must be new Arrivals. Reaching to the side of the riverbank with guarded eagerness, picking up stones from the water's edge, some of them glowed as precious gems. The new Arrivals absorbed themselves in examinations of their stone's character, particularly the etching. Their new names.

Instinctively, he felt his trouser pocket to ensure his was safe and secure. He gave it a bit of a squeeze, and as he did, his heart warmed. Briefly, anyway. *I'm no longer the newish one.*

He'd seen enough now to know, in all likelihood, these new Arrivals would churn into some energy wave, go to that outer courtyard, chitchat with Aivy and that head gatekeeper, and show off their color.

The narrs. Wait till they meet that burly grump.

Then they'd get to enter that gate and hand in their stone. After scratching the back of his head, he patted his hair back in place. Why wasn't he on the same path as all those others? They looked happy. Their lives were probably much simpler than his.

"No, they weren't," a perfectly clear voice in his head replied.

"Who?" He whipped around. He'd heard the response. Aloud, it was, though no one was close by. Someone, some-where, must be watching his every move, listening to his thoughts. Accessing the depths of his being.

He scanned the surroundings. Dozens of eagle couriers milled around by the tree line. All jovial and social they were, polite and smiley.

Guess'n I got the lazy one.

None of them paid much notice to him. And if they did cast a glance his way, they did nothing to acknowledge him. And the many Jophiel-like guardians focused on their own passengers, watching them at the river's edge.

That was okay. Meginhardt hugged himself, used to being alone, not having anyone watch over him. Yet, that voice. Undeniable, someone was paying him attention. Only whoever it be wasn't about to show himself.

An unearthly gurgle in the river bade his interest. With no boulders to break the fast flow, the waters surrounding it appeared deeper. An eerie deep.

He pushed away the account of his mother's drowning. A throng of thick murkiness snaked to the surface. Alarmed by its power, he caught his breath as it gulped swallows of clear waters into its dark drain. The force of its gravity pulled at two nearby watery rotations, a source of burbles and plashes.

He scrambled down the embankment. Then thunder came from somewhere underneath the river. He paused, contemplating a scramble right back up.

"Continue." A voice spoke.

Obeying, without asking why, he searched instead, expecting to find signs of life in those swirls, faces in trapped pieces of rock. And he did, a stone in each, both heading to devastation. That black throng, hungry and seeking to swallow, would suck those living stones into itself.

Meginhardt knew by now what this meant—two beings living out their lives on earth. Did they know they were about to collide? And did they realize a larger and much darker entity was prowling to take ownership of their lives?

A surge of emotion triggered his heart to race. But why

panic? Who were they to him? How was it he happened upon this section of the river anyway? Scolding himself for being silly, he scanned up and down the bank. No beginning and no end. From where the river started and where it ended, was not for him to see. Thunderous warning noises roiled from somewhere underneath, threatening to totter his footing. Surely, someone must hear that roar?

Yet, not a single character, neither the escorts nor the couriers nor the many new Arrivals seemed alarmed. What kind of place was this where no one cared?

Double-checking both ways ensured no one was paying him any mind. The stones in distress sparred as though in some kind of warring exchange. Surely, he could at least grab one of them. If no one in this place was interested, so be it. But he wouldn't stand by and let them drown like Pa did to his mother.

His toes burdened with the crouching weight of his body. Silky wet from the river's spray, he leaned over the waters to snatch whichever of the two stones he could hook first with his reaching open fist.

"Psst."

On the opposite riverbank squatted that same rebel character, striving to get noticed. He strained a flexible neck over the waters. "Hey, bud, psst."

Oops. Meginhardt had nearly forgotten his business, the reason he came back to the river in the first place. Good be it the rebel appeared, reminding him.

"Good to see ya, and hey, you came to your senses." Once he stopped with the happy-footed jig, the goofy sort of character spoke loud and confident. His voice carried well atop the river gurgles, and with some urgency, he waved Meginhardt closer. "Don't go putting your hand in there. It'll sizzle you good, right through your bones."

Quite pleased to see the rebel, Meginhardt pulled his hand back, dropping the idea of rescuing some stone. Hadn't Jophiel claimed some consequence should one stick an unprotected hand beyond the bank's edge and into the gushing flow?

"Yeah, I came to see ya." Meginhardt stood tall.

Something was familiar about this guy, like they already knew each other, more than just their earlier encounter. Someone who understood him well. Truly a good friend.

Butterflies of excitement encouraged the idea of a companion, though decidedly, he produced a stoic response. "You got an offer, ya said? Someth'n about helping me set things right with my pa?"

What might getting things right even entail? He starved for Pa's approval and affection, yet despised how the man lied, leaving him to want nothing but revenge. Either way, his business with Pa was unfinished.

"Sure, sure, 'course, but look, your pa's in trouble." The rebel pointed at the darker of the two ferocious swirls.

That's Pa . . . in trouble?

"Toss me your stone. That'll get you over here. Then we can fix this whole mess. Together. I know how to move things around in this here river, been doing it a long time now." Flashing an encouraging grin, the rebel urged Meginhardt by cupping his hands to a ready position so as to catch Meginhardt's precious stone. "Come on. I'll teach ya."

Meginhardt gave the stone in his trouser pocket a gentle rub with his thumb as he forced a lump to settle in his throat. His stone represented everything and all that he was. It might not be much, but still, it's who he was. Would he give it up for Pa? Handing over his stone would be like giving up on himself.

Nay. There had to be another way. "How about you fish Pa out and toss him over to me?" The negotiation began, but wait! What was he asking? Did he just ask for Pa to die because he wanted his stone fished out the river? Just how did this work? Was it that simple?

"Don't work like that." The rebel shook his head back and forth like an agitated horse.

"So, is that there the girl?" Meginhardt pointed to the second stormy swirl. It was a guess, a good one.

"Yeah, some sister, huh? If she tempers your pa's storm, he'll be hung for sure. But don't worry. Like I said, we got action going on. She's about to become a cake of mud." The rebel winked and chuckled. "Just like ya wanted. And a little bonus fer ya—yer pa's gonna be okay."

"About that." Alternating his hands, Meginhardt pulled hard on his fingers and swallowed a chunk of pride. "Move her away from the bank so she doesn't get lodged."

Lips formed a scary slant across the rebel's face. A sinister cockle burst forth from his throat. "What did that kingdom up there say to ya? You suddenly got a soft spot?" His condescending smirk implied dominance. "You're the protective bro now? Seriously?"

Nay. All stones aside, Meginhardt had made a commitment to himself. Crossing his arms, he'd challenge this bully straight on.

The rebel head-nodded to the location of the stone. "You were trying to save her, weren't you? Is that why you came back? To turn your back on your pa? On me?"

"What's it to you?" Memories of Pa's scornful taunts ran

through Meginhardt's veins, and his jaw tensed. "If'n I wanna spare her, that's my business. It don't mean anythin'."

"Come now. I'm on your side."

Behind the rebel, a clearing appeared, an entire army of like characters to the one cutting the deal.

"Look, we are here for you." He loosened up and offered open hands. "We can help. We can fix it. All of it. Give you another chance with your pa by bringing you here with us. 'Cause this is where he's coming once he's done. He's smart. He's already loyal. And together, we blow your little sister into that riverbank so she stays good and stuck and can't hurt your pa. That's all. We don't want to see your pa harmed. Do you?"

Even the look in his eyes matched the apology in his smile. "You're gonna just let her have the legacy that rightfully belongs to you? After everything you've been through? Really? I'd been told you were dumb, but hey, I don't think you are."

A voice inside Meginhardt's head, quiet but distinct, assured a different message, something about being worthy. He shooed that silly notion away. Had he overreacted with this rebel guy?

"You can give me a fresh start with Pa. How do I know you're not lying?"

"I guess you don't. But those kingdom busybodies didn't help you much all those years before you got here, did they? So, who you gonna believe?"

It was so confusing. Who to believe? Who to trust? His mother had warned him not to be revengeful. But then she skipped away, leaving him a second time.

Enough. He needed to feel in control. "I don't want him hung like a schurke." Though he deserved that. A wind brushed past again, one direction, then the opposite, messing his hair into a frenzy.

The rebel tossed up his hands. "We can do that." Then he paused with a shrug and helpless tone. "But then we gotta do something about that sister. At least temporarily."

Meginhardt patted the mop on his head back into place. More than anything, he wanted the fresh-start part, a whole new relationship with his father. 'Course, that, plus a family of his own. Those were worth whatever he had to give. "Family. What about a family? Can I get that too?"

"Absolutely! We'll teach you how to bring others into the fold. For sure, we're good at that. Do it all the time."

"That's possible?" *Milk me a pigeon. A family of my own.* That was worth everything and anything, no matter who had to suffer. Especially someone he'd never even met.

A cunning smile creeping across an otherwise vague face, the rebel beckoned Meginhardt. "Just toss your stone, bro, and we'll seal the deal."

The business of that girl destroying Pa's future gave him pause. That wasn't right, neither. If she was a threat, Meginhardt ought to do something.

Decision made, Meginhardt reached into his trouser pocket and coiled a fist around his stone. His right arm readied a position to toss it across the waters. "Temporarily, you say?"

"Ah, I told ya—"

"Because"—Meginhardt's snap interrupted the rebel's hesitance—"she don't deserve to exist, and I, Meginhardt Dimietris, wanna be the one to filch her stone right out of that dern river."

CHAPTER FORTY-ONE
SPIRIT OF THE DEAD

In Vereiteln Dorf

LEXXIE KEPT HER gaze downward. Tears dropped and washed her sore, bleeding feet as the bloodthirsty parade ceased at the church stairs. The priest dismounted and pulled his prize witch to his side. Jake guarded in case she'd make a run or—she grunted—some kind of magical fly away. He took the reins of the rope and held on tight so the spirited crowd could witness the tension of her imprisonment.

The priest's next move exuded grace and authority. A simple sign, his hand held high, and the crowd quietened. He appeared to be in his glory with an oh-so-serious heartfelt look. He addressed his waiting audience.

"Our King in Heaven delivers. On this, our Annual Purification Day, the heavens have dropped the greatest impurity of all on our doorstep."

The crowd roared to which he nodded before reinserting his hand into the air for another bout of quiet.

"Some of you say bring her down to the water and test her. But there is no need. For we, your dedicated leaders, have already confirmed a verdict. She has already been tested. Some of you were witnesses."

The crowd began a chant. "Hang, burn, bury. Hang, burn, bury."

Fists pumped the air in rhythm. "Hang, burn, bury."

And so it went in unison and for seemingly an eternity.

Lifting that powerful hand once again to silence the crowd, the priest gave instruction to meet at the gallows in three hours. "Go, my friends, enjoy drink and food and fellowship, for this town will soon, once again, be the purest in the region."

The crowds cheered and dispersed, heading straight for the town's drinking and food establishments to load up their veins and stomachs with courage and relief. Then purchase some souvenirs, the kind they could hang in their home to keep it purified for another year.

"What witnesses?" Lexxie choked out while led to the back of the church via a path outside. She glanced at the burial stones where she first glimpsed that madman, the man who took lives for his own prideful pleasure, the man who destroyed her dreams. She spat a balled-up assortment of spew toward the graveyard.

"Don'ta fret, frilly. You shan't the privilege to be housed here." Jake cackled. His evil sure-footedness moved her along with purpose, the pursuit of riches clinking with each step.

No one answered her question. Who witnessed a trial that proved her so impure she was to be hung, burned, and buried?

Upon reaching the entrance to the rectory, the trio descended a set of outdoor stairs to a heavy door leading into the church cellar. An odor assaulted her nose. Jake gave her a shove when she hesitated to go any farther. It wasn't the odd mixture of smells, livestock droppings and fermented grapes that bothered her, nor even the dank mold, but rather the wafts of rotting meat. 'Twas that odor of human remains?

A glossy sweat sheened the bricked wall of the cellar facing the graveyard. Aye, she must be right. The stank of those bodies rotting in the church burial grounds was leaking into this space. Both hands, still tied in front, met her gagging mouth and did their best to massage her throat.

Though her squint stabbed like daggers, it was her tongue that pierced the air. "Only demons themselves could live in this stink."

Saying nothing, the priest led her down a short hallway to a second heavy door, this one with a lock on its latch. The odor settled once they stepped through.

The surprising décor intrigued her enough to muster her head high to take it in. A moderate-sized space, the ceiling much higher than the hallway was quite telling. A room reserved for celebrations. An elongated refectory table in the center, set for a grand meal. A private banquet with six place settings. At each, a linen napkin folded with perfection atop a pile of three plates with brimming gold rims. Three wine cups per setting also gleamed with a recent polishing. So many forks and knives and spoons to count. Fresh boutonnieres bobbed within finger glasses half filled with water. Engraved crystal wine carafes remained in reach no matter where one sat. An ornate bowl of fruit, a bouquet of fresh flowers, and a basket of breads and cheeses, all waited to be enjoyed. A sideboard equally graced with a soup tureen, crisscrossed serving utensils, and several more carafes. Certain a servant or two would wait upon this secret group of celebrants. Urns chock-full of spices at each corner masked most lingering and seeping unpleasant smells.

"Ah, everything is ready." The priest beamed his satisfaction at the table. Surely, he'd be the host.

A row of painted portraits hung along one side of the room, side by side, each of a woman's fresh face and smartly dressed bodice. Their sad eyes faced the wall-filled mural across the room of a suffering mother, holding her baby tight, who also suffered a digging sadness.

Lexxie frowned—suffering and glory. That concept had been a challenging point for Harmon. He required continual assurances from their priest in Avondale, who was nothing like the one a rope attached her to, that if we were to share in glory, we were to share in suffering.

Was this her suffering? Did she ask for this, simply because she wanted the truth? All of this, so confusing, so dark and evil. Pure deceit. This couldn't be how it ended.

Harmon floated in and out her thoughts. He carried this deep secret for so many years, a dark past.

A short, eager man entered from the opposite end, carrying a wooden box with a pinhole, a heavy gold curtain trailing. A portrait artist. She'd heard of such during one of Grossmutter's lessons. Such a scientific contraption allowed artists to see, then trace, outlines of landscapes. Though some folk rejected paintings from artists known to use it. Well known it was that when one viewed the world from inside the darkened box, the world becomes upside down. Worse, one would witness two realms, the earthly and the spiritual, colliding. All magic. Grossmutter said the latter to be pure unsinn. How

Grossmutter knew so much about the modern world when she rarely left the farmhouse, was a mystery by itself.

Behind him, a scouring woman, bent and physically fragile, bustled in. "Trickster." The old woman shook a finger at Lexxie. "Let's git on with it. Sit. There."

That morning Lexxie first saw her at church seemed so long ago now. This time, instead of a polishing rag, the old woman carried a basket. Ornate pots of red ochre, jars of powder, brushes and small sponges wobbled.

Get on with what?

As though he were a friendly advisor, the priest nudged her by elbow to the row of portraits. His wry lips eager to share. "The old guard kept their hair clips. As for me? Recalling the visage of wickedness—well, that is pure wisdom."

Was she supposed to be impressed?

Each woman sat at the end position of an elegant banquet table, the spot reserved for either the host or guest of honor. Stiff with hands crossed on their laps, hair styled simple and neatly tied. Eyes a despondent longing to message the onlooker. Fifteen portraits in a double row. He walked her past each one, lingering to read the names etched on plaques underneath.

She stopped at L. Dimietris—Lilith.

"Your dear sister Lilith." He twisted a smile.

Witford's drunken, misguided reference swirled anew. Lifting her wrists, Lexxie fingered the etching and studied the face. So very young, couldn't be any older than Lexxie. Her facial muscles challenged to make room for a wee sad smile. *My dear aunt, I wish I knew you.*

The priest tugged her to the next portrait, another Dimietris.

E. Dimietris. *Emmaline. Mother.*

Her dry throat choked. The woman in the portrait presented a splitting image of herself, but more mature. More worn with age and contriteness. Lexxie examined her mother's forehead, her cheekbones, her lips so softly painted across her face. No amount of ceruse or red dye could conceal the pangs of sorrow in those pure eyes. Lexxie lifted her hands, wanting to stroke her mother's face.

But the priest pushed them down, away from the portrait. Same bodice even, her mother was wearing the same frock Lexxie was dressed in. It was obvious what would happen next. They were going to wash and fix Lexxie up for a portrait to hang in this room forever while they celebrated and feasted her demise.

"Curious," she probed. "Why bother with another portrait if I am already on your wall?" Would he reference her as *E* for Emmaline or *A* for Alexandra?

He crossed his arms. "Pity. Indeed, you are a thinker."

"If I be Emmaline, shall you not be frightened?" She gritted her teeth, producing an evil taunt. "I commit to return with even more vengeance—only *you* shall be my most precious target." Would he dismiss her threat and prove he knew well she wasn't a witch?

"You, my dear, are my truth." He spoke without a flinch.

Truth? In light of deceit, perhaps that was true and as much of a confession she'd get from this man, a false priest. Truth was she was Alexandra and living proof he had a hand in a scheme destroying so many lives.

"Ye truth is pure deceit. Lies, greed, power. You don't deserve your position. Ye a lying tongue." Lexxie spoke up for a King she hardly knew, realizing then she wanted to change that. She'd met the devil herself, time to meet the King.

"E. Dimietris, Revenant, if you must know." He chuckled, finally answering about the plaque, and rested his palm on the blank spot beneath her mother's where Lexxie's portrait would soon hang.

His wrathful grimace disgusted her.

Revenant. A return from death. She dizzied, her head weighty, the truths she'd discovered on this journey too heavy to bear any longer. Her eyes rolled up, then back into her head, snatching a gleaming flash from the orange flicker in the elaborate oil chandelier. With loss of all mindfulness, her body fell into a peaceful slice of midnight blackness.

CHAPTER FORTY-TWO
AWAKEN

In Vereiteln Dorf

"GO FROM ME!" Awake from a stupor, Lexxie jerked her body hard, knocking the elderly woman for a tumble. Instinctively Lexxie apologized. Then her senses kicked in, rationalizing her surroundings. She was dreaming. Nay, a horrible nightmare.

This *is* the horrible nightmare!

"Look what ya done," the crippled woman complained. Side-rolling to a bony hip, she negotiated the hardness of the floor, upper body first, then her head. From her hands and knees, she crawled her way back to a crooked stand. "Now that yer awake, sits up in the chair so's I can finish the job."

How long had she been unconscious?

Burly forearms from behind wrapped around Lexxie's chest and hauled her upright and into a proper chair, velvet and with cushion. As she relished the insignificant comfort, a terse headache pounded. *Why couldn't I remain in sleeping bliss? Shall even death forsake me?*

Whatever happened to a soul after one died had to be better than this. Tension around her scalp disturbed her. Wrists still secured, she stomped her foot to loosen the tightness. Hairpins, the cause. This scrubbing-bucket woman had fixed Lexxie's hair with taut pulls and now applied cosmetic paint to her pale, sweaty cheeks. They took advantage of a fainted stillness to prepare her mien, a raving wolf clothed to trick the masses, straight on from the front, anyway.

With the camera-obscura in place, the portrait craftsman chatted with the priest and Jake. She glimpsed yet another man, his humped shoulder and eye patch visible. When did the stonecutter arrive?

Receiving some whispered instruction from the priest, he sneered at Lexxie. "Ree–search. Bugger ya." He and his long dirty fingernail limped out the room.

Of course, he was etching a tombstone. Her grave marker. Er, rather, he was finishing the one he started before she arrived. Someone had to be sacrificed today. What luck for them she sauntered into their dilemma. What name would be used? Perhaps—Ghost of Emmaline, Definitely a Witch.

"I am not Emmaline. You know that, right?" No one paid her mumblings any mind.

Rather, the old woman raised her hands in exasperation. "'Tis the best I kin do. Tell ya the truth, her face sends a chillin' down me spine."

The priest waved the woman out the room with her basket of brushes and powders.

The portrait craftsman grinned. His turn. "Jungfrau, sit yourself over there."

Jungfrau. How sarcastic to be polite and use manners, pretty them up before the slaughter.

Not wanting assistance from that show of muscle who loomed in the shadows, she moved, her sore hips aching for attention. A slow bend forward, she backed into the chair at the head of the banquet table, fit for a queen. Except, she was no queen. She would be a witch the town celebrated with each passing annual Purification Day. Another one caught. Hang, burn, and bury circle-tracked inside her head. But first, a tracing for a portrait painting. How horrid.

Her bound hands neatly folded on her lap, Jake maneuvered a rope around the circumference of her chest inclusive of her chairback. Surely, the rope would be absent from the painting.

Her gaze affixed to the priest. Courage moved to her lips. "How does this benefit you? Him, I get." She gestured to Jake. "It's a big deal out there today. Folks spending plenty. Keeps the town thriving. More for him to skim from the tax purse. But you, a priest, how do you gain from this madness of lies? Such deceit."

Jake drew a sharp yank on the rope, the banding making it painful to breathe.

Oops. Perhaps the timing of her spew had been unwise.

At the word *lies*, the portrait craftsman removed the heavy gold curtain spread across him and his equipment. "What say you?"

The priest shooed off a wave in response, and the craftsman went back underneath to his dark place to work, toying with the box's position to capture what he'd been hired to do.

The priest smiled and clasped his hands before his cassock. "My dear child, no lies hath this tongue been known to speak. I see it my duty to cleanse our town of the likes of you."

"I've no supernatural powers. Tell me, I demand of you, what have you witnessed? Why does this entire town think

me to be my mother, someone to harm them? Lest you lie."
She had nothing to lose with her verbal challenge. *Go ahead.
Choke me again, Jake.*

"Oh, there's a connection you fail to see." Stroking thin
chin hairs on his cocked neck, he produced a serious glare.
"By association, my dear." He strode toward the portraits
and knocked his knuckle on her mother's visage, then added
a second knock, this one on her aunt's. "Your mother and
her sister caused perilous distress to my flock. Well . . ." He
opened both palms wide and high. "You've seen for yourself
what they've done to poor Witford. The man's gone mad.
A shepherd must protect its sheep, keep them safe, remove
anyone who threatens their well-being."

He snapped his fingers in the air and commanded there'd
be no more discussion. Time had run out. She didn't get much
by way of answers.

She gritted her teeth, lips slightly open, as per the portrait craftsman's requirements for a drawn-out length of time,
before Jake shoved a bag reeking of dirty wet stockings over
her head. A heavy door creaked, and a shuffling of boots came
near, bringing with them hot breath that fell on each of her
shoulders. More men arrived. Two grabbed an elbow and
guided her through a long cellar passageway.

Once she stepped outside, the cool breeze did nothing to
ease the flaring rashes on her arms nor refresh the suffocating
heat surrounding her head. Light rays were diminishing as the
sun was falling in the west, nothing to stop its course. If only
she could get a message to Harmon and Grossmutter!

I'm so sorry. A torrent of sadness rushed her veins, then
awakened to anger when a lance from behind poked her to
carry on, like an ox to its slaughter.

Hate-filled hearts lined the path from the church to the gallows. Excitement raged as they approached the platform. Then the crowd exploded when Lexxie, lifted by her elbows, was carried up the wooden stairs, the tops of her swollen feet knocking each step.

The men let go.

She froze. Blinded by the hood, she knew what lay ahead by mere steps.

"Hang, burn, bury." The words circled like a treadle in her ears, pumping to quarter her flesh. A hand, gentle yet pure evil, guided her elbow, positioning her to face the crowd.

As though he himself wasn't possible of harming another, the priest must've held his free hand up to mute the rumbling cheers. "My fellow citizens, my loyal following, all King's children, I say to you ye may rest with peace abounding ye souls tonight."

Lexxie's gut sickened with the adulations. How foolish could these people be?

"You are the evil one." On the heels of her words, the metal tip of a lance dug in between her shoulders. Her wince and groan went unnoticed.

This time, the priest seemingly reveled in glee at the boisterous applause, taking his time to settle the people down as he surely once again raised that influential hand with a godlike manner.

"Hear ye this, my good people, you are deserving of a town pure and safe. I give you my solemn promise, to carry out my duties as your loyal servant." The crowd went crazy. He stopped them to continue. "No matter the consequences. When evil herself lurks, I must cage it and send her back to that deceitful dragon of the universe, the master of all evil, a leader this woman cannot deny." He gripped Lexxie's wrist, and his thrust yanked her arm high. "Recognize this one?"

Another man's arm tore the smelly hood from her head, its wool snatching with it an oily film that had congealed over the reopened wound on her forehead.

Lexxie blinked to lessen the sting in her eyes. If she had a free hand, she could have swiped them clean. The blur of colors, moving bobs with limbs, screaming mouths, thousands of them it seemed. Hundreds anyway. From where had they come? People lined both sides of the lake, known for its depth, said to be ten times deeper than its width she'd heard said. The perfect place for water trials.

She imagined her mother being pushed off the cliff's ledge.

Had Harmon witnessed that horror? If only he would have told her!

The crowd's sound changed. Many gasped, shocked by Lexxie's face. Several chanted the usual ugly wishes for her demise. Others yelled out her mother's name. "Witch Emmaline."

Some doubters grumbled in shock. "The snake awakes?"

They believed she was her mother. Agonizing sorrow Lexxie felt for her mother, yet a privilege to learn she was much like her, not just in looks, but surely by voluminous empathy and bold courage.

At the top of his lungs, the priest himself confirmed it. "She came back once to take her infant child. She'll not take anyone's child this time." He pounded his index finger into his chest. "No, we, my friends, will send her back with nothing but herself."

She imagined a wave of anticipation overtaking his audience.

"We don't simply hang—what do we do?"

"Burn!" the crowd roared.

"And then to be sure they won't return yet again, like this one, what shall we do with the ashes?"

"Bury!" they united, no more gasping.

The hood shoved back over her head. She felt a tugging at her frock. She struggled as two men behind her on the platform removed it from her, leaving her in naught but a shift, adding humiliation to the circling emotions.

"Ye are of your father, the devil," the priest screeched in her ear.

The crowd picked up their chanting again with complete unison and enthusiasm: "Hang, burn, bury. Hang, burn, bury."

She knew their fists were emphasizing each syllable.

Her shoulders weakened from the madness. He'd convinced them her mother came back from the dead and took Lexxie, little Alexandra, with her.

Her head, a heavy boulder, fell forward, her brain swelling with hopeless toxic thoughts. Two men held her so she couldn't faint, for the show was only beginning. Who wanted to watch an unconscious witch be hung? No, they needed her alive. A stiff wallop to the back of her knees was hint enough.

Still, resistance came natural and forceful when they shuffled her to the trapdoor. Her heart palpitated. She swallowed hard. Tears flowed, but no one knew. No one cared. No one could see her eyes under the hood nor know the innocence of her soul. Her toes felt the join between the two flaps, and her chest, the hollowness of death beneath her feet.

CHAPTER FORTY-THREE
DEFEATED

In Vereiteln Dorf

DEFEATED, LEXXIE RAISED her head. The thought of a King, an afterlife, a just world delivered a sliver of much-needed peace. *King, I give ye my life. What's next is up to you. I accept my death.*

Gathering tatters of loose bloomers into balls inside her tied fists, she commanded her breath to slow down. An evening breeze fluttered across her midriff. If only she could will it upward to cool the hot burning skin on her face.

Pages flipped close by. So the priest would read something from his book, quoting and justifying his murderous deed. He repeated a roundabout accusation—she'd come back from the dead and snatched a child once, and now, she'd come back for another.

"Liar," she belted out, her head dizzy from the exertion. The wool cover sucked inside her mouth upon the inhale.

"Did ye hear?" he egged the crowd. "Blasphemy."

So much voluminous chattering, exhausting. Till someone

spoke out employing authority, a man within the crowd. A familiar voice, someone she knew. Her heart skipped. *What said he?*

"That is my daughter. She has not come from the dead as you speak."

The crowd quieted.

Anticipation grew.

The man's voice rang loud and clear.

Lexxie held her breath. Her heart pounded. The organs in her body released their tightness, and she felt a wetness, a relief of urine. Her shoulders dropped as though she needn't be on guard any longer.

Harmon?

She wanted this man to speak again, to promise her she wasn't hallucinating. Be it the nurturing guardian she scolded for his lies in Avondale, then left beaten in Mittel Dorf? *Why come for me? So undeserving am I.*

She shook, this time for different reasons. Had she made better choices she could have avoided this terrible journey.

"Harmon, no," she squealed.

They'd arrest him. They'd hang him alongside her!

For she knew the truth now. He'd taken her, in secret, for her protection. He raised her as his own loving daughter. He gave up their life, their home of wealth and farm of plenty, to take on a poor existence and a lonely life, hiding amid a rural farm community in Avondale. *All for me.*

"Hang me. Get this over with. Send that man away!" She commanded with a muffled but loud voice, hoisting her shoulders back up, her head high. Denying his claim was the only way to keep him alive and unharmed.

A breeze wavered through the crowd, warning a shush.

Amazing, a provoked crowd of so many, and in an instant, eerily tranquil.

Then a sucking sound. Revolting. That priest must be licking his lips. She imagined him clasping his palms together in glee.

"Well, isn't this amusing?" Slow, prolonged steps thudded to the edge of the platform. "Identify yourself."

Careful to avoid any shift of her weight, she leaned an ear forward and willed the scraping and sliding of shuffling to cease.

"This woman is Alexandra Dimietris, and she is my daughter. You know full well who I am."

Gasps and whispers surged through the gathered people much like a swelling rush of falling rocks.

"Har—"

The crack of a whip interrupted her murmur.

She couldn't make out the priest's whisper, a command of some sort, then Jake's aye to follow it. The platform vibrated from a body lurching off. A fury of horse gallops followed. She became aware of the excessive twitch in her fingers. A rhythmic beat pulsed inside her head.

"Harmon, we haven't seen you in years. 'Tis a joyous reunion, indeed." The priest's smoothed his voice over his scherz. "Though, I caution you—answer well. State your business with this woman."

The planks beneath her jilted. Was the priest threatening to trigger? A spear needled into her back, reminding her to hold her tongue. She bit her bottom lip and savored in Harmon's long, exhausted sigh as it wafted upward.

"I took her."

Nay, nay, nay, nay, Harmon. Please let it go. This is my fault. You needn't be punished for my foolish head.

Her courage took its stand. "I know not this man. His voice is nothing familiar." This time, the spear drew blood. "Oh, just end it."

She lost all senses and hope. Who cared anyway?

"Pull that forsaken lever, I say." The hoarse words rasped her throat.

The priest rushed to her side and yanked the hood off her head.

She gasped and relished the freshness of the air soaking her face and entering her lungs. Blinking soothed the sting in her eyes and allowed her pupils to focus. Still, her throat bulged in immense dryness.

Harmon. So desperately, she wanted to get to him, to hear his consoling words, and to receive the fatherly love she missed. Tightening her painted-red lips, she couldn't—no, wouldn't. She shook her head.

He must be made to understand!

He mustn't admit any guilt. They mustn't hang him too. They'd be side by side in an unconsecrated graveyard for souls destined for hell. Fresh tears slipped past her cheeks and down her neck. "Nay," she mouthed to him.

Puffing his chest out made his stand even taller. "I took her as an infant away from Witford Dimietris, that murdering beast." Arms at his side, he pumped his fists and readied to defend if needed. "I raised her as my own. She is my daughter. Not by your law, but by the law of love and common sense to protect."

"Common sense to protect?" The priest spat the words like they were refuse. "This community protects its own." His teeth clenched, his face fiery red. Had the townspeople seen the priest's temper before? He backed down. "She denies you."

He spread arms to the crowd. "This woman has denounced this man with her own lips. His interruption only delays the purification this town deserves."

The crowd roared again, cheering and chanting: "Hang, burn, bury. Hang, burn, bury."

Watching men eager to attack Harmon was torturous. If she could reach and pull the lever herself, she would. "Leave him be! Leave him be. He's done nothing wrong. Please."

"Wait." Another voice rolled above all others. A young scrawny male cleared his way to the front and sprang onto the platform.

GC? The I'm-telling, wild-hare pastor's son? Impossible.

GC cast a glean across the horizon. He had indeed a large audience, all eyes on him. Even with blurred vision, Lexxie sighted his tidy ponytail quivering against his trembling back. Surprised she was when his voice boomed, demanding an answer. "If she doesn't know this man, why does she plead for his innocence?"

The lad's hands spread out questioningly. A deep sincerity in his eyes sought many faces, pausing before moving from one to another. It be evident, that art of oratory came natural from his father. But no one could be aware of his knocking knees.

Frozen midair were the arms and fists welting Harmon. Giving this lad attention, alongside the crowd, all let go, allowing their victim to drop.

Harmon scrambled to his feet, stuffed his shirt into his trousers, and hastily tightened the cord. With a look of faith, he gazed toward this young lad who'd taken the stage.

Mercy me, now what?

Harmon stepped forward and reached for the young lad's hand for a yank up to the platform.

The priest challenged the move, pushing Harmon's chest to topple him backward, laughing at the harshness of his landing. Such a surprising move for a priest in public display.

Dismay trickled throughout the crowd. Many helped Harmon stand and shook their fists, this time at the priest. Questioning shouts rumbled.

Realizing his error, the priest fell to his knees. "Forgive me, King. The evil among us tempted me to harm a man. I've no hatred within my bones. These people"—he swept a wave across his audience—"know I am a man of peace and justice." He stood, apparently trusting his public prayer to erase the unease in the crowd and restore their loyalty to him and him alone.

"We wanna hear what Harmon says," yelled out one townsman.

"Give him a chance. Let 'im speak," commanded another.

Then another shouted, "I grew up with Harmon! He's not the infant steal'n type. A woman for a wife maybe, but not an infant."

Everyone laughed.

The impressive GC kept his hands high throughout the chattering of the masses and encouraged Harmon to join him on the platform.

With obvious reservation, the priest backed down. His face churned a paleness, though Lexxie was not about to stare for a confirming look. His public display of prayer hadn't worked. This would only madden him more.

The spear, nudged secure into her back, released. The slice of freedom felt redemptive.

Perhaps there was hope?

And as for miracles, as slight as he was, GC lifted Harmon to the platform.

The crowd clapped and cheered.

Harmon faced her.

The rope that led her through town like a mule still tight on her wrists echoed a tap, tap, tap against the trapdoor from the quivers controlling her core. If only she could fall into his arms. How could this man ever forgive her? Did he not realize he was giving up his life for her? How could she have doubted his love?

With aggression, she turned her head away. She couldn't let him.

If she welled up inside even a little more, they needn't hang her. She'd simply choke to death on her foolishness. *I don't deserve this grain of hope.*

A scuffing and shuffling of heels from behind stole her attention. The priest stood in a blocking position, intentionally to hide the spear-thrusting man's grip on the trapdoor lever. Opaque red fluid dripped from the metal ferrule held upright at his side. If that man was so eager to draw her blood, he'd be eager to place pressure on the lever and send her tumbling.

GC faced the crowd, obviously excited all ached to hear his words, confirmation as to his own self-worth and, potentially, Lexxie's innocence. *Potentially.* Perhaps all more so to make his pa proud.

The priest burst forward with his hand raised high. "Ah, here comes Witford Dimietris himself. He can clear this up for us. He will testify this woman is, in fact, who we say she is—Witch Emmaline, the devil's daughter herself, back from the dead." He hoisted up Lexxie's arm as if they didn't know whom he was talking about. "And need I remind you why she returned? What is it she wants?"

He shoved Harmon aside and pointed to a galloping horse coming forth, ridden hard by Jake with someone hanging on behind, bouncing like a rag doll.

That someone was indeed Witford.

In truth, whether I live or die will depend on him?

Witford knew the truth. But, with all the liquor in his veins and hatred in his heart, would he choose the reward coin and be the hero of Purification Day? Or would he take the path to his own hanging if all truth were exposed?

CHAPTER FORTY-FOUR
INTERRUPTION OR INTERVENTION

At the River of Times

THE PROMISE OF a new life. Everything Meginhardt ever wanted. What was left to think about? His mother, the one who pranced away at Aivy's snap without looking back? Nay, that dream—the one of a nurturing, comforting mother—had shattered like a cart over a cliff. The rebel's deal, far too tempting to ignore, offered a budding new connection with Pa and a family to call his own.

It was time. Time to forge onward.

Meginhardt had made his decision. All that was left was to toss his stone over the river.

Extending a throwing elbow behind his back, he thrust his chin forward. This was it. No more aloneness. No more lies. He was taking charge for a change. As a matter of fact, for the rest of his existence. His thumb rested on the stone inside his fist as his torso pivoted. His throw must have velocity enough to get the stone over those raging waters.

Hazarding the horror should it fall short was something he preferred not to contemplate. Likely, it would dissolve along with his entire existence. A risk worth taking. Why not? Shan't anyone miss him.

His eyes squared up the target, direct into the cupped hands of the grinning rebel on the opposite riverbank. From his leg muscles to the rotation of his hips, his whole body committed to the throw. A deep breath took the edge off his nerves.

Under the pressure of his thumb, something twisted and moved. His stone was squirming. Reeling, in fact.

Dern it. He tightened his fist. He was going through with this even if remorse cut loose and darted about inside his chest.

"Argh!" Something razor-sharp pierced his neck, crippling his shoulders. His throwing arm fell limp. His fingers suffered a sharp cut. His stone toppled free.

Talons, having gripped him as prey, secured the lift. Long eagle feathers sliced the airflow, enabling an impressive soar upward. Already Meginhardt was above the treetops, staggering vision ablur. His heavy head dangled. His legs swayed as the eagle courier circled freely before preparing to dive as if to attack.

"Secure it," the eagle courier demanded.

Meginhardt battled the gravity drag from the unexpected flight and reached for his stone as they swooped past where it wriggled out from his fist on the bank. "Got it."

Once settled beside a line of oak trees distanced from the gurgling river, he rubbed his neck, sore from the surprise maneuver, a hostile ambush.

"I'm not supposed to give any advice, dude." The courier

slapped a wing across Meginhardt's forehead. "But, duh, you could have lost everything!"

"Ya don't know me." Meginhardt spun to face the opposite direction.

"Don't matter. I gotta tell you, making a deal with those rebels is never a good idea. I've seen plenty in my time." With an awkward gait, the bird stomped till he could yammer direct into Meginhardt's face. "Ask me. Have I ever seen that to be a wise thing?"

"I don't give a rat. Take me back. Yer not supposed to give advice." Meginhardt spun, this time harder, and nearly lost his balance.

Those eagle eyes boring into the back of his head made him squirm. A slight protective layer of defense peeled away.

"Got a better offer?" He pointed to the ugly storm acting up in the river. "My pa's over there. He's in trouble."

"Maybe your pa's the one causing the trouble."

"Shouldn't you be lecturing me on pardoning instead of accusing?"

"Forgiving, yeah. Hitching yourself to the wrong wagon? No." Overplaying a wing wipe as if he had a forehead himself, the bird pushed out a mumble. "Rumor has it you've taken on the stubborn and rebellious kind of loyal."

Heat flushed from toes to ears. The aggressive response was habitual, something he'd learned well over the years thanks to Pa. It didn't take long to calculate, find someone to blame. That girl was the issue. Who was she to put him in this vermin trap? And get Pa hung? On top of that, carry on with the family name like nothing happened?

"If you ask me," the courier intruded, "you're confused."

"Not asking you."

CHAPTER FORTY-FIVE
NEVER HAVE I

In Vereiteln Dorf

LEXXIE SUNK IN dolor. The priest was quick to keep his hold on the audience whilst Jake hoisted an inebriated Witford to the platform.

She searched her birth father's face for a hint of compassion, a trace of regret, even a sliver of guilt. But none brandished themselves. Still, might a tiny voice speak from his heart? Beg her for forgiveness?

"This woman!" the priest shouted, given the crowd's riotous noise. "This woman has already been tried. A mere seventeen years ago, at this very place. Proven a witch by fair trial. Fair, I say, by our lawful practices. We hanged her then. Remember? I know some of you do." He practically sang the last phrase.

A portion of the crowd roiled in agreement.

"She took her infant child with her—away from Witford Dimietris, the child's father, so naught could he have joy nor peace in his life. And now? Now, she's come back." He leaned toward the crowd and scowled a threat. "To take another child from this town. Surely, from a father who stands here with us this very day."

Harmon tried to interfere, to speak up, but fickle was the crowd. Afresh, the chanting began: "Hang, burn, bury. Hang, burn, bury."

With his oh-so-powerful hand, the priest interrupted what he must see as pleasing chanting. "Hark, I present to you Witford himself. He shall testify. We know the horror this woman has cast upon him. And he will stand right here, planting his feet beside this creature, this child of the beast. With my protection, Witford will face this demon he once trusted as his wife, look her in those deceiving, evil eyes, and send her back from where she came. Where she belongs, for she is what the Scriptures call, 'the highway to the grave.' She'll lead you to the chambers of death if ye allow yourself to follow."

Unashamed, he could speak so?

And he wasn't finished. More threats for the doubters. "Go, dare thee proceed. Worthy Gentlemen—seek ye to swoon with her sister, Lilith. Recall ye? 'Tis the daughters of the devil you desire, I ask?"

A firm lean into the crowd, he put forth a challenge. "My dearest Ladies—you want your children to go missing in the night?"

Spew, now he reminds them of the so-said disappearance of Meginhardt, the young lad supposedly taken by his mother who returned as a wolf years after her execution.

Embracing the assembly with open arms, he offered gentle, dismissive nods. "Shall we allow this to happen—again?"

Apparently, he liked that word *again*.

Never once have I died. Never have I led anyone to the grave.

Never have I taken a child. Never have I had an inkling of intent to harm even a swallow in this forsaken town.

Victory was his. "Hang, burn, bury. Hang, burn, bury." Fists pumped in sync as far as she could see. The chant was wearing.

GC shoved his hand high, though the crowd was too far gone into their outrageous desires to witness a hanging. "This is not purification!" he bellowed, using cupped hands around his mouth to intensify the direction of his voice.

To no avail.

Harmon stood on guard aside her, in ready position. Should that lever get moved by hungry hands, he appeared wanting to grab her in time.

Great, now they'd both be hung. Her, a child-thieving witch—he, a child-thieving human.

It didn't matter who they believed. These townspeople were sheep following a wolf who'd tell them anything to retain their loyalty.

She spat the little saliva she could muster, aiming for the priest's feet. It ended as drool down her chin.

The platform was getting crowded. Jake hustled a red-eyed Witford to its front edge, presenting him to the priest—the prize witness in this ridiculous trial of sorts. Witford's shirt was sopping. Jake must have used a bucket of well water to wake him from a state of lethargy. And so much mud caked his hair, they must have fled as lightning to get across town so fast, plenty of dust kicked up by the horse.

As such a sad sight, he looked almost comical.

Yet his presence caused an abrupt flexing of Harmon's muscles and bouts of heavy, shaking exhales. Tense shivers, like missiles of regret, attacked her chest.

Jake held one of Witford's arms tight behind his back seemingly for stability—except from where Lexxie stood, the purpose be more obvious. A threatening measure to ensure Witford's tongue be in alliance. Harmon, they shuffled to the side edge along with GC, their attempts to speak shut down by the priest, who reigned in glory once more.

On his much-loved kiste, the priest continued his execution ceremony. "Witford Dimietris, our esteemed loyal servant, ladies and gentlemen. He served you people as councilman in the day—surely, you remember." Many yeas in the crowd, some doubtful, as the priest wrapped his left arm around Witford's shoulders. "Until—until those sister witches came into his life. Why? To destroy him. To destroy our town. How can a man function when he loses two children and his status in the community? No one wanted to destroy this man, only those witches. And I, to serve and protect the vulnerable, have captured, again, one of these evil creatures. We must end this."

The priest then squeezed Lexxie's wrist, pulled her arm up high, and turned to Witford. "Witford, look ye at this demon dressed as a wife to you. Identify her—who is she to you?"

Witford refused to meet her glance or seek the face he as father never knew, once luminescent with rosy cheeks, without markings from nerve-racking stress. Had he done so, would he have seen her accusatory rage, vanquished hope, dispirited soul? He never knew her nor how she'd invested high hopes in him, was once full of genuine concern, a quester with a giving heart. Perhaps he would have reawakened memories— the same gallows, only he'd see Emmaline's life hanging in the balance. Or even Lilith's, where all this madness began. Perhaps he may have even started to count, adding to the four deaths he'd been responsible for. Two wives, a son, a neighbor. Would he allow another life to be taken under his testimony? The daughter he pined for at her graveside?

It stung. The madman refused to lift his gaze. He'd also refuse her true identity.

Well then, that's that.

Lexxie released her thoughts about Witford, if it be the last words her vocal cords to project. "He speaks to the dead. Ye should hang him too."

She didn't care how Witford would answer. No matter what, she would reject him, owe him nothing. He shan't be the one to save her life. For certain, these townspeople already knew, full well, Madman Dimietris spoke to the dead, another sinful crime punishable by public execution. Except he'd already been excused from it.

"She's a demon. No one to me." He fixed pure hatred on Harmon.

"No. No." Harmon struggled as Jake pushed both him and GC off the platform. "Take me—take me." Harmon's plea rang clear as his body hurtled to the ground.

A pack of men nabbed him as if he would flee as a criminal might.

"Punishment by death." One of them offered Harmon up to be next in line.

The crushing of Lexxie's heart was unbearable.

The man who was her father desired her life be taken to spare his.

The man who adopted her pled for his death to save her life.

Black dizziness came again, and the hood thrust over her head aided the nausea. A heavy rope lay upon her shoulders, circling her neck. Her head shook, and her feet stomped as a doe's might when caught in a noose in sight of her fawn.

"King, please, please take care of Harmon." She gave her final plea. "I beg you."

CHAPTER FORTY-SIX
TURN AROUND

At the River of Times

*D*ERN BIRD, ENOUGH *already.* Meginhardt scowled at the eagle courier and tramped back to the riverbank. With any luck, it wasn't too late to revive the deal.

A thickset curtain of fog slammed like a felled hatchet. The River of Times lopped off in an instant. Far upstream and downstream, a barrier prevented him from getting back to the agreement, a pact for his new life. Too dangerous to feel around a downward climb of the embankment and find that rebel.

They thought they could stop him? Ha! They kin think again. He weren't no simpleton.

An illumination wrapped itself around his shoulders, the odd sensation. Despite its pleasant and homey feel, he fought it. *You ain't got business trying to comfort me now, far too late.*

But a blanket of light wasn't anything he could contend with. There was nothing to grab or pull or even shove. Then it spoke.

"Still got your stone, kid?"

Er . . . He turned to the voice.

What could be worse than seeing Jophiel right now? Aye, seeing Jophiel with a laughing grin.

Meginhardt's side pocket bulged and pulsed. He pulled out his stone to calm it. "Should'a known it was you, the interfering kind."

"Come on, Megs. You'll thank me one day."

Meginhardt huffed, doubting it.

"Too close if you ask me. You do get what you just did, don't you?" Jophiel's words were firm. His head shook. "A deal with the rebels, especially one to harm others? What were you thinking?"

"So I want another chance. What's it to you?" Now, another lecture would surely follow.

"And?"

"And what? Cry me a mercy." Meginhardt shrugged before blinking at least seven times. Better to keep his tongue still and lips shut. Telling Jophiel his desire to join the rebels and cease the chance for his so-called sister to carry on with his father's generational descendants wouldn't raise approval.

"Megs, you are—not this person." Jophiel took to shaking Meginhardt's shoulders, then waved away the eagle courier standing in the distance, releasing him of his duties. "Come. Let's do some genuine work now."

You know nothing about me. And stop calling me Megs.

Jophiel scooped a sulking Meginhardt into his muscular grab and soared straight into the dense fog. Above the river, they lingered long enough for Meginhardt to goggle the two black-water swirls through the intervening veil of haze, far more ominous when viewed above. A sinking, ill-boding mouth at the spot where the two storms sawed against each other, raging rims, one circling clockwise, the other counter-clockwise. Was one Pa and the other that girl?

Surrounding violent waves blustered every which way.

Jophiel nosedived toward the open, hungry maw. Before Meginhardt could resist, they were swallowed and moving fast through an echoing ink-black tunnel now narrowing uncom-fortably. Dark cyclonic winds rotated, the slightest of flinching threatened their welfare. Jophiel masked Meginhardt's eyes with those big palms of his and bounded straight toward the tail of the storm, lunging deep into the river.

It was quick, and it was over. Practically spat from the tunnel's end, Meginhardt's body sacked, secured by Jophiel's forearms. Into a dull, gray sky, they gravitated, falling freely. Meginhardt, relieved to exist still, juddered with a whole-body dog shake.

Soon, they hovered above the earth, the sights impressive and awakened his senses. Until their landing target became recognizable.

He worked his knees as if peddling backward could stop the inevitable. "Nay, stop, not happening, turn around."

A second death would have been better than this. That dreaded water hole where his mother was kept hostage at the bottom with no air to breathe. That gallows platform where his pa had stood and done nothing to stop it.

"I don't need to see the rest of it." He cringed. "Take me back. That rebel's more humane than you."

CHAPTER FORTY-SEVEN
VENGEANCE CALLS

In Vereiteln Dorf

AN EAGER YANK and the weighty noose tightened, eliminating the last bit of freedom around Lexxie's neck.

Silent counting, loud in her head, attempted to drown out the unruly horde. An opposing mix—a sickening unquenchable cheering with an angriness that justice was not served. For once, the people were not mindlessly following each other. They were divided. But none of that mattered now.

Three, two, one. With an unconscious attempt to set free a bolt of stress, her mind reached back to Grossmutter's idea to circumvent an inevitable ruin—marry her off to a boy in Avondale, have babies, and live happily ever after.

Wasn't such a bad idea, Grossmutter. Thank ye for trying.

Yet another intervening voice prevailed over all. Higher pitched, a demanding screech. A breath swallowed and froze at Lexxie's sternum with dire want to hear it again.

"It is true." The voice was loud and resolute, commanding the audience to listen.

A woman. Giselle?

"I kept Alexandra Dimietris as an infant for three months in my boarding house."

What? Mercy.

"Till it was safe, and she'd be old enough to travel. What Harmon Huber says is true. And I was an aid. So, you shall hang me too."

Another voice from the depths of the crowd, a raspy older soul, yelped a challenge. "Lying woman, I be at that digg'n."

"And what did you see but a shut kiste?" Giselle pitched in return.

Thanks to a loud escape of air whistling through missing teeth, Lexxie recognized the voice making the accusation. It belonged to the stonecutter. Made sense. He would've aided with many burials. It would've been quick and haphazard, given it be at the old graveyard.

Hey, that would have been my funeral. The thought be almost funny.

Desperation raised the priest's tone. "Hear ye. This is not a trial. This is an execution. May I remind you—this is *Purification Day*. You want protection, don't you?"

"This woman has never been on trial. Do we not call ourselves a just town?" Giselle's voice resounded now, so clear and close. "This woman is Alexandra Dimietris. Witford's grown daughter, Emmaline's child, raised by Harmon. I swear it to be true. What has this woman done? Her only guilt is to find her forebears."

Yet, you turned me away, watched me struggle?

"Check for yourself," Harmon commanded. "Go to her

tombstone, dig up her box, and find yourself seven rocks, nay any bones. If you want bones, I'll give you bones. Dig underneath the murdering pig's stone pile by his chicken shed. You will find his boy's bones. The only wolf that took Meginhardt's life was Witford—he *is* the wolf."

Not only was digging up one's grave religiously reprehensible but also a serious crime, punishable by execution. Agitation roiled throughout the crowd, people arguing and turning against each other. Dare a grave be dug and the dead disturbed?

The hood stuck to Lexxie's cheeks, wet with her tears. She blew air from her lungs out her mouth to separate it from her face. Heart pounding, she listened. A thread of hope sewed its way through her veins.

"I wist! The truth lays bare." Apparently, Witford had sobered up enough to put his voice forth, rather a spear spewed at Harmon. "I reckon'd ya took her, you and yer good-fer-noth'n mother. You theiv'n, rotten . . ."

"Now, wait a minute." The priest's attempt to regain control seemed unsuccessful. A thud, then another. Were they throwing rocks? At her? Nay. Irregular thumping vibrations continued. They must be aiming at the priest.

An unusually strong gust whizzed across the platform, passing through her flesh and bones. Lexxie reveled at its power. If only it could have scooped her up and taken her far from this place!

Harmon's turn. "You murdered my father in cold blood."

"He was flirt'n with my Emmaline," Dimietris bellied back.

And there it was, another section of the tapestry tied together, long-held secrets exploding in public. Although

Lexxie doubted Witford's flirting perspective, hadn't he just admitted to murder?

The sister witches were not responsible, enough doubt had been cast. A riot broke out, handfuls of townsmen charged to the old graveyard, claiming intent to dig up the faux grave of the Infant Dimietris. Others to the Dimietris farmhouse to dig under the stones in search of Meginhardt's bones.

Witford attempted to escape, but from what she could make of his cussing, he didn't get far. His pathetic cries rang of blackmail. The accusations must be aimed at Jake. That villainous snake.

A throng stormed the platform. Chaotic scuffling, panting, thumps, loud in her ear.

A wry smile beneath her hood, she was certain they snagged the priest. *A day of justice indeed.*

Coins were spilling and rolling every which way, then the distinct sound of a loud metallic groan rang horror.

Someone pulled the lever to the trapdoor.

CHAPTER FORTY-EIGHT
THE TWO SHALL MEET

In Vereiteln Dorf

"SURELY, YOU DESIRE truth," Jophiel coaxed.

But overdone, Meginhardt was, with truth. *Cry me a coin purse of mercies and blow it out yer ear.*

There was no escape, not with Jophiel's grip so tight. They'd soon be landing.

Anywhere but here. How could he watch his mother be shoved into the waters to drown—again. He was trying to put that nasty truth behind him. *Bleak bird man ye are.*

Jophiel's glide, wide and rhythmic, circled around and around until it lulled Meginhardt. Curiosity began to seep. His eyes fixated to the goings-on below.

"Those people." The crowd's size disgusted Meginhardt. "They must have come from other villages. That there's gotta be thrice the folk of Vereiteln Dorf."

But wait. This was no water trial. This be a hanging. A woman's body, dressed in bloomers, hooded and noosed. A dark energy sent waves through the sea of people. "Nay." He kicked wildly. "Now I gotta watch my mother be hanged?"

"Shhst, listen." Jophiel dove to the platform and whizzed through the hooded woman.

Meginhardt caught wind of her energy. *Not Mother. Whew.*

They landed in front of the platform, none of the occupants aware of their presence, not by human eye, anyway. No doubt they felt a current of air brush past if they were paying heed to it.

Meginhardt tipped his head, seeking hints as to the timing. Was this event before his own time in Vereiteln, during, or past?

He must have been mumbling, as Jophiel shushed him again. "Never mind time. Just listen."

A hoarse voice choked an accusation from somewhere close. "You murdered my father in cold blood."

"Harmon?" Meginhardt gasped. Aye, he had aged, for certain, but that same baby face gleamed, though now with dilating nostrils and a sheath of widened blood vessels. "Harmon's father—murdered. By Pa? Cry me a mercy. When did that happen?"

"He was flirt'n with my Emmaline."

"Pa!" Horror tripped through Meginhardt's chest. His father had even furthered with deterioration. When his pa jumped off the platform, several townsmen grabbed him, holding him hostage. Despite his sobering stupor and slight frame, the man could cuss like a crow and gave a dern good struggle, managing to free an arm and punch whatever bobbing head was in his way.

"He blackmailed me!" Pa pointed at Jake, a frequent visitor at their farmhouse.

I knew that Jake was a liar. I could smell it.

Employing those oversized palms, Jophiel churned Meginhardt's head the way of the hooded woman. With an impressive stride, Jophiel next stepped onto the platform and fiddled with the woman's noose while reassuring Meginhardt it was someone he hadn't met.

Chaos ensued, people calling excitedly, dispersing in all directions. Many toward the main road, threatening to dig up graves. Others warned of punishment if they did. A rabble of men lunged forth, keen to secure the priest. The whole scene overwhelming, Meginhardt craned his neck side to side, unsure which way to look.

A growling snarl caught his attention.

Jake. Meginhardt sneered. Why'd Pa behave like a servant whenever Jake came around anyway? Red blotched Jake's face, and his jaw clenched. One townsman had grabbed him by the waist, while another pulled at his bountiful satchel. No surprise Jake threatened to pull the trapdoor lever. It was just like him to bully his way to control. The purse spilled, its contents freed.

Cry me a mercy. Meginhardt had to look the other way. Jake did it. The wroth man yanked the lever!

The only thing left to do was gasp.

Then Meginhardt jumped onto the platform. Could he save her?

The woman's feet flew. Her legs kicked like a wild animal. With constrictions on her neck from the noose obvious, she must be trying to suck in a final breath of air through the hood. Nothing but panic. His own arms to hold her up, useless. A harsh crunch. Her ear pounded into her shoulder. Then she was gone, an expedited tumble through the opening.

His heart wanted to stop beating. His voice screamed for Jophiel to do something, but no sound came out.

Meginhardt stormed Jake with full intention to plow him good. "You beast."

Meginhardt's fists flew straight through Jake's body. Jake, wholly unaware, took to scrambling off ahead of the raging men demanding his capture.

All noise of the hubbub ceased. An eerie silence prevailed the chaos. Mouths opening wide yelling, fists threatening, men running in packs, women using their skirts to hide their children's faces.

One voice, however, came low and clear.

"Now, our work shall begin." Jophiel exuded great calm and lack of urgency. "Come."

Ignoring the black energy of feisty anger aswirl, he pulled Meginhardt through wooden slats and into the gallows' underbelly. They crouched where the woman had fallen and lay crookedly on her back.

Meginhardt knew from his own traumatic death, her face would balloon in redness, her eyes likely still open. Then a deep blackness would fall all around. Would she see countless floating balls of light, as he did? He had to know one thing. "Is Pa responsible for this? For her?"

He didn't want the answer. He was afraid of who she was—his so-called sister, the one he didn't care if she suffered. The one he'd trade so, in turn, he could get the life he'd always wanted. The one he himself wanted to end her existence. Is that what was happening? Was he getting his wish?

Of course, it'd be her. He'd seen those two watery swirls. Waves of instinct, the truth, stormed through his soul. He sickened inside.

The hood over the woman's head pixelated and disappeared, her face exposed only to him and Jophiel. Meginhardt stroked her sticky cheek.

The lid of one eye opened with a flutter. The other appeared more stubborn and stuck. Loose dirt lodged in the edges.

The hanging had failed, something to do with the rope loosening at its knot. Jophiel. Meginhardt exhaled in relief. He did that.

A cawing murder of crows circled wide, visible through the swinging doors still creaking at the joins above her limp body. She rubbed her ear, then her neck and tended to clear out the closed eye. She was lying flat on her back, her knees and ankles twisting in opposite directions. Voices all around. She gave him a curious look.

He reached out to offer his hand.

She took it and sat up with ease. A little lightheaded, a lot translucent, she appeared pleased to feel the airy brightness circulating around her.

"Troublesome day?" It came so naturally. He grinned as he teased. The woman was now in the same form as he.

"You mayest well repeat that." A grand sigh assisted her to collect her senses. "Might ye be from that gathering?" Before leaning on him to be pulled to her feet, she narrowed her brows. "Were you *for* me or *against?*"

Meginhardt wanted to check with Jophiel for help, how to respond, particularly as, certain as anything, this would be the girl he condemned. But Jophiel had slipped out of sight. Meginhardt was on his own to answer.

A mad rush of people arrived with expressions of horror and panic, kicking in the wooden slats of the lower platform.

They passed right through him as though he wasn't there. 'Course, he wasn't, as far as they could know or see.

"Astonishing," she whispered when arms and shoulders passed through her own bodice as well. A snapping of some sort cracked and catapulted her upward, freeing the spirited woman from those twisted corporeal legs. Jumping into a standstill aside him, she placed her attention on the panicked collection of folks bent over a broken body, black hood still on its head.

"I'm dead. Right?" She then bobbed a curtsey. "I'm Lexxie. So, who are you?"

Harmon came rushing, breezing through the transparent version of himself, shoving his way to get to the body sprawled in the dirt. He demanded space and removed the hood with gentle movements. He caressed the wiry dirt-sodden hair, the bloodied tearstained face. He placed his thumb on the side of the neck. He loosened the rope languishing on her chest.

"Harmon." Lexxie and Meginhardt professed their concern simultaneously, both calling out his name.

How was it she knew his friend?

"Will he find a pulse?" she asked, seeming horrified by how Harmon would react if he didn't.

"C'mon over here. Less distractions to talk." Meginhardt beckoned, and she followed around the corner of the gallows to where Jophiel stood waiting for them.

"Gadzooks, my eyes deceive me." She seemed unsure where to examine Jophiel first—his pure size, the glow from this creature, or those wings. Even folded, they looked imposing. "Is he for truth? I always took Harmon to be waggish when he said we don't really die when we die. I need to go tell him his ways are merited." Turning to head back, she muttered at how distraught Harmon would be fussing over her lifeless body and thinking he'd lost her for good.

Jophiel grabbed her arm. "He won't hear you, Lexxie. Nor will he see you. None of them will."

By the look on her face, she found his message quizzical, despite its magical warmth. Meginhardt casted a comforting smile. "Hey, it was the same for me. Took me a while to get used to it but catch this." He walked through a post and then stuck his arm through a passerby.

Smirking at his humorous attempts, she faced him again. "And who might you be? For me or against me? You never did say."

"Meginhardt, at your service, ma'am." Clowning around, he bowed.

"*The* Meginhardt? C'mon, no lies. Are you making a sport of me?"

"You've heard of me?"

"You're the lad under all those stones behind your old farmhouse."

"Aye." He rolled a shrug. "Pa thought it best to shelter me there."

"Shelter?" Lexxie bit her top lip. Giving him a sideways glance, she rocked on her toes, then paused, likely at the realization of such freedom to do so. Her face lit up with some kind of revelation. "To be certain, Witford Dimietris is your father? 'Cause if he is, then you, dear Mr. Meginhardt, are my little brother. You're. . . my family."

Meginhardt thought of the murky swirl in the river, the sister he sold out, ready to let an ugly fate come her way so he could be reunited in a renewed way with Pa. Swallowing hard, he felt small and ashamed. Yet he bowed deeply. Humor sometimes got him out of predicaments. "Well, I am your *older* brother. Technically, I was born first."

"I reckon your mother was my mother's sister."

While Lexxie seemed preoccupied with tallying up the genealogy, Meginhardt suffered an all-consuming uneasiness. Veritable regret. Meeting his sister had thrown him right off balance.

"My mother died giving—" But no, 'tweren't true. He stopped with an awkward abruptness. She was tried a witch and failed. "I never knew her. She was executed when I was just a baby." A pocket of air escaped his lungs, a sorrowful relief.

"Well then, we have that in common."

Out of the dooming gray came a bounding glow of light. Lexxie's genuine interest in him supplied a hope he had never been familiar with. Instead of confusion and revenge, there came great potential for personal growth. And based on truth, there'd be no need to hide. He needed to give her back a glimmer of something. "I remember Emmaline, your mother. She came to cook and clean for Pa and me sometimes. She had plenty o' tenderness. I wanted a wife just like her one day."

Lexxie blinked, as though not knowing what to do. Had he said something bad?

She swallowed hard. "You actually knew my mother?"

"Aye, I like—" He staggered back. Like a shot, her arms wrapped around his torso. Dumbstruck at her whimpering, he held his arms akimbo. Surely, she didn't know anything about his prior state of mind, wanting to kill her and all. *Please, let her death not be my doing.*

"Thank ye." Her embrace went even tighter.

"Ah, nothin'." He dashed a pleading gaze to Jophiel.

Jophiel stepped forward. "I hate to interrupt your family reunion here, but enough chitchat. Since you two know each other, let's get to business. Timing is everything."

A matter of greater importance called.

Meginhardt was careful to be gentle as he loosened Lexxie's arms.

She wiped an emotional tear away. Lowering her head, she whispered, "Should I be bowing to him?"

"Nay." Meginhardt laughed. "But I would listen to what he says if I were you. Believe that." He and Jophiel shared a chin-nod of camaraderie.

"Lexxie, you're going back," Jophiel announced.

"Cry me a mercy." Meginhardt jumped in, his interior thawing on hold. "So, *she* gets to go back?"

When Jophiel cast him a you-gotta-know-better look, Meginhardt backed down. Instead, he had questions to squeeze in. Coaxing himself to a calm, he refocused on Lexxie. "How do you know Harmon?"

Her eyebrows rose. "Of course, I know Harmon. He raised me. He and Grossmutter—ah, I guess to you she was Meredith Huber—they both raised me. They stole me as an infant." She wagged her head, and her shoulders dropped. "I hadn't realized till today what they gave up to protect me."

"Back." Jophiel nudged her. "Now. Let's go."

Animated shrieks and wails elevated underneath the gallows aside the disjointed mound of tissue and bones wrapped in bloomers. Their trio watched Harmon close the eyelids while two others straightened her physical legs and ankles.

"He's distraught." Lexxie brought her hand to her mouth. "May I have a word with him, let him know I am okay?"

But more excitement exploded, interrupting her request.

"A pulse!" a voice lauded. "I'm getting a pulse on this ankle," said the man holding one of Lexxie's physical shins securely.

"Okay, now," Jophiel instructed. "Jump in."

"That's it. That's all?" Lexxie spoke as though she expected more. "I don't want to go back. In fact, I shan't." Arms crossed against her chest, she planted herself firm, not about to budge.

Jophiel smiled. "I just did him a favor." He touched Meginhardt's shoulder. "If he met you, he'd have a change of heart. Plus, it gave me a chance to, you know, play with the rope a bit."

Poor timing for a joke! Meginhardt snickered.

She glared. "You never answered—for or against?" Her hands parked on her hips reminded him of Aivy's determination. "Truth. I demand the truth."

"Okay." Oh how he regretted his prior hardness! "I was against. But that was before I met you. I realize now I am so lucky to have you, kin, my own sister. And I am wholly in now. For, I say."

Huh. His enthusiasm hadn't served him as well as he hoped. Her disappointed expression daggered straight into his heart. Was he to fall into disfavor so fast?

Still, she remained adamant to resist Jophiel's get-going cast. "I prefer to stay this way. May I not? I was just hung. *Hung*—do ye understand?"

A little bold and daring, the girl had spunk. Meginhardt stepped closer to share what he knew. "He rigged the gear, let the rope give. That's why, well, you crashed on the ground. So, you . . . could carry on and . . ."

"Carry on for what?" She wailed as beyond anguished.

"Nay, I feel sprightly. I've nothing to go back for." At that, Jophiel raised his eyebrows, and she ducked her head. The next words came in a whisper. "Well, except for Harmon. And Grossmutter. I suppose I should thank Giselle for speaking up. Maybe even thank Jonne for his help. And I made this promise to a child. . . ."

Meginhardt encouraged her with a hint. "If you go back, you can have a family. Maybe a big one?"

"A family?" Her hearty chortle was followed by a reflective mumble. "To be a mother would be precious."

"But maybe . . ." Meginhardt was about to suggest she not involve Witford in her future. But he sensed her defenses warding off his advice. Best turn to wit, then. "Ah, maybe brush yer hair some?"

Putting more spite at risk, he hoped for another laugh. But she ignored the tease and braved another glance at the mound crumpled on the ground. "Nay, never could a brush pass through that claggy mess."

He caught a glint in her eye, and she must have noticed his surprise at her topping retort. As siblings, they came together with a hearty laugh. Blitheness filled his chest. He crossed his arms and eyed Jophiel. The girl was right. Mirth aside, no way was she going back into that.

"Leave it to the King." Jophiel winked.

"Huh, Harmon used to say that too," Lexxie mused, not noticing Jophiel's crowding, herding her closer to her physical body. She bolted a stiff chin. "Wait. Am I to take care of Witford? 'Tis that my purpose?"

Meginhardt stepped in right away. "Nay, Sister." He blushed at the sister ditty. "Do not make the same blunder as me. Do what you can, encourage and inspire to yer fullest, but naught are ye accountable for another's mind, lest ye harmed it. Remember that."

Amazed with himself, he felt good giving words of advice from the heart. His heart. First time for everything. "And always remember, I am—*for*—you."

He bayed through the flutter of wings and light that enveloped her till she disappeared. He hoped this newfound family member who by some miracle found her way to him, had heard him.

Then some mysterious switch to the sound of chaos must've turned back on. In came cries and yelps, boots pounding and a trapdoor swinging.

How could I have been so selfish to have cursed her as I did?

He leaned down to the crumpled body. "But never you mind that so much." He spoke to the head. "Stay picky about what you think. Don't let some rebel come charging through the gate and bully your emotions." Had she understood his meaning? "It's yer own thoughts that should work for ya."

Finally, he clasped the sides of his face. "Wanting to live in the past don't help. Trust me. Let it go."

"All right, all right." Jophiel urged Meginhardt to step back.

A piercing scream ensued, enough to pale even a ghostly spirit. On the ground, one of Lexxie's legs, swollen and bruised, was being manipulated into a straight position, causing a jolt to her hips. She had reconnected to her body. Both eyelids fluttered open.

He gasped at the concern the eyes of his old neighbor, now a grown adult, aching for Lexxie's well-being.

"Another last thing," Meginhardt called above the ruckus. "Give a nick on the fence ta Harmon fer me."

"Lex, oh dear King! Lex, you're alive. Giselle, get the healer back, quick." Harmon clasped Lexxie's hand. "My dear child, hang on."

"Impressive, kid. Make sure your thoughts are working for you. I'll have to remember that slant." Jophiel pulled at Meginhardt. "C'mon. Don't be a rubbernecker."

"A what?"

"Never mind."

CHAPTER FORTY-NINE
WHAT'S IN A NAME

In Vereiteln Dorf

"SINCE SHE KNOWS me now, I can visit her plenty, right?" Meginhardt beamed as Jophiel drew him beyond the gallows. Surely, Jophiel would allow such. Why else unfold the treasure of kinfolk?

"Nope. Not how it works."

Not the answer Meginhardt sought. His eyebrows came together. His bottom lip fell away. "Will she remember me? What I said?"

"Maybe some, likely not, hard to tell."

Meginhardt dug his heels into the ground. "Stop pulling me. What do you mean? Why'd we bother, then, with all this?"

Towering above Meginhardt, his expression cross, Jophiel bent forward. "Still got your stone? Well, I know you do. Get it out of your pocket."

Meginhardt pulled it out and examined it. A name still etched on its side. Meginhardt directed one searching eye on Jophiel. The other squinted shut. "You won't lie to me?"

He needed something he'd been looking for, hoping for. Assurances. If he were to accept this name etched on his stone, what would it guarantee?

The look on Jophiel's face was telling. "I shan't deceive," came a low, meaningful whisper. "You need to believe you are worthy and wanted." Jophiel's eyes glowed so deep, Meginhardt caught his own reflection like staring at a glassy puddle. "Now, you willing to accept the new name and what it'll bring to you? 'Cause if you do, you must reject that rebel—all of them, for that matter. Walk through the gate, take up your position. Your loyalty to the King and his kingdom."

"And to you?" tested Meginhardt.

Jophiel waved his arms to and fro before his chest and shook his head. "No, and you know it. Intrinsically. Search for it. It's there. You know what I'm talking about. Just like you know there is no guarantee you could have a renewed relationship with your pa—depends on him, not you. But you will be with your mother—she's there waiting for you right now. And you can wait for others. If your pa comes, you'll be there to greet him. If Lexxie comes, you'll be there to greet her. And so on and so on."

Meginhardt read the name on his stone and sounded it out. Meg–ah–lowes. Megalos. It felt right. A wholesome kind of right. Meeting Lexxie had a profound effect. More than anything, he wanted to become the image accompanying the name—strong and mature.

Thoughts shape your life. If so, he could do it. His chest puffed twice its size. "Yes, sir. I am ready. Just call me Megalos henceforth."

"Duly right-minded. It's straight on the path from here. And you shall prepare for what's next."

"Ah, what's next?" The Meginhardt-renamed-Megalos trembled to ask.

"Boss wants you to denounce the rebel right to his face."

CHAPTER FIFTY
THREE DAYS LATER

In Vereiteln Dorf

THICK PIPE-STAINED FINGERS forced Lexxie's right eye open, tunneling a flood of daylight to the back of her pupil. Supreme annoyance of zigzagging flashes paled against the sharp, beating throbs inside her head. Liberating a head roll, she warded off those stubby thumbs from repeating the same act to the other eye.

The traveling physician scribbled some notes with his newly acquired portable writing instrument. "No damage to the brain," he pronounced the diagnosis and added her hoarse and throaty growl were, indeed, encouraging signs. "Vocal cords will be restored."

"Oh, praise be."

Ah, Giselle? Aye, sounded like Giselle.

A hand rested on her forehead. "Rest, my child."

Harmon. Easy to recognize the calluses and the warmth radiating from his palm.

Negotiating bruised muscles, Lexxie managed a slight

twist of her head toward the voices and willed her eyes to open on their own. They fluttered. Shadows lingered around her bed.

Harmon and Giselle in some kind of embrace? Couldn't be. Lexxie must be in a state of madness.

The physician went on, something about compression and constrictions and more rest.

More rest? No doubt there. Her whole body ached. Sections took turns screaming with bolts of tenderness, pain, and tension pulls, her mind just as heavily beaten from emotional exhaustion.

But what was on the ceiling? An intense flash of something celestial, blissful, a flicker of a memory. Then another drain of energy sent her hurtling back into a peaceful darkness, her place of rest and healing.

CHAPTER FIFTY-ONE
SIX WEEKS LATER

In Vereiteln Dorf

"COME ON, GIRLIE, another sip."

"Thank ye, truly," Lexxie said after Giselle lifted the cup brimming of bone broth in sync with her nod. Her vocal cords were still sore, but she received approval to talk.

"Single words or short statements only," the physician had said.

The muscle spasms in her neck and the swelling in her ankles and knees still had some subsiding to do. The vision issues and headaches were settling. Despite the improvements, she remained bedridden. Doctor's orders with Harmon's reinforcements.

Lexxie's well-being boomed with surges of joy. She had three caregivers fussing over her—Giselle, Harmon, and Matilda. Jonne, who decided gossip for the sake of exchanging information was, in fact, suitable, spread word to Matilda in Mittel Dorf and even went out of his way to inform Gross-mutter in rural Avondale.

Now, Matilda scooted into the room and thumped the door closed with her backside as she was wont to do. Her clamoring footsteps sounded too loud for a child, but none else would make such racket.

Lexxie half lifted an eyelid when the bed bounced.

"Fer yer ankles." Matilda held up a cloth-covered plate, then shoved the linens off Lexxie's feet and legs. "When Jonne come to tell me, I was right glad to hear the execution didn't work on ya."

Strong little fingers rubbed Lexxie's ankles. Something warm and wet wrapped around them.

"What be that?" Lexxie pushed the words out.

"These? Cabbage leaves, to heal the swellin'. I soaked 'em real good. So glad he come to fetch me, I was—though he didn't really come to fetch me. I had to beg on that. Beg and beg him to steal me away and deliver me up so you kin keep yer promise."

Her askew braids slapped a sound against her shoulders. "'Course Uncle said nay." The girl dried her hands on her apron. "Till Jonne showed him a fresh pair of boots—fine leather, they were! You should have seen his eyes go all greedy round."

Her tongue jutting out of tightly pressed lips, Matilda tied cloth strips to hold the cabbage leaves in place. "Now jus' leave yer feet still fer abit." She climbed up the bed and took Lexxie's hand in hers. "That Jonne's good folk, ain't he?"

Lexxie mustered up a squeeze, peering up at the child's thoughtful face. Even her calluses could lift a spirit. Was Matilda hurt that her so-called uncle then commenced negotiations to "take the girl for good" in exchange for a purse full of coin? Jonne claimed he agreed in hopes Lexxie's family would accept her. A risk he chose to shoulder the consequence.

Matilda curled up alongside Lexxie and wrapped Lexxie's arm around her. "I've nay intention to return to Mittel Dorf, ya know."

Dear heart. Lexxie squeezed her tight. The child wasn't aware no one there expected her back, and all decided it best not to tell her. Lexxie stroked one of those fraying braids. Seemed Matilda admired her courage. How many times had the child stated plain she wanted to be just like her? She even dressed as a boy and rose on Sadie's back with Jonne, her first big crow of common ground.

Lexxie fixed a glance at the strip of luminance streaming through the window. *Ye home, child,* her inner voice spoke of Matilda. She sat herself taller and cupped the girl's cheeks. "Just don't make the mistake I did, believing courage is adopting a boldness without heart. It's really about seeking the truth and then facing it head-on."

Matilda snugged her head into the hollow beneath Lexxie's chin, leaving quiet for Lexxie's mind to pace.

They hardly spoke more than a few words, she and Jonne. He came often. Once, he even picked a ladybug off her shoulder. So how was the region's post getting delivered? No matter, his presence provided an energized calmness and left her eager for his next stop by.

So swiftly can a mind change.

Over the next few days there had been plenty of opportunities for storytelling, and even though she pled, all she got in return was the surface-style of exchange from Harmon and Giselle. Curious about this odd relationship, Lexxie glare-eyed

Harmon when an opportune moment came once Giselle and Matilda both absented themselves from the room. The icy stare was hard enough he fell back into the only comfy chair, the one beside the head of her bedframe.

Having had enough of his secrets, she made a command. "'Fess it up."

How interesting to watch his chest stiffen until he shifted back, choosing the soft padding to rest his neck.

"I'm no baby anymore. I need to understand what happened." He'd best know she wasn't going to let him off, not this time.

He nodded. "Yes, I've treated you as a child—*my* child." He smiled. "Meine tochter."

Swallowing a lump, he shut his eyes. He must be transporting himself somewhere, a dark place where a seed of trauma grew like wild, weedy underbrush. "Though I had no right."

Here it came, finally. She braced herself and, with a cautious shoulder move, edged closer to hear each word. His side of the story she'd yet to hear, and at this point in the telling, it would be like a grim fable.

"I was there, witnessed the whole thing—well, practically the whole thing."

She propped her pillow to support her head and leaned securely on her elbow. "My mother's hanging?"

"Nay, grateful I was to be spared from witnessing that horror." Both his hands fisted into tight balls. "I should'a stopped the murdering bastard." He raised his head, looking her straight in the eye. "I watched him kick Meginhardt for years, treating him like he be the dregs of society."

Up to this moment, neither Lexxie nor Harmon had yet

spoken the man's name aloud in front of the other. Witford Dimietris. Though, 'twas that man who caused the agonizing disorder that ended with her being raised in a loving home. She did her best to hide a stirring choke and chose to change the story, so as to allow the good within it to flow as a clear river. She hid the tiny smile inside her as she coaxed her attention back to Harmon.

"And Megs, he just took it. Wanting to please his father something terrible, craved his approval." Harmon shook his head and pounded blood-drained knuckles into the armrests. "I told him, said he had to stop taking it. I dared him to stand up to the monster. I should'a never interfered."

That lavender patch, the fence. Megs—Meginhardt. The engraving—M doth sleep. H. Though her mind recollected, her tongue remained still, doing its best to protect her throat from thickening gestures.

Sobs pounded at Harmon's chest. He nodded before cradling his body.

"You couldn't have known." He must've been holding this burden of remorse, well, for her entire life.

"But Megs only shrugged, claiming his ma died because of him, and that was the reason."

Lexxie's head collapsed into the straw-stuffed cushion. Feeling the wetness, her mind, sorting and recalling, she wiped her face. How her heart ached over Harmon aching like this.

Meginhardt. Wait! Didn't she meet Meginhardt? Under the gallows?

"He struck him. He struck him with the iron pan, smashed it on Meg's skull. I can still hear the squeal, the utterings, the howling moan. It haunts me plenty." Harmon's head lay limp on his lap. "I should'a stopped it."

Giselle now stood in the doorframe. Her eyes wrenched with a longing to relieve Harmon of his pain.

What bound those two?

Needing as many connecting threads tied together as possible, Lexxie focused on Harmon, who regained emotional control. A shimmer of something glowing flashed out the corner of her eye, a heavenly being, large with wide, pure-white, and perfect wings. The image, a recollection.

I saw him, that angel. Aye, she recalled it vaguely, right after she hurtled through that trapdoor. And now, a flicker on her ceiling, already gone. She tucked the boggling vision away for now.

"When he got to tell'n a few folks in town a pack of wolves attacked his boy and dragged him out straight through the fields, the whole village believed it. It was a bad year for crops, and wolves were especially hungry. But some folks started saying it was the boy's mother. They called her Witch Lilith, saying she came back to steal the boy away from his drunkard father."

Giselle jumped in. "Folks argued for weeks whether the mother and her boy gone straight to the netherworld or gone to perdition fer punishment. Megs's perishing was the blether of the town, till the priest shut it down. He confirmed it and said Witch Lilith would come back for another if we didn't just leave it all be."

"Good for business, eh, Giselle?" Lexxie's accusatory tongue slipped before she could stop it.

Harmon took an abrupt stand. "Mind yer tongue, child."

"Nay, Harmon, she's got the right to say that." Giselle's fingertips pressed together. "It was good for business. Purification Day grew with more and more attendance from nearby villages after that. I am not too proud to admit." She lowered her head, her braid coils perfect, complete with ribbon. "It turned into a weeklong festival, helped my father keep up with the inn's needs."

Lexxie rolled her eyes and flopped her head back, wincing. "Purification, huh. Such farce." She then propped herself up on both elbows, nodding for Harmon to sit back down. "So, I take it then Gillam, your father, did something about this village-wide deceitful Wit–ford?"

"He did, Lex. But it didn't make any good. Jake took Witford's defense—claimed it had to be Witch Lilith who gathered up a pack, then waited for the opportune moment to attack. Their target was Meginhardt, her boy. Otherwise, they'd have gone after the chickens."

Her eyes widened. "*That* was his defense, that the chickens weren't harmed?"

"Yup. That clay-bank hog was celebrated. Village treasurer and terminer of witchcraft. Doubled on his coin that year, I heard." Harmon stopped. Looked at Giselle as though for some kind of approval, which he didn't get. He didn't wear spew and gossip well.

There was that look again. What tied Harmon to Giselle?

He scratched his head. "Think'n that's enough for today." He tucked Lexxie's blankets up around her neck and kissed her forehead. "Why'd you chop your hair like that?" He poked fun at the uneven cut as he brushed it back with his palm like he did each night when she was a little girl.

"Don't ask." Her fatigue won until a surge emerged. "Wait. I remember now. I saw him. I saw that lad, your friend, Meginhardt."

A spout from Giselle confirmed the absurdness. "What say you?"

Lexxie hurled the covers off and jolted herself into a tall sit, then paused for the dizziness to settle. Yes, Meginhardt, he was with that angel! "When . . ." The effort failed her. She took a deep sigh and clasped her sore neck. "When I was under the gallows, you know, after I—"

"Yeah, yeah, yeah." Harmon raised a hand, spinning it, urging her to continue rather than revisit her time under the gallows. Anxious he was, wasn't he? She must've grabbed his attention fine.

"Well, a boy there came to talk to me. I popped out of my body." Her hands underscored that part. "Then together we went around the corner to tattle."

"To tattle?" Giselle cast looks of doubt.

"It was Meginhardt. I remember now." Lexxie laughed and tugged at her quilt. "I'd forgotten till now."

"Well, go on." Harmon leaned forward and gripped her hands. "What did he say?"

She squeezed back his callused hold. "I—I don't recall all of it, but he did recognize you, Harmon. He said to put a notch on the fence for ya."

Harmon glowed and perched himself on the end of her bed. "Huh. How odd, for nobody could have known he'd been notching the fence as a signal. That was our thing, our secret, our way to stay connected. I started it to let Megs know I was there for him. Aye."

"Guess it means he's there for you now." Satisfaction spread her grin.

"Oh, come now, ridiculous." Giselle swatted at Harmon. "What she's been through would drive any brain to a wild imagination. Stop egging her on."

Egging her on? Lexxie cast her best iron maiden look at

Giselle. What was she doing here, anyway? As if this were any of her business.

Staring at Giselle stirred another vague memory to surface. Just before that trapdoor opened, Giselle's broadcast of guilt. Bodies must have turned her way to listen. Their mouths would've rounded in shock. Lexxie couldn't recall the exact words.

Giselle, discouraged from Lexxie's glare, backed out of the doorframe, inadvertently making space for Matilda to bounce in.

"Get some rest." The stern command came from Harmon as he steered himself and Matilda out the room.

Frustrated, Lexxie concurred, enough for now, and welcomed a wall of sleep to fall upon her.

CHAPTER FIFTY-TWO
STORY TIME

In Vereiteln Dorf

FINALLY, TIME FOR the rest of the story. Lexxie leaned back and gave Harmon the signal. He owed it to her, all of it.

"Back in the day, the church handed out white candy sticks with sugar roses bent the way of shepherd crooks. The general store was the first to modernize with a reckoning board. I was young then, barely fifteen, promised myself to an equally young Giselle, the daughter and only child of the well-to-do Coaching Inn owners. Our plan to marry, a kept secret. The son of a tarnished farmer not being suitable for the daughter of a well-known and respected innkeeper, no sir, even if the farmer owned his land."

Harmon paused for a sigh. His thoughts appeared to be so very far away.

"My mother and father persisted through many hardships. Harsh winters, dry summers, and social discrimination, high on the list. Preferring not to engage with political and religious conflicts, their strife for contented peace was forever at the center of attack. Mutter, poor-mouthed by townswomen for not producing offspring to assist in the field, one son not being enough. Vater, shunned by town officials for slandering his neighbor. 'Ludicrous,' many cried out, giving all of us a wide berth in town. 'How dare they accuse Witford Dimietris, a fine councilman, for mistreating his son,' they said."

The way he rolled his eyes, Harmon must've placed himself back into the day, reliving it all. She reached for his hand, but he wasn't to welcome any such touches of comfort.

"Hadn't Witford suffered enough? Discovering his wife was a witch, much less having to officiate at her execution, and then, of all things, raise their son from infancy on his own." His voice took on a mocking pitch. "They blamed us for Witford's overabundant medicinal drinking. Can you believe that? And then the outrageous story—Lilith, back from the dead, disguised a wolf and stealing Meginhardt away."

Lexxie shifted on the Coaching Inn's soft parlor chair. Digesting this story was healing for her, though it wasn't likely so for Harmon. "I hurt for you, having to witness such horror, Witford slaying Meginhardt. What did you do then?"

Harmon shook his head. "I saw enough. If I told my father, he'd a done something for sure. We were already blacklisted according to many folk. And I—I wanted to marry Giselle. That wouldn't have helped my image in her parents' eyes."

Lexxie blinked only when necessary. Never had she any inkling there was any romance in his life. He just wasn't that sort. And that it be Giselle? "Carry on."

"Besides, my father figured it out. When we noticed Emma-line was with child"—he looked sheepishly at Lexxie—"that's when my father warned her, said she and her baby were gonna be next."

A lump in her throat formed. Scratching the back of her neck gave pause enough to challenge the tears to stay put.

He shifted and drew in long and deep. "Then Witford came after me with an ax. And Vater . . ."

She grabbed his hand and held it in her hers while he struggled. Shaking her head, knowing what happened next, she saved him from explaining Witford's murderous wrath on Harmon's father instead of him.

"Had I only screeched and made noise that dreadful night Megs died, would that have stopped Witford's temper? My father stood up for justice, and what happened? His life, lobbed from us. My mother, burdened with sorrow. How much more could we take? When the town authorities rounded up Emmaline to be tried a witch, she begged Mutter to take her newborn. Mutter said nothin' doing, said he'd come after us too. But I pled for her to help me make things right."

This time, he clasped her hands. "Lex, we did take you as your mother wanted, but we could tell no one. I've burdened deeply over this, but I shan't ever say I regret what we did. And if you hadn't been so determined to yank at that overgrown weed, the lie we lived, roots and all . . ." He stood and sighed, this time with deep relief, his face wet from sogging eyes of thankfulness. "Aye, quite enough to share for the day."

"Wait." She pulled him back to the parlor chair, opposite hers. "What about Giselle?" she whispered. "Did you just leave her?"

He wiped a blushed cheek. "I went to Giselle for help to hide you, so we could . . . fake your burial. If we placed you in the unconsecrated graveyard, no one would question nor care." He lowered his head. "Giselle thought she'd be going with me, to escape to another village, raise you as our own. But Mutter refused, said if we left town with a girl like Giselle, a successful wirte's daughter, folks in nearby villages would recognize her. Find us out. We couldn't have that."

"Did she know where you went?"

Pulling on his beard, he shook his head.

"Did you even say goodbye?"

The same sad headshake.

"You left her . . . for me?"

He stood, heading toward the front door, seeming to have caught a better state of mind. "Aye." He turned and grinned. "I shan't let her go this time, though."

Not only had Harmon and Grossmutter sacrificed their plot of land, their livelihood, their reputation, all for her, but he'd also sacrificed the girl he wanted to marry. There'd be no one who could have cared for her more. She whispered a bewildered thank ye, though he'd already left the parlor to load the wagon with their carry sacks and one large trunk. Giselle, a scorned woman for years. No wonder she wasn't at ease with Lexxie's presence. But now, Lexxie sighed a smile, Giselle would be proud to be a Huber. *As am I.*

Matilda bounded into the room, accepting instructions from Harmon to sit with Lexxie till they were ready to depart. She placed a supportive hug around Lexxie's neck. "Guess," she started, eager to be the one to tell her. "Those bones of that Meginhardt fella got buried right by the church. Soon as the carver has the stone ready, it's go'n up too. Harmon told him to make it the biggest one in the graveyard."

Huh. Here lyeth, my Meginhardt.

Lexxie smiled, a heart full of contentment, pleased to

have Matilda's enthusiastic kindness around her neck rather than a noose. And such an inner connection she'd made with this Meginhardt entity. He stood for courage and patience and faith. She'd have liked a marker for both their mothers erected in a proper place, but that was not going to be. The two pebbles atop Gillam Huber's marker would have to represent the beloved sisters.

And then there was Jonne. Outside the window, the man heaved sufficient quantities of food and supplies and organized them just so. He was smoothing a woolen blanket atop a bed of straw, a place for her to rest while they traveled. The time had come to leave Vereiteln Dorf thanks to rumored threats. Several men came warning that Witford had full intention to ax every member of Harmon's family till there be not a soul left. "So, keep an eye out whilst you sleep," they had said. "Best you all leave town and speak of your plans to no one."

Now, Jake and the priest were being held in chains until a replacement priest could arrive. So where was coldhearted Witford Dimietris hiding out, and which coldhearted folk were protecting him? And what of the celebration table in the rectory set for six? Who were the other four? They were likely to remain hidden, which meant the Huber family would always need to be on guard.

"Yer sweet on him, ain't ya?" Matilda interrupted.

Ah, Lexxie's gaze must've been watching Jonne's every move.

"He's aiding our escape, that's all. I'm grateful." Lexxie wasn't up to being teased. And it was true. Her gratefulness couldn't be overstated.

Being the post rider, Jonne had the privilege of delivering a royal government announcement seeking farmers to relocate.

In return, a plot of land and a generous list of tools would be provided. Instead of sharing the call, he, Harmon, and Giselle plotted new lives. Since Giselle had secretly kept up the taxes on the land Harmon and Grossmutter vacated, Jake hadn't been able to confiscate it. Harmon found a buyer, and Giselle sold the Coaching Inn to a wealthy patron. Jonne left his post-rider position and "lost" the government poster, ensuring the town crier was naught to learn about the opportunity for the time being—enough time to give them a head start.

She yawned while lightheadedness overpowered her, as it continued to do so at least once daily. When she next awoke, she knew where she was. In the back of the wagon, lying flat with a horse blanket beneath her head. Harmon sitting aside her looked most uncomfortable, his arm stretched to keep hold of her hand. Her elbows worked to prop herself up enough to catch her surroundings. Giselle, dressed in men's trousers and dangling chandelier earrings, sat at the helm steering two mares and Matilda right up beside her, but facing backward, wide brown eyes assessing Lexxie.

Recovering from another bout of feebleness, Lexxie winked back to relieve him. If only she didn't collapse from exhaustion so often.

"Smoke. I smell smoke." The acrid stench had likely awakened her senses. 'Twas not that of a cook fire.

The wagon swayed as Giselle steered them onto the road away from the town's center. Plumes of thick smoke climbed in the sky behind them north of the town by the sinkhole. The toxic stink arrested her nostrils. Harmon didn't appear alarmed though normally fire was in the highest category of fright.

"What are they burning?" She stretched upward for a

better look, even grabbed onto the wagon's side paneling to steady herself.

"The platform." He smiled. "Thanks to you, Lex. No more faux Purification Days."

"Mercy." Fighting the excitement, she laid back and nestled into the soft red blanket. But the blanket nay be the reason her whole being warmed. They passed beneath glorious leafage of orange and red, the cloudless deep-blue sky, and the rays of a fall sun pointing the way. "Huh. Guess I did some good after all."

"Guess'n you did." Harmon winked back.

"Wait." She bolted straight up. "Where's Jonne?" Could he have left, just as she was days away from courting age?

"Lex, it's not safe for us to go back to Avondale. Jonne went ahead to help Grossmutter pack. He'll bring her to meet us."

As to where this new pioneering opportunity was, even Lexxie didn't know. Only that it be due south and her family world had grown. Yet, she didn't see Jonne to be much of the farming type and commented such.

Harmon's nose twitched. "Don't go worrying. He'll be back."

Not wanting to let on too much, she moved straight to what had to be nailed to Harmon's sense of protective duty. "I guess Witford is serious about coming after us."

"Guess'n he is." Harmon shrugged. "But I can tell you one thing—yer never gonna be without shoes. That Jonne boy's plann'n to be a cordwainer, got all sorts of crazy plans to craft new designs." He squeezed her hand. "And he's got some keen sense of humor."

This Jonne, the way he kept to himself had made folks not understand him. She played with an earlobe. "Why say that?"

Harmon moved a sack full of gilded beads and buckles belonging to Jonne and exposed a block of something firm and heavy, the etching of "Infant Dimietris" and "likely a witch" visible.

"Nein!" Curiosity flipped inside her. "My grave marker? Why, oh why, are we bringing *that*?"

"Jonne snatched it out of that pit. He wanted you to smash it yerself."

A supernatural feel with a promise of life everlasting flooded warmth through her veins and quivers up her spine. She had a better idea. "Let's place it somewhere by an oak tree when we get assigned our plot, and then grow a patch of lavender around it." She settled back, her whole body relaxing, and her mind confirmed. "That is what we shall do with it."

The settlement they were to be part of had a good-sized river nearby. Surely, a row of oak trees would line the bank.

Although the future was still uncertain, inside her heart were fresh, new, growing seeds of hope and faith. She had caught a fortunate glimpse—there is life following death. And here, we have purpose.

Even bad days from now on, she promised herself to consider good. When the enemy attacked, she'd fly higher. And considering those past dreams, which ceased since she started this self-search, she'd continue to discover much about the woman she was. The horror of a man with an ax and pounding hooves chasing after her carried warnings of Witford Dimietris. And the gilded gold carriage coming from the sky? As much as she pondered whether a future with Jonne was possible, that message was something far, far grander.

Alexandra, her given name at birth.

Lexxie, the name of the woman she'd become.

And one day, she believed with full heart and mind, she would hear again that warm assuring voice calling from the heavens—

Alexien, my child.

CHAPTER FIFTY-THREE
A MIND RULES THE HEART

At the River of Times

EVIL LURKS, LEST you take notice.

If not for the stars disappearing as it snaked past, one would never know such evil existed. An invisible dragon surfing the earth's atmosphere to and fro for opportunities to influence minds, a mouth ready to swallow those unsuspecting. According to Jophiel, all this so-called Space Beast had to do was order his rebel army to sprinkle seeds of deceit at specific targets. It was easy after that. Self-deception perpetuates with mere maintenance, a capability the army excelled at.

Pondering this and his new name written not only on his stone but also across his heart, Megalos arrived at the riverbank, delivered up and guarded by Jophiel. As the waters of the wondrous River of Times flowed downstream, so did measurements of time on earth gurgle and ripple away. Upstream, closer to the celebrated grand fall of waters, was the past, marking out earthly measurements of bygone days and years. He and Jophiel stood at the spot where Megalos, then Meginhardt, had completed his fleeting journey, the time of his great separation.

That friendly rebel stood waiting on the opposite bank. Silent.

Contentment grew inside Megalos and surely glowed up his face.

The two, Megalos and the rebel, peered into each other's eyes. "Not too late. Come work for us," the rebel called.

"You know"—ignoring the invitation, Megalos employed heartfelt sincerity—"I thought you were my friend." As if another, an even more delicate veil was lifted, the vague facial features of the rebel revealed themselves with greater clarity. A screen telecasting that evil dragon, the Space Beast as Jophiel referred, came into view. Offcuts of the Beast's revolting self now were embedded in each member of the rebel army, including this one. The one who Megalos thought he recognized, felt a familiarity with, even a comfort to during his life with Pa. But none of those old feelings survived. Megalos saw through the rebel, ill intentions cloaked in camaraderie. Loneliness had opened the door, inviting the rebel in, so said the past.

Having nothing to say, the rebel turned and disappeared into the masses on his side of the river.

Easier than I thought. Though as soon as Megalos dared to accept such prideful thinking, he acknowledged Jophiel and the kingdom were standing firm alongside him. They were, in fact, his strength, enabling a rejection to this rebel's friendship, a weight chained to a destructive obstacle of unworthiness. Megalos gave up a mind-strong and silent thank-you to his new King, committing his loyalty.

With a chuckle, he added a note of thanks for sending

Jophiel. He turned out to be quite useful. *But don't tell him if ya don't mind.*

Megalos shuddered over what could've happened if his eagle courier hadn't intervened. Recollections of invading thoughts of being alone, unloved, and unvalued. All lies. Bad seeds. No one could know that better than he right now.

"Weeds cannot be pulled away for fear of harming the wheat," Aivy had explained.

He was still chewing on that.

Jophiel tugged at his elbow. "It's time."

After a gentle squeeze to ensure the safety of the stone tucked inside his trouser pocket, Megalos cued his concurrence and offered an unhesitant reply. "Let's go, then."

Next he knew, his footing was no longer on the riverbank. Rather, he was fixed in the center of the kingdom's outer courtyard, the place he landed after his physical separation. A young lad then stripped of any confidence in hope and faith.

The transformation was rather startling.

His grubby flannel shirt and trousers gone, replaced with a strong sense of belonging and self-worth, humility and contentment. Wounds, bruises, and surface grime also removed from his body. An unusual tenderness inside his mouth, a new eyetooth pushing up from pink gums as he experienced a complete transition, a new sense of being, a change beyond comprehension.

Slight panic had him fumbling. His stone—where was it? Unfolding a closed fist disclosed the gem. An emerald rock. His name, Megalos, embedded with bright-orange gold.

"Ready?" Jophiel asked.

"Wait." Megalos needed to take it in. A whole new life lay at his feet, and a fresh gratitude warmed a heart released from a prison of rejection. This was the greatest blessing imaginable.

"Now?" Jophiel probed again.

It was time for Megalos to enter the gate, time to be crowned a kingdom citizen.

Megalos shook his head. Aivy told him many kingdom citizens chose to be oblivious to happenings on earth. Eager to dismiss such from their mind, preferring to carry forth with their new venture. Knowing it was an easy few steps from the kingdom into the outer courtyard, where one could absorb all remembrances and updates for a loved one in an instant, there would be no reason to fear one could forget. One must, however, be prepared to observe their loved one's sufferings, some allotted by the King, some imposed by the rebel leader. That was difficult for many, and the reason kingdom citizens preferred to remain inside the gate.

Could he bear having no longing to recall? Aye, he was considering Pa. He hoped Pa would accept the influences the kingdom sent his way, become aware of the thoughts in his head, turn around, and focus on what was right. As a boy, Megalos dreamed of going head-to-head with Pa. Now, he would wait with the hope to one day have a heart-to-heart instead.

Yes, a kingdom job, one that allowed him to remain in the outer courtyard where he could watch over Pa, egg him on even. Though he didn't have any descendants of his own, there would be those of Pa's. There could be many to come, many to watch over. Franklin, Charles, Maggie, and Sarai— he'd been given the privilege to know a few. And of course, Lexxie. The thought of their brief encounter brought about a rousing affection.

With him deep in imagining the possibility, Aivy snuck up and tapped his elbow. She beamed those crystal-blue eyes, hugging that beloved clipboard. "He is waiting. Come, Megs, my friend."

Megalos had spent considerable time with Aivy as of late. Most enlightening was her dismissal that his curse had imposed a burden upon others. Though she stressed emotions were highly contagious, she insisted true curses were up to the King and the King alone, the same for true blessings.

Megalos nodded, knowing what was next.

Aye.

After entering the gate, he was to attend a special meeting, accompanied by Aivy. At this gathering, he would discover if the King and his Authoritarians had accepted his application. Megalos offered to devote his next three hundred years to serve and protect in the upright post of gatekeeper for the outer courtyard of this kingdom, a place he felt honored to call his home.

"I am ready," he said.

Soon, he would discover his new future.

The story of HERE LYETH hath ended,
though, the characters live on.

Did you enjoy *Here Lyeth*?
Please consider leaving a review with Goodreads or Amazon.
You can learn more about what books are
coming next at JohannaFrankAuthor.com.
While there, sign up to keep in touch! I'm
always eager to hear from readers.

Next are the beginning pages of *Here Lyeth's* novel mates,
other whimsical fiction reads with soulful tales:
The Gatekeeper's Descendants
Jophiel's Secret

*"Because even a little heavenly imagination
can loosen the chains of life."*
~ Johanna Frank

THE GATEKEEPER'S DESCENDANTS

PROLOGUE
FROM THE DESK OF
INTERVENTIONS

Somewhere Inside the Kingdom a File is Opened

THE WAY HUMANS track? I'd say 300 years, give or take. That's when Megs signed on, and he's never looked back. That job is his reason for being. He's the most thankful gatekeeper the kingdom ever had.

I know, I know, things were different then. Such long backups in processing and new arrivals were coming in by the droves. They were desperate to hire, so many jobs to fill. In those days people just had to be eager, show an interest in taking a job.

Now? There's so much competition, people have to stay "on track," as they say. Now they need to develop a particular character while on a humankind tour. As if surviving that tour, a lifetime on Earth, isn't enough.

Yup, those were the good ol' days, more jobs than there were kingdom citizens to take them. Most citizen folk know

Megs as big, strong, and fearless—you know, the kinda guy you'd never mess with and yet the kinda guy whose heart still takes the prize as his biggest feature. But I know him better. I know what made the guy.

You see, Megs, or Megalos, as the king calls him, and I did our journey on Earth together. Actually, that's when we met. I was a few years his senior and a good deal taller, and back then, we were buddies. He was of the scraggly, timid, weakling sort, forever bumping into things. We were farming buddies mostly, friends by association, I guess you could say. When I was milking our cows, I knew he'd be milking his. When I was feeding our chickens, I knew he'd be doing it too. On those unbearably hot, humid days, I'd feel like a pig shucking all that corn, but somehow it was comforting knowing he was over there yonder, sweating it up just as much.

Our families didn't visit. My pa didn't like his pa much, told me to stay away. "Somethin's not right 'bout that man," he would say. "Keep an eye out for his boy. Let me know if he needs protectin'."

I had a perfect view of Megs' yard from the window beside my trundle. Barely a half field away, a stormwater ravine served as the boundary line. A bunch of lavender bushes grew wild on our side while a rotted-out date palm stood beside a big pile of stones on his. I saw Megs' pa kicking him in the behind now and again, and once I saw him get shoved into a patch of manure good and hard. Megs scrambled to get up and slipped even deeper. His pa offered him a hand and then yanked it away, causing Megs to slip again, headfirst. His pa laughed and spat out his tobacco, and Megs, well, he didn't even clench his fists.

I never told my pa. He had a temper, and naturally, I

didn't want to start a feud. But I watched for Megs every day, making sure I caught a glimpse of him at least once, just to be sure he was alive and all. Poor kid, his head always hung in shame. I figured keeping an eye on him was enough, that I was doing good by doing that.

Therein something laid inside me, fresh as thick cement: a foundation of guilt. It was like a prison sentence for the rest of my earth years. *How could I have known what was coming?* I would ask myself. I had witnessed enough. I should have done *something*.

Megs was thirteen. I remember well because it was the year of mud, a time of trials, you might say. The horses and carts couldn't get through most roads. And the harvest that year? It wasn't much. In fact, most folks had diddly squat, including the farm next door. Megs' family's fields were akin to a swamp.

That was when Megs' pa took the beating and punching indoors. He caught me watching from behind our lavender bush once, just as he heaved a fist into Megs' temple. After that I couldn't look no more, was best to forget it all.

One night a couple of weeks later, I heard commotion and some banging around com'n from his way—some muffled yelping too. I did the only thing I thought I could do: I convinced myself all was good. But the consistent haunting *woos* of the eagle owl hinted otherwise. So, I snuck out of the house, crossed the ravine, and crept up to their kitchen window.

There was Megs, on his back, swinging his arms and legs like a wildcat, only his pa had one of his dung-caked boots pressed hard, squishin' his gut. Megs was yelling at him. "I hate you! I hate you!" His pa just laughed, called him a wussy mama's boy.

I'll never forget that shaky look on Megs' face. "Yer no pa. I *curse* you." Megs spat, but I gotta tell you, it didn't get far. "I curse you—and all yer relatives . . . to infinity. I curse you. I curse them all!"

That did it. Megs' pa didn't laugh this time. His eyes grew devil-like and red with hate. "Yeah, you'll never escape me. I'm yer family, but I'm gonna make sure *you* never get yer own."

His pa grabbed the cast-iron pot, still full of hot fat and chops, and well, I didn't see anymore. Chicken that I was, I ran back home and cowered under my bed. Told no one.

The story 'round the village made no sense. "The boy didn't have a chance," people said. "Wolves charged straight through the gate. Jumped him whilst draining out the trough." The incredulous part, "Not a single calf got touched."

Megs' pa blamed the unnatural weather, said it caused wild animals to act like bats in the belfry. Know something? He got away with it. The whole village lapped it up.

But the way my pa looked at me, he knew better. That was no wolf pack. 'Twas a cold-blooded killer, not the kinda pa any kid should have.

I pretty much blamed myself—for not intervening, that is. Things might have been different if I had done something. Maybe I could have stopped it, who knows.

For the rest of my tour on Earth, first thing each sunrise, Megs came to mind. That piercing sound when his pa shoveled gravel around, like it didn't matter. All I could do back then was score some lavender from our bushes and toss it over the ravine, hoping it would land somewhere close to that pile of stones, hoping Megs would know that I knew and cared his body was down there, rotting in the deep.

Now, I know the rule of time—it does not go backwards.

But with the king as my ruler and witness, back then I pleaded with him over and over for a miracle, another chance to intervene, so I could somehow help my dear friend, Megalos.

Well, he heard me. 'Cause now, some three centuries later, Megalos came to me in my kingdom job as head of interventions and him in his kingdom job as head gatekeeper. He was all worked up, didn't know what to do 'bout a situation. He came asking for a favor. An intervention, something I'm darn good at now. And let me tell you, was I eager to pull a few strings!

Wanna hear the story?

EXCERPT CONTINUED
THE GATEKEEPER'S DESCENDANTS

CHAPTER ONE
IT'S HIM OR ME

In the Outer Courtyard of the Kingdom

*O*H, JUST LOOK *at him.* Pipiera squirmed in private adoration. Even now, as he gripped tight the edges of a page and read its message with dedicated focus, simply standing in his shadow assured her. A stern and peculiar expression washed over his face. But none of that mattered. To Pipiera, Megalos's presence was akin to a big, gentle bear hug.

"What's wrong, Papah Moolos?" her voice low and quiet, her eyes fixed upward in hopes to catch his. She knew he loved the nickname she invented, particularly the "Papah" part. It was a sure-fire way to make Megalos pause and grin. Plus, she loved the sense of belonging that came with the pretense she was his descendant, that he was somehow a grandfather to her.

But not today, no sheepish grin. *This is highly unusual. Stress, could that be stress I detect? No, that's strife. He seems worried.* No matter however dreadful the news, she knew he would overcome it in a matter of blinks. He always did.

She considered his face a bit longer, remaining silent and

methodical. *Hmm, could it actually be that bad?* There was a serious crinkle between his thick, dark brows. *It almost appears to be fear. Almost.* She cocked her head a tad. *Surely not!*

She raised her heels effortlessly, shifting all weight to her toes and turning her attention to peek out the only window of Papah's humble living quarters, a single room held high atop the watch post. Nothing but an exquisitely carved bench to sit upon. She scanned the panoramic view. A pleasant aromatic breeze captured her senses and ruffled her bangs. Bored of debating which emotion was plaguing her papah, she decided to settle. Sad. *It's disappointing news. Therefore, he is sad.*

Head gatekeeper was not an easy job. The way leading to the kingdom's main gate saw a continuous hum of new arrivals. Nearly always there would be somebody on the edge of the horizon, heading in toward Megs. He truly shone. He was always prepared, always welcoming, always patient to answer questions and dispel concerns, and, when called for, he could shake his head in a kind and gentle manner. The latter inevitably meant the arrival was to go back. The rules were strict, the orders clear.

Pipiera loved being smack in the middle of the activity, a witness to it all. She teased him about how much fun his job was. He did his best to manage his concern that she did not recognize the seriousness of it all.

The other gatekeepers in the kingdom courtyard respected Megalos for his cautious analyzing, his calculated reasoning, and sometimes, though admittedly rare, his unenthusiastic kindness. But never, ever fear. His comrade, Roly, told Pip she was the only one Megalos would allow himself to banter with. That made Pipiera feel special and, in her own eyes, somewhat of an expert as to his inside track.

Her concern about him and whatever it was that stole his attention lingered. She crossed her arms and offered up some encouragement. "Papah, if you read it even just *one* more time, the words will not jump off the page and change clothes." With both eyebrows arched, Pipiera hoped her teasing would lighten things up.

The mood changed, but not the way she hoped. His facial expression was obvious; he was annoyed. It was the same discerning frown he employed when lecturing her about not taking kingdom business to heart. *I better back off, give him some space. I don't know why he lets himself get so disrupted by these letters from those authoritarians. What's the big deal anyway?*

Megalos often received information in the same manner— a message scribed on official kingdom letterhead, sealed by an authoritarian, and then delivered by that busy little book room keeper guy.

She put her mind on a serious track. *I bet it's an update on a gatekeeper recruit. Papah says it's a good job but really hard to get.* He had explained it to her many times. All his replacement recruits had to develop certain characteristics during their tour, a journey on Earth bookmarked with a time to begin and a time to end. It seemed so easy. All they had to do was recognize how blessed they were, cast their concerns on the king, allow him to keep their hearts clean, and stay loyal. Yet only a few stuck to that on account of all the earthly challenges and whatnots.

The ornate bench creaked as he cast a foot upon it.

Pushing her chin up, she dared a question, attempting to prove she could be serious. "Is somebody struggling?"

"It's a page from Matthew's book." He waved it high

briefly before crumpling it up and shoving the ball of parchment into the pocket of his linen trousers.

So, it wasn't an official message; it was a page from a recruit's book. That can't be right. Since when do they rip pages out of one's book?

It was his turn to stare out the window.

Just being present and silent was the best way Pipiera could think of to support her papah at that moment. But her mind did swirl. Their paths had never crossed, hers and this Matthew's. *I knew it! You had him on a pedestal, you talked about him way too much anyway. I'm glad he's struggling.* Her Papah Moolos talked about him so much that anyone listening would come to know Matthew inside and out. That's if they wanted to. Pipiera preferred to ignore it because she couldn't bear the thought of Papah cherishing anyone more than her. *Just because this Matthew boy chose your footsteps to follow, you think he's so great. C'mon, Papah, he was barely qualified to take that assignment. You said so yourself.* Pipiera hung her head, attempting to hide her thoughts. *Dare I say it?*

"So . . . was doing a tour to become your replacement one day actually the plan for Matthew?" *There, I said it. Because truth be known, I think you want it more than he does.*

His back stiffened and his brows formed a perfect V. "What are you suggesting?"

Okay, here goes . . . "Well, what I mean is, I dread to think if it wasn't. I mean, if Matthew wasn't actually meant to be groomed for your replacement, his earth journey would be . . ." She sucked and tucked in her bottom lip, letting her words trail. She kept to herself the obvious—Matthew's journey would be an impossible one. *Besides, why do you need to retire anyway? What will happen to me? Did you ever think of that? Probably not!*

She could tell his mind was calculating away, surmising the situation at hand. "Matthew must be quite off track," he mumbled whilst rubbing his chin. "Otherwise, Bookie would not have come over like that."

"He's always in a hurry. Everything is urgent with him." She was trying to be helpful. The book room keeper was in charge of all the open books. If one was on a humankind tour, a book was certainly open in Bookie's special room under the special care of his countless scribes, scribbling madly, capturing every thought and action, particularly the details requested by the king.

"Yeah." His finger tapped at his temple while his chin rested in his large, solid right hand. "But he's never ripped out a page from anyone's book before, least not that I know of."

Pipiera watched as her papah continued to think. "Well, maybe he thinks you can have that page rewritten," she said. It was a genuine notion.

Megalos finally broke the silence. "Possibly." Then he shook his head, "I don't think that's it." He chuckled gruffly. "The law clearly doesn't allow for that." Then his lips tightened across his face.

I think that's a half smile. Pipiera took the relaxed muscles around his eyes as resignation to all this silly nonsense about some Matthew boy. *All will work out,* she wanted to assure him.

Alas, he gave the cue. "Let's get back at it." With that, he led the way.

The pair descended the interior circular staircase, seventy-three steps in all. She had counted them many times. Any other day Pip would have fluttered down those stairs, jumping two steps at a time, but today she followed obediently behind her papah. By the time they got to ground level, the heaviness had lifted. Megs paused briefly, flashing a curvy-lipped grin at his little henchman. Then they stepped into the outer courtyard.

Ah, there you are. Back here with me. Where we belong. The two of us. She watched him head to his post by the gate only twenty something steps away. *Our closeness, this life we share. . .* She sighed. "I don't want anything to change."

Pipiera often wondered what drew her to Megalos, why she felt so close and connected, and why they made each other their closest of kin. At least six generations apart, they were quite different. Pipiera could only dream of adventure, but she wasn't certain what that might be, and she lacked the courage to find out. Megalos? Not so much. He wasn't into dreamy adventures. He realized his adventure in the here and now. Pip's bubbly spirit oozed out of her constantly even if her mind did flip in views. Megs stayed on track, by the book, with his inner thoughts tucked neatly inside a serious, all-business exterior. Nevertheless, the two were a pair, together all the time in the kingdom's outer courtyard—him working and her playing. Pipiera didn't take their relationship for granted; rather, she feared it could all disappear one day without explanation. She shuddered at the notion.

Glancing toward Megalos to be sure he was more than an earshot away, she vocalized her grief. "Why should I care if this Matthew boy is struggling? I don't want him, or anyone, to replace you. Why can't you just let the boy struggle and keep things the way they are?"

JOPHIEL'S SECRET

CHAPTER ONE
CHERRY STRUDEL

In the Outer Courtyard of the Kingdom

ONE MORE RUNNING scissor jump. *Goodness, Mother, will you be surprised when you see me!* A graceful landing on both feet and then up again, airborne, straight through the gate and into the outside world—the Kingdom's Outer Courtyard. The place where she grew up from childhood. A couple more sprints to drain the day's nervous energy, then she scampered into a squat. Here, in a patch of lavender, she would watch and wait.

Pipiera's mother was due to arrive.

Papah, the man who had pretty much raised her, was nowhere in sight. Unusual, since he was the Head Gatekeeper and rarely left his post for any length of time. *He can't be far,* Pipiera figured. *I know he wouldn't miss this for anything. . .he knows how I've ached for decades; this reunion means everything to me.*

Legs stretched out, leaning on her elbows, Pipiera admired the wide and majestic horizon, a familiar view that shaped her very existence. A shoreline crested with incoming waves, one after each, powerfully pulling through galaxy upon galaxy, dutifully bringing forth Arrivals from a faraway world, a place the Authoritarians called Earth. A place where she had lived once herself, some years ago, for a mere number of days. The Outer Courtyard was the final stretch of the journey. Arrivals would be gingerly delivered in front of Papah's gate, the Kingdom gate, their delivering wave then taking a deep and gracious bow before gently melting into the ground.

Soon, Mother will come over that horizon, riding on a wave. I will meet her. It shall be grand!

Thankful she wasn't late, Pipiera closed her eyes and let the gentle breezes push her bangs back while she drank the day's aroma, each day different, each day healing. Today's a mixture of citrus and vanilla. She checked the delicate package tucked close to her body, secured by her left elbow. The baked strudel filled with plump cherries hadn't leaked inside its wrapping and didn't appear squished. *A little miracle,* she thought, given all her excited jumps. Well, not too squished, anyway.

Pipiera knew little about her mother, but one thing the ancestor aunties, Serena and Alexien, had told her was a story about their generational line's crazy love for cherry strudel. Pipiera wondered if they had made the story up simply because it was Serena's favorite thing to bake. Besides, who could resist the flesh of the Kingdom's own vibrant selection of sweet, red cherries enveloped inside Serena's hand-stretched layers of paper-thin dough? It was perfect for kicking off a homecoming celebration.

But never mind that—far more splendid would be the long-awaited moment when Pipiera could meet the eyes of her mother. A new page written; instead of sadness and grief, Pipiera imagined joy and happiness. Instead of a story wrapped in a blanket of blackness, her mother could glow freely with abundant light. *I simply cannot wait for you to hold me, Mother. We will never be separated again. Ever.*

The excitement of it all was excruciating. Yet a haunting rush of anxiety coursed through her veins; she couldn't place her finger on any cause for worry. *Surely Mother will arrive at this gate.* Her emphasis on *this.*

This moment was far too precious not to share.

"Now, where is he?" Speaking to her host of lively purple lavender, Pipiera looked around. No Papah Megalos. "Surely, he knows what today is!" Jumping up for a better scan—it was habit—she placed one hand on her hip and buckled her lips, toes dug into the soft vegetation. "Papah. . .*where* are you?" she sang at a pitch only her own ears could appreciate.

Though momentarily absent, Megalos had held his prestigious role for well over 300 years. Head Gatekeeper for the Kingdom. Pipiera was proud of the work he performed day in, day out, greeting and processing Arrivals. Sometimes having to turn them away. Rebels, of course, were mostly to blame for that. Of more personal importance, Megalos was Pipiera's outright favorite relative. Adopted relative, that is—there is quite a story behind the adoption. Another day for that tale. All that mattered now: Pipiera adored Megalos and Megalos adored Pipiera.

Roly, Megalos's faithful second-in-command, emitted a quick hello-nod her way. As much as Pipiera wanted desperately to inquire just where in the blazes her Papah 'Megs' was, she decided that wasn't such a great idea. Interrupting while gatekeepers are in the midst of processing Arrivals was never a good idea. Chuckling, she recalled the few instances when she had marched over and demanded attention at the most awkward of times. *Oh dear,* she shook the memories away. Not funny then, quite laughable now. *I've grown,* she applauded herself. She would have to wait for him, too.

Still searching for Megalos, Pipiera noticed both aunties, Serena and Alexien, sitting themselves down at a picnic table in the citizens' waiting area. She bolted over to join them, nearly dropping the strudel.

"Oh, good. You *are* here," Serena said with zero excitement.

Why the somber tone? Pipiera wondered. *There was no reason for that, not today.* "Of course! Where else, for the Kingdom's sake, would I be? Mother is about to arrive." Pipiera held up the wrapped package with both hands. Well, that got a slight rise of a smile from Serena. Though not from Alexien. *Something's up. Something's wrong.*

Pipiera slipped her legs under the table and settled in. "What's going on?" she eyed the pair, one at a time, not liking the face either had composed. Then her heart sank, pulling her shoulders with it. "No. Don't tell me. She's not coming." Pipiera curtly tossed the wrapped strudel onto the table, cherry guts seeping out.

Dismayed, Serena pulled the package together while Alexien appeared to contemplate an explanation. This day was, in fact, a long-awaited one; the arrival of a family member always was. Completing an Earth tour and returning home? Well, that was something to celebrate.

"No, Pip, that's not it. Maggie will arrive as scheduled." Alexien's voice was dry.

Pipiera exhaled sharp and quick. *Whew.* She took an inhale and looked behind her toward the horizon, where soon her mother would roll in along with one of the Kingdom's escorts. *Toward me. Toward the next forever phase of our lives.* Not sure what the aunties were bothered about, Pipiera wasn't about to let them ruin this moment. *My moment. No, I won't allow anything to interfere. Whatever they are upset about, they will have to deal with on their own.*

She glanced toward the gate. Still no Megalos. Small groups of gathered citizens were excitedly chatting at other tables, waiting for their own loved ones to arrive, all under a myriad of grapevine archways and large blooms of climbing white roses.

Her attention resigned back to the aunties. "Oh, what then? Come on, tell me."

Alexien was the wise and cautious one, at least according to Pipiera. Serena was the creative, scheming one, always having something new and fun up her sleeve. The aunties had taken Pipiera under their wing once she herself became a citizen. They were ancestors, great, great, many-times ancestors, and they, too, had been adopted into a line of descendants now belonging to Megalos. They were all one family now.

Alexien spoke slowly as if the words were painful. "It's—*Jophiel.*"

Serena's mouth twisted about. She was the one who would blurt everything out and then some. But at this particular moment, it seemed she preferred to hold her tongue. Rare.

"Serena?" Pipiera probed. Alexien remained seriously quiet.

This can't be good. It was automatic, Pipiera's fingers clasped in time to catch her chin. *No, please, King, let my Jophiel be alright.*

"Well," Serena tilted her head, readying herself to spill. "There *is* good news. He's coming home early."

"What? No! He can't come home early. I mean, of course,

I would like that. But no, he's got plans, I'm sure of it. He wouldn't have taken a journey without a purpose, I mean, or without a major goal at heart. Why can't he stay longer?" Thoughts racing in circles like a wild rabbit trapped inside a cardboard box, Pipiera continued to blurt out questions as though her aunties were in charge, as though they would have some answers. "Is he hurt? In trouble?" Both hands slapped the table, giving Alexien a jolt. "What and why? Why does the King want Jophiel home so early!?"

Having been somewhat afraid of what Pipiera's reaction would be, Alexien and Serena shook their heads in unison, simply acknowledging her rant.

Ugh. Pipiera hated when they did that, the unison part. Catching her own attitude in the look of caution in the eyes of her aunts, she gave herself a scold. "Trust the King," she whispered softly.

The aunties heard the murmur and nodded, again in unison.

Scratching the back of her head, she twisted about to check on the horizon. It was a legitimate way to stall the discussion—was her mother coming yet? *Nope.* Agitation got the better of her. "Where's Papah Megs, anyway?" *I need him right now.* Her Papah Megs could always put things in the proper perspective, the Kingdom's perspective.

Alexien glanced toward the watch post that towered above the Kingdom gate. Atop it was a room, a humble room with not much but an ornate wooden bench that Papah liked to sit upon when he needed to contemplate. A single window provided a view of the entire horizon, so careful watching never ceased.

"He's up there. With Aivy. I suspect she's telling him to

expect Jophiel soon." Alexien employed her voice of wisdom. Aivy was the Kingdom's transition agent, in charge of the list: the list of all scheduled arrivals. "We thought you could be happy for Jophiel, to know he would soon be on his way. And besides, all journeys have purposes and goals, no matter their length. *You* better than any of us know that, Pip."

Jophiel and Pipiera had a history. They met a mere six years earlier when Pipiera had been elected to take part in an intervention, her one and only mission. He had been the assigned escort to ensure that her travels to and from Earth were free from danger. During it all, they bonded. Supportive and special to each other. Jophiel was now on an Earth tour himself.

Pipiera calculated. He would be six years of age by now, still a boy. A young boy with the gift of intelligence beyond his years, she was sure of that. *Even so, what purpose could he have possibly accomplished?* She pushed the somber dispute down, hard. Though the aunties were right, she should know better than anyone that the length of a tour was not a key measurement.

A dewy wetness soaked her lashes. "I am. Happy for him. Don't get me wrong; I can't wait to see him. It's just. . .just. . ."

Alexien interrupted, "We know, Pip. And we get it." Her counseling tone conveyed an understanding. Neither Serena nor Alexien wished for Jophiel to come home before he could accomplish his tasks and build the character he was meant to build. Serena leaned forward and grabbed Pipiera's elbows, eager to share something else.

Alexien placed a hand on Serena's back as though to caution her words.

Pipiera leaned in. Might there be a scheme of some sort? Leave it to Serena. "I'm listening."

"Risks," Pipiera could barely hear Alexien's voice. "Mind the risks."

So, there is a plan!

Serena's telling face, her mouth twisting all about, eyes artfully churning to a squint, invited Pipiera to lean in even closer.

Whatever it is, it looks like these two might not agree. Pipiera leaned in closer anyway.

"Okay," Serena started. "Three things. You'd have to go now. And I mean now. And you must stay there, like, be an earthling and all, not just coming and going. You'd have to stay there for awhile, maybe even the entire summer. Secondly, you cannot use any powers—no disappearing and reappearing, don't go floatin' about or anything; you mustn't raise any suspicion."

Pipiera's back stiffened as she pulled away. "Me? Go there? Stay there? What? *Why?*"

Before she could reject the plan resolutely, Serena injected with term number three.

"And most of all, Pip. . .are you hearing this? Most of all, do not—and I mean *do not*—create close relationships. No one must discover just who you are. You've a job to do. Get in, stay the course, get out. One summer at most. That's it."

Is she serious? Pipiera examined the faces of her two aunts. Dead serious, both of them. "Am I missing something? Why would I need to go *there*? Besides, my mother is about to arrive." Totally baffled, she cast a firm, "No way!"

Her knee banged the underside of the tabletop but didn't slow her from making a stand. She would have walked away,

but these women meant so much to her. Those two words—
"No way!"—wavered visibly inside the airspace of the three
women, churning into a circular motion, rotating the tension
until it simulated a fierce column, a whirlwind of sorts. They
all watched as it darkened, a soft light growing from its inside.
Then it all disappeared.

Pipiera sat back down. She admired and trusted her
aunties. But their suggestion that she needed to go to Earth
for the summer, pretending she was an earthling? And all of
this right out of nowhere?

Serena rested her head on the table, hands covering her
short, brunette curls.

Alexien offered a resolution. "It's okay, Pip. We really
didn't think you'd be up for it. It's a far-fetched plan, anyway.
We simply couldn't come up with anything else." She then
glanced again at the tower room. Pipiera figured it was her way
of suggesting the deal for Jophiel to end his Earth-journey at
such a tender age and return to the Kingdom was being finalized at that very same moment.

"My mother," Pipiera bullied her defense. "You think I
could leave now? Now that I've waited so long for her arrival?
I've been preparing for *so* long for this moment. You're both
crazy. Seriously!"

The aunties remained quiet, eyes cast downward to where
the whirlwind vision had come and gone.

"You'll have your mother forever when she arrives. Jophiel
won't get another chance. You know that. One Earth-journey
per person. . ." Pipiera could see that Serena really was serious.
And persistent.

Alexien interrupted, "Unless, of course, we cause a commotion, an unofficial interference, a mission."

"Unofficial?" Pipiera gasped. "Uh, you remember how I fumbled the last one?" she added.

"No, no. . .Pip, it all ended well. There was no fumbling. All ended well, remember?" Alexien was being encouraging.

Shifting her seating direction, Pipiera nodded hesitantly. That one and only mission she had taken was something she'd rather forget—except meeting Jophiel, that is. She thought about Alexien's words for a moment. *She's right; it did end well, I suppose.*

Pipiera pushed her back up tall to begin a line of questioning. "Let me get this straight. I'd be a real person, a human earthling whilst there?"

"Just for the summer," Alexien said.

"I have it all figured out," Serena added in a tone full of hope.

"I need more details."

"You'll get them. We don't have time right now," Serena replied.

"Pipiera, dear, you literally must leave now. Now, before Megalos comes down those stairs and out of his tower. We need to tell Aivy and him that you've already left to help young Joppha. They'll *have* to pause his return then," Alexien explained.

"Well, no, they don't." Pipiera was pretty sure they didn't.

"Megalos will insist they wait if it's *you* who went," Serena pleaded. "He'll fight and plead with the Authoritarians. They'll *listen* to him." Alexien moved in closer. "Pip, it *has* to be you."

Oh, I get it now.

Pipiera knew Papah always gave in to her. And though this unofficial plan of her aunties' felt wrong, helping her friend Jophiel, whom she promised to watch over, felt so right.

"Jophiel did say in a letter that he took the Earth-journey knowing he had me to look out for him. What would he think if I disappointed him?"

The two aunties nodded, signaling agreement, in unison. But then Serena crouched low. "Psst, we gotta go. Now! C'mon."

Pipiera scanned the horizon. No Mother.

"C'mon!" Serena grabbed Pipiera's elbow and pulled her off the picnic table. "Alexien will stay behind. She's gonna tell them you've jumped in the main tunnel, all distraught and determined-like. You left to help Jophiel. But we must get a head start!"

Pipiera choked. That tunnel. The last time she jumped in, it was a nightmare. Terror. Trauma. The very reason she'd sworn to herself she'd never go on another mission, despite any promptings from that Intervention team. She had adamantly rejected their repeated invitations to join their group. Though with those words, 'but it ended well,' ringing in her ears, her nod was slight and just enough for Serena to grab her elbow and pull her along till they were both sprinting in the direction of the main tunnel.

Pipiera glanced behind. A leaky strudel on the table, no mother on the horizon, and an absent Megalos to guard the gate. She kept running, though she wondered why. Two people she loved so dearly were about to meet: her adopted Papah Megs and her earthly mother, Maggie.

And I won't be there for the celebrated moment. King, I pray I'm doing the right thing!

TRANSLATION GUIDE

WORDS:

Affray / attack

Ague / fever

Arsworm / slang referring to a contemptible person

Ach du lieber / oh dear

Calf lolly / useless simpleton

Bedlam / madhouse

Bedlamite / madman

Burgermeister / mayor

Dirty beau / slang for an immoral suitor

Dorf / village

Du bist der Fänger / you're the catcher

Forsooth / expression of surprise

Fräulein / miss

Gauchmann / a gullible man

Genug / enough

Grobian / ruffian/boorish person

Grossmutter / grandmother

Guten morgen / good morning

Guten tag / good day

Herr / mister/lord/sir

Hören mich / hear me

Irrsinn / insanity

Jawohl! / an emphatic yes

Jungfrau / maiden

Kinderwiege / cradle for an infant

Kiste / box

Komm / come

Liebste / sweetheart

Mein/meine / my

Mutter / mother

Narr / fool

Nein / no

Notlage / plight/emergency

Rettet / rescue!

Poxed / cursed

Schadenfreude / the pleasure one gets from another's suffering

Scherz / a joke meant to amuse

Schmaltz / chicken fat

Schulze / one with a roll of order

Schurke / villain/rogue/scoundrel

Tochter / daughter

Unsinn / nonsense

Vanderarzt / traveling doctor

Vater / father

Wirte / host/innkeeper

AWARDS FOR THE GATEKEEPER'S DESCENDANTS BY JOHANNA FRANK

2021 – In the Beginning Award – Unpublished Authors, The Word Guild, Canada

2021 – Book Cover Award – BIBA (Best Indie Book Award), International

2022 – Honorary Mention – Young Adult Religious Theme, Readers' Favorite, International

2022 – Finalist – Best Published Novel - Young Adult Fiction, General Market, The Word Guild, Canada

2022 – Finalist – Best Published Novel - Speculative Fiction, Christian Market, The Word Guild, Canada

2022 – Finalist – Book Cover Award, The Word Guild, Canada

AWARDS FOR JOPHIEL'S SECRET BY JOHANNA FRANK

2023 – Winner – Best Published Novel – Speculative Genre, Christian Fiction, The Word Guild, Canada

2023 – Winner – Best Published Novel – Suspense Genre, General Market Fiction, The Word Guild, Canada